WHAT HAPPENED
to Lucy Vale

Lauren Oliver is the author of YA novels *Ringer, Replica, Before I Fall, Panic, Vanishing Girls* and the Delirium trilogy: *Delirium, Pandemonium* and *Requiem*, which have been translated into more than thirty languages and are *New York Times* and international bestsellers. She is also the author of two standalone novels for middle-grade readers, *The Spindlers* and *Liesl & Po*, which was an E. B. White Read Aloud Award nominee; the Curiosity House series; and a novel for adults, *Rooms*.

What Happened to Lucy Vale is her second standalone adult mystery novel.

A graduate of the University of Chicago and NYU's MFA program, Lauren Oliver is also the co-founder of the boutique literary development company Glasstown Entertainment. She lives in Brooklyn, New York.

www.laurenoliverbooks.com
On X @OliverBooks
On Instagram @lauren_oliver_books
On Facebook /laurenoliverbooks

LAUREN OLIVER

WHAT HAPPENED
to Lucy Vale

HODDER &
STOUGHTON

First published in Great Britain in 2025 by Hodder & Stoughton Limited
An Hachette UK company

The authorised representative in the EEA is Hachette Ireland,
8 Castlecourt Centre, Dublin 15, D15 XTP3, Ireland (email: info@hbgi.ie)

1

Copyright © Laura Schechter 2025

The right of Lauren Oliver to be identified as the Author of the Work has been asserted by her in accordance with the Copyright, Designs and Patents Act 1988.

All rights reserved. No part of this publication may be reproduced, stored in a retrieval system, or transmitted, in any form or by any means without the prior written permission of the publisher, nor be otherwise circulated in any form of binding or cover other than that in which it is published and without a similar condition being imposed on the subsequent purchaser.

All characters in this publication are fictitious and any resemblance to real persons, living or dead, is purely coincidental.

A CIP catalogue record for this title is available from the British Library

Hardback ISBN 978 1 473 67274 1
Trade Paperback ISBN 978 1 473 67275 8
ebook ISBN 978 1 473 67278 9

Typeset in Adobe Garamond Pro

Printed and bound in Great Britain by Clays Ltd, Elcograf S.p.A.

Hodder & Stoughton policy is to use papers that are natural, renewable and recyclable products and made from wood grown in sustainable forests. The logging and manufacturing processes are expected to conform to the environmental regulations of the country of origin.

Hodder & Stoughton Limited
Carmelite House
50 Victoria Embankment
London EC4Y 0DZ

www.hodder.co.uk

To my mom:
For putting me back together when it all came apart.

Active Discord Subscribers:

@badprincess Evie Grant
@bassicrhythm Nate Stern
@brentmann Brent Manning
@emheddles Emma Howard
@frenchkissesry Riley French
@geminirising Peyton Neely
@goodnightsky Sofia Young
@gustagusta Jackson Skye
@hannahbanana Hannah Smith (the one in band, not the one who plays soccer)
@heyitsaubrey Aubrey Barnes
@highasakyle Kyle Hannigan
@kash_money Akash Sandhu
@ktcakes888 Kaitlyn Courtland
@lululemonaide Layla Lewis
@meeksmaster Allan Meeks
@mememeup Ethan Courtland
@moonovermatter Scarlett Hughes
@nononycky Nick Topornycky
@pawsandclaws Olivia Howard
@safireswiftly Alyssa Hobbes
@skyediva Skyler Matthews
@spinn_doctor Alex Spinnaker
@stopandfriske Will Friske

Key Organizations and Groups:

The Sharks. Woodward High School's swim team and prevailing obsession.

The Granger Club Team. A storied club team, founded by Jay Steeler and newly helmed by one of his protégés, Coach Jack Vernon. One of the best club teams in the Midwest, if not the country.

Minnows. The school's fresh bait. Typically a title awarded via consensus to the school's hottest freshmen girls.

The Echelon. The beautiful ones. The chosen few. The popular crowd.

Student Leadership Department. Enemy of freedom, champion of academic excellence and perverse school behavioral codes. Arbiter of after-school clubs and student rights. In bed with Administration.

Student Council Mafia. The pathologically cheerful student enforcement arm of the Student Leadership Department. Also, the cheerleader type.

The Strut Girls. Bailey Lawrence, Savannah Savage, and Mia Thompson. Goddesses among mortals. Star members of the Woodward High School Dance Team. Sworn enemies of the Student Council Mafia and the cheerleaders writ large.

Balladeers. The highlight of the Winters Dance. A group of male swimmers who each volunteer to auction off a single slow dance every year.

Important Figures to the Original Nina Faraday Investigation:

Woody Topornycky. Alien enthusiast, alcoholic, and the last person to see Nina Faraday alive.

Tommy Swift. Star swimmer, Coach Steeler's protégé and Nina's on-again, off-again boyfriend.

Jack Vernon. Tommy Swift's friend, teammate, and possible coconspirator. Later, the controversial coach appointed to the Granger Club Team.

Jay Steeler. Former Olympian and fabled architect of the Granger Club Team and the Woodward High School swim program. Coach Steeler would have undoubtedly protected his swimmers at all costs.

"The pizza guy." The critical eyewitness who placed Tommy Swift at Coach Steeler's house during the hours that Nina Faraday went missing.

Sheriff Cox. The longtime sheriff in charge of the initial investigation, related to Jay Steeler through his sister-in-law, Ann Steeler-Cox. Subsequently accused by Lydia Faraday of facilitating a cover-up.

PROLOGUE

We

We were athletes and anarchists, band geeks and gamers, virgins and sluts.

But mostly virgins.

We were dyslexic, and desperate for someone to notice us. We came from a constellation of small towns in the lower left corner of southwest Indiana, all tipped into the gravitational pull of the Woodward Central School District. We came from farms out past the Lincoln Walmart and condos near the College of Southern-Indiana at Housataunick. We came from the McMansions of Granger North, with Byron Park and the golf course, and the trailers of Granger South, with a Waffle House, an IHOP, and a pizzeria rumored to include a dime bag of weed when you ordered a veggie slice with extra green.

We were Christians, mostly. The Sandhus were Sikhs; the Kornsteins were Jewish; Olivia Howard claimed she was Wiccan. We were aspiring politicians and future farmers, violin players and JROTC cadets. We owned guns. We protested guns. We followed each other on Instagram. We wanted more followers on TikTok.

We dreamed of trending someday, for something, going viral for a spontaneous act of courage or for rocketing CHEETOS out of our noses at the doctor's office. We envied Jack Hamlin's older brother, Paul, who had 1.4 million subscribers on YouTube—even before the whole stampede debacle.

We could have told him bulls have no sense of humor, especially during breeding season.

We were hicks. We were pathologically shy. We didn't want to be famous. We wanted to *influence*. To matter, to be special, to stand out. We wanted to be accepted.

We didn't believe in *cliques*. We'd left cliques behind in middle school. But we stuck with our own kind. We believed in friend groups. Common interests. Extracurriculars. Sports. Clubs. Finding your people. To hell with all the rest of them.

We were different. We were ordinary.

We were the roughly thirty-six members of the private Discord server *WoodwardSchoolBored*, and before anything ever happened to Lucy, Lucy Vale happened to us.

PART 1

PART I

ONE

We

None of us know what happened to Lucy Vale. But all of us agree that by the time she set fire to the school mascot in front of Admin, it was too late to do anything about it.

At the time, we weren't thinking about Lucy; we were thinking about dying, and how we really didn't feel like doing it on a random Tuesday in March of our junior year. Shunted into closets, barricaded in our classrooms, sweltering inside the boiler room, we all imagined we were getting stormed by some psycho with a semiautomatic. We heard the fire trucks approach with the shrill of their alarms. We strained to hear gunshots. We speculated about the most likely culprit. Wyeth Boone. Allan Meeks. Lee Mailer. It's always the quiet ones you can't trust.

We texted our parents. There's something happening at Woodward. We're locked inside the art closet. I'm so scared. Are they saying anything on the news?? I think the cops are here. Pray for us. We reunited on Discord and complained about the smell in the art closet. Someone had farted, for sure.

We googled Woodward High School. We had shit service in the boiler room.

We realized we had to shit. We prayed that we wouldn't crap our pants in a closet crammed with peers.

Then the loudspeaker spat out a burst of static, and Principal Hammill cleared his throat across the entire campus. "Sorry, kids," he said. We'll never forget that. *Sorry, kids.* "Looks like someone lit a fire in a recycling bin. We're still clearing the grounds. Back to you as soon as possible."

About sixty seconds later, he was back, this time sounding slightly annoyed. "To clarify, there is no active or inactive shooter. This has nothing to do with a gun. Like I said, it appears someone lit a fire in a recycling bin. Unfortunately we need to wait for the police before we can lift lockdown, so please stay where you are until I give the word."

It wasn't until we were funneled into the parking lot for a school-wide head count that we got a glimpse of the recycling bin, now a blackened deformity with a volcanic residue of char around it. A dozen firefighters and cops milled around the world's most pathetic crime scene. We figured it was an accident, or a hack to avoid class.

We were dying to know who did it.

There was a brief panic when we found out that Connor Williams and Hannah Smith—the one in band, not the one who played soccer—hadn't made it with the rest of the woodwinds into the parking lot. Mr. Cower, the band teacher, was practically molten with panic. He shoved through the crowd like one of us might secretly be concealing Connor and Hannah in our backpacks. We tossed around the idea that these two were the culprits because it was so absurd; they were both the type who actually got sad on weekends when they didn't have any homework to do.

The mystery was short lived anyway. A hastily organized search party of theater geeks and brass hounds homed in on the sound booth, which was locked from the inside. A few minutes later, Connor and Hannah emerged, clearly in a conflagration of embarrassment, and it was pretty obvious to all of us what had happened. We started firing messages back and forth while waiting to return to our classes.

@geminirising: Anyone catching serious walk of shame vibes?
@mememeup: You mean walk of FAME
@badprincess: Is @hannahbanana's sweater on inside out??

It was, actually.

@safireswiftly: omg
@safireswiftly: were Connor and @hannahbanana *hooking up*?

They were.

We found out later that Connor and Hannah were in the bathroom when the alarm triggered. Connor, who'd been in love with her forever, had been desperate to make sure Hannah was safe. It was kind of heroic actually, especially since we had all assumed there was an active shooter on campus at that point. They had bolted to the sound booth, the closest secure space. We heard from Allan Meeks, who'd heard the story from Connor, that they were holding hands in the dark, and one thing led to another. We heard from Willa Barrens, who'd heard from Hannah, that the *one thing* that had led there was Hannah's crashing realization that she did not want to die a virgin.

It was unbelievable. Connor Williams was getting laid, and most of us couldn't even get a hickey.

For a few days, we tossed theories back and forth while the school launched yet another investigation, its second in six weeks. But it didn't occur to us that Lucy Vale's absence the day of the fire might be connected, because by then her absence wasn't special or significant. We weren't even sure that she was planning to finish out the school year. She'd been absent since the Investigative Committee had wrapped its findings about the night of Ryan Hawthorne's New Year's Eve party. Most of us figured she had already dropped out. We didn't know how she *could* come back. Her reputation was permanently destroyed. We figured she would be too ashamed.

We never, ever, ever dreamed that she would be *angry*. It wouldn't have occurred to us in a million years that she would drive to school, sneak into Aquatics, and steal Sean the Shark from storage. That she would take the time to wheel a recycling bin up to Administration, keeping her hoodie pulled low and a sweatshirt zipped over her chin so she was practically unrecognizable.

We didn't believe it at first, even after we heard that the sheriff was looking for her and Administration had leaked security footage from the Aquatics Center lobby to the local news.

Back then we'd worshipped Lucy, envied her, exalted and then hated her. We'd constructed her in pieces. We'd finally solved her like a puzzle. We knew by then that Lucy was a pathological liar, just like her mother. Some of us thought Lucy was an expert manipulator, a covert narcissist, a con artist, or all three. Some of us thought she was just cracked. Damaged, desperate, and suffering from major daddy issues.

But she wasn't *batshit*. And she had no reason—no reason—to be angry at *us*. It didn't make any sense.

Lucy Vale? we all kept saying. *Our Lucy Vale?*

Because even then, after everything that had happened, we still thought Lucy Vale belonged to us.

Then she torched our mascot, and we realized we were wrong.

TWO

WE

Akash Sandhu was the first to talk to the new girl but not the first to hear about her. That honor belonged to Emma Howard. Emma Howard's mom was a real estate agent. It was already late July when Mrs. Howard got the inquiry: a woman named Rachel Vale from Michigan wanted to rent a house. Her daughter, Lucy, would be enrolling at Woodward as a sophomore in just a few weeks' time.

The Vales were clean, quiet, and nonsmokers.

Also, they "might" have a cat.

Whatever that meant.

The news blew up on our Discord server. We were in the hardcore grips of midsummer boredom: we were too young to drive, too hot to work, and too afraid to steal weed from our brothers' rooms. July was crawling on its hands and knees through a heat wave, and so far the most exciting happening was an algae bloom in Byron Lake that temporarily greened the water.

At first we assumed that Lucy Vale would be an athlete, a transfer student who'd slipped under the Indiana High School Athletic Administration's radar. The only reason to move to Granger was to attend Woodward High School, and the only reason to attend Woodward High School was for its athletics programs. Our girls' track team was thriving, and our dance team was no joke. The previous year, Bailey Lawrence and the other Strut Girls had flipped and shimmied and catapulted their way into state championships, and almost ten thousand YouTube views.

And then, of course, there was our swim team.

But the athlete theory got shot down pretty quickly by Riley French; her uncle told her that the school was no longer taking athletics transfers, to comply with IHSAA requirements that might otherwise penalize our teams. Since Riley French's uncle, Judd French, was the assistant director of our athletics department, we figured her intel was legit.

We were so desperate for excitement that we packed this shrapnel of mystery—a new girl, our year, and moving midway through the summer—with as much meaning as possible. We bombarded each other with a rapid barrage, a cross fire of questions we couldn't answer, and theories we couldn't confirm one way or the other.

@ktcakes888: Does anyone know why the new girl is moving?
@geminirising: Does anyone think it's weird they waited this long to find a house??
@badprincess: I was thinking about that. It feels like it must be a last-minute thing
@skyediva: who moves last minute?
@mememeup: maybe her mom got a job
@badprincess: or a divorce?? Do we know if it's just the two of them?
@lululemonaide: Has anyone found her profile?

We had not.

We frivoled away hours searching every Lucy and Lucie Vale, Veil, Vayle, and Vayel on every social media site we could think of for a soon-to-be sophomore from Michigan who looked like she might have a cat. We ruled out most account holders by age alone. But after that, things got murky. We found a handful of Instagram handles that might have been hers, but one was inactive, another had only a few photos, all of them generic, and the rest were set to private.

Alex Spinnaker turned up a Lucy Vale in Vancouver who'd been convicted of a string of low-level identity scams and tried to convince us that we were about to be served by a fugitive con artist and an accomplice posing as her mother.

We were skeptical, to say the least.

@brentmann: served how? Like what's the con?
@mememeup: you mean besides america's higher education system?
@spinn_doctor: Read the article I pinned
@highasakyle: maybe they're planning to rip off the booster funds
@mememeup: this woman is 29, dude
@spinn_doctor: how do you know? She's a con artist.
@ktcakes888: there's a Lucy Vale in Ohio . . .
@badprincess: ew pass
@spinn_doctor: Emma's mom said MI
@mememeup: if she's a con artist, she could be from Morocco
@spinn_doctor: Nope. She's Canadian. Read the article.
@badprincess: I'm so confused
@highasakyle: Wait—the article about cryptocurrency?
@spinn_doctor: read that one too

We agreed on one thing: we'd rather have a Canadian con artist than a Lucy Vale from Ohio. We fucking hated Ohio. We weren't big on Michigan either. But Ohio?

That was the North Korea to our South Korea, the Crips to our Bloods.

Kyle Hannigan suggested someone friend the four most promising Lucy Vale profiles on Instagram. The real Lucy, he figured, would see we went to Woodward and accept.

Obviously that was a no go. We would have sooner volunteered to get a surprise tattoo than friend Lucy Vale before we knew what we were signing ourselves up for. What if she was a sociopath? What if she was *from Ohio*? Or just as bad—in the wrong fandoms? We hoped she wasn't an anime head; we'd had enough secondhand anime exposure as it was—a full six channels devoted to it already, even though most of us weren't even fans.

Hannah Smith—the one who played soccer, not the one in band—eventually tracked down a picture of a Lucy Vale from a volunteer event at an Ann Arbor, Michigan, animal center. But there were a dozen girls our age in the photograph, and Lucy wasn't tagged; her name was just in the caption. We took bets on which girl looked most like a Lucy; we were torn between a super tall, skinny blond with glasses and bad acne, and a heavier girl with a unicorn on her T-shirt. Then @ktcakes888 pointed out that there were twenty-two volunteers named in the caption and only sixteen people in the photograph—which meant Lucy Vale might be excluded.

We were all relieved; the girl with the glasses looked like she had an eating disorder, and the one with the unicorn shirt looked kind of like a Karen. Actually, none of the girls looked much like a Lucy, we decided, which meant we could go back to imagining her. And it turned out we liked the question mark even more than the answer. She was whatever we imagined; she was all things at once. She was short and she was tall, into girls or boys or both, a comic book geek, a theater nerd, a sweeper on the JV soccer team. She was funny, poetic, cynical, and really into Ayn Rand. She was looking for a best friend, or to fall in love, for someone to change her life, and be changed.

Before we knew anything about her—not even what she looked like—Lucy Vale was looking for us.

THREE

WE

In the early days of August, we waited for the new girl and her mother to arrive, maybe with a cat, maybe not. A moving van spotted on Richmond Lane gave us a flicker of hope. So did the fact that a FOR RENT sign had vanished from one of the condos above the Garden Groves mini mall in Lincoln.

But both leads were false, and soon explained by the news that Sofia Young's parents were getting a divorce.

> **@bassicrhythm:** Sofia Young's dad just moved out
> **@bassicrhythm:** that's why the moving van was there. He's renting a place in Lincoln
> **@bassicrhythm:** It's pretty fucked up
> **@frenchkissesry:** I don't understand Sofia's mom
> **@frenchkissesry:** How do you not know that you're a lesbian for 40 years?
> **@ktcakes888:** wait WHAT????
> **@badprincess:** WHAT
> **@badprincess:** is that why her parents are getting separated?
> **@badprincess:** Because Sofia's mom is a lesbian??

@highasakyle: I don't get why Mr. Young has a problem with that...
@highasakyle: ...now he and his wife both like to bang other women
@nononycky: maybe Mrs. Young likes them to be of legal drinking age
@goodnightsky: wtf you guys this is so fucked up
@bassicrhythm: it really is
@highasakyle: My cousin took a class with Mr. Young
@highasakyle: He said the guy grooms a new girl every semester
@goodnightsky: no, I mean what you said
@nononycky: he teaches poetry. Enough said
@goodnightsky: this whole conversation is beyond fucked up
@ktcakes888: poor Sofia. I feel so bad for her
@badprincess: @goodnightsky is right. We shouldn't be talking about this.
@badprincess: Especially behind Sofia's back
@goodnightsky: OR IN FRONT OF MY FACE

That's how we found out that Sofia Young was on Discord with us. It was high-key awkward.

The problem with Discord was also the great thing about it: since our server was invite-only, we were lazy about tracking usernames. On Discord, usernames were like Instagram filters, slight alterations in tone and aesthetic that varied with our moods. Before we accidentally told Sofia her dad was a serial cheater with a taste for teenagers, for example, most of us just assumed @goodnightsky was Skyler Matthews because her old username was @goodskyelf, and @goodnightsky joined only a couple of weeks after Skyler said she was going to change it.

Ironically, we always figured it was safer to avoid our real names. We'd all heard horror stories about the time Harper Rowe was catfished by her friend Reese Steeler-Cox pretending to be their *other* friend Charlotte Anderson. "Charlotte" baited Harper into talking shit about Reese and got Harper permanently iced out of the in crowd. Poor Harper started middle school as one of the Echelon girls and ended it as a musical theater geek, all because of a friend's Discord server and her misplaced trust in a username.

Then there was the rumor that Ryan Hawthorne's creepy older stepbrother, Luke, had used Ryan's name to make it onto a private Discord for the Woodward cheerleaders and solicit topless photos of at least three of the girls. Although, there was controversy about whether it was actually Ryan Hawthorne's creepy stepbrother pretending to be Ryan Hawthorne who did it, or Ryan Hawthorne pretending to be his creepy stepbrother pretending to be Ryan Hawthorne. Either way, it made for crazy drama our freshman year and nearly got Ryan Hawthorne suspended from the swim team just before state championships, which would have been tragic.

Besides, our real names came with trip wires of social expectation. We couldn't use our real names and interact honestly. That's the other thing about Discord: we were all friends on the server, but we were *only* friends there.

High school wasn't a hierarchy; it was a habitat, an ecosystem. We all had our places and our roles to play. School was a little like being onstage, acting out different parts in a play, reading different lines, following a script everyone knows but doesn't remember learning. In the play, some characters are friends and some aren't. Some characters act all their scenes together, and some are never onstage at the same time. No one knows why, and it doesn't matter. That's just how the play is written.

The Discord, to us, was the greenroom: a place where all the actors hung out before going onstage again.

That's why we were lazy about usernames. Our real names were part of the script. They were characters we played every day.

On Discord, we could finally be our real selves, and no one would ever know.

∼

After the whole mix-up with Sofia Young, conversation about the new girl began to sputter, like a star burning through all its gas. By then it had been almost a week with no new information. Emma Howard hadn't logged on to the server in weeks. According to Hannah Smith, Emma was coy the first time Hannah asked whether the Vales had found a house yet and seemed annoyed the second time. After Hannah asked a third time if Emma's mom had shown the Vales any houses, Emma *literally* burst into tears, like there was a water balloon behind her face and Hannah's question had popped it. She didn't know, she wished Hannah would stop asking, she wished Hannah would maybe ask about Emma for a change, because it felt like Hannah only talked to her when she wanted something and it really wasn't fair, she was super stressed, she was assistant stage director for the youth theater's production of *Peter Pan* opening in three days, like did Hannah even know what a stage director *was*, and she hadn't even *seen* her mom in like a week because she was so busy planning her dumb wedding to that totalitarian freckledick she was engaged to.

@hannahbanana: Emma doesn't really get along with her mom's fiance.

@lululemonaide suggested that we buy tickets to *Peter Pan*. @mememeup told her that he would rather have an actual freckle for a dick. @lululemonaide logged off in an obvious huff. We felt kind of bad about it. But we were already short on fun things to do. We weren't trying to go full deficit.

Thank God the Sharks were getting back in the water. We'd noticed a welcome banner for the new team season hanging outside Aquatics, and Ethan Courtland had spotted Coach Radner sporting a ferocious sunburn and vacation stubble, talking on his cell phone outside the pool entrance while Ethan was practicing three-point turns in the Woodward lot.

We could always count on the boys' swim team for distraction; being consumingly, pathologically obsessed with the Sharks was as fundamental a requirement at Woodward as wearing pants to class.

That year the Granger Club Team, the all-year training team that pushed most of the best swimmers to compete for the Sharks during the high school swim season, had gotten a new coach: Jack Vernon. He'd trained under the infamous Coach Steeler and competed with Tommy Swift during the all-star season that was derailed by Nina Faraday's disappearance. We knew little about him beyond that he was leaving a position with one of the Granger Club Team's fiercest rivals. We agreed that his appointment was a coup for the Steeler family; they'd been pushing to restore Coach Steeler's legacy and reputation since his death from colon cancer the year before we got to high school.

We wondered what Coach Vernon would mean for our season. We obsessed over the status of Jeremiah Greene's elbow injury. We scoured Instagram, Snapchat, TikTok, and Twitch for video proof that JJ Hammill, a sophomore, and Ryan Hawthorne, a junior, had really challenged the senior cocaptains to a 200-meter relay at Byron Lake—and possibly even *won*. We couldn't find proof one way or another; there was some confusion about whether the race had actually happened.

August slurped toward September.

We played video games and watched YouTube. We scooped ice cream and rotated hot dogs. We mowed lawns and painted sheds. Our older siblings went back to college. Nick Topornycky's uncle was back in jail.

We heard Sofia Young had gone to stay with her grandparents for a while.

We heard from Administration: the Aquatics Center might soon be under renovation again. We wondered if the girls' locker room would finally get a Jacuzzi and steam room like the boys' had.

We dreamed of roiling water and woke up in a sweat.

We had so many weird dreams in August that we made a channel to talk about weird dreams. In some of them we were swimming, flashing through water that felt like air. In others, we drowned.

@lululemonaide had a dream she was in trouble. She was trying to charge her cell phone so she could call for help, but the charger was always a strawberry by the time she was trying to fit it into the wall.

@hannahbanana had a dream that she was on a boat with Principal Hammill, filming a scene from *Jaws*. Principal Hammill, the director, was instructing her to jump from the boat, which was a diving board, into a pool filled with hundreds of extras dressed in shark costumes. But she realized right as her feet left the board that the whole thing was a setup, a trick by the sharks, who were real, only pretending to be actors.

We didn't know what any of it meant. We suggested meditation podcasts.

We were anxious and suddenly regretful for all the time we'd spent being bored. We got nostalgic remembering that we'd been excited about the new girl weeks earlier. We felt nostalgic for July and the promise of change.

Emma Howard's mood, at least, had improved after the three-day run of *Peter Pan* successfully concluded and earned a generally positive review in the county newspaper. She logged on to Discord, finally, to offer her theory about what had happened to the new girl.

@emheddles: Maybe the Vales changed their minds about moving
@emheddles: my mom said that she wasn't helping them anymore

That part turned out to be true, although not in the way we, or Emma, had interpreted it. Later we figured out that when Mrs. Vale called saying she was interested in renting a house, she meant a *specific* house, one they'd already seen plenty of times, at least online. All Emma's mom had done was get the Vales in touch with the owner.

But Emma wasn't the type to ruminate on semantics, and neither were we. So we assumed that her explanation—that the Vales had changed their minds—was right.

We were almost offended. It felt like we'd been ghosted. The shared spark of interest we'd been carrying went right down the toilet bowl. It was like the lights came up on a really good movie, and we all suddenly remembered we were sitting in third-period English. Embarrassed somehow. A little lonely too.

But we were used to falling a little in love in our imaginations and getting our hearts broken in real life.

Facts were facts: Lucy Vale wasn't coming.

Until, one day, she did.

FOUR

Rachel

Lucy made a playlist for the drive, an eclectic mix of artists that Rachel had never heard of and old favorites that Lucy had absorbed from her, a kind of musical transfusion. They drove mostly without speaking. Every so often Lucy's left hand went to her eyelashes and Rachel said, "Chicken tenders," which was a code word the therapist had recommended. Lucy's eyelashes were light brown, feathered white in the sun. But they'd grown in again, thank God. Last year she'd had none. Without them she looked sick, almost reptilian. But recently Rachel had found little bunches of them on Lucy's pillow again, and piled next to her laptop. They'd returned to their ritual of reminders. Whenever Rachel observed Lucy plucking, she said, "Chicken tenders," and Lucy would stop.

She hoped moving was the right decision.

Lucy sat with the stray, Maybe, balanced in a cardboard box on her knees, periodically peering in and whispering words of comfort that Rachel couldn't make out. She supposed that the undersized tabby was, officially, no longer a stray. Before they left Lansing, Lucy had insisted that Maybe—who for months had been showing up outside their apartment, rubbing provocatively against the front door and mewling for food and attention—be given the chance to opt in to or out of the move. It was no use trying to persuade her that the cat might not have the cognitive sophistication to forecast its happiness. Recently Lucy had been obsessed by new research into animal cognition, consumed with ideas of self-determination and the agency of all living beings. She hadn't yet announced her vegetarianism, but Rachel suspected it wouldn't be long.

That was Lucy. She always seemed to have a cause, to hand her heart away to an idea, a principle, a way of sectioning the world into right or wrong. When Lucy was eight or nine, she announced a hunger strike after seeing gruesome images of the food crisis in South Sudan. Rachel expected her to cave after a few hours. Instead, two days later, they were engaged in a blow-out fight over a slab of lasagna. The beginnings of an eating disorder, Rachel was sure. On day three, Lucy fainted in the halls of her elementary school, and Rachel threatened her with hospitalization unless she abandoned her campaign.

The next month, it was something about dolphins. As smart as humans, Lucy said. *They can even beat us at video games.*

Lucy was like that. Protean and obsessive. Fitful and intense. Like she was always stretching, reaching for something, desperate to hold on to a scaffold that would give the world its shape.

"I think Maybe might throw up," Lucy said. They were the first words she'd spoken since Grand Rapids. Mostly she'd sat with her head tilted toward the window, face invisible while the sun played on her hair. Thankfully the purple streaks had faded almost to invisibility. To Rachel, Lucy's hair color was a metaphor. She was finally getting her daughter back.

"Why do you think she's going to throw up?" Rachel asked. Her impulse, what she might once have said, was: Maybe is fine. She's a cat. But their family therapist had encouraged Rachel to respond with patience and curiosity, help Lucy explore her perceptions, and witness her point of view.

"She looks anxious to me," Lucy said. She had developed a tendency to project complex mental and emotional states onto the cat. In the lead-up to the move, Lucy had mostly been concerned about the quality of Maybe's mental health and whether she'd be able to adapt. But when Rachel asked Lucy whether she was worried about adapting, she'd only shrugged.

"And she's drooling."

"Would you like me to pull over?"

Lucy squinted out across the slur of flat scrub grass pinioned between I-69 and the sky. "She might run away."

"She might," Rachel agreed.

Lucy readjusted the box on her knees and said nothing. So much for self-determination.

They'd made it to Indiana. So far the landscape looked universal to this portion of the Midwest: broad highways, flat as a shovel end, and billboards that pointed to tobacco superstores, rest areas, sex shops, and Jesus. Rachel remembered that on her childhood drives to Indiana, every Bible verse provoked some explosive reaction from her mother. *Opiates for the masses,* she would say, drumming the wheel with her palm, and Rachel would drop her eyes as if she might be lulled to sleep by mere exposure.

It was only noon, but Rachel was already exhausted. The moving truck had arrived at 6:00 a.m., and there was a last-minute scramble to load the rest of Lucy's books, still towering in her bedroom, organized meticulously by color. Then Lucy had spent an hour outside, monitoring Maybe's behavior, trying to determine her ultimate desire to accompany them to Indiana. For weeks she'd been trying to prepare the cat for the relocation: leaving her open suitcase on the porch for Maybe to explore, rubbing catnip on the cardboard box that would serve as a makeshift carrying case, then slowly moving it by increments closer to the car. The day before the move, she at last moved the box into the back seat and sat for hours on the front porch, watching Maybe sniff around the vehicle, raise herself on her back legs, and peer into the interior before ultimately walking away, tail high. Lucy had reported all of this in great detail. *Maybe's undecided.*

That's very on-brand, Rachel responded. She was just happy that Lucy wasn't on her phone. The year before . . .

Well, the less she thought about the year before, the better.

They stopped at a gas station somewhere between Fort Wayne and Indianapolis to use the bathroom and buy some cold water for Maybe. Lucy went in first while Rachel waited in the idling car, watching the sun beam off her windshield, turning the little lot the color of chalk. Minutes later, Lucy reemerged with the water, a bag of Sour Patch Kids, and a new hat—an over-the-top display of rainbow stripes with sequined stars glittering against a brim of purple. As Lucy crossed the parking lot to Rachel's waiting car, two men unloading a pickup truck glanced at her. It made the breath tighten in Rachel's chest. Lucy was now at that age; she seemed to shift seamlessly between child and adult. One second, Rachel saw in the slope of her nose and the fullness of her cheeks the baby she'd been fifteen years ago, her face turned into the warmth of Rachel's breast. The next second, Lucy might toss her hair, and Rachel would get quick flashes of a stranger with long legs and a stubborn mouth, eyes that darkened into anger.

"Check it out. Only six ninety-nine," Lucy said, presumably meaning the hat, as she opened the door.

Rachel adjusted the rearview mirror. One of the men was watching again, lingering at the gas pump, gazing at Lucy as she bent over to pour water into Maybe's travel cup. She resisted the urge to shout at him, to tell him to fuck off, to peel his eyes away from her daughter's legs, freckled from the sun.

"I think you should have saved your money," Rachel said, and Lucy grinned. Rachel was encouraged. Lucy's mood was changing, lightening, as they got farther south.

Maybe the problem was Michigan. Rachel should never have sent Lucy to that private school. Too much wealth. Not enough parental supervision. And Rachel had been working too hard—consumed with her career, consumed with the slow deterioration of her relationship with Alan. That had been hard on Lucy too. Alan was the only father she'd ever known. She'd been eighteen months old when Rachel and Alan had begun dating midway through graduate school. By the time she celebrated her second birthday, Alan and Rachel were living together.

"This will be an adventure, you know," Rachel said. "A real mystery."

Lucy said nothing. She maneuvered the box back onto her lap. Maybe rustled in her box, gave a plaintive cry, and then settled down again.

"We should go," Lucy said. "Maybe wants to get there."

They backtracked to State Road 37 and continued south, and then west.

It was another sixty miles before they started seeing sharks.

FIVE

We

It was an ordinary Thursday. Muggy. Full of mosquitoes. Even Discord was listless.
Then, suddenly, our phones went hysterical with notifications: one after another, rapid fire, belling our brains into shock.

@moonovermatter: New girl
@moonovermatter: Here
@moonovernatter: Lucy
@moonovermatter: Just moved
@moonovermatter: Heard music from my bedroom this am
@moonovermatter: shitty
@moonovermatter: *shitty music
@moonovermatter: looked out my window, saw the moving van across the street
@moonovermatter: Went out back to yell
@moonovermatter: girl came outside
@moonovermatter: saw me
@moonovermatter: fuck I was dumb
@moonovermatter: but I was in shock
@moonovermatter: like why FH

@moonovermatter: why would you do that
@moonovermatter: she doesn't seem crazy
@moonovermatter: mom's sus
@moonovermatter: garden gnomes etc
@moonovermatter: we'll see I guess
@badprincess: what the fuck is happening?????
@mememeup: is this a joke? I don't get it
@moonovermatter: shit gotta go at work
@skyediva: WHO IS THIS???????

It was a scandal. It was chaos. Who was @moonovermatter? Why were they on Discord? How did they know about Lucy? What the fuck was the deal with the garden gnomes?

Spinnaker was losing his mind, of course, over compromised cybersecurity and lax protocol for changing usernames. We figured we only had a few minutes before he started expounding on cryptocurrency again and tried to cut his paranoia off at the pass.

@highasakyle: does anyone know who @moonovermatter is?
@badprincess: isn't @ktcakes888 an admin??
@ktcakes888: yeah but I don't have an updated list. Akash does
@badprincess: this is so fucking creepy
@skyediva: Where's AKASH WHEN YOU NEED HIM
@moonovermatter: That was Akash on my phone. We're at work
@moonovermatter: he forgot his cell
@highasakyle: my brain is melting
@badprincess: doublefuckingcreepy
@nononycky: who the fuck are YOU
@moonovermatter: oh sorry
@moonovermatter: This is Scarlett!
@moonovermatter: I changed my username
@moonovermatter: Do you like it?

Scarlett was, presumably, Scarlett Hughes, who did in fact work with Akash. But we were in no mood to give her feedback on her hippie-ass username, and still suspicious that we were being trolled for reasons unknown.

Meeks suggested that we go to Blue Hills Mall, where Scarlett and Akash worked, which was a great idea except we (a) had no cars and (b) had no licenses, permits, or ability to drive. We texted Akash to confirm and heard nothing. We DMed him on social media with no luck. We lost our minds trying to find someone who knew Scarlett Hughes's cell phone number. Nick Topornycky texted Sahara Richards, which did nothing but confirm that Nick and Sahara were hooking up. Sahara redirected us to Hope Gonzales, who was visiting her grandparents in Mexico and had turned off her phone.

We had a stormy few minutes before @lululemonaide thought of simply calling the mall, but that was a dead end too. We couldn't just ring up the food court, and the number listed for mall security was out of service.

We started poring over the messages again, parsing every letter for legitimacy. We couldn't see why anyone would go out of their way to impersonate Scarlett *or* Akash, let alone both of them at the same time.

But the claim about meeting Lucy Vale made no sense. The geography of the story, the blocking of it, fell apart under scrutiny. Akash's house was at the very end of a cul-de-sac, first of all; he *had* no neighbors across the street. Plus, @brentmann pointed out that Akash's bedroom was at the back of the house, overlooking the deck. He couldn't even *see* the street from his bedroom window. All he could see was his backyard.

@meeksmaster: and the Faraday House lol
@brentmann: true and FH
@lululemonaide: Akash lives next to the Faraday House??
@spinn_doctor: yeah. Their backyards are almost touching
@badprincess: wait—Akash mentioned FH in his messages????

No. No way.

We scrolled up to double-check. But for a minute, we couldn't believe it. Even as the messages splintered into proof—FH, across the road, behind the house—we couldn't believe it. It was impossible.

One of the server bots kicked back a welcome to @gustagusta, who'd just logged on.

@gustagusta: THE NEW GIRL IS LIVING IN FARADAY HOUSE !!!!!!!!!!!

For more than a minute, the words just hung there, floating in black space, waiting for a response. But none came.

@gustagusta: ??
@gustagusta: um hello ?

Our brains went dark, tapped out of battery.

@gustagusta: HELLO??
@gustagusta: I said Lucy Vale just moved into the FARADAY house
@gustagusta: Any comments? Concerns? Ideas? Questions?

Actually, we had only one, and @mememeup said it perfectly.

@mememeup: why

SIX

We

The Faraday House on Lily Lane was two hundred years old, scabbing paint, and losing ground daily to the steroidal growth of a famous garden gone feral, fifteen years untended. It was missing shingles from its roof and one of the front windows. If it were a dog, it would have fleas and visible scratch marks, patches of fur missing. Inside it was no doubt a nirvana of mice, an orgy of spiderwebs, a wet dream for all termites.

Also: the Faraday House was haunted. Some of us claimed to have seen a phantom Nina Faraday wandering the rose garden, dressed in a long pageant gown, seemingly searching for something. There were some people who passionately believed that Nina had never disappeared—at least not like her mom claimed. Those people thought Lydia had gone crazy and killed her daughter in a fury of rage, or as a puritanical sacrifice, or just because she was psychotic. Some people believed that all her subsequent ravings about the swim team, and Coach Steeler's involvement, proved that she had gone around the bend. Others thought that Nina had never left the house at all, that she was buried under the floor somewhere or in one of her mother's flower beds.

Whether Nina's ghost was still wandering the place or not, we couldn't say for sure. We didn't even know that Nina was dead. Plenty of us thought she'd run away, maybe to be with a secret boyfriend, one of the older guys she was rumored to have been seeing on the side.

But we knew that Lydia had never left. We'd seen her. Everyone had. It was a known thing: Lydia Faraday's tormented spirit hung forever in the apple tree, twisting around her madness. As kids we'd dared one another to sneak up to the gates at dusk, press a palm to the cold iron, and summon Lydia to appear.

Nina, Nina, where did you go? Lydia, Lydia, what do you know?

Most of us had learned terror at those gates, as the shadows under the apple tree began to condense, thickening to the form of a woman with her neck crooked around a rope.

For years the house had been graying behind a thickening curtain of trees and growth. We assumed it would stay that way until the wilderness of vines and climbing ivy toppled it for good.

Who in their right mind would ever choose to live in a place like the Faraday House?

You'd have to be dumb, crazy—or a sucker.

We needed to know.

We needed Akash.

We needed him back on Discord.

SEVEN

We

We waited. We watched TikTok videos. We checked Akash's socials. We scanned the horizon anxiously, as if the new girl might appear in a sign.

After the initial informational blitz, @moonovermatter was silent. We picked our teeth and popped our pimples. We scrolled through TikTok some more and crawled out of our skin. The normal cadence of fitful summer conversation kept skittering to the same, repetitive question.

Had anyone heard from Akash?

Had anyone heard more about the new girl?

Our patience thinned as the hours limped by, as if time itself had come down with full-body arthritis.

Finally, just after nine o'clock, a moderator bot welcomed @kash_money to the conversation.

@kash_money: I'm baaaaaaack faaammmmmmm!!!!!!!
@badprincess: TELL US EVERYTHING YOU FILTHY HO
@kash_money: oh wow
@kash_money: Hi Evie

@badprincess: OR I WILL CURSE YOU TO FIND A PUBIC HAIR IN EVERY COOKIE FROM NOW UNTIL ETERNITY
@kash_money: man I missed the internet

Akash's first encounter with the new girl was pretty much as he'd described via @moonovermatter's account. According to Akash, he'd woken up to loud music—"1970s headbangers, like you'd hear at a strip club," he told us, which just showed he'd never been to one—sometime before 9:00 a.m.

Originally he'd assumed that the source of the noise was the utilities van he'd spotted, parked on the gravel service road that divided his property from the backyard of the Faraday House. He didn't think anything of the fact that a satellite TV operator was parked just outside its gates. Plenty of delivery trucks and service vans parked there rather than in the cul-de-sac where Akash's trigger-happy neighbor was always threatening to shoot out the windows of any vehicle that obscured his driveway. So Akash had stomped over expecting to find some dude with a mullet napping in the front seat, only to find the van empty and a girl marooned in the wilderness of the Faraday backyard, cheerfully breaking down boxes with a straight razor.

Lucy Vale, Akash said, seemed pretty nice.

We asked if Lucy Vale was pretty. Akash said she was pretty enough. We asked what that meant. Spinnaker suggested he give us a number, one through ten.

Akash refused. We attacked Spinnaker for sexism. Lucy wasn't a used car model.

We asked Akash to describe her. His response was unsatisfactory: Lucy wasn't tall, and she wasn't short. She wasn't thin, and she wasn't plus. Her hair was brownish. Not long. Not super short. But shortish. Maybe. We suspected Akash was biased. The Sandhus were Sikh, and when they said long hair, they meant long. His older sister Rivka's ponytail swung like a metronome, all the way down to her ass.

@nononycky: so . . . Lucy Vale is a girl
@nononycky: with a face
@nononycky: and some hair
@nononycky: that's what we got so far
@safireswiftly: no offense @kash_money, but this is why you suck at creative writing

Akash took offense. He said if we wanted to know what Lucy looked like, we could follow her on Instagram. Shoot, we could introduce ourselves in person. We all knew where she lived.

No, he absolutely was not going to introduce us. How would he introduce us? He'd met her for all of ten minutes.

Yes, they were following each other on Instagram. She'd asked for his handle, so she would feel like she knew someone.

But she didn't. Know him. Or any of us. Or anyone.

She wasn't shy. But she wasn't, like, crazy talkative. They'd talked a little bit about music, and a lot about garden gnomes. But the whole conversation was ten minutes. Maybe less. He was still in basketball shorts, the T-shirt he'd slept in, and flip-flops he'd grabbed on his way out the door. He hadn't even put in his contacts yet. We'd never seen Akash in glasses, and he wouldn't send us a picture.

Layla Lewis asked if, in fact, the Vales had brought a cat.

@kash_money: yes. Maybe
@mememeup: which is it?
@kash_money: I mean she does have a cat, Maybe
@mememeup: bro
@lululemonaide: I'm confused
@kash_money: I mean Lucy Vale has a cat, named Maybe. Lucy introduced me
@nononycky: oh god. She's one of those.
@skyediva: what is THAT supposed to mean?
@kash_money: Idk. She seemed cool

>**@nononycky:** the girl? Or the cat?
>**@kash_money:** the girl. The cat seemed like a cat.

She hadn't said why they'd moved. She hadn't said why they'd moved to the *Faraday House* of all places.

We wondered if it was because the Vales were poor. Maybe they were too poor to afford anywhere else.

But Akash didn't think so. They weren't squatters. As far as he knew, they were official renters of southern Indiana's most infamous residence, i.e., actually paying money to be there. He'd seen a Toyota hybrid in the garage and mountainous volumes of moving boxes on the porch. Plus, he'd noticed a price sticker stuck to the back of Lucy Vale's T-shirt—for a forty-dollar garden gnome, no less.

He knew because Lucy had asked Akash to remove it.

The point was: What poor person shopped at Pottery Barn? What poor person would buy a forty-dollar garden gnome, even if it was a gag gift? *Especially* if it was?

We agreed that they would not.

We asked Akash if he was going to tell Lucy about the Faradays, in case she didn't know.

>**@kash_money:** Are you crazy? First off, I barely know the girl
>**@kash_money:** And also, still no

We asked him if he was going to try and go inside.

>**@kash_money:** of course not
>**@kash_money:** See: "Are you Crazy" and "I barely know the girl" above
>**@kash_money:** And also...
>**@kash_money:** *I'm* not frigging crazy.

EIGHT

Rachel

On their third day in the new house, Lucy entered with a potted philodendron.

"Someone left this at the front gate," she said.

Rachel immediately thought of the neighbor Lucy had described—Cash something or other. Sikh, according to Lucy. A nice guy. Cute too.

But not like that, Mom, she'd quickly clarified, reading her mother's look. They'd made a pact: no more secrets, and no boys. No dating at least. When Lucy was in middle school, just as Rachel and Alan's relationship was collapsing, caving in like some slow-moving sinkhole, Lucy's various romantic obsessions—her desperation to be liked, or loved, or at least valuable to someone—had almost consumed her. They'd agreed that here in Indiana, Lucy needed to focus on her schoolwork. Develop her interests. Find her friends.

"Is there a card?" Rachel asked.

Balancing the philodendron in the crook of one arm, Lucy excavated a card from her back pocket and opened it one-handed. A tumble of leaves cascaded down her forearm. Lucy's cheeks were splotchy from the sun, her hair swept behind a knotted bandanna. She already looked healthier. More alive. The previous year, Lucy's life force had seemed to leach away into her phone, as if some digital parasite demanded constant feeding, tending, nutrition from its host. *The Picture of Dorian Gray*, with Bluetooth. Lucy's skin had taken on a gray tinge, as if the upward-casting light from her screen had left it stained.

A nightmare. It had been, in the end, a nightmare.

"A small gift to welcome you to the neighborhood," Lucy recited. "Looking forward to meeting you soon. Signed, the Steeler-Coxes." Lucy looked up. "Steeler," she repeated. "We saw that name on the golf course."

Rachel said nothing. She hadn't told Lucy about the Steelers and their stranglehold on this corner of Indiana. She had been hoping that things had changed. But change, she thought, usually followed money, not the other way around.

"Great. Just what we need. One more plant to take care of," Rachel said instead. She took the philodendron from Lucy. "I wish they'd gotten us a hacksaw instead."

Lucy giggled. "Or a machete."

"Or that," Rachel agreed. She thought of dumping the plant in the trash but instead tucked it into a corner by one of the decorative stained glass windows in the dining room.

"I wonder why they didn't ring the bell," Lucy said.

"I doubt it's working," Rachel said. Wendy Adams, the house's longtime owner, had prepared her for electrical problems, but they were worse than Rachel had anticipated. Only a few outlets on the ground floor functioned. The representative from Rockland Electric who'd been dispatched to examine them told Rachel that mice were the likely culprit. *They like to chew the wires,* he'd said, casting his eyes around the walls uneasily, as if they were surrounded. *Best bet is to open the walls, rewire the place.* Rachel told him she would think about it. For now they would make do with power strips, a jumble of sprouting extension cables that ran through the first floor like veins. "Besides, people are superstitious."

"Maybe isn't. She went all the way up to the attic today. It took me an hour to find her," Lucy said. "And cats are very sensitive to things like that."

"Things like what?" Rachel asked.

"Energies. Ghosts." Lucy shrugged. "But I did hear footsteps last night. I swear I did. Up and down the hall, and to the top of the staircase. I got up because I was thirsty. The water from the tap tastes mossy, by the way. Still, I don't think it's going to hurt us."

"The water?" Rachel asked.

"Whatever was making those footsteps," Lucy corrected her. And then, tilting her head, she added, "Can't you feel it?"

"The only thing I *feel* is about eighty," Rachel said, neatly sidestepping the question. She had little interest in the paranormal; she found plenty inexplicable about the way humans behaved, and what they did to one another. Still, she couldn't deny that the house where Nina Faraday and her mother had lived for nearly two decades had its own kind of pressure, or maybe a pull; from the time she had heard that the house was available for rent, she had almost felt a compulsion to experience it, to walk the mystery herself. Nina had been only a handful of years younger than Rachel when she'd gone missing. Her disappearance had rocked southern Indiana and left a permanent impression on Rachel's early adulthood. She remembered that her aunt and uncle began locking their doors after Nina went missing; in the brief, chaotic early days of the investigation, rumors swept lower Indiana about a serial killer preying on young women. That was before people began to whisper about the swim team's involvement.

Rachel and her cousin had followed the early news coverage obsessively. In retrospect, Rachel thought that Nina's disappearance, and the competing visions of the case presented in the press, were key drivers to her desire to become a crime journalist. Nina's case had taught her an early and important lesson: there could be no crime without a victim. Too often, the victim was eventually erased, obscured by judgments and finger-pointing. And so, too, the crime got erased, slowly scrubbed of its significance and power. Uninvestigated. Unresolved.

But Rachel needed to be careful about what she said to her daughter—so quickly absorbed by fascinations and fantasies—about the Faradays. "My lower back is killing me. And I also *feel* like you haven't set up the bookshelves yet. You promised to do it yesterday."

Lucy rolled her eyes. "Okay, okay." She started to pass into the living room but paused in the doorway, running a hand along the casing trim carved with ornate rosettes. "It's lonely," she said abruptly. She glanced back at her mother, and for a second she looked like someone else. Someone much older. "That's what it feels like."

She went out, humming.

NINE

WE

We all knew someone who claimed to know something about what really happened to Nina Faraday. Rumors grew fast in our corner of Indiana, and in the sixteen years since Nina Faraday had disappeared, we'd had an infestation.

Back then, everyone had an opinion. We had cousins who'd been in school with Nina. Aunts who'd babysat Nina when she was only a few years old, when Lydia Faraday was still working periodic night shifts at the hospital in Clarion. Neighbors who'd worked the night shift with Lydia remembered mostly that she was a good RN, but tough and someone who kept to herself. Nate Stern's cousin had done gymnastics with Nina. Alyssa Hobbes's mom had sung in church choir with Lydia. It was a known thing that Mr. Rowe, who taught us social studies and coached the girls' JV soccer team, had dated Nina Faraday back in middle school. The tragic association, we imagined, clung heavily to him even now; we often speculated that regret for his early love kept him single and living with his mom, allegedly in the basement of her house.

Over the years, we'd heard murmurs that the Faradays had been deep into drugs. That Lydia Faraday had trafficked narcotics for an ex-boyfriend and was entangled with Mexican cartels. We'd heard that Nina Faraday had a history of making up stories and had, as a little girl, claimed variously that her father was a spy, a military pilot, and a member of the Italian Mafia.

We knew that she'd been well liked. Popular. Too popular, some people said. According to rumors, Nina had been cheating on her boyfriend, Tommy Swift, in the months before she vanished, possibly with a much older man, possibly with a handful of them—any one of whom could have abducted her.

Then there were the whispers—insidious, peripheral, like the hissing of a snake camouflaged inside the green—that Tommy Swift might have known more than he'd said.

The facts of the case were few and unstable. Even the facts deteriorated over time, molting like radioactive particles into new uncertainties. Nina Faraday had stayed at school late the day she disappeared. She was seen walking to her car, which was parked just outside Aquatics, at around seven o'clock.

Woody Topornycky, Nick's uncle, had actually been the one to spot her. We'd long speculated that this last encounter, the burden of it, was part of why he was always in and out of jail, sometimes for using, sometimes for brawling or selling or driving drunk. Granted, he was already pretty tapped when he was in high school, and his memories of that evening were colored by an OxyContin and marijuana haze. In the past, he'd insisted that the coyotes in the woods were microchipped by the government and spying for a capitalist cabal of unnamed powers. By the time we were old enough to cross the street when we saw him, Woody was telling anyone who listened that he'd been abducted by aliens, not once but twice, as punishment for his knowledge that they were behind Nina's disappearance. For years he claimed to have seen strange flashing lights descending behind the building not long after Nina arrived. Whatever he'd seen or imagined that night, it had scared him enough to run his first solid mile since getting booted from the football team.

At around seven thirty, Nina had texted her mother that she was heading home. Lydia Faraday returned to the house just after eight o'clock and found her daughter missing. Sometime in that half hour, Nina had presumably packed her gym bag and stepped outside again—to meet someone, go somewhere, do something—and never returned. The final cryptic text from her cell phone, sent to Tommy Swift, came from somewhere out near the entrance to the state park. It read simply: I know you want me out of your life. I'm leaving for a while. Don't look for me.

Over the years, there had been sporadic sightings of Nina Faraday. Once, when we were still in elementary school, a girl turned up in an Oregon police station claiming to be Nina, and we remembered the news sweeping like a current across our awareness. For days, no one talked about anything else.

But in the end, it turned out she was just another runaway, a heroin addict trying to escape an abusive boyfriend, start over with a new identity. Why not Nina's? After all, everyone was looking for her. Everyone wanted Nina to come home.

But she had not, not so far.

Woody Topornycky wasn't the only one with a crazy theory about what had happened to Nina the night she disappeared. Over the years, there had been as many theories as there were idle nights to cook them up, and dozens of investigative leads pursued and then unraveled. A rival swimmer from Jalliscoe was briefly suspected in her disappearance. A drifter who'd settled on the creepy commune where Olivia Howard and her parents lived was brought in for questioning after he claimed to have seen Nina hitchhiking on State Road 44. But in the end, the police decided he was just lonely or looking for attention. Some people thought Nina had been taken by a cartel. Nina's friends suggested that she'd been involved with a married man who was never identified. Others thought that Nina Faraday had been murdered by her overprotective mother.

They figured that *guilt* was enough to explain Lydia's suicide.

A little more than a year after Nina's disappearance, Lydia's body was pulled down from an apple tree in the front yard. It had been discovered hanging by one of her neighbors. Lydia had left no note. Only clues. Deteriorating mental health. Wild accusations against Tommy Swift, and Coach Steeler, and the rest of the swim team. A lawsuit that would never be filed. Bottles of liquor under the sink. Overflowing trash cans in the kitchen. Nina's room pristine, untouched.

After that, the doors of the Faraday House had been permanently locked, festooned with **No Trespassing** signs. For as long as we'd been alive, the Faraday House had been uninhabited. Off limits, except to squatters and the occasional ghost hunter, arriving to scale the gates and try to record proof of malevolence for their YouTube channel.

For as long as we'd been alive, no one in their right mind would dream of stepping foot in the Faraday House. For as long as we'd been alive, the gates to the Faraday House had been padlocked shut, its rooms empty, lifeless, a dark and hollow space in our imaginations. We'd packed up the mystery, and all its lingering, troublesome questions with it. We'd left it to molder in the dusty dark of our childhood terrors.

Nina, Nina, where did you go? Lydia, Lydia, what do you know?

Then the Vales moved to town and turned on the lights.

TEN

Rachel

The town of Granger had grown in the decade and a half since Rachel had last visited with her cousin, then a student at the modest campus of the College of Southern-Indiana, located in Housataunick to the east. Since that time, the college had swelled to accommodate ten thousand students, burnished by a solid athletics department and a brand-new gym. Housataunick, once a slurry of feed shops and used car lots, had transformed in the interim; Rachel and Lucy had passed a Panera Bread, a Chipotle, and two competing Subway shops driving in.

But Granger North still had the cozy feel that once charmed her. A local Dairy Queen was advertising five-dollar Blizzards as a thank-you to the local fire department. Most of the big chain stores were well concealed, located on the thick veins of county roads that ran to Granger South and the rural hamlet of Lincoln beyond it. Still, Rachel picked out a Jamba Juice, a Jimmy John's—even a McDonald's housed tastefully inside a brick building that might once have been a bank.

But there were plenty of local businesses too. Lucy recited names aloud as they walked: Second Time Around, a thrift store; the Hook-Up, an upscale bait and tackle shop; the Everything Store, which seemed to sell souvenirs, most of them related to swimming. They crossed into Byron Park, where Rachel pointed out a memorial fountain dedicated to Tommy Swift.

"Tommy Swift." Lucy slid her sunglasses down her nose, an affectation she had picked up somewhere. Rachel wasn't sure where. "Isn't he the one who killed Nina Faraday?"

"Maybe," Rachel said. "Maybe not."

"That's what the internet thinks," Lucy said pointedly. She stared hard at the fountain again, as if she disapproved of it. "How did *he* die?"

"Car crash. He was in pretty bad shape after Nina disappeared. Drugs. Alcohol."

"Guilt," Lucy said knowingly.

"Or grief," Rachel said.

Lucy turned to her. Out of the blue, her face changed. "You know something," she said. "You know something you're not saying. You have a theory."

Lucy could be like that: vague and noncommittal one second, then suddenly sharp, penetrating. Sometimes she was exhausting.

"Yeah, well. A theory and five bucks will get you a cup of coffee," Rachel said. It was an expression she'd picked up from her first real boss, Becky Adams, at *Michigan Metro News*. What she knew about the Faraday case didn't even amount to a theory anyway. Not yet. All she had was a storm cloud of ideas gathering slowly in her head, as if condensed by the pressure of proximity and the memories it returned.

"Not even, depending on the coffee," Lucy said, and tapped her sunglasses back into place.

For lunch they chose the diner. The back wall was covered with framed photographs. From a distance, they looked nearly identical. Stepping closer, Rachel identified every generation of the boys' swim team, dating back to the late eighties. Jay Steeler was in roughly half of them, aging in freeze-frame above a line of red vinyl booths. Rachel had the sudden, frantic urge to tell Lucy not to look. But she had moved on to scrutinize a display of signed swim caps pinned behind glass, floating like strange marine creatures toward the ceiling.

No secrets. That promise kept niggling around in the back of her mind like festering larvae newly exposed to the sun. She didn't want

Lucy to feel betrayed. She didn't want her to question Rachel's intentions. Their connection, their relationship, was still too fragile.

But soon, she thought. *Soon.* Once Lucy had settled in. Once she had found her way. Once she had finished high school.

A waitress with the alarmed look of an exclamation point showed them to a booth. Lucy slumped down in her seat, disappearing behind the oversize menu. "Everyone is staring," she said.

Rachel felt it too—the ripple of attention sliding their way as soon as they walked in the door. Two girls who looked to be about Lucy's age were huddled near the windows, phones out. Rachel could still hear the sibilant hiss of their whispering.

"It's a small town," Rachel said. "Especially with the college students gone."

"Small towns," Lucy corrected her. "Woodward takes students from across the county."

"So you did read the website," Rachel said teasingly. Lucy shrugged.

"They're not going to like me," she said. Somewhere between the park and diner, her mood had soured. It was Rachel's fault. She'd made the mistake of mentioning that Alan had called—looking, as ever, to speak to Lucy. Lucy had refused his calls, cards, and emails ever since he'd moved in with his new girlfriend. Whenever Rachel encouraged her to talk to him, she only said, *He made his choice.* Lucy's therapist had described Lucy as *rigid*. Once she made a decision about something, it was almost impossible to change her mind.

"The whole school is obsessed with sports," Lucy said. "Sports, swimming, and some stupid thing called Shark Week. All the girls look like pageant princesses."

"My cousin was a pageant princess," Rachel said. "She was Miss Southern Indiana two years in a row."

"And now she's a trad wife," Lucy said.

"Kelly is not a trad wife," Rachel said. "She runs her own business."

"Selling *candles*," Lucy said. She poked ferociously at the ice cubes in her water, dunking them toward the bottom of the glass. "I bet all the cheerleaders at Woodward are blond."

"What's wrong with blond cheerleaders?"

"A time warp," Lucy said. "That's what's wrong with it. It's a time warp, and a cliché."

"Well, maybe you should try out for the team. That way they'd have a little diversity."

Lucy rolled her eyes.

The waitress returned for their order: a tuna melt for Lucy, a salad and black coffee for Rachel. It was good to see Lucy eating again. She'd gotten so skinny last year, her breasts had all but vanished, snuffed back into her rib cage.

"What about Akash? Akash isn't an athlete. And he seems to like you." Rachel had a good feeling about the Sandhus. A quiet family, thoughtful. Respectful. They hadn't asked a single question about what had brought Rachel and Lucy to the area, and to *that house* specifically. And yet, Rachel had felt the topic resting carefully beneath their conversation, like a courteous absence.

Rachel was less enthused about their neighbors on Lily Lane. She'd caught one of them, a balding man with a liver-spotted complexion, snooping around their gates. She could have sworn he'd been into their mailbox too. And the postman had warned them about Mrs. Gorsuch at number 82.

"Yeah, that's true," Lucy said, brightening a little. "I could be friends with Akash."

"Maybe you can join the coding club," Rachel said. "You like computers."

"I like video games," Lucy corrected her. "There's a difference."

"Well, maybe you could start a video game club."

"Or an anticlub club," Lucy said. "We don't know what we like, and we never have any meetings."

"Just be yourself," Rachel said, hating the words even as she said them. She sounded like one of those posters she'd seen hanging around the school's Student Leadership Department when they had submitted Lucy's paperwork. "You'll be fine."

"Oh, Mom." Lucy sighed. "It's high school. That's, like, the one thing I'm *not* supposed to be."

ELEVEN

WE

We were dying to meet the new girl. Even seeing Lucy from a distance counted as gossip, and launched frenzied speculation about the possible significance of the Vales' clothes, car, groceries, gas station purchases. It felt like the beginning of a game, like online Mafia, or one of the escape room experiences they built every Halloween in the old Sears on 87. It felt like an obvious cue, an imperative to look for *something*, so that we would know what we needed to find.

We found excuses to hang out on Lily Lane. Kyle Hannigan spent so long pretending to stretch a cramp outside the Vales' front gates, hoping to catch a glimpse of Lucy, that a woman with a rifle shouted to him from number 82 to ask if he needed help with something. Harper Rowe lost her nerve with one foot on the front path when she saw Lucy's mom aggressively pruning the honeysuckle bush around the infamous apple tree where Lydia Faraday's body was found swinging. Will Friske stuffed the mailboxes on Lily Lane with promotional flyers for his cousin's landscaping business, even though we all knew it was a front.

> **@badprincess:** Does your cousin even have a landscaping business?
> **@badprincess:** I thought he just sold weed

@stopandfriske: weed is a plant
@stopandfriske: You have to grow it
@stopandfriske: on land
@brentmann: when do you scape it?

Akash, we agreed, had gotten stupid lucky. He reported almost daily interactions with the new girl and her mother. He'd observed Lucy Vale on her hands and knees, trying to coax Maybe out of the overgrown thicket that almost entirely concealed the screened porch. He'd spotted Lucy Vale pumping air into her bike tires, and she'd waved and shouted hey. He'd seen Rachel Vale sweeping debris off the back porch, and she'd come down to the service road to introduce herself.

We wanted to know what Lucy's mother was like.

@kash_money: young
@spinn_doctor: he means hot
@kash_money: if I meant hot, I would have said hot
@spinn_doctor: you did, on our group chat
@brentmann: dibs on the milf
@skyediva: wait, @spinn_doctor and @kash_money have a group chat?

We tossed around how we might engineer a chance meeting with the Vales. Since Akash refused to introduce us, we suggested congregating en masse at his house, hoping to at least catch a glimpse of them. He strictly nixed the idea, claiming that his parents still suspected him of dealing drugs and that they'd been running a borderline surveillance state ever since he'd received his devices back.

We grew resentful. We suspected Akash of playing favorites. When we heard that Meeks, Spinnaker, and Kaitlyn Courtland had been invited over for a game night, had actually been midargument about the relative powers of ogres versus giants when a voice at the back door announced a paint-splattered Lucy Vale, out of the blue, live and in need of masking tape, we seriously regretted not getting into D&D, or at minimum Catan. It was nepotism; the gamers were cashing in on their friendship with Akash to unfair advantage, and there was nothing we could do about it.

It took forever to learn D&D.

After days of debate, we decided that the only reasonable thing was to throw a party. The problem was that (a) we had no idea how because (b) we weren't allowed to have parties, although granted (c) we'd never asked our parents because (d) we were usually too busy on Discord or Tumblr or Twitch.

Then Peyton Neely noticed that Olivia Howard and Lucy were mutuals on Instagram. Layla Lewis confirmed that Olivia had helped Lucy pick out a cat gym at PetSmart, and since then they'd been exchanging cute animal memes.

Also: Olivia was open to the idea of throwing a party and was sure her parents would be cool about it.

@mememeup: don't her parents have like a commune or something?
@lululemonaide: NO
@lululemonaide: It is NOT a commune
@lululemonaide: Think of it like a family farm/farmstore
@lululemonaide: But there are a bunch of families who live there
@lululemonaide: And run/own the whole thing together
@ktcakes888: um . . .
@ktcakes888: how is that different from a commune . . . ??
@lululemonaide: because they don't have like a creepy leader
@lululemonaide: And practice weird rituals
@lululemonaide: And like sacrifice animals to alien lizard gods
@lululemonaide: Or have sex with cows
@gustagusta: that's a cult
@gustagusta: Are you thinking of a cult?
@lululemonaide: omg YES sorry
@lululemonaide: Hahaha

@lululemonaide: she DEFINITELY lives on a commune!!
@lululemonaide: Sorry
@geminirising: omg she's so lucky
@lululemonaide: I was thinking cult
@geminirising: because the commune bought land from that guy who ran that cult for vengeful livestock or whatever
@ktcakes888: waiiiitt
@ktcakes888: You mean the Nature's Blood cult????
@ktcakes888: Like 1970s/80s era??
@badprincess: literally put my phone down for five minutes and I come back to a full on what the fuck
@nononycky: were they the ones that were cutting up stolen corpses and packaging body parts like groceries to make a point?
@ktcakes888: they put tainted meat on the shelves too
@ktcakes888: People got really sick
@highasakyle: oh right
@highasakyle: the ones who like basically all shat themselves to death
@lululemonaide: yeah, there was cross-contamination
@lululemonaide: e. coli on surfaces, etc.
@lululemonaide: they didn't believe in chemical cleaners
@nononycky: or doctors
@gustagusta: wait hang on
@gustagusta: The cult was still around when Nina Faraday disappeared.
@gustagusta: one of them was a suspect, remember?
@gustagusta: Let me see if I can find the article . . .
@meeksmaster: I remember. The creepy drifter.
@meeksmaster: someone saw him with a shovel and a duffel bag walking on SR 44 the night she disappeared
@lululemonaide: okay first of all his name is Brian
@lululemonaide: second of all they wasted a week digging up roadkill

@lululemonaide: even though precisely zero of the teeth he uses are human
@highasakyle: um
@highasakyle: ...
@highasakyle: ...
@highasakyle: ...
@highasakyle: What?
@badprincess: teeth????
@skyediva this is like watching a crime podcast
@skyediva: Don't want to know / can't stop listening
@lululemonaide: it's actually really pretty when it's finished
@lululemonaide: You can totally see why it sells
@ktcakes888: when what sells ... ????
@mememeup: damn it
@mememeup: Unsubscribe
@lululemonaide: the jewelry
@lululemonaide: It's really nice, actually
@lululemonaide: I'm sure Brian will show you
@lululemonaide: He's super friendly
@lululemonaide: He still lives on the commune

Olivia Howard's house, we agreed, was just too far from town for a party.

Spinnaker proposed a deal: forty bucks a head to cover expenses, an additional twenty to be held as collateral until after clean up, and we had to be out by eight o'clock. In exchange: a four-hour pool party that Akash would invite Lucy Vale to attend. Conditions were as follows: no alcohol, weed, or illegal substances; no song requests or manipulation of the playlist; Meeks would DJ.

We were fucking outraged.

Forty dollars? To hear Meeks DJ?

How dumb and desperate did he think we were?

We all knew the answer: exactly as dumb and desperate as we, in fact, were, which is why we were so scandalized. It was flagrant extortion. It was Mafia shit—especially since Spinnaker's family was *insanely* rich.

The fact that we would probably end up paying was the worst part.

@highasakyle: This is why nobody likes you
@highasakyle: You should be paying us
@bassicrhythm: doesn't your dad have like three BMWs?
@spinn_doctor: one of them's a Porsche
@spinn_doctor: And my dad didn't get rich by spending money
@nononycky: True. Just by inheriting it
@hannahbanana: Can you justify that cover price?
@hannahbanana: Would love to see a list of expenses
@skyediva Maybe we can trim the budget
@hannahbanana: Transparency = trust

Hannah Smith, alto saxophonist, was also the treasurer of DACS, Diversity in American Culture and Society, and the daughter of an accountant and an elementary school principal. No one could mine a balanced budget for meaningless motivational slogans like Hannah could.

We were still bartering with Spinnaker on the general thread when a new message popped up under #ANNOUNCEMENTS.

Sofia Young was back, and she'd apparently forgiven us.

@goodnightsky: check it out
@goodnightsky: my mom's going on a "work trip" this weekend with some slut she met on WLW
@goodnightsky: I can't believe this is my life now
@goodnightsky: soooooo....
@goodnightsky: party Saturday night??

We weren't happy Sofia's parents were divorcing, obviously. But we were glad that Sofia had found the silver lining.

TWELVE

Rachel

It took them a week of cleaning before they were ready to tackle the second floor. Still, they kept their air mattresses blown up in the living room. It wasn't bad, sleeping together in the open space. It felt like camping, Lucy said. To Rachel, it felt like starting over; she remembered sleeping on an air mattress for most of her first year of graduate school in an apartment cohabited by four other students.

Upstairs they wandered the empty rooms, observing the claw-foot tub in one bathroom, making note of the paneled doors and the strange decorative flourishes particular to Victorian houses.

The walls were covered with graffiti. Mostly kid stuff. Penises and curse words, nothing too bad. And in one room, painted huge and in red: *RIP Nina*. Rachel traced the letters with her fingers, thinking of smooth highways that led to nowhere. Thinking of a girl, evaporated like paint fumes sometime after school.

They bought paint. They bought painter's tape. They sheeted plastic across the floors. Lucy thought every room should be a different color. She picked out lemons and limes, eggshell blues, rosy pinks. Happy colors. Rachel thought it was a good sign.

They changed into old clothing and armed themselves with rollers and foam brushes. Lucy consulted instructional videos on YouTube, sitting cross-legged on the plastic, while Rachel poured out the paint in a shallow pan.

"This says we should start with the ceiling," Lucy said.

"We'll do the ceiling last," Rachel said.

"Okaaaayyyyy," Lucy said, dragging the word out into a question. "But YouTube never lies."

"If only that were true," Rachel said. "Open the window, will you? We need some ventilation in here."

Lucy stood up in one fluid motion while Rachel tested the ladder. She made an experimental stroke on the wall and felt a thrill as the color unfurled.

Lucy made a sound. "There's someone out there again," she said.

Rachel glanced over her shoulder. From this height, she had a clear view of the service road through the window. "Same guy?" Lucy had reported someone hanging out there earlier that morning. *Another lurker,* she'd said. Every day there seemed to be a few more of them.

"Or girl. I can't tell. They're wearing a hat. But I recognize the bike." Then, "Oh my God. Now they're taking *pictures*. Does this mean we're famous?"

Rachel carefully backed down the ladder to switch from a roller to a brush. She glanced out the window just in time to see a figure in a baseball hat pocket a phone and push off on a green bicycle.

"The house is famous," Rachel said. "We're just adventurers." She went back up the ladder again. Lucy returned, leaning an elbow on one of the treads to stabilize Rachel's weight.

"Have you started writing yet?" Lucy asked after a bit.

Rachel chuffed. "When would I have started writing? Yesterday I spent four hours on the shower grout."

"You're procrastinating," Lucy said in a knowing tone. "Because you don't know what the book wants to be."

"I don't even know if it *is* a book," Rachel said. "It's just a feeling."

Lucy thought about this. "I bet if we look hard enough, we'll turn up clues in the house," she said. "Secret cupboards. Something tucked beneath the floorboards. That's how it would go in a movie. We'd find Nina Faraday's diary, with the name of her killer written in it."

"So far I've mostly found mouse droppings and dead ladybugs," Rachel said. She didn't want to admit that she, too, had fantasized about discovering some remnant evidence of Nina and her mother in the house. Not a diary necessarily. But little details: glow-in-the-dark stars on the ceiling, like the ones Lucy was so fond of; pencil marks in the doorframe where Nina might have stood to measure her growth. Details that might help Rachel draw closer to the girl and her mother at the center of so much gossip and speculation, a furious storm of language that had by now almost completely occluded the truth. "But let me know if you turn up a smoking gun."

"I think she ran away," Lucy said. "I think Nina's mom was driving her crazy, and she just packed up and started over somewhere. That's what *I* would do."

Rachel turned around to give her daughter a look. "Except that your mom never drives you crazy," she said. "She's absolutely perfect. Right?"

Lucy grinned. "Obviously." Rachel drifted back to the window, running her fingernail around the flaking paint, chunking it to the floor. "I wonder what *he* thinks," Lucy said, gesturing to the stranger still wheeling his bike slowly just beyond the back gate.

"Well, maybe you should go out and ask him," Rachel said, only half joking. She was curious to know, actually, what locals thought about the Faradays now, all these years later.

All these years later, without a word from Nina Faraday.

"Yeah, right," Lucy said. She stuck out her tongue, made a gruesome face through the window, and waved.

THIRTEEN

We

We had to tell Lucy Vale that it was Olivia Howard's birthday so she would agree to come. We were ambivalent about the lie, which immediately brought headaches. For one thing, Sofia was salty that she was suddenly responsible for throwing Olivia's birthday party when Olivia hadn't even *invited* her to her real birthday celebration a few weeks earlier—and, even worse, had completely missed wishing Sofia happy birthday in February.

We pointed out that it was probably only because Sofia and Olivia weren't friends.

@goodnightsky: exactly
@goodnightsky: Hosting a pretend birthday party for a fake friend is just as much work as hosting an actual birthday party for a real one
@goodnightsky: Cake is cake
@goodnightsky: You know?

We couldn't argue the point. And ultimately, we had no choice but to go through with the fake birthday celebration. Akash had warned us that Lucy Vale didn't seem like a *party* kind of girl, an impression that only a cursory glance at her Instagram account confirmed. Since moving to Indiana, she'd mostly posted stories about her cat, Maybe, sleeping in different boxes, plus a few shots of the wild roses crawling up the collapsing trellis on the east side of the Faraday property.

Obviously we couldn't explain to Lucy that we weren't exactly party people either—not without confessing to entrapment. But Olivia Howard figured that Lucy Vale wouldn't miss a birthday party for one of the two Instagram mutuals she had in Indiana, and she was right.

On Tuesday, we heard through Layla Lewis, who'd heard through Olivia Howard, that Lucy accepted her invitation.

On Wednesday, we heard through Akash, who'd spoken to Lucy Vale, that she'd asked whether they could bike over to the party together.

On Thursday, it stormed. Rumors that the bad weather was going to last through the weekend started a brief hysteria of meteorology on the server. We swapped weather maps and resources, skimmed Wikipedia, and used "fast-moving pressure-system" in average conversation. Sofia reassured us: rain, shine, sleet, or shitstorm, her mom was leaving town to have sex with some slut named Jill, and we were having a party.

That week there was record collaboration and cooperation on the Discord server. We were excited about the ice-cream cakes Kyle Hannigan had scored from Baskin-Robbins—a low-key flex, since his dad was the regional sales manager. But we had no idea what to do about presents. Layla Lewis wasn't very much help; it turned out she was still annoyed about the sterling silver bracelet she'd bought Olivia last year, which Olivia hadn't worn even once.

Topornycky suggested that next time she add a pair of molars.

On Thursday, Aubrey Barnes offered Sofia Young her Party Supply discount card, and Peyton Neely scored a ride for them from her older brother, since Party Supply was only a few streets over from his dealer's house and he needed to buy weed anyway. The marching band geeks volunteered to blow up the balloons, as if the risk of death-by-balloon were too great for anyone who hadn't spent a decade huffing into a trombone.

On Friday, it was still raining, and Olivia Howard joined our Discord. Gifts, she told us, were *absolutely* not expected. Cards were welcome, of course.

> **@pawsandclaws:** but seriously, guys
> **@pawsandclaws:** your presence is enough

We planned our Saturday night maneuvers like a military campaign—partly because Jackson Skye was a huge military history geek, and he was the one who started the thread about carpooling. Will Friske's cousin, Josh—the one who ran a semifake landscaping business and a very real weed distribution center—offered to shuttle on Saturday night at a fair rate of five bucks a head. Nick Topornycky's older brother, Dylan, threw in a free ride with the purchase of one of the six-packs that had been baking in his trunk.

By Friday afternoon, the rain had slowed to a drizzle. By Friday night, it had turned to a slow-moving drift of mist.

On Saturday, we woke to blinding sunshine and couldn't believe our luck.

Normally, things didn't work out like we wanted them to. Normally, *disappointing* was the only luck we could count on.

But that was before. When we were in middle school. When we were freshmen. Bottom-feeders. Children.

Before we were about to be sophomores and had parties to go to, and throw, and lie about. Before the new girl came to town. Before the gates of the Faraday House opened again.

Maybe, we thought, our luck was changing.

Maybe Lucy Vale was a sign.

FOURTEEN

Rachel

Rachel kept track of all the names that began to bubble up in conversations with her daughter, writing them carefully in her notebook, the kind she'd carted around since graduate school. Lucy joked that Rachel's notebooks were an extension of her brain, a repository for all the to-do lists, reminders, and observations that buzzed ceaselessly in her head like swarms of delirious flies. *New GP? Submit Lucy's ID to Woodward. DMV—Monday. Advanced copies—when?* Hieroglyphs, Rachel thought; symbolic notations that pointed to every important moment of her adult life, and plenty of the spaces in between.

The year before, she'd been tracking Lucy's meals. The margins were packed with terms such as *cognitive distortion* and *control mechanisms*, remnant wisdom from their endless parade of therapy appointments. She'd filled pages and pages with a careful timeline of Lucy's developing compulsions: showering, plucking, scratching her skin with scissors. Not cutting, not quite. But close.

She'd been glad to shelve that notebook.

Now Rachel found a clean sheet of paper and made careful note: *Akash Sandhu—good kid. Alex Spinnaker—coding club. Olivia Howard—works at PetSmart.*

In Lansing she hadn't known any of Lucy's friends. She *thought* she had. There was sweet little Erica with braces and spotty skin, and Dhara, who was some kind of chess genius—girls whom Lucy had known since fifth grade. She hadn't thought much of it when they stopped showing up for monthly sleepovers and Erica's mother turned frosty, cold, when they occasionally bumped into each other at parent-teacher events. She'd been so busy—distracted with work, with the clamor surrounding her second book, with the slow, catastrophic fallout of Alan's affair. Lucy was fine, she thought. Too much on her phone, yes. Too often locked up in her bedroom alone. But fine, dependable. Grounded. Wise, in some ways, for her age. She was the one who'd told Rachel, *You don't need Alan. Alan needs you. That's why he resents you.*

And she was right; Rachel was sure that Lucy was correct. Rachel had loved Alan. But she had never *needed* him. Alan was just a familiar feature of her life, like the comfortable reading chair she'd had since her twenties, the one whose cushions retained the permanent impression of her thighs. For years they had simply lived their lives in parallel, coming together less and less frequently for sex, rising and sleeping at different hours. But always saying I love you. Touching hands, briefly, when they passed in the hall—Rachel on the way to her desk, Alan on his way . . . somewhere. Rachel hadn't thought to ask. She hadn't thought to worry about his frequent absences from home.

She hadn't thought much about Alan at all, if she were honest about it. *Or* about Lucy. She had taken them both for granted.

Then she began finding all those eyelashes, and Lucy's dinner balled up in her napkin and discarded with the trash. It was then she realized that something had gone terribly wrong.

On the afternoon she sent Lucy off to her first party in Indiana, Rachel finally made it up to the attic. The house felt strange in Lucy's absence. When Rachel imagined the move, she'd always envisioned the two of them cocooned inside this project—transforming this notorious, long-neglected house, revitalizing it together. She'd imagined Lucy selecting wallpaper, or hanging curtains. She'd imagined skating down the wide, sleek hallways in their socks. Making pancakes on Sunday mornings. Watching horror movies while the winter rain rattled the old windows.

But already, after only ten days, Lucy was ebbing away, drawn back into the world of her peers.

Well. That was as it should be.

Still, Rachel was afraid.

In the quiet, with the shafts of sun pinwheeling through the windows, the first words of a book fell into her head.

At first, everyone agreed that Nina Faraday was a good girl. Later, they began to have doubts.

As if on cue, her phone trilled in her back pocket. Her agent, Marc.

"How's my favorite client?" he said when she answered.

"How often do you say those words per day?" Rachel said. She had to lean her shoulder hard against the attic door so it didn't pop open like a cork released from a bottle. Up here the heat was sweltering. It smelled like wet mice.

"Depends on how many clients I call," Marc said easily. Rachel had known Marc since she was twenty-five, fresh out of graduate school and freelancing for *VICE Magazine* while toggling two jobs. They'd met at an industry conference in Chicago, and he'd recognized her name from an article about a sex scandal at a local Catholic school. He was only two years older than her but already wearing a suit, looking pressed and sleek and adult, as if someone had run him across an ironing board. He carried business cards in a silver case.

She disliked him, at first. She didn't take him seriously when he asked if she'd thought of writing a book. Lucy was a toddler. She and Alan, then a law student, survived mostly on ramen. She'd earned fifty bucks for the article that went viral.

But Marc had persisted. He'd monitored her bylines, sent her flowers when she got a job at the *Chicago Tribune*. He helped her shape her first book proposal. He even selected her pen name—a necessity, Rachel had decided, given the subjects she chose, and the attention that could follow.

"How's the heartland?" he asked. "Plant any corn yet?"

"I'm mostly worried about *un*planting things," Rachel said. From this height, the garage below buoyed up on a single tapestry of green, disrupted only by the narrow river of gravel running down to the back gate. "You should see this place. It's like the Amazon."

"How's Lucy doing?" Marc's voice softened a bit.

"Lucy," Rachel said, "is at a party. Not that kind of party," she added quickly. "A barbecue for someone's birthday. The kids around here seem nice." There were initials etched into the windowpane. She had to crouch and position herself at the right angle to make them out. *NF + TS*. Nina Faraday and Tommy Swift. Her heart gave a small thrill.

"That's great," Marc said. The weight of what had happened at Lucy's old school hung temporarily between them. Then Marc cleared his throat. "I've got an update on those ARCs. Good news is, they'll be ready in time for sales conference . . ."

They chatted a bit and then said their goodbyes, leaving the topic of Rachel's next book untouched. After they hung up, she stood for a while, running a finger over the trace impression cut into the glass. Someone had gouged several hard lines through the initials, as if in regret for putting them there. Was it Nina? Her mother? Or Tommy himself?

She roused and turned her attention to the miscellany of junk that had been left undisturbed in the attic for God knows how long. She doubted any of it had belonged to the Faradays, the last legal tenants, so far as she knew. More likely a generation of squatters and trespassers, junkies and ghost hunters, had wound their way up these stairs. At least there was no graffiti disturbing the old wooden beams and the rafters, mossy with spiderwebs. It would be a handsome room—an aerie of sorts—once it was scrubbed and sanitized.

She put on a mask and a pair of old gloves and began filling trash bags. The floor was covered in old newspaper, all of it hopelessly spotted with mouse turds. A festering mattress was gutting springs onto the floor. There were cardboard boxes, too, stacked around the room, slowly disintegrating into pulp. She opened one and saw more mouse turds covering a haphazard pile of old paperbacks. All of it would have to go down to the dumpster.

Up and down the stairs she went, sweating freely in her mask until it felt clammy on her skin. The whole time her mind kept pinging between Lucy at her first social event and Nina Faraday standing at the attic window, holding a penknife in her hand, eking out the initials of the boy she loved—then, at some point, furiously crossing them out.

It's always the same story with a few modern updates, Marc had said when Rachel told him about Lucy and her old school, all her problems the previous year. *It always comes down to a boy.*

A simple, and not entirely accurate, assessment. But there was some truth to it.

Rachel wondered whether there had been some truth to it for Nina Faraday too.

FIFTEEN

We

Whether or not Lucy was pretty, hot, beautiful, or some or none or all of the above was a matter of furious debate. After the party, we argued about the most basic facts of her appearance. Her hair might have been mousy brown, or dirty blond, or auburn. The word *caramel* was thrown around pretty freely.

We couldn't agree, it turned out, on even her basic physical characteristics. Allan Meeks, five foot four and one of the shortest boys in our class, swore Lucy Vale was even shorter than him and threatened to measure her to prove it. But most of us thought Lucy Vale looked average, and the Hannah Smith who played soccer swore that Lucy Vale was at least five eight. It was the same with her eye color, which varied between brown and hazel, the color of honey and the look of cheap weed, depending on who was reporting on it.

We tried to deconstruct Lucy's face, to triangulate the symmetries, to understand them, without success. When Spinnaker pointed out that her nose was a little too short for her face, and her ears a little too large, we couldn't disagree factually. Although we disagreed with what it implied: that Lucy Vale had flaws.

Some of us thought Lucy was a dead ringer for Jade Goodwin, the model who'd gotten her start parodying runway shows on

TikTok. After the party, Brent Manning made a composite image of legendary twentieth-century beauties such as Marilyn Monroe, Audrey Hepburn, and Gisele Bündchen to prove that Lucy's features corresponded perfectly to a recognizable Western standard of female perfection. The experiment was flawed. The composite image looked like a creepy CPR mannequin, or a doll that might be possessed, and it launched an enormous argument about racist beauty standards and the twentieth-century American eugenics movement.

Point was, Lucy didn't look at all satanic. At least we could all agree on that.

Otherwise, there was no consensus. Peyton Neely, for example, insisted that Lucy looked exactly like a white-tailed mongoose.

@badprincess: WTF is a white-tailed mongoose?

Peyton Neely posted a link to the mongoose's Wikipedia entry to the "New Girl" Discord channel. We were skeptical. Mongooses looked just like ferrets. Peyton Neely thought Lucy looked like a ferret?

@geminirising: No. I think she looks like a mongoose.
@geminirising: Do you not see it?
@mememeup: dude
@mememeup: Put a mongoose and a ferret in a police lineup, and there's no way anyone could tell the difference
@geminirising: why would you need a ferret or a mongoose in a police lineup?
@geminirising: They're different species. You could just take DNA samples

She had a point. But we all felt that if Peyton really thought Lucy looked like a ferret, she should have the balls to say so, not get sneaky with euphemistic mammals.

The first hour of the party was as awkward as the average cafeteria lunch. Sofia Young's house had been emptied by Mr. Young's departure, and we wandered the living room idly and filtered onto the deck, studiously ignoring all the missing family portraits and furniture. We were thrilled, and alarmed, to see everybody from the server in real life—none of us could remember inviting or approving Sean Douglas, for example—and we quickly knotted into groups and subgroups, collecting like lint around the fabric of our usual social sets. The anime heads and the gamers got into heated debates about manga we'd never heard of. The band and orchestra geeks dominated the chip bowl. The chorus and drama crowd swapped TikTok favorites and threatened to rope us into a video.

It was a relief when Nick Topornycky showed up with Sahara Richards and, more importantly, beer. Slowly we coalesced under its liquid power, and the novelty of awaiting the tenant of the Faraday House. The mystery had come alive for us again, animated by new blood. Kyle Hannigan asked Olivia Howard whether Brian, the creep who lived on her family's commune, had ever spoken about how the sheriff's office had considered him a suspect in Nina's disappearance. Olivia told us that (a) Brian wasn't a creep, (b) her family lived on a farm collaborative, not a commune, and (c) she'd never asked him because it was none of her business.

Nick pointed out that minding your business didn't seem very *collaborative*.

Before Olivia could respond, Sofia Young trumpeted, *She's here*.

A sudden crush of movement drove us to the front patio, where we waited, frozen and breathless, to catch our first glimpse of the new girl.

The sky was a pale, leached blue, the clouds the raw pink of entrails. We suffocated on our own excitement. It seemed to take forever for Akash and the new girl to move out of the trees. But at last, they did, and our anticipation collapsed around the reality of Lucy Vale. She had a wrapped present for Olivia under one arm—a pink sweatshirt with a stitched cat on the chest next to the zipper, we later saw—and as she and Akash started across the lawn, she kept freeing one hand from the box to tug at her shorts.

She wasn't tall, and she wasn't short. She wasn't thin, and she wasn't plus. Her hair was brownish. Not long. Not super short. But shortish.

Afterward we could never quite agree.

That was the thing about Lucy Vale. That's what frustrated and baffled us about her, and later drove us crazy trying to figure her out, twisted us into knots trying to get our hands around her shape. That's what drives us crazy even now, so many years after it happened: the neither-here-nor-thereness of her.

It wasn't that she was shy exactly. We soon discovered that Lucy had plenty of questions about Woodward, and our extracurriculars, and which teachers we thought were the hardest. She wasn't afraid of controversial opinions—such as hating ketchup, which was close to insane, or feeling ambivalent about swimming as a sport, which was wrong and would have to change. She told Will Friske that the best hot dogs came from Chicago but she didn't believe in deep-dish pizza, which was more like calzone cake.

The real problem with Lucy Vale was that she *wasn't one thing or another*. She told Riley French that she'd played soccer in middle school but wasn't very good. She couldn't even say what kind of music she was into; she told Meeks that it was *all over the place* and *depended on the vibe*. She talked a lot about her cat, Maybe, but denied being a cat person. But when Brent Manning asked if she was a dog person, she said no, definitely not. Too slobbery. Plus, she'd been bitten by a neighbor's terrier when she was a kid.

But she liked some dogs. She liked some cats. *Really,* Lucy said, *it all depends.*

On the one hand, Lucy's answer was totally reasonable. The Thompsons' chihuahua was an actual reincarnated serial killer, for example. And Mr. Mole, the now-obese tabby who lived in the Student Leadership Department Tutoring Center, would sit purring and drooling on our shoes until we gave him scratchies. Mr. Mole was the friendliest cat we'd ever met.

But the question wasn't actually about preferences. It was about personality. It was about *being* cat or dog people. Dog people were, for the most part, extroverts. They were social and fun, and possibly narcissistic. They might be sporty. They probably had nice hair. Cat people, on the other hand, were smart, shy, and prone to dreaming. They might be into theater or fan fiction. They wore scarves and loved thrifting.

The question was: What type of person are you?

And Lucy's answer—*it depends*—was a cop-out.

Lucy did like horses—from a distance at least. We couldn't believe it, but Lucy had never been on a horse before, unless a pony ride at the petting zoo counted, which it didn't. She was equally shocked to find out how many of us had horses. Scarlett Hughes's family stabled broncos for the rodeo in Pewter Falls; the Howards rehabilitated rescues; Kaitlyn Courtland and her cousin Ethan both competed in junior rodeo and stabled their horses with the Hughes. And that wasn't even *counting* the working farm horses.

Well, Toto, Lucy said, *I guess we're not in Lansing anymore.* We couldn't tell whether she sounded disappointed. We didn't figure out until after the party that Lucy Vale had moved from a university town, practically a city. That explained why she couldn't ride a horse.

The Vales were northerners.

We were desperate to know how she and her mom had chosen the Faraday House, and whether Lucy knew its history. But none of us were brave enough to straight-up ask her, even after the three six-packs were divided among all of us. It was hard to find a casual way to ask if she'd noticed a body hanging from the apple tree yet, or if there was any disembodied weeping coming from the attic. We were even afraid to use the words *Faraday House,* in case it led to awkward questions. If the Vales really didn't know about the Faradays, and the storm of theories about what had happened to Nina, we didn't want to be the ones to tell her.

Instead we edged as close as we could to the topic, hoping that Lucy Vale would take the hint and open up on her own. Jackson Skye pointed out that his dad had a paint and tile business, if the Vales needed help getting the house in shape . . . ?

When Lucy only said, *Thank you,* Evie Grant tried to salvage the opportunity, jumping in to say they must have their work cut out for them, seeing as the home had been so long *abandoned.*

But Lucy Vale simply replied that the inside of the house was a thousand times better than the outside made it seem. The owners, she said, had made sure to keep it clean and had hired a caretaker to regularly turn on the lights, flush the toilets, and run the heat so that the pipes didn't freeze in the winter—all of which was news to us.

Still, we refused to give up entirely. Even if Lucy didn't have much to say about the house, there was no way she could duck the topic of the garden: a ravenous, colonizing jungle that crawled up the front porch and snaked up the colonnade porch and looked as if it were determined to haul the house down into a grave. Between the apple tree, the ghostly apparition of the tormented Lydia Faraday, and rumors that a phantom Nina Faraday still wandered the old rose garden, the Faradays' ruined gardens were the most haunted botanicals in the Midwest, possibly the whole country.

We persuaded a stoned Will Friske to mention the flyer he'd slipped into the Vales' mailbox, the one advertising his cousin's landscaping business that largely served as a front for growing weed, in the hopes that Lucy might admit to knowing more about the property and why it had fallen into such disarray.

But it was useless. Lucy simply thanked Will Friske for the offer of help and told him that her mother had big plans for the garden. Then she told us a random story about the time her mom had planted false sunflower instead of Maximilian in her college co-op garden and, over the next two years, watched the Napoleonic conquest of the entire quad by colonies of yellow blossoms.

My mom learned her lesson, for sure, Lucy said.

Plants were social beings, just like people. They lived in carefully calibrated balance with their neighbors.

Introducing a new one could be dangerous.

~

After the party, we tried to hold on to an impression of Lucy.

What resurfaced again and again was the memory of Lucy Vale and Akash, arriving on foot from the direction of Hickory Lane, blurred at first behind a kaleidoscope of leaves that cut them into moving colors.

She looked nervous.

And for that first second when we saw Lucy Vale—nervous, pretty, and holding a wrapped gift, while the sun bled out into the trees behind her—we hated ourselves for lying.

But we hated her even more for believing us.

Then Olivia freed herself from the crowd and plunged toward Lucy, arms outstretched.

Perfect timing, she had said. *We were about to do the cake.*

Her voice canted over the music. Like a tailwind, the words swept away the momentary pressure of feeling bad. *The cake,* we echoed, *the birthday cake.* Like an incantation to ritual magic we all knew by heart.

We complimented Lucy on her wrapping job. Sofia suggested that she put the present with all the others, leaning a wink into her tone. Kyle Hannigan went to get the cake from the freezer. Evie Grant chased after him with the birthday candles.

We sang "Happy Birthday," loudly, with drama. We were horribly off-key. But at least we all sang together.

We were athletes and anarchists, band geeks and gamers, virgins and sluts. We were actors and magicians.

We lied, and we protected our own.

PART 2

ONE

We

School didn't start so much as engulf us, tsunami-style.

Three years ago, Principal Hammill had pledged to overhaul our academic program and bring improvements to Woodward's overall ranking. This year he was on a bender of new initiatives through the Student Leadership Department, and determined to make every one of them our problem.

Mrs. Steeler-Cox, our SLD head and chief propagandist, was hellbent on mind control. The Student Council, gestapo to Mrs. Steeler-Cox's Adolf Hitler, frog-marched to the endless rhythm of *participation*. We were cordoned with reminders, permission forms to forward to our parents. Health and vaccine certification notices attacked us with bold type. We were clobbered with opportunities for involvement—in new extracurriculars, in volunteer clubs, in petitions and information sessions and future bake sales. The student portal caved to a ritual onslaught of new rules and mandates, terms and conditions we scrolled through with our eyes crossed.

Our teachers were delusional with homework. The seniors were despotic. They colonized the student lounge. Senior pennants sprouted between the rafters; over the year, they would grow, a thickening of colorful felt, scrawled over with inside jokes, drawings, and iron-on patches. Freshmen overran the halls like an infestation of rats in rotten corn.

We auditioned for *The Crucible*. We pined for the dance team—to join it, to date its members, to get close to Bailey Lawrence, Savannah Savage, and Mia Thompson, the three sophomore Strut Girls, the most beautiful girls we'd ever seen outside TikTok. We signed up for Model UN and signed a petition to return saltshakers to the cafeteria.

We could not *believe* that Mrs. Jennings assigned Spanish II an essay on day one. Never mind that it was only a few hundred words. She clearly required medication.

Questions assaulted us from our homework; they startled us at our desks. We couldn't get through dinner without an attack of hows and whys.

We rolled our eyes at the announcements and swiped memes under our desks. We juggled new classes, new clubs, and outrageous episodes of acne. We claimed our assigned lockers and bartered for better ones. We swapped stories that didn't belong to us. We were Woodward insiders and professional informants. Bailey Lawrence and JJ Hammill were on again. Savannah Savage was dating girls now. Calum Caloway knocked a girl up over the summer.

September was for signing up, and signing in, and sleep deprivation.

But most of all: September was for Sharks.

After Labor Day, an infestation of team pride swept the county. The Four Corners, our collective constellation of towns, molted its summer skin and broke out in school colors.

We gossiped about Coach Jack Vernon and the Granger Club team, one of the best club teams in the Midwest. We imagined tension between Vernon and Coach Radner, an ossifying Woodward fixture who'd coached the high school team—and been vying for a position with Granger Club—ever since Coach Steeler was forced to abnegate both positions. We argued about whether Coach Steeler should indeed get his name on a memorial pavilion proposed for the Aquatics Center. We agitated for a sauna in the girls' locker room under the guise of gender equality, as we'd done the year before. We gossiped about the new swimmers and about Noah Landry, who'd shot up another four inches over the summer and would be competing for the high school team for the first time.

The county was invaded by swarms of great white sharks: sewn onto jackets, ironed onto T-shirts, painted in the windows of downtown Granger, swimming across the frosty windows of the fish aisle at Kroger. Pennant flags in our school colors—orange, yellow, and black—went up between telephone poles, suspended overhead like downward-pointing flames. The diner advertised its new autumn specials: Man-of-Steeler fish-and-chips and Shark Bait shrimp tacos. The post office was offering special edition Shark stamps. Spinnaker started talking about NFTs.

For the most part, we forgot about Lucy Vale. With our focus on surviving a new year, and on dominating a new swim season, we absorbed her into the mass of our student body with barely a ripple. We bounced her between the gamers and the vegans, left her oscillating between lunch tables. She was Akash's problem, and his special project.

We figured they would get together any day.

Lucy Vale joined chorus, then switched to band, and then returned to chorus. She refused to sign up for mock trial, waffled about trying out for the soccer team, but ultimately opted instead to volunteer with the Student Justice League. She caved to Skyler Matthews's pressure to join the literary magazine, which, as far as we knew, had never published an actual issue. She volunteered for the yearbook committee with Kaitlyn Courtland, challenged Evie Grant and Hannah Smith to games of Words with Friends, and shared Spotify playlists with Olivia Howard. She dropped in periodically to the after-school meetings of the coding club, mostly to kill time with Akash before they took the late bus home together.

Still, she didn't quite belong. We wondered about who her father was, for example. Akash said that Lucy never talked about him, although she'd once mentioned an "ex-stepdad" and talked about having aunts and cousins in nearby Everest. We tracked with distanced curiosity the evolution of the Faraday House, its softening transformation under the Vales' workmanship.

When Olivia proposed inviting Lucy to join our Discord, we quickly axed the idea. Akash was stridently against it. For one, he didn't want Lucy Vale to know that we all participated in selling homework to the athletes. He doubted she would approve.

For two, if Lucy Vale joined our Discord, we couldn't talk about her anymore.

In those early back-to-school weeks, when we saw Lucy Vale hunched over her laptop in the back of the student commons during free periods or heard her name over the loudspeaker, it was surprising, like a touch of static. Lucy Vale was still a foreign object, a misplaced LEGO underfoot.

September was a bad time for new girls and old ghost stories.

In September, we had other things on our minds.

TWO

We

The news that half a dozen Sharks had been jumped by a rival team on their way out of Lucky Strike bowling alley ricocheted around social media and blasted onto Discord on a Sunday, twelve hours after the county sheriff had allegedly been called to break up the fight.

We were just trickling out of various church services, and our outrage that day was appropriately biblical.

The Jalliscoe Wolverines were one of a handful of Indiana high schools that counted a roster of excellent club swimmers on their teams, and we hated them. The whole town was a hellhole of fork-tongued devil-worshippers. Their mascot represented a clear psychic attraction to the beast, a magnet for the deceitful and corrupt.

The general channel that day was a ruin of informational shrapnel. Contradictory facts sparred for screen space. The Wolverines had used a baseball bat. A beer bottle. Both. It had taken two deputies to break up the fight. One of the Wolverines was in the hospital. Aiden Teller was in the hospital. The Wolverines' head coach was threatening to press charges. Coach Radner was going to suspend Ryan Hawthorne for throwing a punch at a deputy. Coach Vernon was going to boot Teller from the club team.

We rushed to the *County News* website to check the police blotter. But the most recent post was from Friday: a handful of misdemeanor possession charges, a suspected arson reported on Donahue Road, half a dozen DUIs. We pretended not to notice that Topornycky's uncle had been booked again; it barely counted as news anyway. We obsessively hunted down accounts for the Wolverines and shadowed anyone they'd recently tagged in their photos.

Sofia Young logged on.

She wanted to know if it was true that Jeremiah Greene had been arrested.

We freaked the fuck out.

@badprincess: Jeremiah was arrested????
@mememeup: wait wait wait
@mememeup: Are you positive?
@goodnightsky: I'm pretty sure one of the Sharks was arrested
@goodnightsky: This girl at Waffle House said her stepbrother works at Lucky Strike
@goodnightsky: And she mentioned Jeremiah
@badprincess: wow
@badprincess: institutionalized racism much
@nononycky: #defundthepolice
@brentmann: we need to get all the facts before we start jumping to conclusions
@nononycky: the criminal justice system says otherwise
@brentmann: so Greene was arrested because he's black?
@safireswiftly: I don't think so
@kash_money: watch out, your white privilege is showing
@safireswiftly: I'm literally Black
@safireswiftly: I'm saying I don't think Jeremiah Greene was arrested
@safireswiftly: He was at church at like 9 a.m.

@ktcakes888: ?? You're supposed to message me when you change handles, Alyssa
@skyediva: your church starts at 9 a.m.??

In the absence of hard facts, we floated suspicions of conspiracy. Lucky Strike was right on the border of Willard County, only twenty minutes from the pool where the Willard Swimming Club trained. A solid portion of Willard Club swimmers competed for the Jalliscoe High School team during the fall season. Maybe the whole fight was a Jalliscoe plot, a ploy to get the Sharks suspended, or to break Alec Nye's elbow, Tonya Harding–style, with a baseball bat. It wouldn't be the first time Jalliscoe had plotted to take down the swim team. As far as we knew, every deputy on the Willard side of the county line was protective of their home team, and as crooked as the teeth of a zipper.

Then Nick Topornycky reminded us darkly about That Time with Will King.

Meeks sent him a question mark.

Ethan Courtland asked whether Will King was the alien abduction guy. Scarlett Hughes said that she could totally imagine Jalliscoe full of aliens. Alyssa Hobbes accused her of racism. Scarlett clarified that she meant ETs, not illegal immigrants.

Nick Topornycky clarified that *Warren* King was the alien abduction guy. Will King was a swimmer who graduated with his older brother.

Friske made a joke about anal probing.

Olivia Howard wrote at the same time as Meeks to ask about the alien abduction.

Alyssa Hobbes wanted to know what happened That Time with Will King.

THREE

WE

The Thing with Will King happened when we were still in middle school. Will King had just broken up with his girlfriend and was on the rebound. The girl he met online was older. Gorgeous. A beauty queen, she said.

She said she was from Prairie Lakes.

Which was true. By *then*.

What she didn't say was that she'd been expelled from Jalliscoe High School her sophomore year when it turned out she and two friends had been giving head to any athlete who would give them oxy.

She also didn't mention that she was now working both sides of the market, getting bulk from a friend's cousin, a con job who sold "miracle supplements" to competitive athletes who wanted an edge.

It was preseason, Labor Day weekend, when she finally invited Will to hang out. Her college friends were throwing a party off campus. King noticed that a few guys from the Wolverines had showed up, along with some bottom girls from Jalliscoe. But it was a big party, and he was worried about drawing out the cops. Again, it was preseason. There were plenty of drugs floating around, and everyone was getting wasted. He had practice in the morning.

Luckily the girl was ready to go home, so they left together.

He admitted later that he'd seen her take a bunch of shots with her friends. But she wasn't slurring, and it never occurred to him she was high as a kite. She'd told him she was an athlete. He figured she knew better.

So he drove her home and walked her in, and they hooked up for a few hours. By then it was almost two o'clock in the morning, and he was tired.

So he split.

Monday morning, Will King woke up to find two Willard County sheriff's deputies in his living room. Afterward Will King said he wasn't sure whether the pills discovered in his console had been planted by his date or by the deputies who'd been authorized by his father to search the car; the Kings later found out that one of them was the girl's cousin by marriage.

The subsequent investigation turned up plenty of proof that the girl's initial claims to the police were bullshit. In the end, she recanted her accusations and dropped all charges against him. But by then Will King's acceptance to Wisconsin had been rescinded, he'd missed the entire season, and the Sharks had lost out on the state trophy.

Will King was a cautionary tale. The thing is, he'd been naive. Too trusting. A good kid.

And being good could get you in serious trouble.

The problem was that not everyone was trustworthy.

And the thing about girls from rival counties?

They lied.

FOUR

Rachel

Rachel hated being a liar. But it was part of her identity, an aspect of her career—of her history, even, and of Lucy's. So she'd found ways to skirt the truth, to skim past it in conversation, to refract her words slightly around their real intention.

To the freckly librarian at the Granger Public Library, she merely introduced herself as new to the area and explained that she was interested in learning more about the history of the house at 88 Lily Lane.

"Oh." The librarian, whose name tag identified him as Ted, looked immediately nervous. "What sort of history?"

"I understand there have been deaths in the house," Rachel said, and he flinched. Quickly enough, however, he recovered. "The main house was built in the late 1880s," he said and began keystroking at his computer. "The Adamses were major landowners. Pioneers of the area's early agribusiness. At one point, all the land in that area belonged to the family. Generations of them lived and died in that house. I can see what we have, but you might have better luck with the historical society . . ."

"I meant more recently," Rachel said. "I understand that everyone refers to it as the Faraday House . . . ?"

Ted the librarian stiffened, cleared his throat. "Yes, well, its most recent history . . ." He trailed off. "Well, you can read about it in the old

Rockland County Register. The paper folded a few years back. But we've got almost every copy loaded up in our archives. I'll show you how to search it. But it makes for grim reading."

"That's okay," Rachel said. "I'm a grim person."

Ted the librarian didn't seem to appreciate the joke. But he agitated out from behind the desk and gestured for Rachel to follow him. They passed through careful displays of popular fiction titles and carved a left to the library's multimedia center. Rachel noted that it had been gifted by the Steeler family. The Steelers were inescapable in this county. Their money and influence were everywhere, like the invisible pressure of a bad smell.

It had been a mistake—childish, really—to alienate the Steeler-Coxes. She'd meant to send a thank-you note for the philodendron. She'd at least thought about it. But she'd never been good at that kind of thing: social pleasantries, mannered niceties, the back-and-forth social rituals that preserved a kind of suburban equanimity. Her mother, an academic and former punk rock musician who boasted of doing heroin with Gregg Allman, had often told her that manners were invented by Louis XIV for the purpose of keeping the aristocracy too preoccupied to rebel. Rachel hadn't even learned to properly hold a fork until she was in college.

So she hadn't sent a thank-you note. Then she'd discovered that Ann Steeler-Cox, Jay Steeler's only niece, was the administrator of something called the Student Leadership Department, which seemed to have some obscure role in both student academics and the athletics department. There had been an unpleasant incident regarding Lucy's enrollment paperwork and Rachel's refusal to list her daughter's religious affiliation. Eventually, losing patience with Ann Steeler-Cox's repeated insistence, Rachel resubmitted the paperwork with the family's religion listed as "pagan."

After that: silence.

The multimedia center was large, windowless, and faintly antiseptic. Rachel selected a computer far from a small cluster of teenagers who appeared to be mostly playing with their phones. Ted showed her how to navigate the library's digital archives and then left her alone.

There were, she discovered, 123 references to *Faraday* in the *Rockland County Register* from the time that Nina was first reported missing to the date of the newspaper's last edition. By contrast, the Sharks had gobbled up more than a thousand references; the Steelers, another four hundred. Tommy Swift alone had found his way to print more than sixty-seven times.

She opened a few articles at random, starting from the older headlines. Tommy Swift Flies into State History. Tommy Swift—the Next Indiana Olympian? There was Tommy Swift doing service work with his church youth group, and Tommy Swift dressed in a tux with his teammates ahead of something called the Winters Dance. Balladeer Auction for Tommy Swift Fetches $1000, the caption read.

A short twelve months later, the coverage took a turn. Tommy Swift Issues Statement Regarding Disappearance of Ex-Girlfriend. Tommy Swift Defends Against Doping Allegations. Tommy Swift Disappoints at States. Almost unconsciously, she slotted each article into a growing mental timeline, a reverse hero's arc.

Next she loaded up results for *Faraday* and performed the same desultory review, this time moving backward from the most recent articles. Family and Friends Gather for Vigil, Ten Years After Nina Faraday's Disappearance.

Backward: Coroner Pronounces Lydia Faraday's Death Suicide.

Backward: Lydia Faraday Brings Simultaneous Charges Against Woodward High School and Rockland County Sheriff's Department.

And again: Where Did Nina Go? Swim Team Rocked by Suspicions.

"The Sharks will eat their *faces*."

Rachel startled at voices across the room. Two high school girls were sitting elbow to elbow at the same computer terminal, scrolling a social media site and lobbing their conversation cavalierly through the otherwise silent space.

"No, but literally. How stupid can you be?"

"Alec Nye is literally going to kill someone. Like, he might actually commit homicide."

"He actually should."

A memory pulled at her: a long-ago Halloween party on an unseasonably warm October day at the off-campus residence of a group of College of Southern-Indiana fraternity brothers. Her cousin had begged her to go. She already felt old among the crowd of undergraduates. Old and sad. She'd just broken up with Dan. Or was it Max? She'd been drinking too much that first year out of college. Drinking and smoking too much weed.

She drank too much that night.

She remembered a massive unfurnished basement pulsating with bodies, and music so loud it blew out one of the speakers. She remembered squatting in the woods to pee after both bathrooms backed up onto the floor, taking sips from a full SOLO cup even as the urine ran between her sneakers. She had cat whiskers painted on her cheeks with mascara. Her cousin was dressed as Artemis and carrying her father's longbow.

She remembered the crowd agitating around a surge of new arrivals and a single syllable rising, repeated all through the yard like wind passing through an undulation of grass. *Sharks. Sharks. Sharks.* High school kids. At the time, she hadn't known what it meant.

She closed out of the archives. She wasn't ready to go back there yet. She wasn't ready for the research, for the agonizing crawl across the past. She wasn't ready for the Faradays, and what had happened to them here.

Somehow Nina had dropped out of the world—swallowed up, vanished, inhaled without a trace. Collapsed into dead typeface, an endless march of stories about who she was and whether she was worth looking for.

But it was Lydia Faraday that Rachel felt for the most. She had tried so hard to get justice for her daughter. She had tried to hold the right people accountable.

The problem was, they were the wrong people to cross.

Stupid woman.

She hadn't had a chance.

FIVE

We

Shark Week that year was violent with school spirit, and anti-Administration passion.

By then we'd figured out that it wasn't Jeremiah Greene but Aiden Teller, one of our cocaptains, who'd been arrested. Even worse, we heard that Ryan Hawthorne had injured his shoulder in the fight.

> **@mememeup:** welp, there goes the season
> **@bassicrhythm:** should we be having a vigil or something?
> **@kash_money:** for the season?
> **@bassicrhythm:** for Hawthorne's shoulder
> **@gustagusta:** which means, for the season
> **@badprincess:** how are you guys making jokes about this?
> **@badprincess:** I'm sobbing rn
> **@geminirising:** me too
> **@mememeup:** co-sign on that

It didn't matter, in our minds, who'd thrown the first punch. Clearly the whole thing was an ambush, and Jalliscoe was to blame.

> **@spinn_doctor:** I'm telling you, this was coordinated

@spinn_doctor: Jalliscoe masterminded the whole thing
@highasakyle: Wouldn't that require a mind?
@highasakyle: What is "too smart for the inbred bootsuckers who live in Jalliscoe?"
@spinn_doctor: apparently not, @highasakyle, since it worked
@spinn_doctor: This is straight out of *The Art of War*
@spinn_doctor: If you guys were actually literate, this wouldn't surprise you
@ktcakes888: not the time, Spinnaker

The next day, half the Sharks came to school looking like rotten vegetables kicked around a field. The whole team was alternating between stoicism and grief, like prisoners facing a morning execution. Meanwhile, not a peep from Administration. Mrs. Steeler-Cox was allegedly locked up with Principal Hammill all morning, and none of us even had the heart to make a joke about what they might have been doing all that time.

Slowly we cobbled together a timeline. The swim team had gone for pizza with Coaches Radner and Vernon. This in itself was newsworthy, and suggested a new era of cooperation between the Granger Club Team and our high school Sharks, something that could only bode well for the state title—and make our competitors hysterical.

Afterward, some of the guys had gone bowling. Cocaptains Alec Nye and Aiden Teller were in one car. Ryan Hawthorne had Jeremiah Greene and some of the juniors in his jeep.

JJ Hammill was driving his dad's 4Runner, even though it was after 9:00 p.m. and he technically didn't have his driver's license yet, only his permit. Hammill left the bowling alley early and was first out of the parking lot. According to Nate Stern, who heard it from Conrad Lyons, whose cousin Liam had just made the swim team, Hammill was turning onto the road when the Wolverines arrived. The two cars nearly collided. An argument broke out, then escalated. At some point, one of the Wolverines exited their car with a baseball bat and aimed it for

Hammill's headlights. Hammill gunned it, and another Jalliscoe goon hurled a bottle at his fender.

Nye, Teller, Hawthorne, Greene, and a handful of other Sharks were just filing out of the bowling alley when they saw the bottle fly by Hammill's car, missing it by inches. All hell broke loose: eventually three deputy cars dispatched to the scene.

By dinnertime we'd heard that one of Jalliscoe's swimmers was in the hospital, claiming the need for stitches and alleging he'd been hit with a bottle. Meanwhile, the Wolverines and their loyalist stans were already grumbling about a lawsuit. The worst part was that, for once, we couldn't dismiss Spinnaker's ranting as paranoia. More and more, it was looking like the Sharks were under attack by coordinated forces.

We were so desperate for news about Aiden Teller, we even turned to our parents. Eventually we confirmed through Evie Grant's aunt, who knew Aiden's grandmother from the historical society, that Aiden had in fact been sprung from jail. But his socials were ominously quiet. *None* of the Sharks were posting, and that made us more nervous than anything. In the silence, we sensed a hefty dose of Administrative influence.

We didn't trust it. We knew we could defend the Sharks' behavior only to a point—especially if it turned out that some of the swimmers had been drinking like a few people were saying online.

Then, midmorning, Jackson Skye spotted Vice Principal Edwards ushering two Willard County deputies into the office, and we started hearing the poisonous whisper of *disciplinary action*. The words soured the atmosphere and filled us with dread. First Meet was in less than a month, and Aiden Teller was one of our best swimmers.

We didn't know what was worse: that Jalliscoe now had Administration in a headlock or that we had to admit that Spinnaker was right. We *should* have read *The Art of War*, or at least skimmed it, or skimmed the SparkNotes online. Because that's what this was. Not a competition. An attack.

Jalliscoe was trying to take what was ours by right.

The Sharks weren't a symbol. They were a line in the sand.
We vowed to protect them, no matter what.

~

Over the weekend, an epidemic of school colors turned the campus violent shades of yellow and black. An infestation of shark decals gnawed the walls of the cafeteria, followed us to our lockers, and leered at us from the bathroom mirrors. A local news crew suddenly materialized in our parking lot; college recruiters drifted into Vice Principal Edwards's office. Reese Steeler-Cox and the Student Council Mafia were sutured to their cheer uniforms.

Woodward pride was so extreme, it bordered on punishing. We were a seething, concentrated force of *winning* and grimly determined to have the greatest week ever.

At the same time, we noticed symptoms of a surprising change: somehow, when we weren't paying attention, Lucy Vale had started nudging toward *popular*.

Layla Lewis first reported that Savannah Savage had invited Lucy to sit next to her in math class. We felt a sudden premonition of dread, as if some key fact about the new girl had eluded us. As soon as we were alert to the possibility that Lucy Vale had attracted the attention of the school's Echelon, we saw proof of it everywhere. We tracked Lucy's rising clout by the people who said hi to her—or went out of their way to give her dirty looks—in the hallway. Eli Franklin, the best player on the admittedly mediocre basketball team, started circling around her locker. The rest of the team hooted her name whenever they saw her in the cafeteria.

Most telling was the way Reese Steeler-Cox and the Student Council Mafia started side-eyeing her. Gone were the veneer of friendliness and the fake smiles spackled on in the new girl's direction.

The final proof of Lucy Vale's new popularity hit like a stomach virus: suddenly, violently, and in the bathroom.

At issue: whether Lucy Vale was wearing the wrong shark.

What Happened to Lucy Vale

~

We didn't know that the Student Council Mafia had cornered Lucy Vale about the hammerhead shark on her sweatshirt until Aubrey Barnes saw her crying between third and fourth periods.

Akash lost his shit.

@kash_money: WTF what do you mean crying??
@kash_money: what happened??
@kash_money: where is she??

No one knew; Lucy Vale wasn't answering her texts.

We were outraged, appalled, and stymied by helplessness. We drowned in our respective seats across campus, fending off the assault of irrelevant education coming at us from our teachers. We thumbed messages under our desks. Ethan Courtland managed to send a desperate SOS before Mr. Harte confiscated his phone for the remainder of the day. We observed our customary moment of silence when we lost him on the chat.

Within the hour, details of the confrontation began to materialize. We constructed a picture from discrete facts, dropped at random like errant pieces of a jigsaw puzzle we had to fit together without a reference. There was the fact that Lucy Vale was absent from fourth period, and Aubrey Barnes reported that Lucy had been wearing nothing but a tank top by the time she was seen red-faced and puffy-eyed outside the cafeteria. There was the backed-up toilet in the girls' locker room and the janitor called to clean up the water seeping into the hall. There was Scarlett Hughes's cousin's text asking if Lucy Vale was okay. There was the shrill, hysterical voice of Mrs. Steeler-Cox piercing our eardrums through the loudspeaker, reminding all students that we at Woodward had a code of conduct that we would pledge to obey or risk losing our school privileges—e.g., the right to attend.

Our best intel came from Ceecee, a Woodward graduate and our Administration mole. Ceecee was related to the Steeler-Coxes through marriage to Lieutenant Steeler, which made her pretty much unfireable. She was also a raging alcoholic who dosed her sodas with vodka stashed in old Pepto-Bismol bottles and was so lazy that she rolled her chair from the filing cabinets to the copy machine and the front desk like an oversize Ping-Pong ball.

But she was a willing accessory to most of our usual misdemeanors, largely because she was so lazy—the forged late notes, which she pretended to believe had actually been signed by our parents; the claims of nonexistent symptoms that kept a rumored pop quiz off our schedules and landed us in the nurse's office for a forty-five-minute nap.

Plus, she had access to all the school's disciplinary files and a front-row seat outside Vice Principal Edwards's office. She was the one who leaked the news of Aiden Teller's four-week team suspension, for example—days before it was made public in the local news—and had long hinted that the Steeler-Coxes had plenty of skeletons in their closet. Although we were never sure if that was just the vodka talking.

According to Ceecee, Lucy had been cornered by the juniors between periods and forced to turn over her sweatshirt. We found out later that Charlotte Anderson, Reese Steeler-Cox's sworn appendage, had shoved it into the toilet—*after* she'd peed. Topornycky joked that this explained the cleanup in Stall 12. But we were too furious to think it was funny.

Technically every class was allotted a particular variety of shark: reef sharks for the freshmen; goblin sharks for us; hammerheads for the juniors; and for the seniors, great whites. We couldn't have told you who'd made this rule or how we'd learned it. It was just one of those unspoken laws that we absorbed together, like a giant oxygenated lung.

Nothing but wearing the seniors' great whites was a serious infraction. For example, Lana Mueller, a sophomore, was always parading around in her boyfriend's work jacket that had a hammerhead patch sewn on to one shoulder, and she'd never been aggressed by a marauding pack of juniors.

Clearly something deeper was at play.

The mystery was resolved before last lunch, when the Sharks and Minnows list was leaked online. None of us knew who'd drawn it up. Ultimately the authorship wasn't important. The Sharks and Minnows list, we understood, was bigger than any one person. It represented Consensus. It represented What People Were Saying—or more specifically, Who They Were Talking About.

It was a small scandal to see that Lucy had grabbed the tenth spot on the list of Minnows; all the other girls were freshmen. But it was only a small scandal. Given that Lucy Vale was new, we supposed she technically counted as fresh bait.

> **@ktcakes888:** is Lucy hot now? I thought she was just cute . . .
> **@moonovermatter:** I think she's so hot
> **@brentmann:** This list is a sham
> **@brentmann:** Bailey Lawrence is number one goddess
> **@brentmann:** She is perfection
> **@brentmann:** She melts glass
> **@mememeup:** the Minnows are new to school, dude
> **@brentmann:** I don't care. It's false advertising
> **@brentmann:** Bailey torches everyone on this list
> **@highasakyle:** maybe you should file a complaint
> **@kash_money:** This list is SO FUCKED
> **@kash_money:** Minnows are fish bait
> **@nononycky:** Sharks are trophies
> **@nononycky:** What's your point?
> **@kash_money:** My point is that it's sexist
> **@skyediva:** so is mansplaining sexism
> **@badprincess:** if you want to be offended, may I recommend the school's "Style Guide" for Shark Week themes

@bassicrhythm: you mean because 90 percent of the models are white girls??
@badprincess: I mean
@badprincess: Because 100 percent of the models
@badprincess: Are GIRLS
@nononycky: remember, Ladies
@nononycky: Shark Week is for everyone
@nononycky: But only YOU can prevent Unwanted Sexual Harassment
@geminirising: does the style guide count?
@mememeup: well for sure no one asked for it

Sofia Young, who was getting rebellious, insisted that Lucy Vale wasn't actually that pretty.

@goodnightsky: we just see her as pretty, because she acts like the kind of person who should be pretty
@goodnightsky: it's an optical illusion
@lululemonaide: ?? she is definitely pretty
@goodnightsky: see? that's what you think
@goodnightsky: so of course you see her as pretty
@goodnightsky: because you're expecting her to be pretty
@goodnightsky: It's called confirmation bias
@kash_money: I think it's called jealousy, actually

Sofia Young signed off.

Some of us messed around trying to circumvent our biases, to see if we could trick our brains into seeing the real Lucy. A few excruciating minutes of early American history, and we were easily falling off the New World into a thick fog of boredom so complete, it felt almost like clarity. Then, when we'd for sure cleared our minds of all Lucy thoughts, we'd sneak a glance at her. Or we'd try and rearrange Lucy's features in our heads to imagine her ugly, bunching her nose and eyes and mouth together in our imaginations, doubling her forehead and sharpening her chin to a knifepoint, whittling her nose into a hook. We'd carry this image with us in the halls, between classes, into the cafeteria, holding it like a shield against our expectations, hoping to startle off the mask of Lucy's prettiness whenever we first saw her.

The exercise was fruitless. None of us could be sure that the Lucy Vale we saw was, in fact, the real Lucy.

The day after the Sharks and Minnows list made the rounds, Lucy's name made a sudden leap through the loudspeaker just before third period: Bailey Lawrence, Savannah Savage, and Lucy Vale were to report to the vice principal's office immediately.

The announcement touched the whole school like a cattle prod. Some of us were in D-wing, looking across the slope of pavement to the Aquatics Center and the single construction trailer moored next to the fence. Some of us were in the cafeteria, teetering on the threshold minutes of our last free period of the day. Some of us were pulled back from a daydream. Some of us, from a doubt. Some of us were thinking of Jalliscoe. Others of the Sharks.

Lucy Vale, Bailey Lawrence, and Savannah Savage, please report to the vice principal before your next class.

The school shivered. We froze. Some of us held our breath.

Lucy Vale, Bailey Lawrence, and Savannah Savage, please report to the vice principal's office.

A surf of noise rose toward the halls from every classroom across campus, like the throaty gasp of an approaching wave.

Lucy Vale, Bailey Lawrence, and Savannah Savage, please report to the vice principal's office.

It was done. We agitated into motion and poured into a wave of movement without noticing that the binding spell had worked on us, instantly cauterizing the three names into a single concept, a joint action.

That's how all magic works: a spell that binds words to a belief. A belief that binds the world to the word, and the power of its magic.

Right away, we flooded onto Discord, unified by a single thought and a question mark. But Evie Grant beat us to it.

@badprincess: wait wait
@badprincess: Is Lucy Vale a Strut Girl now????

It made sense of what had happened to Lucy Vale in the bathroom, and why the junior girls were suddenly giving her the stink eye; obviously Lucy was a threat.

In the silence, we all said a brief prayer for Akash and his chances with Lucy Vale.

SIX

RACHEL

Lucy wanted to know when her mother was going to make friends.

"I have friends," Rachel said. "I speak to Billy Flescher almost every day."

"He's your *handyman*, Mom," Lucy said, rolling her eyes. "I mean *real* friends."

It was seven o'clock on a Tuesday. They were eating dinner at the wrought iron table they'd dragged out into a cluster of azalea bushes. For more than a month, the boys from Friske Landscaping had been working to clear the overgrowth of weeds, bushes, and Jurassic-size ferns from the two-acre property. They'd filled half of four dumpsters with yard debris: fallen branches, pulpy leaves, snarls of kudzu, armfuls of uprooted dandelions, which Lucy had mourned for their cheerful faces. Now, slowly, the garden was reemerging. Lanes of mulch wound in rivulets around the house, mounded softly like tended graves where dozy perennials could sleep until springtime. Rachel was surprised by all the beautiful plantings they'd uncovered, quietly withstanding the encroachment of hungry neighbors: a peony bush, for example, and a slender Japanese maple. Valleys of climbing rose bushes, so overgrown they hadn't flowered in years. And a semicircle of azalea bushes forming a natural enclave that opened out toward the service road.

Lydia Faraday had been a master gardener.

"Hey," Rachel said in her best *GoodFellas* voice. "You don't worry about me. I worry about you. Capisce?"

"I have friends," Lucy said mildly.

"Well, according to Ann Steeler-Cox, you don't have enough of them," Rachel said, only half kidding. She'd spent the morning sequestered in Ann's office at the Student Leadership Department, ostensibly to discuss Lucy's issue in the bathroom. She'd had trouble concealing her growing dislike of the woman who burnished her last name like some badge of honor. Ann had a long narrow face that reminded Rachel of a perpetual finger wag, and a vacant smile that never quite touched her eyes. *We just want to be sure that Lucy finds her place in our community,* she'd said in a hushed kind of half whisper, as if they were discussing something shameful. *It's our responsibility to help her.* As if there were something wrong with Lucy and not the girls who'd stripped her and shoved her sweatshirt in the toilet because of some stupid shark.

Still, it bothered Rachel that Lucy didn't seem more upset about her showdown with the older girls or the fact that she'd been summoned out of class to meet with Mrs. Steeler-Cox and the vice principal. If anything, Lucy was in a *good* mood. It had been her idea to eat outside—*in our fairy circle,* she'd said—and she hadn't once complained that Rachel, the world's most inept cook, had managed to scorch their frozen pizza. She'd even offered to make a salad, propping her iPhone on the counter, brow furrowed in concentration, following along to a YouTube video as she carefully measured vinegar into a tablespoon.

"Mrs. Steeler-Cox is a troll," she said now.

"She's just doing her job," Rachel said, although she tended to agree.

"Her job is to get money for the swim team booster fund. It's, like, her sole purpose in life. The Student Leadership Department is a scam. It's just shellacking."

"Who told you that?" Rachel asked.

Lucy shrugged. "No one told me," she said. "It's just a thing. Everybody knows."

Everybody. The word dropped casually from Lucy's mouth. For weeks the students at Woodward had been a *they*, as in, *They all want me to join a stupid club.* Or, *They're all freaking out because someone tried to steal their mascot.* Occasionally singular identities bubbled out of the monolith—Akash and Olivia and, more recently, someone named Bailey Lawrence—but for the most part, Lucy had cast herself stubbornly apart, at least semantically.

Maybe, despite what Mrs. Steeler-Cox had said, things were changing. Rachel had noticed that Lucy picked up more friends recently on her Instagram. She'd even angled for a TikTok account again. So far Rachel had refused, and she continued to monitor the photos her daughter was posting, even though it made her feel like a helicopter parent. No selfies. No full-lengths.

Nothing she might later regret.

"Maybe we should make you a dating profile," Lucy said, swiping pizza crust through the puddle of vinaigrette on her paper plate. "You're not too old." Then, squinting: "How old are you again?"

"Thirty-seven," Rachel said.

"That's definitely not too old," Lucy said, although she sounded uncertain. "You're not even *forty* yet."

"I feel too old," Rachel said. It was true. After the heartbreak with Alan, a collapse at the center of her adult life, and then all of the trouble at Lucy's old school, Rachel felt like she'd broken across the terrible shores of midlife. Like she'd washed up in this remote corner of Indiana as wreckage. That's why she was drawn to the Faraday House. She understood it.

"That's just because you're holed up here every day," Lucy said. "You need to get out more. Meet people. People who are alive," she added when Rachel began to protest. "And don't work at the library."

"We could join a church," Rachel said teasingly, and Lucy made a face.

"I'm thinking of becoming Wiccan," Lucy said. "Olivia Howard is Wiccan. She said my aura is orange."

"Oh yeah?" Rachel remembered what the family therapist had told her about being *present* for Lucy. That meant trailing after the meandering course of her conversation. "And what color is my aura?"

Lucy held her hands up, making a picture frame with her hands, and squinted at her mother. "Sad," she said finally. "Sad and worried about something."

"Blue then," Rachel said.

Lucy leaned across the table and grabbed Rachel's phone. "Here. Let me take your picture. You'll need them for Bumble." Lucy giggled.

"And what kind of man should I be looking for?" Rachel asked as Lucy slid around the table to fuss with her hair.

"Ew, Mom. I don't *know*."

Across the road, Rachel saw the doors to the Sandhus' back door slide open. Akash drifted outside to fiddle with a garden hose. Rachel suspected from the deliberately casual and unnecessary errand that he was really looking for Lucy. It was the third time he'd drifted onto the back porch since they'd started eating. She saw him angle slightly in their direction and lifted a hand to wave. Let him know that he was busted. He ducked back inside, looking sheepish. Poor kid.

"I think Akash might have a crush on you," Rachel said.

Lucy was still finger-combing Rachel's hair, arranging it to spill over her shoulders. "He's just a fussbucket," Lucy said.

"A fussbucket?" Rachel repeated. She had no idea where Lucy picked up her lingo—half of it a patter of italicized slang, the other half pure Lucy. "And what's he fussing about?"

"It's Shark Week, Mom. It's, like, the most important week of the whole year." Lucy leaned a heavy dose of sarcasm into her words. "He just wants to be sure I'm okay."

Rachel felt a tug of something in her chest. That old pain, the Gordian's knot of worry that had seethed in her chest for the past year and a half. She turned to Lucy and impulsively grabbed her wrists. They were still so small, so fragile feeling. She thought of bird bones, breaking against the sky.

"Are you okay?" Rachel asked. "Do I need to worry about you?"

Lucy looked at her for a moment. Then she belted a laugh, clear and loud, startling two wrens from their perch. Rachel watched them fleck up against the waning light.

"I'm fine," she said. She sounded triumphant. "I'm the new Lucy. Besides," she added teasingly, "*I* have friends."

She wrapped her arms around her mother's neck and kissed her.

SEVEN

We

In the end, no one could prove that the Strut Girls had filled Reese Steeler-Cox's gym locker with cat litter. In a way, it didn't make sense, not as retaliation for what had happened in the bathroom. Technically Reese Steeler-Cox hadn't been on-site, although Aubrey Barnes swore she saw Reese texting outside the bathroom at the same time Lucy was getting stripped down inside. But this was controversial; Aubrey Barnes was a notorious pick-me girl and always trying to insert herself into drama.

Some of us suspected Olivia Howard, for obvious reasons. She had ready access to cat litter and lived on a commune with a guy who made jewelry out of scavenged deer teeth. There was no telling what she was capable of. On the other hand, we didn't think she'd necessarily be motivated to revenge on Lucy's behalf. She was devastated that Lucy Vale had punked her invitation to join the Humane Society Club and blamed all the attention of the Echelon for changing her. Olivia even suspected—correctly, it turned out—that the reason Lucy Vale was hedging about yearbook was because she'd been invited to audition for the dance team by Bailey Lawrence, even though she'd technically missed the window for new recruits. Plus, we didn't know when Olivia would've had time to get to the gym before homeroom since she rode the longest bus from

Housataunick, and Nick Topornycky insisted they'd arrived just as first bell was sounding.

The evidence against the Strut Girls, on the other hand, was circumstantial but damning. The crime had been committed sometime between 7:30 p.m. on Monday, when Reese Steeler-Cox locked up after cheer practice, and 8:30 a.m. on Tuesday, when she'd run down to grab face paint from her gym locker and found the lock clipped with bolt cutters. Since the gym complex was locked every night at 8:00 p.m., and accessible only via the Aquatics Center, also locked from the outside, the window of opportunity narrowed to the hours before second period on Tuesday morning. Unfortunately—or maybe by design—Bailey Lawrence, Savannah Savage, and Mia Thompson had called the dance team to an early rehearsal for their pep rally routine in the auditorium. From there it was just a short sprint down the hill to the gym complex.

It didn't help that Savannah Savage's last TikTok included several cat emojis in the caption, or that Bailey and Mia had replied with devil and tears of laughter emojis, respectively.

The fact that the whole dance team swore they'd walked up from the locker room and back as a group might have saved the Strut Girls from suspension but was ultimately meaningless. The Strut Girls owned the dance team, like everything they touched. We knew the team covered for them.

In their favor was the fact that none of the girls had a cat or easy access to a litter box. Unfortunately this wasn't definitive; Mia Thompson had been lingering in the Student Leadership Department Tutoring Center, which had both, on Monday afternoon. Mia claimed that she'd simply been waiting on her boyfriend to finish a tutoring session. This was highly suspect, however, since her boyfriend bought all his homework through Spinnaker and Akash.

It wasn't clear whether the cat litter had for sure gone missing from Mr. Mole's box in the SLD Tutoring Center, but that was the general assumption. The school's sixteen-year-old tabby, Mr. Mole, had been rescued as a kitten from an underground cistern during the last major renovation of the Aquatics Center and found a permanent home in one of the unused conference rooms just outside Mrs. Steeler-Cox's office. According to Ceecee in Admin, who'd been a student at the time, Mr. Mole had found his way into the sewer drainage system during construction of the new pool, which is how he'd gotten his name. There was some debate about whether Mia could have smuggled the cat litter out of SLD and, if so, what she had bagged it in overnight. But we had no doubt the Strut Girls were capable of anything they put their minds to, especially when it came to retaliation.

Lucy Vale, on the other hand, was technically alibied. She'd skipped out on an after-school yearbook meeting on Monday and taken the early bus home; Akash confirmed that he'd walked with her to the parking lot after final bell.

All in all, it was a nearly perfect crime.

In the end, the announcement linking Lucy Vale to the most popular girls in our class did nothing but add to the buzz around the new girl and the growing feud between the junior Mafia members and the sophomore Strut Girls. Without hard proof, Admin couldn't penalize any of the girls. We made jokes all day about the dangers of *litter*ing, especially when Mrs. Steeler-Cox was within earshot, and we imagined that Reese Steeler-Cox looked a little bit wilted. For once, it seemed, the Student Council Mafia had taken a hit and reached the end of their power. For once, the Student Leadership Department was ineffectual.

We should have expected Admin to retaliate.

EIGHT

Rachel

On Tuesday, Lucy came home flush with excitement, bouncing her backpack on her shoulders as she trotted, breathless, from the bus stop. Rachel was sitting on the porch, lost in old reporting, trying to get her hands on an image of the mother and daughter who'd come before her. And then there was Lucy, bounding like a puppy up the newly laid walk, cleaving through the muddle of the past.

"You won't believe it," Lucy said, dropping cross-legged next to her backpack and pulling out her laptop. "Admin has gone fascist. All because of a stupid T-shirt."

"What are you talking about?" Rachel said, setting aside her reading. Still, she felt the Faradays skirting like a black spot at the edges of her vision, calling her attention back to something huge and bright and terrible, something so large it could not be looked at directly. "What T-shirt?"

"Bailey's T-shirt," Lucy said. Her face was white with heavy pancake makeup and her eyes lidded with thick, dark eyeliner. It was Come as You Aren't Day. The night before, Lucy had spent an hour debating all the things that she wasn't: an athlete, a cheerleader, a beauty queen, a band geek. But finally she'd determined to go emo. She still had the wardrobe and makeup, Lucy pointed out. Besides, it would be a kind of trick.

Come as you aren't anymore, she'd said. Rachel could hardly stand to see her daughter morph back into the sullen, pale replica who, for two years, had seemed to swallow her daughter whole. At the same time, Lucy was delighted to wear her old clothes and posture like a costume. *I can't believe I thought this was actually okay,* she said. *I look like a Halloween prank.* Rachel had forced a smile that felt more like a grimace. It was still too painful to be funny.

What she wanted to say was, *I thought I almost lost you.*

"Who's Bailey again?" Rachel asked, her fingers fidgeting toward her notebook.

Lucy gave her an incredulous look. "Bailey Lawrence? She's captain of the dance team. As a sophomore. She has like four thousand followers on TikTok."

"And what was so wrong with her T-shirt?"

"Savannah and Mia wore them too. It was from an old Madonna tour. It said 'Like a Virgin' on the front."

It took Rachel a beat to get it: come as you aren't, a virgin. She made a face.

"It was a joke," Lucy said quickly. "Mia's definitely a virgin."

"What about Bailey and Savannah?" Rachel asked.

Lucy gave her a stern look. "Mom," she said. "Don't slut-shame."

"I'm not slut-shaming. I'm just asking," Rachel said. Then: "Why? Are they sluts?"

"They're legends," Lucy said. "And their T-shirts were *funny*. But Admin freaked out. Now they're saying the whole dance team can't perform at First Meet. They said team members had violated Woodward's code of conduct."

She passed her laptop to Rachel. The student portal now included a two-page bullet point list of student infractions. Rachel scanned them quickly, amused.

"You can't have gum in class?" she asked.

"You can't *chew* gum in class," Lucy corrected her. She stood up, then leaned over her mother, letting her sleek ponytail swing down over one shoulder. "They've gone totally insane. See? *No improper use of waste receptacles*. What does that even mean?"

"Maybe they're trying to promote recycling," Rachel said mildly. Most of the rules didn't seem that objectionable: no phones in class, no using the bathrooms for selfies, no vulgar language, no bullying. The usual stuff.

"Wait until you see the new dress code," Lucy said, reaching over her mother's hand to scroll the keypad. "You'll lose your shit."

"Lucy."

"Sorry," she said, not sounding sorry at all. "But seriously. *Read* it." She nudged the computer screen a little closer on Rachel's lap.

Rachel quickly scanned the dress code. Shorts, skirts, and dresses must be no more than four inches above the knee. No translucent items of any kind. No slogans promoting violence or sexual activity. No "spaghetti strap" or strapless tank tops. No midriff-bearing shirts. Appropriate undergarments.

"It's a little extreme," Rachel admitted. "Especially the part about undergarments."

"It's more than extreme." Lucy yanked back her laptop and glared at the screen with such a punishing intensity that Rachel almost laughed. "It's completely sexist. These rules only apply to *girls*."

Rachel felt a little shock; she hadn't noticed. "Let me see that," she said and read the list again more carefully. Lucy was right. Other than the prohibition against graphic T-shirts, the rules only applied to traditionally feminine clothing.

She thought then of something she'd just read about Nina Faraday, a comment from one of the sheriff's lieutenants who'd defended the investigation of her disappearance against charges of indifference. *Look, as far as we know, Nina's off somewhere with some secret boyfriend. She wouldn't be the first.*

Rachel wondered what he had meant to say. The first *what*? The first girl to go missing because of her bad decisions? The first girl to cause headaches for the sheriff's department? The first girl who wasn't worth chasing down?

Rachel handed back the computer, slightly repelled by the idea of Mrs. Steeler-Cox hovering behind the font, keystroking her way into Lucy's closet and onto her body. Onto her *undergarments*, even.

Things changed, she thought, and then they didn't. They moved the way that drowning people tread water: temporarily and without real hope.

"Savannah says we should sue," Lucy said. "Do you know that Steeler-Cox told Bailey that her leggings were too tight last week? She said that Bailey might give people the wrong *idea*. That's sexual harassment."

"We're not going to sue," Rachel said, exasperated. "For God's sake, Lucy. We moved here for a fresh start. Just ignore it. Wear what you want."

"Wear what I want," Lucy repeated slowly. Then: "Are you sure about that?"

Her eyes were bright, sparking with the kind of energy she got when she had landed on a new cause or a new passion. Like miniature police lights were flashing a warning somewhere deep inside her.

Rachel knew then that she'd been somehow outmaneuvered.

"Why?" she asked warily. "What did you have in mind?"

NINE

WE

The next day, Lucy Vale came to school in a SpongeBob SquarePants costume, and we all lost our shit.

We snuck photos of Lucy trying to fumble her locker open with enormous white gloves and maneuvering the crowded hallway in a six-foot-tall cube of smiling Styrofoam. We got a video of Lucy sidling through the portico doors sideways. We bowed to her in the hall.

We couldn't get enough.

We found out that Nick Topornycky did the best SpongeBob impersonation in school. We were shocked by how good it was. How did a committed gamer with a known alien fetish pull off a SpongeBob impression like that?

We asked him if he even liked SpongeBob SquarePants.

@nononycky: who the fuck doesn't like Spongebob squarepants?

It was a good point.

Word spread quickly to Admin about Lucy's costume; it wasn't exactly the kind of thing that went unnoticed. We would have given anything to see Vice Principal Edwards shit a brick when he realized that Lucy was not technically in violation of the school's new standards for dress, had reported to all of her usual classes, and was taking notes as usual—kind of. Her costume was so unwieldy that she couldn't actually fit the Styrofoam bulk behind a desk, and bulbous white mitts made it impossible to type or hold on to a pen.

Still, she played the whole thing straight. She requested that someone help her press record on her iPhone at the start of every period. And she wasn't milking it for comedy or attention either. When she raised one of her bulbous hands, it was because she had to ask a question, always on topic.

It was absolute legend.

Lucy made it all the way to third period before she was once again called to Vice Principal Edwards's office. This time she was sent home to change. By the afternoon, the dress code had been amended by hand—sad work for Keith, the school's head janitor, who had to go flyer by flyer with a Sharpie—to include a prohibition against costumes. Administration posted a hysterical new message to the portal. Mrs. Steeler-Cox oozed into the font selection, a serif-heavy mess that reminded us of her signature on the summons she had her army of recruits distribute with increasingly liberal abandon.

Lucy's punishment galvanized a miniature revolt. It was Bailey Lawrence, in fact, who led the charge. Lucy Vale's outfit, Bailey argued, violated none of the new dress code rules. So what was the problem? Why had she been sent home?

To us, it reeked of sabotage. Was Admin trying to divide us, to repress our spirit, to bury us under so many rules and restrictions that we couldn't even focus on the upcoming swim season? Somehow the idea got floated that Mrs. Steeler-Cox was having an affair with someone from Jalliscoe and trying to rig the season in their team's favor.

Admittedly, it didn't make a lot of sense. Jalliscoe was solid, but they weren't as good as, say, Willow Park, which almost always made states alongside us. And Mrs. Steeler-Cox was clenched so tightly around her uncle's legacy, it was a miracle she hadn't shat out a state trophy by now. On the other hand, we knew that behind the veneer of school solidarity, affirmed with soul-deadening regularity on the official school social media accounts—which we followed only out of fear of reprisal—were political currents squalling over huge sums of money. Occasionally tension bubbled into view; the Tellers, for example, were considering bringing a lawsuit against the school board, and tension was ratcheting up over the planned construction of the Jay Steeler Legacy Pavilion in the Aquatics Center and whether his name would still grace the frontispiece. And for all the attention on the Woodward Sharks and the Granger Club Team, the swim teams and their operations were obscure to all of us, sheeted behind the warping influence of committees, subcommittees, boards, and the legacy booster fund.

Still, on an emotional level, the conspiracy theory was compelling. Besieged by homework assignments and laws about how we talked and dress and even chewed, trapped in the eddies of a system that turned us to its will, we suspected an unseen current of power was at work beneath the surface of our lives.

As freshmen, we'd tolerated it. What choice did we have? We were fresh meat. We were newly hatched. We were the Minnows, finning frantically around a threshing of dangers, just trying to survive.

But things were different now. We'd had a party. We'd even had alcohol. Topornycky knew where to score Adderall. Nate Stern sold weed out of his locker. Hannigan could get us a discount at Baskin-Robbins.

We were sophomores. We were turning sixteen and getting our learner's permits. We were practically adults—and just before swim season, we were all coming down hard with a violent case of giving-zero-fucks.

Forget our rivals. Forget the championships.

We entered October at war.

TEN

We

On Pajama Day, Lucy showed up wearing an enormous grain sack that covered her from shoulder to ankle. We had no idea where she'd gotten it or how she'd made it into a dress overnight. We didn't yet know that Lucy Vale could be like that sometimes: focused. Maybe she didn't know whether she belonged in chess club or debate, yearbook or the dance club. Maybe she liked most kinds of music.

But when she set her mind on something, Lucy Vale could be savage.

This time Admin acted quickly. By the end of first period, Lucy Vale was missing from biology and the rumor had whipped through the school: the new girl had been suspended for the day.

Bailey Lawrence spoke of fascism, a concept we'd recently studied in European history. She talked about freedom of expression, sexism, double standards, and the fact that the dance team had been unjustly banned from performing at the pep rally, which meant by syllogism that we wouldn't get to see any twerking. But mostly she talked about the Student Leadership Department's growing campaign of terror: the new rules and hall monitors, the new system of merits, the dress code, and the random locker searches.

It was all adding up to some serious Mussolini shit.

Bailey and Savannah led the charge into Vice Principal Edwards's office. Most of the dance team rallied behind Bailey Lawrence—no surprise—as well as some other Echelon girls we suspected were using the excuse to skip class. A handful of us went with them. Kaitlyn and Ethan Courtland had decent leverage with Administration; they had both volunteered to be parking lot ushers for the season's home meet and swore to report everything back in real time.

The rest of us followed the action the way we usually did: through our cell phones. Tucked into textbooks, palmed under desks, our phones were our tethers to reality and an antidote to the blunt-force trauma of ritual education.

According to Kaitlyn, Principal Hammill had to be called in to serve as backup. With students packing every square inch of available space in his office, Edwards had the desperate look of a fish trying to tail its way across fifty feet of sand.

Principal Hammill, a college football star and former marine, was famously implacable; when a raccoon got loose in the cafeteria the previous year, Hammill instructed everyone to clear the place and lock the doors, got in his car, drove home, and returned with a shotgun to plug the thing. But even he lost it after nearly an hour of back-and-forth. "Just . . . dress like normal people. Okay? That's all we're asking. Dress normally, in normal clothing, like you'd wear with your family."

That directive was, as it turned out, a fatal mistake.

Friday, Fancy Dress Day, fell with a heavy hand of gray mist. The weather was locked in an atmospheric stalemate somewhere between rain and evaporation. It put us in a strange mood; we felt as if we were waiting for something to happen.

Lucy Vale wasn't in homeroom, and even Akash couldn't tell us where she was. He hadn't spoken to her since the night before, and we wondered if something terrible had happened—if Lucy Vale had even been expelled. The arrival of a local news crew, and the sight of the deputy's vehicles straddling the bus drop-off lane, gave us phantom premonitions of school shooters. The patrolling staff members had doubled overnight. The atmosphere before first bell was disconcerted, and disconcerting; with the Sharks, the Student Council, and the cheerleaders preparing for the pep rally, the school felt like it had been gutted of all its life force.

Bailey Lawrence and the other members of the dance team huddled, unusually quiet, at their table in the cafeteria before school, glaringly conspicuous in jeans and hoodies, as if to shock us into constant awareness of their exclusion from the pep rally lineup. It worked. We drifted aimlessly, in meandering silence, through the cafeteria in our fancy dress, unmoored without the Echelon's gravitational pull. Suddenly we felt stupid in our long gowns and contour makeup, felt the pinch of our dress shoes and heels or the scrape of collared shirts on our necks.

After homeroom we were directed to the gym. Normally the march from main campus down to the athletics complex was triumphant. That day, sutured in between teacher chaperones and the hawkeyed student monitors serving as SLD rats, the girls wobbling on their heels and the boys twitching in their suit jackets, the procession put us more in mind of a funeral. We could hardly bear the sight of Aiden Teller, walking head-down with the boys' basketball team, or muster up a fake smile for the *County News* photographer who paced next to the flow of students, snapping pictures with a cigarette clipped between his lips.

The familiar smell of the gym and the pressurized squeeze of the bleachers shook us out of our oppression. We had to give Student Council credit for their decorations, which had seemingly exploded like a molting of cicadas all over the gym. The walls were shaggy with yellow and black bunting. Thick ropes of matching balloons strapped between the ceiling lights made colorful clouds overhead. Principal Hammill gave his usual speech, the bald dome of his head reflective in the glare. Then Vice Principal Edwards took the stage to a scattering of boos, quickly dwarfed by thunderous and deeply ironic applause. After that, the improv troupe performed a boring skit that was salvaged by the intercession of Mr. Harbinger playing a psychotic villain from a rival swim team, which earned him a standing ovation.

After that it was time for the cheerleaders. There was no denying that the squad was good that year—Reese Steeler-Cox was a savage flyer, and the tumbling happened in perfect synchronicity—but we didn't miss the venomous glances the Student Council Mafia tossed off in the dance team's direction. Theirs was a rivalry that extended deep into the pageant circuit, and this time the cheerleaders had clearly notched a point.

It was the only time in our lives we could remember feeling sorry for Bailey Lawrence and the Strut Girls.

Lucy Vale arrived just before the cheerleaders had finished their routine. She was dressed normally in jeans and a T-shirt. She looked tired at first—and then, when she realized that everyone was staring, embarrassed. She probably hadn't meant to bang the door so loudly when she entered, and it was only coincidence that it happened during a split-second break in the music. Still, half the school turned in her direction at once.

As she stood there, scanning the crowd for a familiar face, a place where she belonged, Sofia Young half rose from her seat and began to wave.

Then Bailey Lawrence stood up and yelled, "Over here, Luce."

Luce.

That was it. *Luce.* In just a split second, Lucy Vale transformed.

A towering human pyramid was stacking into shape on the gymnasium floor, and Reese was finding her balance at the top. We didn't see her fall, but we were aware of a tremor that rippled through the formation, and we heard Reese shout before she dropped. There was a moment of confusion while the pyramid shifted underneath her—and then she disappeared behind a wall of bodies.

By then Coach Radner had taken the microphone to announce the swim team, the county photographer had dropped to a knee to snap their entrance, Reese was back on her feet, and so were we—cheering, roaring, thundering our applause as twenty-four members of the boys' swim team flowed to the gymnasium floor, *appropriately* and *normally* dressed in knee-length skirts and women's tank tops with regulation-width straps.

It was epic. It was an amazing time to be alive and on Discord. We agreed afterward that the best picture went to Will Friske, who'd ignored the swim team completely and zoomed in on Mrs. Steeler-Cox's face, clenched like an asshole around a fart.

It was the first time we'd fought back against Admin—and won.

After that the dress codes came down, and we declared victory.

We were proud of that.

ELEVEN

Rachel

Lucy settled, finally, on a bedroom in the attic. For weeks Rachel had joked that her daughter was like Goldilocks, carting her mattress and box spring between both spare bedrooms on the second floor, including the one that shared both a bathroom and a view of the backyard with her mother's—then, after a few nights, declaring that they didn't have the right "vibe." Maybe wouldn't settle in either one and instead kept finding her way to the attic. It was a sign, Lucy said. The energy was better just below the roof.

"Is that what your friend Olivia told you?" Rachel asked, remembering that Lucy had mentioned that Olivia Howard was Wiccan.

"Olivia's not my friend, Mom," Lucy said. That was news to Rachel. "We're friendly. There's a difference. Bailey and Savannah are my friends."

"What about Mia?" Rachel asked. In the dwindling days of September, Lucy had seemed to bloom these new ties overnight. Pretty girls, all of them, especially Bailey with a slim ballerina body, proportioned face, and expertly applied makeup.

"Mia's a noodle. All she cares about is Taylor Swift and getting a boyfriend," Lucy said. Rachel was amused to hear the note of scorn in

Lucy's voice. "But we're friends," Lucy conceded after a pause. "She won't even go to the bathroom without us."

"Well, as long as they're nice to you," Rachel said.

"The *nicest*," Lucy affirmed.

Rachel had met her daughter's new friends several times by then. The first time Lucy invited them over, all three arrivals had shuffled wide-eyed through the house, cooing over details that Rachel had grown to love: the carved wooden paneling, the large fireplaces, the bay windows that bowed out over the front porch. They were conspicuously courteous, almost to the point of irony, eager to please, quick to say ma'am and thank you. Polished, Rachel thought. Used to performing for a crowd. Bailey, Lucy gushed, had been crowned Miss Southern Indiana two years running and was the youngest dance team captain ever. Rachel didn't point out that only weeks earlier, Lucy had lamented the idea of going to school with a bunch of beauty queen types, just like she barely blinked when Lucy, famously unathletic, suddenly announced that she was joining the dance team. Secretly Rachel had been hoping that Lucy might wind up with friends like hers had been at that age: artist types, theater geeks, kids who slurped along the edges of the high school social ecosystem and then seemed to blossom in college. But at least Lucy had found a group.

So Rachel helped her clear a place in the living room to practice. She put on headphones whenever Lucy and her friends started thumping around. She said nothing when Taylor Swift started leaking down from the attic at all hours.

Girls Lucy's age were mutable. Their affections changed in an instant. She took it as a sign of progress. Lucy was changing.

Lucy was coming alive again.

Later Rachel would remember that time—late September and into October—as one of the happiest of her adult life. The weather was glorious in early autumn, crisp and vibrant and still full of color, as if every day were lightly caramelized in the oven. Slabs of sunlight fell like butter through the curtainless windows. Lucy hung string lights from the rafters in the attic. One weekend they crisscrossed three counties visiting different yard sales and antique stores, selecting side tables, resin lamps, wall tapestries, and a miniature figure of a horse and rider that Lucy wanted for the dining room.

Mornings were slow for Rachel with no deadlines to meet, no producer or editor to report to. She luxuriated in a bathrobe. She did the *New York Times* crossword in bed after Lucy caught the bus in a chaotic flurry of activity. She researched shade plants and garden follies. She stretched inside the emptiness—room after room of quiet, empty space. The house felt, on those cool fall mornings, like an animal, creaky with arthritis but warm-blooded, full of memory and grace. She'd never cared much about where she lived—she and Alan had furnished most of their first apartment from Target—but now she found herself fretting over damage to the banister, scouring, sharp-eyed, for signs of wood rot, dreaming of damask curtains that would pool like liquid on the floor.

She still hadn't made any real friends. But she had acquaintances. The manager at the diner, Kelly, knew her name by now. Ted the librarian had advised about her peony beds. She kept a text thread going with two friends from graduate school, both scattered at different universities. She and her cousin spoke almost weekly; twice already she'd made the drive to Willard County to visit her aunt and uncle, still living in the sprawling bungalow where Rachel had been exiled on so many holidays and vacations. Rachel had been an adult before she'd understood that her mother, a functioning alcoholic and indifferent caretaker, had fobbed her off on relatives as often as she could.

But to Rachel it had never felt like a punishment. Indiana for her had been filled with freedom. She'd kissed her first boy in Indiana. Her first girl, too, during a game of spin the bottle.

And, of course, Indiana was where Lucy was conceived. Rachel had been twenty-two. Only six weeks from starting her graduate studies.

She remembered weeping when the pregnancy test registered positive.

Just get rid of it, her mother had said when Rachel finally told her.

It. That word, *it*, had needled Rachel. It. A collection of cells budding into body parts, into a heart and blood to beat it, into lungs and a liver, into fingers and feet. How long before *it* became a *he* or a *she*?

She didn't know. But as the days went by, she started to imagine her life dividing, splitting into a new life growing deep in her stomach. Like a flower was opening inside her. She started toggling a new reality in her head, imagining when she might breastfeed between classes, how she might afford diapers on her student stipend. She started juggling possible names. Nathan. Lucian. Lucy.

She hadn't called the clinic after all.

Lucy had never expressed much curiosity about her real father. She'd bonded quickly with Alan, who took to parenting her with such practiced ease and obvious delight that Rachel resented him for it sometimes. Lucy called him Daddy Al, and they were close—so close that, at one point, Alan floated the idea of getting married and adopting Lucy officially. When Lucy eventually asked about her father, Rachel told her the truth: that she'd met a guy at a party and failed to use protection.

It was mostly true. There had been so many guys, and so many parties, the summer after she graduated. She'd been drinking so much then—self-conscious, desperate to appear sophisticated, desperate to be someone, to matter to someone. The truth was that Rachel didn't know which of her bad decisions had resulted in her pregnancy.

But when she told Lucy that she'd never regretted it, not once—that was true. Motherhood had worked on her like an anchor on a rudderless ship, rooting her somewhere secure, tethering her to schedules and rhythms, calming the frenetic inner churn that, for much of her life, had kept her reaching—for another Adderall, another hit of weed, another drink. Another guy.

In the afternoons, Rachel rode her bike the four miles to the library. She wasn't officially working, but she had emails to write, interview requests to answer. Her first book had only recently fallen off the bestseller list. Still, flickers of a new story—or maybe an old one—kept sparking to life in her head, trailing words like the phantom tail of a comet. *There is no crime without a victim. No one can agree whether Nina and Lydia Faraday count. Some believe that the real victim was Tommy Swift.*

She hadn't explicitly moved Lucy to Indiana, or to the house at 88 Lily Lane, because she'd intended to write about Nina Faraday's case. In many ways she *didn't* want to write about it. It was too domestic. Too predictable. It touched too close to her own history, especially that final trip to Indiana to visit her cousin during her cousin's last year of college. Besides, she was supposed to be taking a break. Learning to garden. Bonding with Lucy, helping restore the family ties she'd neglected for years while hustling her way up the journalistic ladder.

But living in the old Faraday House, Rachel felt slowly absorbed into the mystery of its previous occupants—as if the house were a membrane inside of which the past was still alive. Sometimes, standing in her kitchen after breakfast, she had the sudden sensation of falling through space and time, plunging into the body of Lydia Faraday performing these same ritual tasks—loading the dishes, sweeping crumbs from the counter—and worrying about the very same things that worried Rachel. Who was her daughter texting? What was she texting about? What happened during the hours that her child was out of sight, sealed behind the implacable doors of some building at school, porously absorbing her classmates' opinions and attention, cultivating friendships and enmities?

What was going on in her daughter's life, at school, in her mind? Then she would feel a kind of gravitational pull back to the growing accumulation of research about the Faradays and find herself scouring old newspaper articles and interviews as if she might find the answer there.

How does a girl simply go missing?
How does she vanish into thin air?
Surely, surely, there must be a way to find her.
There must be a way to bring your daughter home again.

TWELVE

WE

It's hard to explain what we felt about Lucy Vale—the obsession that took hold after the assembly. We tracked her outfits, posts, and extracurriculars. We alerted each other whenever she popped up in one of the Strut Girls' stories, like she was some exotic bird we were tailing across the wilderness of social media. In a way it felt like watching a movie, one of those fairy tales in which an average girl, someone like us, discovers she is secretly a princess and gets whisked off to another world to claim her crown and marry a prince.

Somehow we were changing. Woodward was changing. And Lucy Vale was central to all of it, an invisible element of volatility, an extra pressure that gave friction and spark to buried tensions.

Of course, not all of us were fans. Alex Spinnaker still distrusted the Vales, mostly because he couldn't find any dirt about them online. It was dubious logic but undeniable: Lucy Vale might have burst into existence only when Akash first spotted her behind the Faraday House, like one of those physics experiments when something becomes real only at the moment of being observed.

Spinnaker hunted for information about Lucy's relatives and turned up a Susie Vale who lived right on the border of Willard County, putatively on the Jalliscoe side. He investigated every rumor filtered to us about Lucy and her mom—specifically that Lucy was the product of an affair with a married man and that Rachel Vale was *that* kind of woman, a suggestion that whipped around after she declined an invitation to join the PTA. He threatened to collect Lucy's DNA and have it tested for genetic links to our rivals, oscillating wildly between hypotheses that the Vales were living under an assumed identity and that they were Jalliscoe moles.

Scarlett Hughes floated the idea that Lucy Vale and her mother were in witness protection—which would explain, she claimed, why their social media identities were so recently constructed. Lucy's dated from only a few months before the move.

> **@moonovermatter:** people in witness protection have to build a whole new identity
> **@gustagusta:** people in witness protection don't have any photos online, dude
> **@moonovermatter:** They do if they changed their appearance. They get all new socials
> **@gustagusta:** As a cover. They're not sharing reels from the pumpkin patch, believe me
> **@geminirising:** when was LV at the pumpkin patch?
> **@gustagusta:** she went with her mom this weekend
> **@gustagusta:** It was all over her Instagram
> **@kash_money:** wow, stalk much?
> **@gustagusta:** not all of us can just peep her bedroom at night, bro
> **@kash_money:** that's not funny
> **@nononycky:** . . . cuz it's true?

We mined facts about the Vales like panners for gold. We picked through the silt of a thousand everyday observations and interactions, selected certain facts, certain stories, and polished them over and over until they became meaningful. Until they shined, at least to us.

What Happened to Lucy Vale

Lucy Vale collected socks and sometimes wore mismatched pairs deliberately. She had her ears pierced—Olivia counted two holes in her right ear, at least—but never wore earrings. But she liked bracelets a lot and putting tiny stickers on her nails. She doodled on her Converse during class. She claimed to be allergic to asparagus. She loved peach yogurt.

> **@gustagusta:** really? peach? Are you sure?
> **@hannahbanana:** positive. She literally eats peach yogurt in third period every day

We were baffled. Our cafeteria carried only a small selection of yogurts: plain, vanilla, and strawberry. Occasionally a blueberry made its way into the batch, for reasons unclear. So where was Lucy Vale getting peach yogurt?

> **@hannahbanana:** IDK. She brings it from home I think
> **@hannahbanana:** She brings a tiny spoon too
> **@hannahbanana:** She's like really into small spoons
> **@heyitsaubrey:** Small spoons? Or small utensils in general?

Hannah Smith didn't know the answer. But Olivia Howard confirmed that Lucy Vale used regular-size utensils at lunch, unless she was, you know, eating a pizza or something. But when she needed a fork, she definitely used a regular-size fork, and she never looked unhappy about it or anything.

We agreed this was far from definitive since the cafeteria offered only regulation-size silverware.

Eventually Olivia agreed to ask. It turned out Lucy's mom was a tea drinker and had a collection of very small spoons she used to stir her tea. Lucy had started using them when she was a little girl. Now she just thought they were cute.

Unless, Lucy said, she was eating cereal. Eating cereal with a small spoon was insane.

We completely agreed; cereal should be eaten with the largest possible spoon that wasn't officially a ladle.

Some of us began to seek out peach yogurt in the grocery store. Some of us imagined that the smell—a rush of chemical sweet, the faint tang of bacterial sourness—was how Lucy would taste if we ever kissed her.

Which, obviously, we never would.

History is written by the victors. High school, by consensus. But fate is written by the gods, and ours swam for the Sharks.

If the team thought Lucy Vale was desirable, she was too desirable for us.

Free will was an illusion, and consent was not ours to give.

PART 3

ONE

We

The Church of Noah Landry formed quickly, almost overnight. One second Noah was just another solid swimmer, loping through the halls giving fist bumps to teachers, including thousand-year-old Mrs. Constantine who would reach out to grip his fist instead of grazing knuckles; or reconfiguring his six foot four inches around a desk he almost looked like he was absorbing into his rib cage; or hunching over his laptop in the SLD Tutoring Center, headphones on, jogging his knee in time to a secret rhythm.

The next second, suspicion was everywhere, like bacterial mold, or a stain on the bathroom ceiling we couldn't unsee once we'd spotted it. Noah Landry had gotten good. Noah Landry had gotten very, very good. Noah Landry was something extraordinary.

That's why Jalliscoe was freaking out. That's why our rivals were poisoning the internet with accusations of cheating and dredging up old rumors about Coach Vernon, Tommy Swift, and Nina Faraday. It was all to make our swimmers look bad. It was because of Noah Landry.

It was because he was going to help us win state.

It was because he was going to qualify for nationals.

For once it turned out that no one was exaggerating.

Even before we first saw the video of Noah Landry swimming in the Ohio River, we'd been curious about him simply because he was swimming for the Sharks for the first time. Since seventh grade, he'd trained with Coach Vernon on a club team based in Waukaumet, a full hour-and-a-half drive into Illinois. We knew, vaguely, that he'd been something of a star—but in exile, swimming on one of the B-tier club teams, Noah Landry had been peripheral to our collective obsession.

That began to change when he returned with Coach Vernon to the Granger Club Team and agreed to compete for the high school during the fall season. For one thing, he'd grown into his shoulders over the summer. For another, it was obvious to us that Reese Steeler-Cox was angling to date him. They knew each other from church; both were Hoosier back to the 1800s. And once Noah Landry made the Sharks and Minnows list, Reese hung on his attention like a coat on a peg.

By then we were all convinced: the sweet, serious Eagle Scout was a full-on snack.

We didn't know why the video of Noah Landry, Alec Nye, JJ Hammill, and Ryan Hawthorne racing in the Ohio River had taken so long to circulate or who had made the original recording. We could tell from the white caps that a stiff wind was blowing up that day. Even the voices closest to the phone got snatched away intermittently by the wind. Down river, boaters steered bloated sails across the widening churn of water. A **No Swimming** flag snapped back and forth near the dock, cracking a rhythm into the audio track.

Six swimmers entered the mud-colored water; we recognized Nye, Hammill, Hawthorne, and Noah Landry, plus two other guys we later identified as cocaptains of the Willow Park swim team. Even Nye and Hammill were fighting for speed. We could tell the effort of every stroke by the churn of the water. But Noah Landry . . . the first few seconds he lagged behind, almost floating. Like he wasn't in the water exactly but suspended slightly above it, hovering on the surface tension where the current was nothing but a shiver down the spine. Not pressure. Information.

Then, after a second, maybe a second and a half, he just . . . moved. There was no other way to describe what his body was doing. It wasn't swimming. It was . . . flowing. It was flowing across the river like a current moving sideways, barely kicking up any resistance when he stroked. Next to Landry, the other swimmers looked like they were drowning.

Within seconds, he'd pulled ahead. Then he was leaving Nye and Hammill behind. His body in the dark water looked fluid and long, fishlike. There were times watching him when we had the distinct impression of a tail.

Whoever recorded the video had maneuvered onto one of the docked speedboats to get a better view. Even so, Landry and the others soon became nothing but dark specks in the water. Then they were returning, with Noah a full three body lengths ahead. We counted three and a half full seconds after Noah stood up, raising his arms and grinning toward the camera, before Nye made it back to shore. Three and a half seconds, at *least*. Spinnaker insisted it was 3.86, Ethan Courtland argued it was pedantic to try and ascertain that level of accuracy without a touch pad, and Nate Stern wanted to know what *pedantic* meant.

Either way, it was unthinkable. Nye was the best swimmer on the team. He was one of the best swimmers in the *state*. And yet Landry had thrashed him.

Which meant that Noah Landry was something different.

Noah Landry was unstoppable.

And that meant, in some small way, that we were too.

TWO

Rachel

The Sharks' first swim meet of the year took place on a Saturday, and it seemed to Rachel as if the entire county had turned out to attend. Traffic snarled to a crawl a quarter mile from the school entrance. As they nudged closer, Rachel saw a grizzled old man wearing a Styrofoam fin on a headband, inspecting the arriving cars as they turned down to the lower parking lot.

"That's McVeigh," Lucy said. "He's a legend."

"A legend for what?" Rachel asked.

Lucy paused. "I don't actually know," she said. "He's just been here forever." She waved as McVeigh eyed their vehicle warily, as if he suspected them of smuggling in anti-Shark sentiment, before gesturing them on. "I bet he's checking for Wolverines," Lucy said, twisting around in her seat to watch him proceed down the line of cars, scowling. "I heard they might try and sabotage the meet."

"The Wolverines . . . ?" Rachel noted, uneasily, two sheriff vehicles parked directly in front of Aquatics. The image flashed of a sullen kid in a trench coat training a gun meant for the military at the crowd, then she quickly forced the idea from her mind.

"They're swimmers from Jalliscoe. They hate the Sharks. They got Aiden Teller suspended from competition for *six weeks*. We're all freaking out." Rachel noticed, with some amusement, that her sports-indifferent daughter was once again including herself in the group. "His season is basically over."

"There was a fight, wasn't there?" Rachel had seen reference to a scrape among members of the boys' swim team and some of their rivals in a recent police blotter. She'd been curious about the swim team and all the rumors attached to it over the years. Tommy Swift had been suspected of relying on a regimen of performance enhancers; Coach Steeler of encouraging him. A boy named Will King had dodged accusations of sexual assault. Several boys had been arrested for drunk driving. Only two years earlier, team captain Alec Nye's name had come up in connection with an interesting case of revenge porn. But nothing ever stuck; nothing was ever proven. Woodward's star swimmers remained, it seemed, impervious to legal trouble.

Now, sandwiched between cars festooned with team colors, shark decals, and swim team bumper stickers, Rachel thought she knew why. She had seen this kind of devotion once before, when she'd attended a University of Michigan football game with her college boyfriend. They'd been squaring off against Ohio State, their sworn rivals. At certain moments, Rachel had truly feared a crowd riot.

Inside the lobby, the air was heady with the smell of bleach. They funneled in through the first glass doors, past a life-size bust of Jay Steeler that startled Rachel with its cold, bald gaze. She noticed people touching it as they passed, skimming its forehead lightly, almost reflexively, as if in religious deference. Sweat gathered at Rachel's neck, but there was no space even to remove her jacket. She had the sudden urge to escape, to run back into the fresh October air, away from this crowd and its worship.

But it was too late. Seconds later they were inside, pummeled through the lobby doors and into a long hallway jostling with student greeters with sharks painted on their faces and narrowed by folding tables filled with baked goods. Rachel thought she recognized Reese

Steeler-Cox leaning on a pair of crutches and directing a small handful of acolytes to deliver welcome brochures.

Then they were swept down the hall, shuffling after the crowd past elaborate displays of trophies, ribbons, and photographs of the boys' swim team through the years—from early-nineties photographs of the original Granger Club Team clustered at the edge of the old YMCA pool to newspaper articles about the early wins and triumphs at counties; the original blueprints of the Aquatics Center, framed next to a headline announcing the beginning of construction; dust-colored images of the construction site and a small army of bulldozers and excavators mowing the ground, raising their steel jaws to the sky. Rachel checked the date engraved on a silver plaque beneath the frame. That, Rachel thought, must have been right around the time Nina Faraday disappeared.

The whole walk, Rachel felt, had the feeling of a religious pilgrimage. She caught sight of a framed photograph of Coach Jay Steeler, then in his early 50s, tan and relaxed, giving a thumbs-up to the camera from inside the gigantic dirt pit where the pool would soon take shape. Further on, the modern Aquatics Center rose out of the dust of sepia-toned photographs, ending with a full-color image of Coach Steeler getting tossed into the deep end by the boys' team just after opening, permanently frozen in midair just before hitting the water.

To Rachel, Coach Steeler's smile looked more like a grimace.

Finally she noticed a framed memorial plaque dedicated to Tommy Swift, the protégé who'd placed the Granger Club Team, Woodward Sharks, and Coach Steeler's methods firmly on the map of American swimming. Nina Faraday, on the other hand, seemed to exist only in her absence, even here, in the gaps between the visual story lines.

It occurred to Rachel again, *There is no crime without a victim.* Somehow, in the sixteen years since Nina Faraday had disappeared, even the notion of her victimhood had vanished.

Just past the boys' locker room, they wheeled left, flowing onto the pool deck. The air was soupy with humidity. Already the bleachers were filling up. To Rachel, the crowd was an undifferentiated mass, an amoeba-like blob of constituent black-and-yellow components. But Lucy, with that teenager's finely tuned instinct for social particularities, easily picked out her classmates from the throng.

"There's Akash and Nate Stern. See? Oh. They've got *Spinnaker* with them. He's kind of tragic. And look. There are my friends in the front row, right across from the team bench." She said this with a certain amount of pride, waving furiously at Bailey, Savannah, and Mia.

"Do you wish you were sitting with them?" Rachel asked.

"Mom, no," Lucy said. "I sit with the Strut Girls every day."

"The what girls?"

Lucy giggled. "That's what everyone calls us. It's from one of Bailey's videos. I'll show you."

Lucy pulled out her phone and began swiping. It was dizzying, the way Lucy toggled back and forth between the *real* and the *virtual*; Rachel thought of long invisible tendrils growing from one to the other, enmeshing the two worlds permanently.

As if sensing what Rachel was thinking, Lucy glanced up. "I'll show you later," she said. Unexpectedly she put her phone in her back pocket and reached for Rachel's hand, intertwining their fingers.

It had been Lucy's idea to attend First Meet together—an olive branch, Rachel thought, after a stormy argument several days earlier about Lucy's social media use. Lucy had accused her mother of toxic narcissism, of invading her privacy, of denying her *right to even exist as a separate human*—language she had picked up, undoubtedly, from the same sources that Rachel had tried very hard to monitor. Later Rachel found Lucy in the attic, sobbing piteously into her pillow. She sat down and placed a hand on Lucy's back, felt her spine rise and fall like the ravaged mast of some shipwreck on a swell.

If you really want a TikTok account again, you can have one, Rachel had said. *But you know the rules. No challenges. And I'm going to need the password.*

Abruptly, Lucy stopped crying. For a long second she lay so still that Rachel might have worried she'd stopped breathing except for the continued motion of her back, warm under Rachel's palm. Rachel remembered then when Lucy was a little girl and used to climb in her bed whenever Alan was traveling. In the middle of the night, Rachel would wake up and find her daughter so motionless, curved like a small parenthesis in the darkness, that she would feel spikes of sudden terror. Only when she touched her Lucy, felt her small body expand and relax with every breath, could she sleep again.

I'm just trying to keep you safe, Rachel had said then, a little desperately. And finally Lucy answered, her voice still muffled by the pillow, *I know, Mom. But you can't.*

She had prepared as best she could to be a mother. But she hadn't prepared for the love. Nothing could have prepared her.

People kept streaming in. The stands were soon so packed, Rachel felt like a grain of sand in a swell of dunes. Every time someone moved in the bleachers, the whole crowd seemed to move with them, spitting out a single body, then rapidly filling the gap from the overflow of spectators waiting at the open doors. Rachel was glad she'd used the bathroom before they'd left the house.

Her eyes landed on an older couple seated in the first row of the observation deck, tucked among knots of college recruiters and scouts. They stood out for their formal, almost somber dress, and for how they waved stoically down to the stands, like royalty greeting fans during a funeral procession. She heard the woman on her left point out "the Swifts" to her husband, and then she understood. Tommy Swift's parents were both thin and stooped, haggard before their time.

Rachel wondered why they'd come.

Moments later, she had her answer. The pool was cleared of swimmers. Finally they were ready to begin. People were still jostling for seats, a crowd pressing in from the hallway.

"Is it always this crowded?" Rachel wondered out loud.

"God, no." It was the woman on her left, her cheeks painted with Sharks colors. "We're all here for Noah Landry."

It was the first time Rachel ever heard the name.

THREE

We

Seeing Noah Landry swim in person was nothing like watching him on video, where distances were warped and the energy of the spectators, tilting in his direction, blurred into pixelation.

Seeing Noah Landry live was breathtaking.

He was a sleek arrow leaving the starting block. Then he submerged almost soundlessly, and his body turned to a dark torpedo under the surface, rippling halfway down the length of the pool before surfacing a full body length ahead of Nye.

Later we couldn't remember screaming his name. We couldn't remember rising to our feet. All we remembered was the feeling of tilting, tipping down as a vast group toward a central thrill, and of certainty: Noah Landry was the best swimmer since Tommy Swift. Along with Coach Vernon, he was resurrecting Jay Steeler's legacy.

It wasn't Lucy but Noah Landry we'd been waiting for all along.

~

After First Meet, the drama with Jalliscoe metastasized.

First a graffitied penis appeared on the statue of Jay Steeler in Byron Park. A few days later someone hacked Jalliscoe's official Instagram account and linked their bio to a pornography website. Spinnaker denied responsibility, but that was no surprise; he simultaneously pinned a description of *self-incrimination* to a #badideas thread on the Discord server, which many of us took as a confession.

Jalliscoe hit back with a litany of bad press. Mostly it was the usual bullshit: snide commentary, vague insinuations of cheating, and veiled references to the Faraday case, plus the occasional Looney Tune claiming that the Steelers' fortune was due to an unholy pact with Satan. Jalliscoe went trawling for old yearbook photos of Coach Vernon with Nina Faraday's ex-boyfriend, Tommy Swift—as if the fact that Coach Vernon competed under Coach Steeler were proof of a secret conspiracy rather than justification for his hire.

Coach Steeler had been controversial, maybe. He'd had a reputation for inappropriate comments. He'd had a weird sense of humor. Maybe he'd even been a creep. But no one doubted that he'd turned out champion swimmers, or that he'd put Granger on the map.

Still, the infestation of negative press gave the Student Leadership Department leverage to announce new student initiatives. We weren't surprised to find out that Mrs. Steeler-Cox was milking the rivalry for her own purposes. She couldn't hear the word *infraction* without going full Stalin. A hysteria of new links, SLD tutorials, and updates swept the student portal. We gave permission for so many new abuses of the school's authority, we wouldn't have been surprised to find out that rectal exams were being added to the protocol.

Even our parents got embroiled in the controversy. Patti Hargrove, Derek Hargrove's mom, was cautioned by police after tailing the mother of a Jalliscoe cheerleader home from the Walmart Supercenter and making "threatening gestures" with her carton of eggs; and Peyton Neely's dad, who worked for the fire department, posted a rant about Jalliscoe that got him cautioned by the union.

The same week, someone supposedly took a dump in a lane of the Wolfe Swimming Club's Olympic-size pool. Of course, Jalliscoe immediately started pointing fingers. We all agreed it was an act of absolute desperation, and to save face. If someone had dropped anchor in Willard County waters, ten to one the asshole was native to town.

A few days after that, three Wolverines broke into Aquatics and tried to steal our mascot, Sean the Shark. We assumed the Wolverines were to blame anyway, since the three vandals were wearing rubber werewolf masks. Of course, the Wolverines insisted it was a frame-up job. The question was whether the Jalliscoe swimmers were stupid enough to disguise themselves in an incriminating costume.

Opinions were divided.

Whoever it was, the Wolverines or someone trying to set them up, only got as far as the display case. The dumbasses might have gotten away with it if they'd had the patience to look for the key in the director's office. Instead they broke the glass and triggered an alarm that brought security down on Aquatics. We would have paid good money to see Old McVeigh, the night guard, probably oozing the stink of whiskey and hopped up on God knows what he usually snorted, crash through the doors swinging a tire iron and shouting apocalypse and revelation. We would have dropped at least a bill to see McVeigh chase those motherfuckers into the parking lot. We almost felt bad for them.

Almost.

Will Friske suggested we break into the Jalliscoe pool and sub in arsenic for one of the chemical cleaners. Ethan Courtland, a chemistry nerd, pointed out that to have any effect, you would need at least fifty micrograms of arsenic per liter, which was roughly 167 micrograms of arsenic per gallon. Given that the average pool contained six hundred and fifty thousand gallons of water, you were looking at more than ten kilograms of arsenic.

@highasakyle: yeah, that'll land you on a no-fly list
@spinn_doctor: Please unsubscribe me from this thread
@spinn_doctor: How many times have I explained that private and secure are NOT the same thing??
@spinn_doctor: If anyone wants to talk, find me on Signal

> **@hannahbanana:** sorry to be basic, but what about we just steal the Wolverines mascot?
> **@badprincess:** do wolverines even KNOW HOW TO SWIM???
> **@skyediva:** maybe that's why they went after our mascot
> **@skyediva:** Theirs sucks

About a week after First Meet, a fifteen-year-old hit piece about the sheriff's investigation of the Nina Faraday case resurfaced online. We were certain that another Jalliscoe apologist was to blame, that this was yet another attempt to sully the Sharks' reputation before the competition season kicked into overdrive.

But this time our enemies hit the jackpot and went viral.

The article featured a photograph of Nina and her on-again, off-again boyfriend, Tommy Swift, partying with Jack Vernon. This coupled with Aiden Teller's recent arrest detonated an explosion of new outrage online, half of it from people who'd never even been to Indiana. According to the internet, Tommy Swift had gotten away with murder. Jack Vernon had helped him. The Sharks, both past and present, were violent sociopaths, coddled by a system that cared only for their wins. Coach Vernon got a flood of anonymous abuse posted to his personal Facebook page and briefly had to go private on Instagram. Even Student Leadership and Mrs. Steeler-Cox got dragged.

We were so consumed by the tension with Jalliscoe, we didn't even notice that at some point we'd stopped referring to 88 Lily Lane as the Faraday House. Maybe it was because Will Friske's fake landscaping flyer had resulted in a real landscaping job, and he and his cousin Josh had been working at the Vales' house for a month, and that's what he called it: the Vales' House. Maybe it was because, under the Vales' stewardship, the house was changing—liberated of its stranglehold of weeds and climbing ivy, exfoliated of its scabrous paint, opened up and turned out and exposed to fresh air and Instagram photography. Maybe it was because of the wicker porch furniture, or the new pastel trim, or the bikes that rarely made it all the way into the garage. Maybe it was the reappearance of the yard itself, looking shockingly exposed without its overcoat of weeds, like someone robbed of a toupee. Maybe it was because of the Vales' bird feeders, or the fairy lights in the apple tree, which surprised us the first time we saw them in one of Lucy's Instagram stories and thought, *Beautiful.*

Maybe we simply didn't have time for ghost stories; we had Wolverines.

Or maybe it was that Lucy Vale had finally found her place at Woodward. She had locked into orbit at a small but meaningful distance from us where we could observe her in peace, as we did all the Echelon girls. Slowly we accumulated a mental tally of her habits, likes, and quirks, a drift of information that familiarized her in the mental landscape of our lives. We got used to the way she sat in class, with one leg tucked beneath her, picking at the frayed cuff of her jeans. We got used to the way she waved, keeping her hand close to her hip with a sudden explosive flurry of her fingers. The more familiar Lucy Vale became, the harder it was to imagine her living inside a mystery, much less as a protagonist.

Maybe it was because we trusted Akash, and Akash trusted Lucy, even after she became a Strut Girl.

Whatever the reason, day by day Lucy Vale's house had molted its association with the Faradays, peeling away from the legend like an old sticker losing adhesive.

Then, in mid-October, came a plot twist.

FOUR

Rachel

In retrospect, Rachel should have expected intruders. The Faraday House was, after all, a sort of tourist location, frequently listed on "Indiana's Top Ten Most Haunted Places." On some websites, the house even gained national notoriety. Even before they'd left Michigan, Lucy had tracked down YouTube videos, some of them with thousands of views, on accounts with names like Ghost Hunter and Urban Explorer. Typically the videos were filmed at night, sweeping an eerie luminescence across the yard and porch. (One creator even filmed himself breaking in through an open window and tagging an upstairs wall, where Rachel and Lucy subsequently discovered it; when they repainted, Lucy joked they should start a home renovation channel of their own.) And, of course, the owner Wendy Adams had warned them about the problems with squatters over the years and recommended a new security system, maybe some cameras at the gates.

That was all on Rachel's list. She just hadn't gotten around to any of it yet. But she hadn't failed to notice the unusual quantity of traffic on the quiet dead-end street—from cars that wheeled around slowly in the cul-de-sac, to bikers that unaccountably required long rests when they drew close to the gates, to kids slurping along the service road with iPhones held high like miniature idols. But that's who she'd assumed they were for the most part: kids. Teenagers, friends of Akash's, high school students with nothing better to do than trade in gossip.

Lucy didn't seem concerned about the attention. She even found it funny. Already a Halloween enthusiast, Lucy had elaborate plans for decorating the house. She'd made a Pinterest board full of fake skeletons, plaster tombstones, ghoulish-looking mannequins, and oversize spiders perched in feathery cotton webs. *We might as well lean in to our reputation,* she'd said, a little gleefully. *If it's a haunted house they want . . .* She trailed off, leaving the provocation unfinished. So they went on a rare shopping spree while Rachel tallied the expenses carefully against her budget, too enchanted with Lucy's vision, her enthusiasm, to say no.

Then came the strangers in the middle of the night.

It was a Sunday. Rachel had gone to bed late, just before midnight. She'd started working again in the evenings, after Lucy was fast asleep in her attic room and all the other houses had darkened their windows. When she finally crawled into bed, she was still thinking of Nina Faraday's cell phone pinging off a tower not far from the state park forest several hours after she'd sent her last text: I know you want me out of your life. I'm leaving for a while. Don't look for me. It was so on the nose, so dramatic. Almost formal. Surely she knew that Tommy Swift would immediately alert someone—his parents, her mother, or even the police. Surely the text made it more likely that Tommy would start searching for her. Maybe that was even the point.

But he hadn't. As far as anyone knew, Tommy Swift hadn't told a soul about Nina's final cryptic message—not until several days later when it became clear that she wasn't coming home.

Why?

She was thinking of Nina and Tommy Swift; then she was standing in the middle of a river full of eels. Alan was angry at her for something; she had lost her earrings in the water because she'd been distracted with work. She didn't want to tell him about the eels, threshing the water with their slippery, dark bodies, or about her certainty that the earring was gone, lost for good in the current. She was afraid to move, and there he was pacing the bank, shouting at her. Lucy too. *Mom,* she was saying. *What are you doing? Mom!*

"Mom, get up."

She startled awake. A wheel of light through the window briefly touched Lucy's face, her hair wild, her eyes huge in the dark.

"Get up," she said again, breathless. "Someone's trying to get in the house."

"What?" Rachel was shocked alert. Suddenly the room and reality, came rushing at her. The light had vanished from the window, but she could hear laughter and muffled conversation from outside the house. "What do you mean, someone's trying to get in the house?"

"There are people outside. They must have climbed the gate." Lucy was rocketing from the room. "Call the police."

"Lucy, stop!" Rachel could hear Lucy pounding down the stairs, shouting. She bolted out of bed, doubled back and snatched her cell phone. "Lucy! Get back here!"

It was too late. By the time Rachel got downstairs, Lucy was flinging open the door, brandishing what looked like a bicycle pump and one of her flip-flops.

"Lucy!" Rachel nearly pitched off her feet at the end of the living room where Lucy had gutted the storage closet looking for a weapon. She was punching 9-1-1 and calling for Lucy to get inside, and suddenly she heard a high scream, so sharp it seemed to bring down the night. Seconds later, as she reached the door, she saw lights blink on in windows along the street.

"Lucy!" She wheeled outside, ignoring the dispatcher on the other end of the telephone indifferently requesting her place of emergency.

"It's okay, Mom." Lucy was carved into silhouette by the blazing light set up behind her. "She was just scared."

Rachel's mind stuttered over the scene: the four strangers, one of them still trembling next to her daughter. The audio recording equipment. The shovels. The case of beer. And mounds of earth overturned in the garden, now rutted with holes. She couldn't make sense of it; for a second she wondered if she was still dreaming.

"Ma'am, are you there?" The dispatcher's voice was still piping from the cell phone in her hand. "Ma'am?"

The stranger standing next to Lucy sniffled. Lucy reached out and placed a hand on her arm, comforting her. She turned back to look at her mother.

"She thought I was a ghost," Lucy said simply.

FIVE

We

The story coalesced like usual, in dribbles on Discord and in homeroom. First neither Akash nor Lucy showed up for the bus. Then Layla Lewis logged on to ask if anyone knew why there had been cops at the Vales' house in the middle of the night. Kyle Hannigan tagged Sofia Young to ask whether she'd heard about a disturbance in the neighborhood. Hannah Smith messaged Nick Topornycky to ask if he'd texted Akash. Scarlett Hughes messaged Alex Spinnaker, who went on a rant about Akash's dismal performance under the onslaught of demonic attackers the night before. And Will Friske got a message from his cousin, who was pissed.

Apparently they were going to have to resod the Vales' whole fucking yard.

> **@stopandfriske:** motherfuckers
> **@stopandfriske:** those dipnuts dug up my whole weekend
> **@ktcakes888:** what dipnuts?
> **@stopandfriske:** the ones who turned up at the Vales' last night
> **@badprincess:** ???
> **@highasakyle:** gonna need some context, buddy
> **@ktcakes888:** what do you mean *turned up*?

@badprincess: what do you mean *dug up*?
@stopandfriske: He didn't tell me much. Just that there were trespassers at the Vales' last night. Lucy's mom called the cops when they wouldn't leave
@safireswiftly: What were they doing there?
@nononycky: yard work, sounds like
@ktcakes888: in the middle of the night??
@stopandfriske: alright. Here's a pop quiz
@stopandfriske: Three strangers with two shovels can dig fifteen holes an hour
@stopandfriske: If they all met on the internet
@stopandfriske: Then what do you think they were digging for?

For a second, no one answered. We floundered on the edge of Lucy Vale's front lawn, rutted now with imagined holes, trying to see a pattern. But there was no reason to dig up the Vales' yard. There was no reason for three strangers to arrive carrying shovels.

Not to Lucy's house anyway.

Then, in an instant, the mental distance between the past and the present, the Vales and the Faradays, collapsed, and we understood.

We channeled our shock into another second of silence.

@gustagusta: shit
@stopandfriske: nope
@stopandfriske: try again?
@badprincess: please tell me it doesn't have to do with the Faradays
@stopandfriske: no hints allowed. Anyone else?
@highasakyle: * hits buzzer *
@highasakyle: I'll go with *bones* for five hundred
@stopandfriske: ding, ding, ding

By midmorning, everyone in school knew about the trespassers, strangers from Montgomery County who'd come digging for Nina Faraday's remains in the middle of the night. From the beginning, the operation wasn't exactly professional. One of the intruders broke the latch on the front gate before realizing it hadn't been locked. They'd brought a six-pack, headlamps, and portable recording equipment.

Of course there was a podcast involved.

Some gossip had to travel, and some had to breed like bacterial mold in wet showers. But some stories simply hit everyone at once, like landmines laced underneath our awareness that exploded in a single instant.

The news about the intruders was like that. Suddenly no one could talk about anything else. Maybe it was because so many of us had a farming family somewhere in the blood, but trespassing on someone else's land—and disturbing the ground, no less—was deadly serious business in southern Indiana. The NRA crowd made jokes about home security systems manufactured by Glock. The gun control faction lashed out at them for trivializing the impacts of gun violence on young people. As usual, jokes about trigger warnings abounded.

As usual, we weren't sure if we really found them funny.

Akash arrived just before the end of third period with his first ever late pass and new social currency. Since Lucy was still out, Akash temporarily absorbed the role of leading star. We could barely get near him at lunch. The Echelon crowd was suddenly interested in his friendship with Lucy Vale. Even Sam Harris, who in seventh grade tried to cut Akash's hair with a pair of garden clippers he'd smuggled in his gym sweatshirt, was acting friendly.

Akash confirmed that, yes, the trespassers had come looking for evidence of a violent crime. Yes, the Friskes would have to resod the whole yard; it looked terrible, like it had fallen prey to a small army of oversize gophers. Yes, the trespassers had brought shovels, headlamps, and a variety of podcast equipment. No, Akash didn't know the name of their podcast.

We'd heard through Evie Grant, who'd heard from Mrs. Rowe at 4 Lily Lane, that there had been a verbal altercation, a shouting match that had drawn the Vales' neighbors onto the street. Akash confirmed it. But according to him, it was mostly Lucy Vale doing the shouting.

> **@kash_money:** can you believe that the ass wipes who broke in thought the Vales were the ones trespassing?
> **@kash_money:** I guess they thought the house was still vacant
> **@gustagusta:** really? the welcome mat and the porch furniture didn't tip them off?
> **@kash_money:** they actually wanted to search the basement
> **@moonovermatter:** are you KIDDING ME???
> **@geminirising:** so which conspiracy camp are they in—do they think a mystery man snatched Nina or that her mom axed her?
> **@kash_money:** neither
> **@kash_money:** They think it was Tommy Swift
> **@kash_money:** And that Coach Steeler alibied him
> **@gustagusta:** Coach Steeler, every other swimmer, and the pizza guy who delivered a pepperoni pie to Steeler's house that night?
> **@kash_money:** all liars
> **@badprincess:** poor Lucy.
> **@badprincess:** Can you imagine finding out that way?
> **@badprincess:** Like about your own house??
> **@kash_money:** she didn't
> **@kash_money:** Apparently the Vales know all about the Faradays
> **@kash_money:** Lucy told my dad that's why they took the house

We were stunned. In the sharpening silence that followed, our ideas about Lucy Vale siphoned off into a question mark and an imprimatur of wonder.

Clearly we'd underestimated the girl.

SIX

WE

Lucy Vale came back changed the next day. For a month, she'd been notching up Woodward's social strata. But after the Vales' yard got ripped up by the would-be justice league, she made a final, dramatic leap into the spotlight.

There was no doubt about it: Lucy Vale was a secret badass, and the most desirable girl in high school.

We were delirious with curiosity. We attacked her with questions. Was it true that she'd threatened the trespassers with a tire iron? Was it true that her mother eventually invited them in for a tour? Was it true they'd turned up a buried time capsule in the yard?

The answers were, in reverse order: no, yes, and kind of. It wasn't a tire iron but a bicycle pump, and she hadn't threatened them with it. She'd grabbed it from the closet without thinking as soon as she and her mother had realized what was going on in their yard. While her mother called the police, Lucy Vale catapulted out of the house brandishing a six-dollar plastic air pump and a cell phone. She hadn't realized it wasn't recording until after the police had arrived.

By then a small flock of neighbors were drawn over by the commotion, which at one point devolved into an argument about Indiana's recycling practices. Lucy Vale's neighbor Mrs. Gorsuch stalked over in a silk nightgown and a pair of waders with a rifle crooked over one shoulder. The cops arrived and managed to defuse the tension. Unbelievably, Lucy's mom eventually offered up a tour of the house. Afterward they'd joked with the cops about selling tickets to pay the rent.

In the end, the Vales decided not to press charges. Lucy told a few of us at lunch that she actually liked the podcasters and was considering an invitation to be interviewed for their show, *Blood in the Water*. They'd recorded a two-part series on the Faraday case earlier in the spring. Apparently the Faraday episodes had been so popular that the producers decided to devote their entire next season to Nina's disappearance and her mother's subsequent suicide.

We tried to listen. But most of us jumped ship early. Hearing them dissect Nina's disappearance, and then her mother's death, was too weird. We didn't like one of our stories voiced by a stranger. It was like a voice from a dream speaking suddenly from behind you. Personal and weirdly violating. Like the internet had taken a shovel to our subconsciouses.

Funnily enough, we'd never actually googled the Faraday case. There was no reason to search the details because it wasn't that kind of mystery. At least, it wasn't for us.

But after the crime-hunting podcasters broke onto the Vales' property, we found out that Nina Faraday's case had grown increasingly famous online thanks to the continued agitation of an estranged aunt, Ellen Faraday, whom we'd never heard of. Ellen Faraday was convinced that Nina was murdered at home by Tommy Swift and that the rest of it—the cell phone data proving she'd been out near the state park at 8:00 p.m., the missing gym bag from her closet, the fact that there was no proof she'd been murdered at all—was a blind.

Ellen Faraday was persuaded most mysteries weren't actually very mysterious at all; no one liked to dig up dirt when it was close to home.

Jackson Skye joked that, in a way, it was too bad that Nina's bones hadn't turned up. It would have implicated Lydia Faraday and proved that Nina's ex, and the rest of the swim team, had been telling the truth all along.

> **@kash_money:** not necessarily
> **@kash_money:** Some people think that Tommy followed Nina home from Aquatics
> **@kash_money:** And killed her before Lydia got back from work
> **@bassicrhythm:** Tommy was with the rest of the team at Coach Steeler's
> **@bassicrhythm:** The pizza guy confirmed it
> **@bassicrhythm:** That's like a twenty-five-minute drive from Nina's house
> **@kash_money:** I'm not saying I agree with it
> **@kash_money:** don't shoot the messageboard

Lucy Vale told us about the Discord server *Still Seeking*, which had more than five hundred thousand subscribers and had pinned Nina Faraday's profile under its featured cases.

We found the server. None of us wanted to subscribe.

A few of us went down the rabbit hole, though. There were always a few of us going down the rabbit hole, jumping ship, jumping the shark, stanning ships; sending memes or spawning jokes. That's how it was with us: spirals, spam, streaming a whole season of a show we'd already seen three times when we were supposed to be doing our homework. We learned that there had been supposed sightings of Nina everywhere from Santa Fe, New Mexico, to Bangor, Maine, but that all of the leads had been busts. We stared at a creepy photograph digitally aged to resemble Nina sixteen years after her disappearance, as if it might tell us something about what had happened to her a decade and a half earlier. Will Friske declared a personal crusade to solve the mystery of Nina Faraday's disappearance once and for all because he'd been victimized by the interest around the case. Akash was similarly inspired because

Lucy had been victimized; and plenty of us revived our interest in the case because Lucy Vale was interested.

The question was: Why?

Lucy's explanation about why her mother had wanted the house was unconvincing and quintessentially vague; her mom was a true crime fanatic, she'd told us, as if that made sense of it. A lot of us were into true crime, but that didn't mean we wanted to take a shower in the middle of a cold case.

Peyton Neely straight-up asked Lucy in homeroom if she believed in ghosts, figuring that she would say no. But apparently Lucy had to think about it. Finally she said she definitely believed in energy. They'd once lived in a house where there was some kind of dark energy, for sure. They'd moved after only a year, when Lucy started having nightmares.

But Lucy Vale claimed the energy in the Faraday House wasn't like that. If anything, she told Peyton Neely, it felt heavy, a little sad. Abandoned.

Besides, she added, *it's never the dead ones you have to worry about.*

Peyton didn't know what she meant by that, and neither did we.

Knowing that the Vales had consciously chosen to live inside the Faraday mystery changed everything. Overnight, Lucy Vale and her mother fell through the veiled mysteries of that inscrutable house and returned sheened with its glamor. Suddenly Lucy came bearing secrets, middle-of-the-night dramas, and a high tolerance for ghosts. If at first she'd been Other, the blank space for our imaginations, in October Lucy Vale became Object, a source of endless fascination, a riddle of contradictions, both an encryption and the key to unlocking it. At the heart was a question of not just who she was but what that *meant* and how to make sense of it. Suddenly the baggy sweatshirts, the Converses that rotated with her moods—it all seemed like camouflage, like a deliberate attempt to mislead us. The scrunchies she layered on her wrist, on the other hand, might be significant.

Now she was more than a mystery. She was a riddle. In need of a secret code.

Over the years we'd seen the kinds of people who gravitated to the Faraday House. Ghost chasers and horror junkies. YouTubers who'd scaled the gates. Goths and druggies, people who identified as vampires, at least on their social channels.

Dark people. Fringe people. Outsider types.

People with demons, and shadows, of their own.

Sure, maybe the Vales were a little bit city; maybe their hands were a little soft.

Maybe they weren't like us. But they weren't like that either.

They weren't *crazy*. They weren't even that interesting.

That's what we thought anyway.

And even after we knew we were wrong about the Vales—even when Lucy Vale became a kind of obsession—it never occurred to us to wonder about her demons.

Or ours.

PART 4

ONE

Rachel

Lucy did persuade her mother, at last, to make an online dating profile.

"You know, we had an agreement," Rachel said "We said *no boys*." Rachel still couldn't think about the high school boy who'd roped Lucy into a monthslong nightmare—*sexploitation*, they called it—without the urge to explode something. She still felt they should have pressed charges. Lucy was still a *child*.

"You don't need a boy, Mom. You need a *man*." Lucy dropped her voice dramatically and then giggled. They were sitting side by side at the kitchen table. Lucy was stringing together Halloween lanterns—little paper pumpkins with devilish grins. Rachel was drinking her third coffee of the day and scrolling through an assortment of available men in the area. "Besides, not all boys are bad. Some of them are nice."

Rachel heard a lilt to her daughter's voice and looked up, suspicious. "Like who?" she asked.

Lucy kept her head down. Her hair, loose, concealed the half arc of her smile.

Rachel went back to scrolling. She wasn't seriously looking for a boyfriend—she still couldn't imagine having sex with anyone but Alan, and she was even beginning to forget what *that* had been like—but she thought a little flirtation, a little attention, wouldn't hurt. The past few years had been so *serious*. First her relationship with Alan, withering like a plant from being poorly tended, leaving him moody, remote, and secretive. She hadn't noticed—or maybe she hadn't cared? Not until it was too late. And then the problems with Lucy: all that bullying, the disordered eating, the self-harm.

She was still young, as Rachel's mother was always reminding her, somehow marking the words as tacit criticism. It wasn't normal for her to be holed up in the middle of nowhere, letting her career languish just as it was exploding, isolating herself as some of her best years were slipping by. To Rachel's mother, southern Indiana might as well have been Siberia. "Here's a man who owns three Papa Johns franchises," she said, pretending to be impressed.

"You like pizza," Lucy said with a smirk.

"Wait. Forget it. He has an Ayn Rand quote in his bio."

"Picky, picky." Lucy held up the miniature lanterns, evaluating them intently for a moment, and then put them aside and reached for her mother's laptop. "Here. Let me see."

Rachel got up and dumped the rest of her coffee in the sink, startling a sparrow from the windowsill.

"Ooooh, look. This one's a cop." Lucy began to read, "'Twenty-two years with the Willard County Sheriff's Department. Actually, scrap that. Willard County is enemy territory."

"Willard County is where your great-aunt and uncle live. Let me see that." Rachel leaned over Lucy's shoulder, contemplating the broad, flat face of Danny Wilkes, forty-seven. Immediately she wondered what he thought about the Faraday case and the Rockland County investigation, such as it was, into Nina's disappearance.

This was her problem. Her interests ran her, again and again, back to work. It wasn't all her fault; the Faraday case was inescapable in Granger. There were threads, connections back to Nina Faraday and her mother, everywhere she looked. In the surnames of Lucy's friends, which raveled her back to the names of former witnesses and classmates.

In the Steelers themselves, of course—a sprawling clan, linked to politics and real estate, the sheriff's department and the school board. In the Granger Club Team, now training under Jack Vernon, a man who'd actually swum with Tommy Swift. Rachel imagined a gigantic web, or a root network, extending through much of the county, anchoring everyone back to the same mystery.

"They don't know better. You do." Lucy nudged her mother away with an elbow and hunched over the laptop again. A second later, she made a noise somewhere between a cough and a snort. "Oh my God. No way. That's Topornycky's uncle."

"Topornycky?" Rachel recognized the unusual name immediately. Her heart rate spiked.

"Nick Topornycky's uncle, Woody. I can't believe he's actually trolling for a girlfriend." This time when Rachel reached for the laptop, Lucy actively fended her off. "No, Mom. You cannot go out with him. He's literally insane."

"Relax. I just want to see what he looks like." Lucy finally relented, yielding her chair to Rachel. Woody Topornycky looked older than his thirty-eight years. Still, he was handsome in a weather-beaten way, at least in his profile picture.

Lucy was now agitating around the kitchen, going nowhere in particular like a moth caught in a lamp. "He's a total alcoholic. He dated Bailey's mom for, like, one minute and completely destroyed their Christmas. Bailey said he was so hungover in church, he literally threw up into the nativity scene."

"He was also the last person to see Nina Faraday alive," Rachel said.

Immediately Lucy stopped pacing. "Really?" she said. "Where?"

"At school. She was crossing the parking lot. According to Woody, it looked as if she were heading to the Aquatics Center." Woody Topornycky had a Substack and, from what Rachel could tell, a devoted community of readers who liked their local history dashed with conspiracy theory.

"According to Woody, aliens have military bases under the poles. He's a nutcase. You should see his YouTube channel." Then Lucy added, "He didn't see her after that?"

"If he did, he's never admitted it," Rachel said. It was an odd thing. At the time, the new Aquatics Center was still under construction, the pool unfilled. It seemed unlikely that Nina would have gone there looking for Tommy. On the other hand, Woody Topornycky wasn't, as Lucy pointed out, the most credible witness. And he hadn't actually seen Nina *enter* Aquatics. Maybe he'd simply been wrong about where she was heading.

"Maybe *he* killed her," Lucy said.

"Maybe," Rachel said. "The police thought it was possible."

"The simplest explanation is usually the correct one," Lucy said sagely. "My bet? Tommy Swift killed Nina in a fit of rage, and Coach Steeler lied for him afterward."

It was, from what Rachel could tell, the predominant opinion everywhere *but* Rockland County.

"Is that what Arianna thinks?" Rachel asked. Arianna was the postgrad student who'd screamed so piercingly when Lucy rocketed out of the house brandishing her bike pump—thinking, Arianna later confessed, that they had triggered the old curse and reanimated the spirit of Nina Faraday to take her bloody revenge. After the confusion abated—after Arianna and her friends accepted that Rachel and Lucy were neither ghosts nor trespassers—they had proven to be polite, thoughtful, and appropriately sheepish about their illegal entry. Ever since the podcasters had broken through the gates, attempting their dig for proof of murder, Lucy had been emailing back and forth with the production team. Rachel wasn't sure it was a good idea; Lucy already seemed to be in Mrs. Steeler-Cox's crosshairs, frequently reporting hallway demerits for things as minor as spitting her gum in the trash or lingering in the cafeteria after first bell.

Rachel blamed herself. She should have made more of an effort to fit in. She should have joined the PTA, or the Woodward Moms'

Association, or one of the other acronyms that Mrs. Steeler-Cox chaired. At the same time, she enjoyed being an outsider. An uncategorizable element. Something, and someone, who Didn't Quite Belong.

"Tommy's the one with all the motive," Lucy said, ignoring the question. "Nina dumped him, didn't she? She had a new boyfriend."

"No one knows that," Rachel said. "That's what people said *after* she disappeared. And besides, Tommy had an alibi."

"Right. He was with Coach Steeler."

"And the rest of the club team," Rachel said.

"That doesn't count," Lucy said. "They could have lied too." She took a handful of candy corn from the bowl on the table and began siphoning them one by one into her mouth. "You know, there's a psychic online who says that Nina never ran away. She says Nina was killed and buried next to water."

"That's very helpful. Maybe we should drain the Ohio River and look there."

"I'm just telling you what she *says*."

"Don't you have other things to think about? Halloween? Dance rehearsal? Your homework?"

Lucy gave her a look. "I'm just saying, if Coach Steeler really did cover up for Tommy Swift, I don't think Woodward should build a whole big memorial to him. Not until we know for sure."

Rachel's scalp prickled. "What memorial?"

"I don't know. It's some pavilion named after him. There's a message about it in the portal. We're all supposed to vote." Lucy yawned. "And just so you know, I'm done with all my homework."

"Really? Even French?"

"Oui, oui, madame."

Outside, someone honked. Lucy immediately pivoted for her jacket, sweeping her phone into her pocket. "That's Bailey. I gotta go," she said. She leaned over and kissed her mother's cheek. She smelled like honey. "Love you."

"Remember, you promised me a pumpkin!" Rachel called after her. Lucy turned around and gave her a thumbs-up. When the front door opened, Rachel caught a glimpse of her daughter's friends: beautiful, smiling, dressed in shrunken T-shirts despite the October chill. Cool, Rachel thought. Her daughter's friends were cool.

"Bring a jacket!" she shouted. But the door was already closing, snuffing out the sound of laughter.

Moved by a sudden impulse, Rachel went to the living room windows and watched the four girls move in a giggling pack toward Mia's brand-new BMW. A gift, Lucy had told her, from Mia's father, once a swimmer himself.

She found herself thinking again about webs, about veins of money that ran from Aquatics to the sprawling Steeler clan and back again. She thought about connections, and pack animals, and Tommy Swift's alibi. Twenty-two members of the swim team and their coach.

She wondered why Nina had lingered at school so long on that final day. She'd had no practice. No tutoring session. No after-school club. No one had seen her at all—not until Woody spotted her crossing toward the new Aquatics Center, still barely architected, ostensibly closed to students. Only an hour later, she had texted her mother that she was on her way home, and Tommy that she was running away.

So what had happened in that hour? What had Nina Faraday seen, or done, or chosen that had upended her life, sent it leaping from its tracks?

And more importantly—who else had seen Nina Faraday?

TWO

We

As we nudged closer to Halloween, a steady stream of tragedy tourists began their pilgrimages to 88 Lily Lane. It happened every year but not to this degree; the break-in at the Vales' house winched interest in Nina Faraday's cold case to a record high. Akash reported out-of-state license plates on Lily Lane almost every day; he even saw an overzealous YouTuber trying to scale the fence one morning when he walked out to catch the bus.

That was around the time that people started whispering that Lucy Vale and her mother practiced witchcraft.

In a way, it felt inevitable. We still had no solid explanation for why the Vales had chosen to live in the Faraday House. And the Vales' response to their intruders—the fact that they'd offered to take the podcasters on a tour of the house, and even into Nina's old bedroom—struck some people as odd.

Even worse, Rachel Vale wasn't looking for a church. That was practically unheard of in southern Indiana. With the exception of the Kornsteins and Akash's family, everyone we knew had a church, even the families that barely went. Church was part of life in southern Indiana—like going fishing in the summer, or buying a Christmas tree from ACRES Lawn & Garden right after Thanksgiving, or loving the Sharks.

We initially tried to downplay the rumors of midnight sabbaths and blood rituals. Sure, maybe the fact that Lucy Vale linked a countdown to Halloween on her socials was a little extra. Maybe Lucy's insistence that she and her mom spend weeks decorating for the big night was a little weird. But we dismissed the throwback picture of Lucy and Rachel Vale costumed identically as witches as coincidence. Just like the fact that she'd posted it on a Friday that happened to be the thirteenth.

Or maybe it was a message. A clue. A hint. A wink in the direction of the rumor.

The question was: Which direction?

Things escalated once Lucy Vale brought an H.P. Lovecraft book to school and soon afterward posted to social media professing a love for Cthulhu. Part of the problem was that we didn't know who H.P. Lovecraft was and initially misidentified Cthulhu as a pagan deity, thanks to Allan Meeks. According to him, H.P. Lovecraft was a necromancer who, along with Nikola Tesla, had been indoctrinated into an occult secret society known as the Council of Eleven, devoted entirely to the resurrection of the dead.

It turned out that Meeks's information was entirely ripped from a vast wiki dedicated to a cult Japanese manga and subsequent RPG community. But by the time we separated fact from fiction—to the extent that we could—the damage was done.

Suspicions of occultism cast an obscuring cloud over the Vales' motivations and seemed to touch Lucy with a special, awesome, unseen power.

@badprincess: Does anyone know if Lucy and her mom did a séance to try and contact Lydia Faraday?
@hannahbanana: omg. I think I did that in sixth grade
@hannahbanana: With a ouija board
@hannahbanana: Do you remember that @ktcakes888?
@ktcakes888: I remember your mom threw out my Ouija board

@ktcakes888: And told me that only Jesus had the answer to all my questions
@nononycky: interesting. did Jesus tell you what happened to Nina?
@geminirising: lol you guys. People are saying that Lucy Vale cast a spell on Noah Landry
@geminirising: And that's why he's so into her
@kash_money: Noah Landry is not into Lucy Vale
@kash_money: He's just in some cock-fight with Alec Nye
@kash_money: it's a bet to see who can pull the most Minnows
@kash_money: All Noah cares about is winning
@nononycky: uh-oh
@nononycky: Looks like LV put a spell on @kash_money too
@kash_money: fuck off, Nick

Unfortunately the idea that Rachel Vale and her daughter were occultists wasn't a hard sell. The Vales, as a unit and collective idea, rubbed plenty of people the wrong way. We could feel it, like the static charge of electricity just before a bad thunderstorm. Maybe it was because Lucy's mom was so pretty, or because she was single. Maybe it was because Rachel Vale never shopped at the Costco or the Walmart and instead supposedly drove thirty miles to the Whole Foods in Redding. Maybe it was because she had the time and the gas money to drive thirty miles, even though none of us knew what she did for a living. We suspected family wealth. We threw around snark about trust funds and alimony and the liberal elite.

We wondered what Rachel could possibly get up to all alone in that house while Lucy was at school.

Neither Lucy nor her mom knew how to fish; they didn't go to football games; they didn't hunt, as far as we knew. They weren't country. But they didn't fit in with the establishment either. They didn't apply to the golf club or volunteer at the historical society or turn up at the Rotary Club brunch to benefit local veterans.

And: they were vocal opponents of the new Jay Steeler Legacy Pavilion.

Then there were the Vales' Halloween decorations, which over the course of the month had become an increasing cause for concern. First cotton spiderwebs, slung artfully from porch rail to roof, skeined the facade. Days later they began colonizing the azaleas like a fast-growing mold. Plaster gravestones sprouted among the browning stalks of the perennial garden. Skeletal arms twined between the spires of the iron fence; decapitated heads leered from their tops. It was as if time were turning in reverse, tunneling us back toward the Faraday House of our childhood nightmares.

We had to admit the effect was impressive. But once the Vales roped a ghost to the apple tree in the front yard, we agreed things had gone too far. Some of us began to feel that old sense of dread when we drove past Lily Lane on the way to school, or when we turned our bikes onto Burton's Way after leaving the Sandhus' and saw the lamps burning in the upper windows of number 88 against a smoke-colored sky, casting miniature aureoles of light against the ever-quickening darkness. Some of us were startled by the appearance of a silhouette against the windows and felt our breath hitch against our hearts, a sudden leap of terror, before remembering that it was only Lucy on the stairs or her mother moving around the kitchen making dinner.

But for a brief second, before the past peeled away from the present and left Lucy and her mother alone in the house, some of us forgot.

For a brief second, from out of nowhere, the certainty came down on us like the touch of a hand: that Nina and Lydia Faraday's story wasn't over.

That, somehow, it was happening again.

The question was: What to do about it?

Most of us didn't really believe in witchcraft, of course. We knew that Olivia Howard was into Wicca obviously, and we didn't want to give her the excuse to start waving her sagebrush in our direction and talking about auras. Crystals and nature worship was one thing. But demon-conjuring, occult sacrifice, and satanic possession was another.

On the other hand, we all had our moments. Our nighttime impressions of shadows shifting in our peripheral vision. We'd heard stories: a ring of decapitated dolls turned up by groundskeepers in Byron Park; the pile of charred animal bones heaped in a mysterious crop circle that had appeared in the middle of the Topornyckys' alfalfa field; strange rhythmic chanting deep inside the state park. We'd heard of shadow people, and the time Ethan Courtland swore he'd seen a half man, half dog startle on his way home from the river on his dirt bike. We knew about the handprints that had materialized suddenly on the windshield of Mr. Spinnaker's BMW when it passed over the bridge on Old Derrick Road. And we'd all known the sudden invading chill that gripped us out of nowhere when we rode past the abandoned cemetery on State Road 26, its splintered headstones leering like broken teeth inside a tangle of greenery. We'd all felt our breath freeze in our lungs, convinced while alone on an empty street that we'd felt the touch of a hand to our backs, or a breath that had scraped our bare necks, or a heavy presence falling soundlessly behind us. Plenty of us had felt it on Lily Lane, staring up at the Faraday House, waiting for Lydia's restless ghost to appear.

We didn't believe in witchcraft or black magic. About Satan, we were undecided. But we believed that some people believed.

And *that*, we knew, was dangerous.

THREE

We

A week before Halloween, a package showed up on the Sandhus' front porch for R.C. Barnes, a name none of us recognized. Akash later swore he'd opened the package before checking the delivery address; he'd been waiting, he claimed, on a delivery of new computer speakers.

> **@mememeup:** who the hell is R.C. Barnes?
> **@kash_money:** apparently, someone who lives at 88 Lily Lane
> **@mememeup:** And writes books

He sent a photograph of the package's contents: a dozen copies of a single book titled *The Monster in the Basement: The Abduction of Grace Wallace*, authored by R.C. Barnes.

> **@safireswiftly:** Who is Grace Wallace?
> **@badprincess:** are you kidding?? There was an entire Netflix documentary about her
> **@mememeup:** can we stick to one mystery at a time, please?
> **@mememeup:** WHO IS RC BARNES??

The question temporarily united us in a shared digital crawl across the internet. R.C. Barnes, we learned, was the pen name of an investigative journalist who had, among other things, gone undercover for years to investigate the mafia's continued connection to Chicago politics and who, early in their career, had been nominated for a Pulitzer Prize for their work exposing the serial rapes committed by a prominent businessman in Akron, Ohio.

@hannahbanana: soooo . . . why are his packages coming to the Faraday House?
@lululemonaide: do you think RC Barnes is Lucy's father??
@goodnightsky: ummm, sexism much?
@gustagusta: not really. Pretty sure you still need a father to make babies
@ktcakes888: that is very transphobic
@spinn_doctor: okay, snowflake
@goodnightsky: I meant that RC Barnes isn't necessarily a man
@pawsandclaws: Didn't Lucy say her mom was a journalist?

We racked our brains. Had Lucy mentioned her mother's job? There had been so much speculation about Lucy's mother and what had motivated her to move to the area, and to the Faraday House specifically, that we had trouble separating the threads of fact and fiction. Lucy's mother was an escaped criminal, an impoverished ghost hunter, and an eccentric heiress, all in different retellings; she had been a tragic divorcée, a hot lesbian, and even the escaped acolyte of a Chicago-based cult that had briefly swept national attention after a raid in late summer of their Evanston-based compound.

But Olivia Howard was insistent: Lucy had certainly mentioned that her mother worked in journalism at the fake birthday party. Skyler Matthews backed her up. She remembered talking to Lucy about her mother's career on a crime desk, back before Lucy Vale became a Strut

Girl, back when she was still alternating between the gamers and the literary geeks at lunch.

We tracked all the biographical parallels to Rachel Vale we could find in descriptions of R.C. Barnes's career path. The more we rooted through details about the author, the more compelling connections we found to the Vales—including an obsession with privacy that might explain the Vales' pathetic digital footprint.

@ktcakes888: check it out. RC Barnes used to write for the Chicago Tribune
@ktcakes888: Didn't Lucy say that she and her mom lived in Chicago?
@hannahbanana: she's definitely *been* to Chicago
@kash_money: no mention of a cat
@gustagusta: no mention of a *kid*
@meeksmaster: this article says RC Barnes is the pen-name of a Michigan-based journalist
@nononycky: It's gotta be her

Within twenty-four hours, Skyler Matthews and Kaitlyn Courtland had made an impressive graphic—modeled after the murder boards they'd seen while binge-watching old episodes of *Law & Order*—to compare all the points of biographical intersection between Rachel Vale and R.C. Barnes. Their work persuaded us: Rachel Vale had a secret identity as a *New York Times* bestselling author.

As soon as we knew, it seemed inevitable, the only possible resolution of all the mysteries that had surrounded the Vales since their arrival. For example, the fact that Rachel Vale didn't seem to work but could afford to buy Halloween costumes for her shrubbery; the fact that she had so many tattoos; the fact that the Vales leaned progressive. According to Spinnaker, it was impossible to make it in media these days unless you voted Democrat or took to Twitter.

Sensing a forthcoming rant about the deep state, @ktcakes888 briefly muted his account.

Our excitement snowballed quickly into hypotheses about the Vales' net worth and what the rumored Netflix docuseries based on R.C. Barnes's first book meant for the rest of us. We wondered if she had been to LA, had met any of our favorite YouTube stars, or could get us our own series. Skyler Matthews, who was by then floating the idea of her own podcast, suggested she might invite R.C. Barnes on for an interview. Olivia Howard outrageously claimed to have known all along that Rachel Vale was an artist just from reading her aura. Jackson Skye countered that journalists weren't artists. Allan Meeks fired off a dozen eye-rolling emojis in a row.

@meeksmaster: what are you talking about?
@meeksmaster: All they do is creative writing
@spinn_doctor: never trust the #fakenews
@geminirising: okay qanon
@geminirising: Put the crazy down

Will Friske reminded all of us, irrelevantly, that he'd dropped a deuce in Rachel Vale's toilet back when he and his cousin were clearing their yard.

If Rachel Vale was famous, then so was her toilet.

Then Peyton Neely introduced a new line of conversation. Wasn't it odd that only months after a famous writer had moved into the Faraday House, a bunch of supposed strangers allegedly broke onto their property to try and excavate the yard for Nina Faraday's body and then made a podcast about it?

Wasn't it . . . *convenient*?

@badprincess: you think it was a setup??
@badprincess: Like some kind of publicity stunt?
@safireswiftly: omg

@safireswiftly: Did Rachel Vale PLAN the podcast???
@geminirising: what do YOU think?
@mememeup: I think that makes zero sense
@mememeup: If Rachel Vale is RC Barnes
@mememeup: and she wanted to blow up a story about Nina Faraday
@mememeup: why wouldn't she just write one herself?

Ethan Courtland's question was meant to be rhetorical. But it shuddered us all into silence, struck down by a heart-stopping idea.

@badprincess: oh my god
@badprincess: Do you think that's what she's doing???
@mememeup: wow
@skyediva: welp, I guess that would explain why she moved into a literal crime scene
@skyediva: Maybe she wanted to get closer to the subject matter

The idea was thrilling, and terrible. We didn't believe it could be true.

At the same time, it made an awful kind of sense.

We had to confront Lucy about her mother. We had to force a confession from Rachel Vale. Alex Spinnaker suggested that Akash hold the books hostage until Rachel Vale fessed up. Evie Grant suggested that Coraline Winters contact Barness publisher pretending to be Rachel Vale. Olivia Howard suggested we write R.C. Barnes a fan letter, deliver it to the Vales, and see if we get a response.

Akash logged on and apologized for disappearing for a few minutes. We hadn't noticed and were gracious about it.

@kash_money: sorry guys
@kash_money: Guess who just rang the doorbell??
@badprincess: Lucy???

@kash_money: nope. Her mom

@kash_money: She wanted to know if we got a package of her books

We recovered from the shock in record time, then rushed to spread the news. Of course we did.

That's how Discord was.

That's how we were.

Swapping messages, shit-talking, hoarding our phones like gateways to a secret world. We clung to the threads like they might lead us somewhere—out of our bedrooms, out of Indiana, out of our skin. We unraveled the world into sound bites. Everything was just talk.

Everything was just a topic.

In boredom, we burned everything into the bones of a story.

We had no way of knowing that, someday, Lucy Vale would burn right back.

FOUR

Rachel

Danny Wilkes, twenty-two-year veteran of the Willard County Sheriff's Department, agreed to meet Rachel for lunch at the Old Mill, a hundred-and-fifty-year-old landmark outside the township of Jalliscoe. Rachel remembered it from the occasional dinner with her aunt and uncle. She was almost positive they'd celebrated her cousin's graduation at the Old Mill. Or was it Kelly's eighteenth birthday? Either way, stepping into the wood-paneled room and across the wide plank floorboards buckled with age and creaky with the pressure of every step, she experienced a sudden, almost vertiginous nostalgia for the teenager she'd once been. She'd had plans to backpack through Europe, fall in love with a man named Claude or Sergio. She'd dreamed of breaking stories, of wartime, corruption, and injustice. She'd dreamed of Pulitzers, cargo planes, and the dusty back roads of distant countries.

That was before college. Before the parties, and the pills, and the pregnancy. Before Lucy arrived, dense and grasping, with a gravitational force that reoriented her entire world.

Danny looked older in person than in his profile picture. No surprise there. Still, he had a nice smile.

"I should have known when you first pinged me you weren't looking for a date," he said, a little ruefully. She'd introduced herself as a journalist on their first phone call and asked him explicitly whether he might instead be willing to meet and talk about the Faradays, even though Willard County hadn't been explicitly involved in the investigation. Still, cops talked. "You're way out of my league."

They chatted a bit—about the weather (glorious), Danny's divorce (amicable), their respective children (teenagers all). At some points, Rachel thought, it really might have been a date.

But after they ordered, Danny leaned forward and squinted at her. "So you're writing a book about the Faraday case, huh?"

Instinctively Rachel looked around as if someone might be listening. But the restaurant was full—boisterous with families, truckers, and wizened couples who looked as if they'd been there since the restaurant's heyday—and loud. Besides, she reminded herself, she was in "enemy territory," as Lucy put it: a place free of fanatical devotion to Woodward's club team or the Sharks. The contrast between how the adjoining counties had reported on Nina's disappearance and her mother's suspicious death was amazing. In Rockland County, all the coverage had pointed to some unknown stranger—a drifter, a drug runner, a mystery boyfriend from parts unknown—or back to the Faradays themselves. Nina had run away with one of her many admirers or because her mother was too controlling. Lydia Faraday had waged a vindictive campaign against Tommy Swift because she was obsessed with Coach Steeler, whom she had briefly dated in high school.

In Willard County, the headlines—and subtexts—were very different. Tommy Swift, or one of his swim team buddies, had killed Nina Faraday. Coach Steeler, and possibly the entire Administration, had helped cover up his involvement.

And Lydia Faraday's death was no suicide, and no accident.

Rachel said, "I'm thinking about it. For now I'm just doing some research."

"And how's that going?" Danny's eyes carried a glint of amusement. "Rockland County Sheriff's Department being helpful?"

"I haven't asked," Rachel said, which was true.

"Wouldn't be much use if you had," he said frankly. Then he added, "You might have more luck when Sheriff Cox steps aside. It won't be long now. He just doesn't have the support he used to."

"Sheriff Cox," Rachel repeated. "Any chance he's related to the Steeler-Coxes?"

"Sure. He's one of the clan," Danny said. Seeing Rachel's face, he added, "You see why some people had doubts about the way the disappearance was investigated."

"What about you?" Rachel asked. "You remember. What do *you* think?"

"I think it was three days before they'd even opened an investigation. Even then, they treated Nina like a runaway."

"I take it you don't think she ran away," Rachel said.

Danny shrugged. "Most runaways come back," he said simply. "Look, the truth is, it's easy to play Monday morning quarterback on this stuff. I don't know what they had to go on. I wasn't on the case. That was, what, sixteen years ago? I was still writing speeding tickets. We didn't even know who Nina was until Cox asked for our help bringing in Joaquin Turner." Rachel wrote down the name. "He was a senior at Jalliscoe then. Another swimmer. Apparently he'd been hanging around with Nina."

"I bet that didn't make Tommy Swift very happy," Rachel said.

Danny tipped his head in acknowledgment. "All those kids—all those boys on the club team, Steeler's boys—they like to win."

It seemed almost like a non sequitur. But Rachel heard the implication in his words.

"Do you think the school protected them after Nina went missing?" she asked.

"I think the school still protects them." Danny suddenly grew more agitated. "Look at what happened a few weeks ago. Some of our kids get jumped, beaten up outside a bowling alley. One of them winds up in the ICU. And what happens to the kid that put him there? Nothing."

"You're talking about Aiden Teller?" Rachel asked, and Danny nodded. "He got suspended from competition," she pointed out. "My daughter tells me that his scholarship could be in jeopardy."

"It's a slap on the wrist. He should be in prison. He's a menace; they all are."

Rachel reflected. There might not be a single person in southern Indiana who could be objective when it came to Granger's steady stream of swim stars. But she didn't say so.

"So why does everyone protect them? Is it the money?" Rachel knew that the Woodward High School Athletics Booster Fund was one of the largest in the state. The vast majority of it went to their Aquatics department.

"Oh, sure. It's partly that." Danny shrugged again. "I grew up outside of Gainsberg. For us it was the football team. Our quarterback could have driven an 18-wheeler into the church, and he'd be welcomed back on Sunday morning for Communion. And you know, that whole area—what they call the Four Corners—had nothing going before Steeler came back to build the swim program. The whole county was depressed. Main Street was bleeding businesses. No one wanted to move there. Now . . ." He shook his head. "Well, let's put it this way. I'm surprised you found a house so quick."

"I found a house that no one wanted to move to," Rachel said. Danny raised his eyebrows but didn't prod any further. Rachel leaned forward. "What do *you* think happened to Nina Faraday?"

Danny's eyes slid away from hers. Like any good cop, he didn't answer directly. "Like I said, I don't have all the information. I don't know what was investigated, what wasn't. I don't know who they spoke to. But I think those boys knew something, for sure. Whether Tommy put hands on her, I can't say. But my bet is he knew just exactly where she was. It usually is the boyfriend, you know. The boyfriend or the ex. Tommy was both, from what I understand, depending on the week."

He was right, of course. Rachel knew from her brief time covering the crime desk for KWMC out of Detroit. People craved real mysteries—juicy suspects, major twists—but they were surprisingly hard to come by. Most crime scenes traced back to the same sad story. An angry husband. A jealous wife. Someone who needed money.

Most mysteries weren't very mysterious in the end. They didn't make for good stories. They were just sad.

Still, Rachel found herself strangely resistant to the idea that Tommy Swift was, after all, to blame. There was the issue of his alibi. Even if all his teammates had lied for him, she didn't see how a random pizza delivery guy could be persuaded to get in on the cover-up unless he'd been bribed—or possibly threatened. Still, it seemed implausible; that kind of loose end tended to unravel with time.

Then there was the fact that Tommy had seemed devastated by Nina's disappearance. He'd dropped twenty places in the national rank within six months; a year after that, he was kicked off the University of Arizona team, moved home, and got arrested for drunk driving. Meanwhile, his old teammates were flourishing. Coach Steeler had moved on to a lucrative position at Indiana State University. Tommy's old friend Jack Vernon placed third at nationals.

Guilt, some people said. To Rachel, it didn't quite fit. If Tommy had done something to Nina, if he'd murdered her and staged her disappearance, he wasn't likely to be the kind of person who felt bad about it later.

But maybe Rachel didn't want to admit that after sixteen long years, the Faraday mystery might simply die out with a whimper, relegated to the compost heap of obvious stories. In a weird way, she wanted more for Nina. Maybe they all did—the clamor of internet sleuths, the podcasters who'd come digging for remains, even the locals who insisted that Nina must have run off with a stranger.

Maybe they were all just looking for a better story.

"Can I ask you a personal question?" Danny said.

"Sure," Rachel said. "But I may not answer."

"Teenagers go missing every day in this country. Girls turn up dead. There are hundreds, thousands of unsolved cases, and a lot of them aren't sixteen years cold. So why this one?"

Rachel hesitated. She wondered whether to tell him the truth. She wondered whether she even knew the truth herself. Finally she said, "I met her once."

Danny looked surprised, but only for a second. Just as quickly, his expression shuttered into a kind of attentive neutrality. "Nina?"

Rachel nodded. "It was only in passing. I didn't know who she was at the time. My cousin put it together later." It was at that same Halloween party, the one that Kelly had dragged her to off campus. She remembered the way the news had shuddered around the party when several high school boys arrived with their girlfriends. Swimmers, someone had mentioned. *Sharks.* One of them had some family connection to the host. Still, their presence leaned the crowd into unease. Everyone was afraid that the sheriff would arrive.

"She must have made quite an impression," Danny said.

"She didn't," Rachel said. "But the Sharks did." She was sure that Tommy Swift must have been among the handful of boys clustered on the front lawn trying to wrestle a drunk friend to his feet. She could still see it: the shouting, the urgency, the knot of teenage girls standing birdlike several feet away, agitating with nerves. She remembered the way those girls had eddied across the lawn when the boys' coach arrived, the soft pitch of their voices explaining, excusing, asking for help. Rachel watched the whole scene play out from the hood of one of the cars logjamming the driveway. At one point after the crisis had passed, the boy on the lawn revived and the teenagers dispatched into respective cars, Jay Steeler had spotted her struggling to light a cigarette. She had never forgotten the cool way he slid his gaze over her bare legs.

You're too pretty to smoke, he'd told her.

Rachel was drunk enough to be flattered.

After lunch, Danny and Rachel returned to the parking lot together. After the dim cloister of the Old Mill, Rachel was shocked by the sudden brightness, surprised to find the afternoon still intact, still puttering on busily without her. Danny offered to put Rachel in touch with a friend who'd covered the case once Nina's disappearance had become state news.

"And Rachel," Danny added after they'd already fumbled through an awkward hug. "You be careful, okay?"

Rachel reassured him that she would. Minutes later, back in her car, she wondered what had compelled him to say that. What possible danger could there be in investigating a sixteen-year-old cold case? She shrugged it off. No doubt Danny had made the comment out of a misguided attempt at chivalry. He seemed the type.

She drove home feeling grateful, and also guilty. She hoped Danny Wilkes would find a nice woman someday.

Lucy was home early, stringing cobwebs between a display of plaster headstones. They'd spent an obscene amount on Halloween decorations for the house. Lucy had sworn that she would start babysitting as soon as possible so she could contribute—*if* anyone trusted her with a child after learning where she lived. Rachel had pointed out that the forty-five-dollar severed heads that Lucy had insisted on for the gates wouldn't do her any favors on care.com.

"Guess what?" she announced as soon as Rachel got out of the car. "The podcast episode dropped today. I got *eighteen* new follow requests."

"And you'll say no to all of them," Rachel said, hefting a bag of birdseed from the trunk. "I don't want any strangers looking at your pictures."

"Why does it matter? You barely let me post anything," Lucy said. Rachel gave her a look. "Okay, okay. Fine. There go my dreams of a brand deal. Also, you got a letter. I think it's from your publisher. For some reason they left it on the porch."

Rachel set the birdseed on the back porch and picked up the letter addressed to R.C. Barnes from the mat. She barely registered that there was no return address.

Inside was a folded piece of paper with a simple typed message: *We don't want you here.*

"What is it?" Lucy asked, studying her mother's face.

"Nothing," Rachel said quickly. "Work stuff." She found herself scanning the yard as if someone might be hiding behind the trees. Her gaze landed on the Sandhu house across the street. She thought she could see movement in Akash's window. How often did he watch them? She thought of all those cars making slow U-turns on Lily Lane. The strangers who showed up to snap pictures of the house. Just the other day, a neighbor had walked her toddlers down from two streets over to admire the decorations.

"B-o-o-o-ring," Lucy said with an exaggerated sigh. She was on her knees now, carefully nudging a plastic spider into place on a pillowy nest of cotton.

Rachel balled the note in her hand and glared across the empty space.

Too bad, she thought. *We're staying.*

FIVE

We

All of us hate-listened to *Blood in the Water*, the podcast produced by the three amateur sleuths who'd stormed 88 Lily Lane.

We hated to admit the podcast was well produced. Episode 3 made us feel as if we were ourselves trespassing on the Vales' property one misty October evening, listening to the whine of the old gates as they were scaled and the repetitious bite of shovels in the dirt. Soon Lucy Vale was shouting dimly into our headphones, threatening to call the police.

One jump cut and a short bit of narration later, she was sitting down for an interview.

Lucy Vale's segment was less than three minutes long. Still, it was a revelation. That's how we found out that Lucy Vale knew even more about the Faraday case than we did, that the Rockland County Sheriff's Department was apparently besieged with requests to reopen the investigation into Lydia Faraday's death, and that the internet was confused about where Lydia Faraday's body had been found hanging. According to the producers of *Blood in the Water*, Lydia Faraday's body was discovered *inside* the house, hanging from the second-floor landing and roped to the banister.

Even weirder, Lucy Vale confirmed it.

The news shuddered our Discord server and quickly ricocheted around our group texts.

At first, none of us believed it. A small hysteria seized us. We fired back Reddit messages that we regretted the moment we hit post. We were sure that Lydia Faraday's body had been pulled from the apple tree in the front yard. We were positive. It was a known thing. As kids we'd biked to the gates of 88 Lily Lane at sunset and stood with the wind lifting a chill on our arms and legs as the sunset deepened shadows in the yard. We'd whispered *Nina, Nina, where did you go? Lydia, Lydia, what do you know?* We'd waited in the evening stillness, the wind hissing a message back through the wild clutch of growing things, until a sense of deep terror gripped us: eyes watching us from somewhere in the tangle of shadows. Kyle Hannigan had actually seen her and nearly pissed himself—the silhouette form emerging, taking shape like a breaching whale from an ebb of twilight, with her neck crooked over the rope, wild, sightless eyes, and the slow pendulum of her feet groaning the branches. Some of us were there, watching from a distance as Kyle turned with a yelp and came sprinting back toward Elizabeth Street, breathless and bloodless. Peyton Neely's camp counselor had told her about a girl who took an apple from a strange dark-haired woman she saw standing beneath the tree one day, and almost died.

But the Vales, and strangers all over the internet, claimed otherwise. We even found a leaked 9-1-1 call that seemed to confirm it. Surely, we thought, they had made a mistake. We theorized instead that the report was fake. We *insisted* it must have been doctored.

@spinn_doctor: here's a tip: never trust anything you read online
@gustagusta: right. Except conspiracy theories
@spinn_doctor: Exactly. It's all Russian misinformation

@mememeup: ah, yes. The old Russian operative cold case campaign

@mememeup: Sewing American dissension over the mishandling of suicide cases

@brentmann: #bluelivesmatter

@geminirising: please stop

We might have asked Lucy Vale. We might simply have leaned over in homeroom and mentioned the podcast and the police report. We might have casually corrected her about the facts of the Faraday case and explained that we knew for a fact that Lydia Faraday had hanged herself in the apple tree because we'd all been terrified of the apple tree growing up, which only made sense if it was, in fact, where Lydia Faraday had been found hanging.

In desperation, we did the unthinkable and turned to our parents. Did *they* remember how and where Lydia Faraday had died?

This, unfortunately, only muddied the picture. Astonishingly, Mrs. Courtland seemed to think she'd overdosed. Mr. Hannigan, who'd provided an ice-cream cake for Lydia Faraday's memorial service, which only a handful of people had attended, could only vaguely indicate that he thought a gun was involved.

It turned out neither of them was entirely wrong.

According to *Blood in the Water*, a gun registered in Lydia Faraday's name was discovered in an unlocked gun safe by the police who recovered her body. A toxicology report returned proof of both alcohol and prescription barbiturates. The two facts together inflamed conspiracy theorists still speculating that there was more to her death than the police had let on. Why, the theory went, would a woman with a handgun choose to rope herself to a banister when she could have taken an easier, more painless way out? A pair of YouTubers, both amateur criminologists, had even consulted both a physics professor and a forensic scientist and filmed an entire twenty-six-minute video about how the evidence from the medical examiner's report proved that Lydia

Faraday must have been pushed or thrown off the second-floor balcony, launched over the banister headfirst.

It was suspicious. It was convincing. It was clickbait.

We were sure it was just clickbait.

Luckily, Halloween gave us the excuse to find out.

SIX

Rachel

It was Lucy's idea to have a Halloween party, an open house for trick-or-treaters, neighbors, and friends with hot cider and prizes awarded for the best costumes. But the night before, she began to have doubts.

"What if nobody comes?" Lucy's attic room had, over a month, slowly accumulated a detritus of Halloween decorations: snarls of colored lights, stacks of construction paper, even a severed hand randomly dangling next to her blow-dryer from a hook in the closet. Rachel had to sidestep an enormous trash bag of cotton fluff and several rubber spiders just to make it to Lucy's bed.

"Of course they'll come," she said. "They're already coming." It was true. For days people had been gravitating to Lily Lane from all over to take pictures of the house.

"I don't mean randos," Lucy said. "I meant my friends." Her hand fluttered to her eyelashes, and Rachel remembered at the last second to say, "Chicken tenders."

Poor Lucy. Even before she'd met the seventeen-year-old who had promised her he loved her, that he would keep her pictures private, she'd been struggling in middle school. In sixth grade, her old friends had suddenly turned on her—an inexplicable cruelty but part of the inevitable striving for social ascendancy that Rachel remembered from her early adolescence. Lucy hadn't had good friends, *real* friends, in so long.

Rachel cleared a space on her daughter's bed and sat down. With her hair wet from the shower, wearing an oversize T-shirt that had once belonged to Alan, Lucy looked much younger than fifteen. Like the wide-eyed, stick-legged nine-year-old who'd begged to adopt a manatee for Christmas.

"Of course they'll come," Rachel said. "It was Bailey's idea, wasn't it?"

"I didn't mean Bailey either." Lucy squirmed away from her mother's hand. "Forget it."

Rachel didn't move. She sat there scrutinizing her daughter's profile, the way she twisted and fidgeted in her body as if it were a costume that didn't quite fit. On the bed, Lucy's phone kept lighting up with messages. An endless stream of texts and group chats, memes and photos. A world inside a world inside her daughter's head. Rachel had a sudden realization: this was about a boy. She felt a sudden clutch of dread.

"Is there anyone in particular you're worried about?" Rachel asked.

Lucy didn't answer for a second. Then she twisted again, casting off the dark mood and giving her mother the slender arc of a half smile.

"I'm not one of your mysteries, Mom," she said, lilting the words into a taunt. "Don't try and solve me."

SEVEN

We

Halloween fell on a perfect Sunday in October. The sky was electric blue. The trees were burning off the last of their leaves.

By the time our parents dropped us off on Lily Lane, the street was packed with cars we didn't recognize. At number 72, a woman puttied to a rocking chair was chain-smoking next to a jack-o'-lantern and a bowl of Halloween candy. Trick-or-treaters prowled among the houses, shaking down their residents for candy.

Most of the houses had Halloween displays in the yards. But they were nothing like the Vales'. The gabled roof pointed like an accusation to the overhang of clear blue sky. The porch was dotted with leering plastic jack-o'-lanterns. Toothy graves splintered the ground on either side of the front path. Mechanical skulls cackled at us from denuded garden beds. Black-and-orange crepe paper hissed in the trees and concealed lanterns projecting ghostly silhouettes across the windows.

We spotted a few people we knew milling around the house, including Mr. Henderson from freshman-year biology. He was sweating in a Cowardly Lion costume and huffing after three of his kids. There were plenty of children dressed as great white sharks, like there were every year. Even Mrs. McCullen, the school librarian, was wearing a cardboard fin and felt cowl studded with teeth.

We'd agreed to arrive just after lunch and voted unofficially against costumes, fearing somehow that we would get them wrong. But several of us broke rank. Alex Spinnaker arrived in his father's BMW dressed as a 1970s pimp; Meeks cosplayed a character from a manga series we'd never heard of; Olivia Howard wore cat ears and whiskers painted on her cheeks.

We almost didn't recognize Lucy, who was dressed as the ghost of Marie Antoinette. We joked that we'd been hoping for SpongeBob again, but we all agreed she looked beautiful even with a ring of fake blood around her neck. We couldn't believe the details of her costume. She'd taken care to whiten her skin down to her fingernail beds and wore a powdered wig daubed with more fake blood at the hairline. We could hear her skirts whispering around her legs when she walked. We speculated that the dress alone must have cost hundreds.

Ever since we'd found out that Rachel Vale was a famous writer, Lucy had taken on a new sheen of notoriety. We couldn't say whether we were the first people or the last to know about Lucy's mom. But as soon as we found out about R.C. Barnes, the news was everywhere. Gossip about "that writer woman from up north" bloomed like an infestation of markweed across the Four Corners. To many people, a career in liberal journalism was just as bad, if not worse, than the suspicion that the Vales were practicing witches. Either way, opinion about the Vales began to coalesce into a drumbeat of consensus: the Vales were keeping secrets.

To us this only exoticized Lucy Vale, setting her apart from the other girls in school. She was as close to famous as anyone we'd ever met, except for Jack Hamlin's older brother, Paul, who had 1.4 million YouTube subscribers. But Lucy Vale's notoriety was different. It was deeper, more dangerous. It ran close to the Faraday mystery and sidled up to rumors that Lydia Faraday's case would soon be reopened. It skimmed town controversy and deep politics. It dipped into podcasts.

It was about us, or against us, or for us—we still didn't know.

Rachel Vale was dressed as a witch and distributing hot apple cider from a cauldron on a camper stove. We weren't sure whether her choice of costume was tongue in cheek, a nod to all the rumors about her, or a tacit confession.

A crowd of children at the picnic table clamored for miniature Snickers, small bags of candy corn, and themed stickers. We edged close to the table, shooting looks at one another. We'd all agreed before the party that we needed to know whether Rachel Vale was writing about the Faradays—and if so, why? Alex Spinnaker insisted that we deserved the truth. But we felt suddenly shy in Rachel Vale's presence and reluctant to speak with her. Instead we accepted Styrofoam cups of apple cider and joked about being dressed up as kids who hated Halloween. We took handfuls of candy corn and squinched them with our teeth.

We gathered under the apple tree almost by accident, compelled to the spot where a ghoulish figure writhed at the end of its rope, turning on cold sluices of wind. It was the first time we'd all been together since the party at Sofia Young's house, when we'd sung Olivia Howard "Happy Birthday" and shared our first group secret: a trick we'd played on Lucy Vale.

Now it was the specter of Lydia Faraday connecting us, and an unspoken question about where she'd died. For years we'd felt the apple tree almost like a pressure, like the pull of hidden gravity working on us from our dreams.

But standing beneath the cloth body of a Party Supply ghost in the branches, we felt nothing but a curious emptiness and the bite of the wind touching our exposed skin.

We wondered why Lydia Faraday had done it. Why that day? Why that moment? Why a rope?

If she'd done it.

If she'd picked a rope.

We weren't conscious of it then—not yet—but a new element had forced its way into the old ghost story. The Faraday tragedy was alive again and spawning—birthing strangers who came in the middle of the night, YouTube videos and theories that took shape in their comments, questions that pointed to something unfinished, unnoticed, unexamined.

Holes. The Faraday case was full of holes.

And for the first time ever, we were full of doubt.

We entered the house together.

EIGHT

We

Inside 88 Lily Lane for the first time, we felt strangely oppressed, like the oxygen was thinning. A skeletal family was arranged in front of the television, and the way they'd been posed—as if rotted in their chairs—gave us all a bad feeling.

If the Vales were, in part, poking fun at the house's reputation, we were outside the joke. To us, the curtains drawn against the sunlight and fake cobwebs veined over the furniture felt ominous, like a staged reproduction of the Faradays' history, our history. The deep shadows and the atmosphere of quiet, the strangers wandering room to room in silence, reminded us of a memorial service.

We wandered into the kitchen aimlessly and picked through Halloween candy on the table where Nina Faraday had eaten her last breakfast. We drifted into the den, now full of the Vales' books, where Nina and her mom used to watch TV. We paused in front of the windows Nina had passed on her way out the door, peering out through the lattice panes that cut the outside world into a neat geometry.

Nick Topornycky was the first to suggest we duck the rope blocking off the staircase so we could get to the attic where Nina had slept. Alex Spinnaker tried to claim the idea as his own, and Meeks seconded him. The argument quickly devolved into old grievances about Topornycky's rejection of his former Dungeons & Dragons group. Olivia Howard suggested that it would be nice to meet Lucy's cat, Maybe, who was probably hiding upstairs. Akash firmly reminded us that we were all invited guests. Sofia Young pointed out that we'd technically never been invited.

Someone said the word *police*, and again it was repeated. Alarmed and guilty, it took us a minute to understand that someone had called the sheriff's department to complain about all the cars in the road.

Then Lucy Vale was there, pushing past us, muttering something about her neighbors. We sprang away from the staircase as if she could read our intentions by the proximity. She latched on to Akash, and we saw the way she squeezed his hand, as if for reassurance, and briefly smiled up at him.

We were envious, and afraid for Akash.

We followed Lucy onto the porch and watched her maneuver toward the road to join her mother by the police car, passing through the long clutch of afternoon shadows. We recognized both deputies: Nate Stern's cousin, confusingly dressed as a firefighter, and Deputy Martinez, a Boy Scout troop leader and organist at the Episcopal church.

We stood there with our hands in our pockets to keep our fingers from bloating in the cold, watching the exchange from a distance.

Akash wagered that it was the Hollands at number 66 who had called the sheriff. They hated the Vales.

Why? We wanted to know.

Akash only shrugged.

"They're different," he said.

The cars had thickened on both sides of Lily Lane and formed a natural runway for the procession of new arrivals. We saw the Strut Girls coming up the street in a group with Alec Nye, JJ Hammill, Ryan Hawthorne, and Jeremiah Greene. To our disappointment, Noah Landry wasn't with them. Meanwhile, departing families slowly thinned toward their cars. Mr. Henderson herded his children through the gates, pausing to say goodbye to the Vales and offer his paw to the deputies.

We couldn't hear what he said, but one of the deputies laughed, and Lucy Vale cracked a smile that flushed her whole face beneath the pancake makeup.

She was beautiful, especially for a ghost.

Suddenly a sharp wailing erupted in the garden. A little girl in a unicorn costume stood motionless beneath the apple tree, only a few feet from where the dummy was noosed to the branches, clutching her ratty rainbow tail in both fists and howling open-mouthed. Two older kids were just scampering off down the garden path when we turned around to look, and we caught the faint whisper of their giggles as they disappeared around the garden.

A gigantic fairy came flapping across the yard to enfold the girl in her arms. We figured it was the girl's mother. Still, the child kept wailing, so loudly that several other trick-or-treaters plugged their ears.

Then Rachel Vale was hurrying back from the street, looking harassed. Up close, we could see faint lines etching her forehead and the corners of her mouth. Still, she was beautiful. Her eyes were a vivid blue, the kind of color that people tried to reproduce with tinted contact lenses, and her hair was practically the color of pitch.

We had to admit, visually speaking, she made for a very convincing witch.

"Unbelievable," we heard her say as she came up the porch steps. Her eyes barely skimmed over us until they landed on Akash. "Kash, run and grab the ladder from the garage, will you?"

Akash peeled away wordlessly.

"It'll be easier just to take the whole thing down," Rachel said.

"Take what down?" Olivia Howard asked.

Rachel Vale squatted to fish a toolbox from beneath the wicker settee. "It's so ridiculous," she said. "I never would have hung it in the first place . . ."

"Hung who?"

"That dummy over there. I just thought the tree seemed like a nice place for it. Visible from the road, kind of creepy . . ." The toolbox was chaotic, and it took Rachel a minute to locate the garden shears. "I had no idea it would be considered disrespectful."

"People say that Lydia Faraday hung herself in that tree," Sofia Young blurted. We were all impressed, and embarrassed.

"So I gather," Rachel Vale said.

"Did she?" Sofia pressed. We suspected her of being a little drunk. Her parents' divorce, we agreed, was changing her. She had pink stripes in her hair now and often came to school smelling like weed. We weren't sure what to do about it, and we couldn't exactly ask her parents. "Did she kill herself in the apple tree?"

Rachel Vale pointed her garden shears at Akash who was returning with the ladder. "Lydia Faraday was found in the house," she said firmly. "She was hanging from a belt tied to the banister."

That was it. That was the whole story. We watched her cut the dummy from the branches in silence. The little girl in the unicorn costume was gone; her mom must have taken her away. We saw the Grim Reaper on his hands and knees, searching for something in the grass. A vampire crouched nearby was moving a hand through the rhododendron. Something was lost.

In the street, Lucy Vale was modeling her costume. We heard the Strut Girls shrieking laughter as Mia Thompson tried to shunt them into a photograph for a selfie. Alec Nye and the swimmers hung back a few feet, watching them.

We felt suddenly invisible, and cold. Lucy Vale looked somehow as if she were receding, drawn out by the tide of attention.

Or maybe we were the ones pulled backward. Behind us, in the recesses of the house, something dark gathered force in our imaginations. An idea taking form on the staircase; it swayed on the upstairs landing as if hesitating.

Rachel Vale, we realized, had answered Sofia's question only in part.

"There's Noah Landry," Evie Grant announced into the silence, as if we'd all been waiting for him.

His arrival sent a visible ripple through the party. Everyone stirred slightly, angling toward the street. A kid dressed as Batman nudged shyly toward him, clutching a piece of paper for an autograph.

We saw Landry's eyes gloss toward the other swimmers as they registered each other. Maybe we imagined the brief pause before he extended a fist to Alec Nye, the way his smile snagged slightly before touching his eyes.

We watched him greet Lucy with a one-armed hug. He was so big, she practically disappeared in his embrace. Whatever he said made her laugh, a sound that touched us all the way up on the porch.

Akash turned away and banged inside the house.

"Poor Akash," Peyton Neely said.

"Where's Spinnaker?" Sofia Young asked.

That was when we realized that Spinnaker, Meeks, and Topornycky weren't with us on the porch. But we didn't know for sure that they had, in fact, slipped past the rope and made it upstairs until hours later, when we saw the proof on Discord. By then we were all home, still working the chill out of our fingers, safely scrolling through photos of the attic.

We were scandalized when we found out that Spinnaker had peeled off from the others to venture not just into the attic but into Lucy's bedroom. We called him a stalker and a creep.

@kash_money: seriously, wtf is wrong with you?
@spinn_doctor: hey. Don't look at me. They're the ones who decided to have an open house
@badprincess: you went into her drawers??
@meeksmaster: he got some of her drawers
@badprincess: omg
@badprincess: @spinn_doctor is seriously going to wind up on the news someday
@spinn_doctor: thank you
@gustagusta: it wasn't a compliment, dude

Still, we were interested to find out that Lucy Vale was on birth control. Lucy Vale wasn't necessarily a prude, we felt. But she wasn't like the other Strut Girls. She wasn't a partier. She wasn't *like that*. She claimed she wasn't even interested in having a boyfriend, and we privately doubted she ever had. She wasn't necessarily naive. But we all felt she was somehow an innocent: a girl so pure, she didn't even know to be afraid of ghosts.

If she noticed the pair of underwear missing from her drawer, she never said anything to us.

PART 5

ONE

Rachel

On Thanksgiving, Lucy spoke with Alan for the first time in a year and a half. Well, maybe *spoke* was too strong a word. She was passing Rachel with a blow-dryer, headed for the bathroom, while Rachel was on the phone.

"Is that Alan?" Lucy asked. "Tell him I said happy Thanksgiving."

"Did you hear that?" Rachel asked him after Lucy had slipped into the bathroom.

For a second Alan seemed too overcome to speak. "Yeah," he said, half choking the word. "Yeah, I heard."

"It's a start," Rachel said, and he drew a quick breath, as if the idea had knocked the wind out of him.

It was a good day.

At lunchtime they piled in the car and made the drive to Rachel's aunt and uncle's house in Willard County. Rachel's cousin Kelly—the so-called "trad wife," according to Lucy—had made the drive from Columbus with her husband and three children. Rachel's grandfather, who had moved into an assisted living facility in Kentucky after his last stroke, was positioned in the living room like some kind of beneficent houseplant, smiling at everyone, occasionally slurring a remark that only his nurse could interpret. Kelly's children darted through the familiar rooms waving imaginary weapons at one another until Lucy wrangled them all to the floor to try a puzzle together.

"If you ever need a babysitter . . . ," Rachel said to her cousin, indicating Lucy and the children soberly sorting through the pieces.

"Yes, please," Kelly said. She dropped a hand on her belly; she was pregnant with her fourth. "Does she give discounts for volume?"

After Thanksgiving dinner—served buffet-style for the chaotic assortment of friends and neighbors who'd also been invited—Rachel lay with Kelly on Kelly's old bed like they were teenagers again, sneaking away from the crowd to listen to music or gossip about boys. The room still had trace evidence of its former life: a gigantic stuffed turtle; Kelly's old vanity, once cluttered with makeup and perfume and photographs of her friends; a corkboard where she'd pinned all her concert tickets. Rachel was happy and sleepy and full. Half a glass of wine, undrunk, sat warming on the nightstand. One summer she and her cousin had kept a bottle of SoCo in the bottom drawer of that nightstand, concealed behind a jumble of bras and tampons under the theory that Kelly's dad would never fish through it. Now they were old. At least, Rachel felt old.

She inched down until her ear was level with her cousin's warm belly, listening for the sound of the life stirring there, thinking of seeds sleeping underground for winter.

"So how has it been?" Kelly asked. Rachel realized, with a start, that she had been on the verge of falling asleep. "Does Indiana feel like home yet?"

"I think so," Rachel said. "I love the house."

Kelly moved her hand up and down the swell of her stomach. "Lucy seems like she's doing well," she said. "You must be so relieved."

Rachel tutted her. "Don't jinx it," she said, only half joking.

Kelly turned on her side with a grunt. "What about your special project?" she asked, keeping her eyes fixed on Rachel. Rachel had always loved Kelly's face: long and aquiline, almost noble, like some old Flemish portrait from the 1600s.

"Little Girl Lost?" Rachel said. She didn't remember when the nickname for Nina Faraday had dawned on them. More than a decade ago probably—back when Nina Faraday, the girl they'd briefly encountered at a party the autumn before she vanished, was only an incidental topic of interest, a shared point of connection. It was only in the past few years that the moniker "Little Girl Lost" began to haunt Rachel in the way that writing sometimes did, peeking around corners of her attention, shadowing her thoughts as she drifted off to sleep. It would make, she thought, a good title for a book. "Slowly," she admitted. "There's so much bullshit to sort through. And I'm getting stonewalled by the sheriff's department." She shrugged. "I'm supposed to wait for the changing of the guard."

"But you're still going through with it?" Kelly asked. "You still think there's a story there?"

"There's definitely a story. There are plenty. That's part of the problem." Then: "Why?"

"Nothing. I just thought you might change your mind after you and Lucy got settled, that's all."

It wasn't lost on Rachel, or on her therapist, that her growing interest in Nina's case had coincided with the worst year of Lucy's life—the worst year for both of them—when it seemed that Lucy might simply slip away from her, lost to her agonies and her obsessive rituals, lost to the punishment of her peers.

But Lucy was better now. And Rachel still wanted to know what had happened to Nina Faraday.

Rachel poked her cousin in the navel. "You think it's a bad idea."

"I didn't say that," Kelly said. But she was making a face. "You've had a hard few years," she said after a beat. "Maybe you can just relax for a bit. Let go. Nina's been missing sixteen years. Another few years won't hurt."

"Tell that to my agent," Rachel said, and they laughed. Rachel propped herself up on one elbow. She realized she wanted Kelly to understand. To bless her, in a way. "Look, I just want to know for sure whether Tommy Swift was involved. I want to know if Jay Steeler helped cover up for him. I mean, for fuck's sake, the school's trying to turn the guy into Gandhi. They're dedicating a whole building to him. It's not right. Not if he had information about Nina. I just want the truth."

"Are you sure that's the only reason?" Kelly gave her a look. She knew about Rachel's brief, pathetic affair—if you could call it that—with the much older and very married Jay Steeler. But even she didn't know how Rachel had unraveled after the night they'd spent together, how often she'd called him, how she'd once driven all the way down from Chicago just to sit outside his house, trying to work up the courage to confront him.

"This isn't about revenge, if that's what you mean," Rachel said.

"Good. Because you know what my mom would say." Kelly sat up with a grunt, leading with her stomach. "It's okay to glance in the rearview mirror. But start staring, and you'll veer off the road."

Rachel sat up too, stretching. Unbelievably, it was only four thirty in the afternoon. "I'll remember that on the way home," she said.

∽

They had one more stop to make.

The Sandhus had invited Lucy and Rachel to join them for dessert when they returned from Willard County. Rachel had agreed, partially out of guilt; in the paranoid days after she'd received a second anonymous letter in the mailbox, she had briefly suspected Akash. He so clearly had a desperate crush on Lucy.

Heartache could do funny things to a person. Especially a teenaged boy.

Rachel and Lucy parked the car, and Lucy ran inside to get the cookies she'd insisted on baking. She emerged moments later, her cheeks whiplashed from the wind, her hair standing up with static as if alarmed by the change in temperature. They tromped across the service road and cut across the Sandhus' backyard. The grass cracked with ice. It was the kind of cold that shocked every breath into the pantomime of a ghost.

Inside, Aman and Sabrina Sandhu were in the kitchen, working diligently through a wreckage of dirty dishes.

"Thank goodness," Sabrina said. "You're right on time. I don't think I could hold off the kids much longer. Leila has been asking for pumpkin pie since before we carved the turkey."

"The kids" were Akash and his two older sisters, both home from college with several friends in tow. Lucy kicked off her shoes and bounded into the living room to join them. Rachel heard a vocal flurry of greeting—introductions, laughter—and felt an immense sense of gratitude, true thankfulness, flame to life inside her. Kelly was right. This was where life happened: here in the present, with friendly neighbors and warm kitchens and stacks of dirty dishes.

Rachel should be content to stay here.

She peeked her head into the living room and saw Lucy comfortably settled next to Akash on the couch, one arm slung casually behind his head, leaning close to look at something on his laptop screen. Akash, meanwhile, sat rigid, as if afraid he might shatter their proximity by breathing.

Poor Akash. He was a good kid.

As she set out the small plates, Rachel latched on to snippets of conversation from the living room. The kids were discussing something called "Market Catch." She kept hearing a single name, repeated like a bass line under some growing disagreement.

It was that swimmer, the one everyone was excited about. The one she'd met on Halloween. A tall, goofy-looking kid with sloped shoulders and hands too big for his body. Noah Landry.

They were arguing about Noah Landry.

Then Akash stormed into the dining room, speaking over his shoulder.

"He's *not* that nice," he said. "It's a front. He's putting on a good front."

He blew past Rachel without a word and disappeared into the kitchen. He had a brief exchange with his mother, then returned, still looking sullen, carrying a coffeepot and a handful of dessert spoons.

"You okay?" Rachel asked. She could tell Akash was still seething.

He didn't answer right away. He went around the table depositing a spoon at every plate, slightly harder than was necessary.

Then he said, "Noah Landry isn't the guy everyone thinks he is. He's a narcissist. He just hides it."

"Okay," Rachel said. She had no idea why Akash was telling her.

Akash straightened. "Tell Lucy," he said. "Tell her that Noah Landry always wins."

So. Rachel had been right about Lucy. She was anxious about a boy—about *the* boy, the great Noah Landry who everyone was talking about—and Akash, poor kid, was obviously heartsick about it.

Noah Landry always wins. It was a funny thing to say. Inconsequential, in a way. Still, as Akash turned out of the room again, Rachel wondered why it felt like a warning.

TWO

We

For a month, we plowed through the competition. For a month, there *was* no competition. We were unstoppable, and we loved it.

Noah Landry wasn't the only one making record times in November. Alec Nye, Ryan Hawthorne, JJ Hammill, and Jeremiah Greene knocked half a second off a state record for the men's 200-meter relay, and Hammill set a new state record for the 50-meter fly.

But Noah was on a different level. He burned through the state records in five different events and broke two national records in the month of November alone. It was like something in him morphed the second he hit water, a transformation of pure kinetic power. We'd never seen anything like it. Swim meets were always packed, but that fall the crowd swelled with every new record smashed. We could pick out more and more outsiders: recruiters with their baseball hats and pinky rings, deep pockets down from Bloomington, and even farther, with perfect teeth and hair that looked shellacked.

The word *Olympics* lingered in the halls like perfume. It infected our consciousness, worked its way into our dreams where we were swimming with sharks or twisting in bands of bright blue ribbons. In November, the dream of seeing Noah Landry qualify for the Olympics unified us, repairing the rift that had temporarily gutted our Discord of key members. The girls from yearbook, and Topornycky and the gamers, logged back on.

We became used to seeing news crews next to Aquatics, and headlines about the Granger Club Team and Steeler's legacy uploaded almost daily to the student portal. There were so many links about Noah Landry we couldn't keep up with them.

He was the best swimmer to come out of Indiana since Mark Spitz. He was a revelation in the pool. He was born for the water.

An Olympian.

Noah Landry was an Olympian in the making.

That's what everyone was saying.

~

Meanwhile, the holiday bunting went up along Main Street, and Christmas displays cluttered the storefronts. Downtown Granger was hijacked by Winter Blues: a weeklong, countywide celebration that came toward the tail end of the regular meet season. To us it heralded the approach of the Winters Dance—and after that, championship season. The gigantic plaster shark outside the post office got pinned with its annual fur-trimmed hat and roped with a stranglehold of tree lights. At Woodward, Student Council members wore matching elf hats and pushed holiday cheer and bake sale items on the school between classes. Coach Radner had to carry around a pineapple for an entire week, an inside joke we didn't really understand, and the Sharks wouldn't explain.

Noah Landry had just taken down another national record, and Jay Steeler's younger brother, an Evanston-based city council member and one of the booster fund's biggest donors, had gone on record with the prediction that Landry would be the best swimmer of his generation. We were high on a record-breaking season and a clear path to sweeping regionals and then states.

The more media coverage Noah's times attracted, the more the Sharks were compared to the all-star team that had twice swept nationals under Coach Steeler. The parallels between Tommy Swift and Noah Landry were obvious and inescapable. They excelled at all the same events. Tommy still held state records for three events—100-meter butterfly, 50-meter breaststroke, and 200-meter breaststroke—but Noah Landry had already burned through his times in the 50-, 100-, and 200-meter freestyle, and he was closing in on Tommy's breast and fly times. Both boys even attended the same church, and Pastor Marks, who had presided over Tommy Swift's funeral service, showed up at half a dozen swim meets.

Maybe because of Coach Vernon's appointment to the club team, or because of the historic times Noah was clocking, or because of constant references to Tommy's records in the press, it seemed to us that the Swifts were suddenly everywhere. We picked them out at almost every home meet. We saw them leaving church, clutching one another on the stairs. Riley French saw Mr. Swift scrutinizing salad dressing labels in the IGA. Olivia Howard saw Mrs. Swift maneuvering a cat crate out of the veterinary clinic and murmuring reassurances to the Maine coon hissing inside. We wondered how they felt seeing their son's name so often used in connection to a new star swimmer.

We wondered how they could tolerate the resurgence of attention around the Faraday case.

Coverage of Coach Vernon was mixed. From the beginning, we saw just as many articles that dragged him for his relationship to Coach Steeler as praised him for it. We attributed the hate to online conspiracists, those wackadoodles who kept pushing theories about Tommy Swift and hypothesizing that the team had covered up his involvement in Nina's disappearance. It didn't help that someone had unearthed old photos of Coach Vernon back when he swam with Tommy Swift and, as a result, frequently hung out with Nina. It wasn't clear to us how close they'd actually been, but one of their Halloween photos blew up online; in it, Tommy had one hand wrapped around Nina's throat while pretending to bite her neck. Jack Vernon, dressed like a Viking with a battle-ax stained with fake blood, was laughing. It wouldn't have been such a big deal except that Nina's face was purple, and she appeared to be grimacing. We all agreed she was probably just really drunk—we could tell from the unfocused look of her eyes, which were sliding away from the camera—but the internet was whispering about sadism and sociopathy and debating whether or not Tommy's hand was actually restricting her breathing.

Then there was the yearbook debacle.

The same day that Coach Vernon and Noah Landry appeared on a state news segment, the *IndyStar* published a piece about the murky legalities of booster funds and public school sports using the Sharks' record and endowment as a case study. We skimmed most of the article but obsessed over its most controversial section: a two-decade-long litany involving current and former members of the swim team, including a few unfortunate sexual innuendos unearthed from the yearbook bios of some of our very best swimmers in the past twenty years.

We didn't condone the jokes, obviously, especially the year the seniors all kept a public count of the Minnows they'd netted. At the same time, we acknowledged that the decades before ours were backward, and regressive, and still besmirched by the throttling choke hold of the patriarchy. Enlightenment had come belatedly, only with our generation.

We couldn't fault the past too much for its ignorance.

And we knew it was only an unfortunate coincidence that the same year Nina Faraday disappeared, a trio of club team swimmers—including Jack Vernon and Tommy Swift, two of the team's stars—had earned a violent nickname in the pool, and their senior yearbook had gone to press with *murdersquad* printed in each of their senior bios. The online uproar about the name was understandable, if totally overblown.

If anything, the moniker was further proof of their innocence.

Senior bios were due at the end of January.

Obviously, they'd had no way of knowing that Nina Faraday would disappear in March.

But the backlash was ferocious. Rumors of drug use among the boys on Coach Vernon's club team crowded the comment section beneath every article almost as soon as it was posted. Vernon's mailbox was defaced with penises—twice. Someone keyed Principal Hammill's new car, although we were undecided about whether one of our swim team rivals or Bailey Lawrence was more likely to blame. (Supposedly JJ Hammill had cheated on Bailey with some suckerfish from Edwards County over Thanksgiving, and the car was his to inherit.)

Still, no one but a rival swimmer would have dreamed of defacing the plaster bust of Jay Steeler that sat just inside Aquatics, the bald chrome of its head worn smooth by half a generation of hands rubbing it down for good luck before swim meets. Yet, horrifyingly, someone had managed to scrawl *LIAR* just above his eyebrows—a thick, ugly worm of text that janitorial spent God knows how long trying to remove.

Days later, someone called in a bomb threat to the Allentown YMCA just before counties, and everyone was forced to evacuate, including the swimmers doing warm-up laps. We weren't fooled by the selection of targets. We knew that disrupting our win was the real aim.

After that our server was infiltrated, and then came the scandal of Market Catch.

～

Market Catch was an online auction sponsored by Student Leadership and the athletics department, ostensibly to raise funds for local youth sports teams. It was also our favorite part of Winter Blues. Bidding was open to the public, and every year the SLD managed to bully, bribe, terrorize, or blackmail roughly three hundred separate donors into posting goods and services to a Market Catch web page that temporarily replaced our student portal online. Offerings were typically diverse, ranging from the practical (a new chainsaw from Ace Hardware, a full emergency kit put together by the guys at TM Outdoor) to the edible (venison from Huckabee Farm, a catered Sunday dinner from Ribs & Roast) to the silly and all-out bizarre. That year an "heirloom" taxidermy frog dressed in a top hat was listed for $200. Five yodeling lessons from Mr. Ridges started at ten dollars. We couldn't believe it when both sold within hours.

Most of what went up for auction didn't interest us except as fodder for potential memes. But traditionally, members of the swim team volunteered as Balladeers, and each auctioned off a slow dance at the Winters. The Balladeers' Auction was the single biggest moneymaker—the previous year, the winning bid to secure an Alec Nye dance was more than $1,000—and also its most controversial item. Supposedly any registered student could bid on the Balladeers, provided she was female and had parents wealthy enough to drop serious cash on three and a half minutes of slow, shuffling revolutions and sweaty public palming around a gym floor. In reality it was an oligarchical sham, not to mention completely heteronormative—a nepotistic tool of the elites and the handful of rich Student Council girls who almost always wrangled the top bids from the rest of us.

Still, we loved it.

Watching the bids notch toward ludicrous was its own spectator sport. As soon as Market Catch went up, we waited for the Balladeers' Auction to go live. The big question was whether Noah Landry had, in fact, volunteered as a Balladeer, as some people were saying.

Of course, that was the hope—and, we suspected, a reason for the enormous volume of ticket sales. On the one hand, Noah Landry was devoted to charitable works, and the raffle nominally counted. We knew him as a devoted church kid, an Eagle Scout, and a member of the school's United Service Club, even if he was always busy training and never actually went to meetings, at least according to Evie Grant, whom we suspected had joined only after she saw that Noah Landry was listed as a member and who, to our knowledge, didn't give a shit about homeless people.

On the other hand, Noah Landry was, outside the pool, averse to the spotlight. He was quiet—possibly even shy—and avoided most social events. In fact, the biggest proof that he was interested in Lucy Vale was that he'd bothered showing up at her Halloween party. Swimming, church, homework, and a little bit of sleep—from what we could tell, that was Noah Landry's life. Some of us doubted that he would come to the Winters at all, even though the Sharks were its centerpiece.

It all depended, we felt, on Lucy Vale—whether she would go and whether she'd enter her name in the raffle.

We placed bets on how much money a dance with Noah Landry might rake in and joked about how salty Alec Nye would be when Landry torched his going price. We imagined their rumored rivalry might break out into open warfare. We made puns about Alec Nye going off the deep end.

But in the end, we never had the chance to see it.

The night before the Balladeers were due to be listed online, Scarlett Hughes sent a worried message through Discord. Market Catch had vanished mysteriously from the internet; the site was returning an error. At first we assumed that a rush of traffic had temporarily crippled the server.

But the following day, Market Catch was still offline, and our suspicion coalesced into certainty: we'd been hacked. The flurry of contradictory and apologetic statements from Administration confirmed it.

Spinnaker speculated that one or more bad actors were assaulting the server with invalid requests. Valiantly, the coding club offered their help to defend Market Catch from attack. Typically Administration rebuffed them, claiming some obscure series of technical glitches was responsible for the outage.

We knew better. And soon we had our proof.

At first we celebrated the email blast alerting us that the Market Catch website had been restored. It was a few hours before Olivia Howard raised the alarm; the offerings now included hardcore pornography, a handgun, and, even more shocking, information concerning Nina Faraday's whereabouts, listed for the price of one hundred dollars.

We were panicked. We were outraged. We were paralyzed, watching bids pour in on the counterfeit items. We discussed mounting a sting operation and frantically tallied whether we could find enough cash to place a bid ourselves.

We couldn't.

We debated calling the police or the FBI. We hunted for clues to the hacker's identity in the descriptions of the foreign items, which Skyler Matthews pointed out contained many of the same grammatical quirks. All we determined, however, was a propensity for semicolons.

It was a cataclysm.

We reached out to Alex Spinnaker and the coding club for help, then had to endure a lecture from him about penalizing cybercrime.

@gustagusta: so let me get this straight
@gustagusta: What I'm hearing is
@gustagusta: You're not going to do shit
@spinn_doctor: of course I'm going to do shit
@spinn_doctor: I already told my dad

Nate Stern claimed to have heard from his cousin that the sheriff's department would have to investigate the false tip, even though we were sure they would only find a giant time suck. On the plus side, Nate further insisted that whoever had posted the porn and the gun for sale might end up in federal prison. We prayed that it might turn out to be one of our most vocal rivals—like the Wolverines' head coach, who'd been insinuating for years that the Sharks dabbled with performance enhancers, or the captain of the Elgin High School football team, who'd spat on Noah Landry in the parking lot after a meet.

As restoration of the Market Catch website stalled, the Student Leadership Department scrambled to salvage the Balladeers' Auction. In the end, Mrs. Steeler-Cox, working with the Student Council, determined that the slow dances should be sold by student raffle. We were pretty outraged by the change until Skyler Matthews, who was back on Discord, reminded us that auctioning off human beings had connotations that our ancestors, who had proudly supported the Union against the Confederacy, would have been ashamed of.

It was a logic we didn't dare contradict.

Still, we grumbled, especially the girls. There was no way to guarantee a dance *or* bid on a specific Balladeer. The nineteen volunteering members of the swim team weren't identified. For twenty bucks, a girl could buy her name onto a raffle ticket and the chance to dance with the Shark who pulled it. It was, we had to admit, a far more democratic system—at least superficially.

Of course, the Student Council Mafia still had a way to tilt the odds in their favor. There was no limit on how many times one girl could enter her name into the raffle, provided she was willing to shell out. The bulletin board outside the cafeteria was refitted daily with a tally of tickets sold. Beneath was a table where two Student Council shills rotated time with school iPads, heckling everyone who passed to get in on the action. In the days leading up to the dance, we attempted to identify which swimmers had volunteered by voyeurism, observing those trying to persuade all the cute girls to put in for more tickets and falling stonily silent whenever a bottom-feeder shuffled by. *Eight hundred tickets* sold within the first week, more than double the entire female population of the school. And the numbers kept climbing.

The raffle system, we soon discovered, was bedeviled by the problem of all new democracies; we suspected that the results would be manipulated. There was no way that the Steeler-Coxes would keep their clutching hands out of the ballot box—or the ticket roll, in our case. If no one was monitoring and controlling the entrants, the logic went, what was to stop any of the boys on our server from snapping up a block of tickets and scoring a dance with one of the Sharks?

@gustagusta: besides the fact that SLD would murder us?
@nononycky: if Nye didn't get to us first

As the Winters approached, Akash's mood grew erratic. He tracked Lucy's every interaction with the swim team, especially Alec Nye and Noah Landry. He posted a heart eye emoji under the photo of the dress she'd bought, then immediately added a string of arbitrary emojis to soften the messaging. He spoke about skipping the dance. He wondered if the DJ would take requests. He suggested asking Lucy to the dance—as a joke. There was a kind of manic desperation in his use of exclamation points.

All along, he swore that Lucy hadn't entered her name into the raffle. He insisted that she had zero interest in buying a dance with one of the Sharks.

@kash_money: Lucy's not a fan
@kash_money: she only goes to meets because everyone else is so into it
@nononycky: so . . . she's cosplaying fandom?
@kash_money: yeah, exactly. Like an anthropology experiment
@mememeup: how meta
@spinn_doctor: I don't buy it
@spinn_doctor: she's playing you
@spinn_doctor: she loves the attention
@kash_money: Lucy's not like that
@kash_money: she just wants to fit in

We didn't bother to argue with Akash. But privately, we were beginning to have our doubts.

Later that would prove important.

THREE

RACHEL

There was, according to Lucy, only one place to buy a dress for the Winters Dance: Angela's Formal, an emporium-size outfitter of tuxes and formal wear that had been in Granger "forever, like since the eighties." In fact, the day Rachel accompanied Lucy and her friends Bailey and Savannah to the store, she saw a pack of boys she immediately identified as swimmers looking over rental tuxes. With some amusement, she observed the odd, coded way the boys and girls acknowledged each other—lots of shorthand and arch glances, a studious attempt to appear disinterested. The boys turned their eyes on Rachel next with a curious, flat kind of detachment that she did, in fact, find vaguely sharklike. But maybe that was just in her head.

"That's Jeremiah Greene," Bailey informed her. Bailey was growing on Rachel. She was bright and bold and energetic. A little bit wild, Rachel suspected, but she took her schoolwork and the dance team very seriously. And she seemed loyal to Lucy. "He just made the club team this year. He's not half as good as he thinks he is."

"And Mia's obsessed with him," Savannah said, giggling.

"And Mia's obsessed with him," Bailey confirmed.

They moved into a thicket of dresses: floor-length prom gowns with ruffles and trains, skintight minidresses with plunging necklines, lots of sequins.

"No," Rachel said firmly when Lucy reached for a scrap of cloth so sheer and insubstantial, it hardly counted as clothing.

"Mom, I was just *kidding*." She rolled her eyes and turned to Bailey. "See what I mean about her? She's so *easy*."

"Don't worry, Ms. Vale." Bailey put her arms around Lucy and gave her a kiss on the cheek. "Lucy's one of the good ones."

Savannah laughed. Lucy blushed. She shot Rachel a pleading look, as if Rachel might otherwise be tempted to blurt out the truth: Actually, Lucy almost failed eighth grade. *Actually, she was buying off-script antianxiety meds from some loser she met online who called himself her boyfriend. Oh, yeah. And she sent him naked pictures on her thirteenth birthday* . . .

While the girls loaded up a shared dressing room, Rachel wandered through the racks. She found herself wondering whether Nina had shopped here and what kind of dress she might have chosen. Something modest probably, to appease her mother. But with a small hint of rebellion—a slit up to the thigh or a plunging back. Something she could easily conceal with a shawl or a safety pin before she was out of the house. A normal teenage girl, pinioned like a butterfly between childhood and adulthood, doing her best to appease both worlds.

She thought again of Nina's two final texts, sent within minutes of each other. To her mother: I'm on my way home now.

To Tommy: I know you want me out of your life. I'm leaving for a while. Don't look for me.

Had Nina sent one? Both? Neither?

Why had she lingered at school so late? Where had she been for the hours before Woody Topornycky saw her in the parking lot? Who was she with?

Rachel felt certain that if she could just reconstruct Nina's final afternoon, she would know what had happened to her.

"Mom." Lucy's voice carried over the Byzantine arrangement of clothing racks from the dressing room. "Mom, come look."

Rachel returned to see Lucy showing off in a hot-pink dress with beaded straps.

"Option number one," Lucy said, doing a twirl. "What do you think?"

Before Rachel could answer, a voice at her elbow said, "Very pretty."

Rachel turned, expecting a salesperson, and instead got a shock: next to her was Tommy Swift's mother.

Lucy must have recognized her too. The smile fell from her face. She glanced at her mother uncertainly.

"It's cute," Rachel said, keeping her voice light. Her heart was beating very fast. "Let's see the next one."

Lucy withdrew behind the curtain. Tommy's mother didn't move. She just kept standing there, smiling blandly at Rachel. Rachel reached for her first name. Nancy.

"Your daughter's very pretty," Nancy said. She had a soft, slightly raspy voice that was inflected with a deep southern drawl. "I'm Nancy Swift. You're new to the area, aren't you?"

They shook hands. Nancy's grip was soft, practically limp. Her hands were tiny like the rest of her. Rachel remembered that an article in the *Rockland County Register* had remarked upon that fact. Somehow this five foot three woman had given birth to a boy who grew to be six foot five.

"Newish," Rachel said. "We've been here since the start of the school year." She didn't mention that she had relatives in Willard County, had been visiting southern Indiana since she was a baby. She never did.

Nancy nodded. "You're in Lydia's old place, aren't you?" Rachel was surprised by the easy way she said Lydia's name. As if Lydia Faraday were an old friend, a mutual acquaintance, someone who'd simply moved away. "I hear you're a book writer."

Rachel shouldn't have been annoyed, or even surprised. She'd tried as hard as possible to steer away from the term *journalist*, a word that startled and set people on edge even under the best of circumstances. And she'd been careful about using a pen name for her first book and making sure there were few identifying details about her online.

Still, the truth had a way of getting out, especially when it was inconvenient. She was at least partially to blame; there was no way to assemble research about Nina Faraday's disappearance and her mother's death without poking around, stirring up questions, chasing down people like Danny Wilkes.

"I've written *one* book," she said simply. She searched Nancy's face for judgment or suspicion and found nothing. Nothing but a benign, slightly dazed expression, as if her soul had been drained of all opinion before it could touch her eyes. It gave her the innocent look of a deer in headlights, and Rachel didn't trust it.

Lucy flounced out of the changing room again, this time wearing a dark-blue dress with a twinkling pattern of silver threads that looked like stars. She seemed surprised to find Nancy Swift still standing there.

"Number two," she announced and did a slow twirl. Rachel gave her the thumbs-up. Lucy frowned briefly and withdrew again, swishing the curtains closed on an efflorescence of whispers.

"If you ever want to talk to someone . . ." Nancy let the words trail off just before they became an invitation. "I know it can be hard to get settled in a new place. Especially a place like this. So many of us have been here since before the cows."

Rachel's spine stiffened. Was this, she wondered, Nancy's subtle way of reminding Rachel that she and Lucy were outsiders? She had a sudden paranoid suspicion that Nancy knew about the anonymous notes that had shown up in her mailbox. Maybe, she thought viciously, Nancy had even put them there.

Maybe she was worried about what Rachel, the book writer, would uncover.

Either way, she realized, Nancy Swift had given her an opening.

"Actually, I'd love to talk," Rachel said, keeping her voice bright and friendly. It was true. She'd love to hear what Nancy Swift had to say about Nina Faraday and her son's erratic behavior after her disappearance. "We can have lunch."

Nancy looked taken aback but obediently provided her cell phone number and email. Afterward she briefly took Rachel's hand between hers. Her palms felt like paper, brittle and fragile with age even though she couldn't be seventy yet.

"Tell your daughter I like number two better," Nancy said with a little smile. She gave Rachel's hand a final pat and moved off, engulfed by the next canyon of taffeta and silk. Rachel felt confused and slightly guilty. Had she *imagined* the threat inside Nancy's remark? Was it possible that Nancy Swift was simply being friendly—that it was she who, as usual, was hunting for hidden motives? Either way, Nancy Swift had given her an opening.

"What was that all about?" Lucy reemerged from the dressing room, this time wearing pale blue. Bailey and Savannah trailed after her, all ruffles and whispers of fabric. All three girls were barefoot, wide-eyed, conspiratorial.

"She was just saying hi," Rachel said. She spun Lucy around in a circle. "This one's cute," she said.

"Mom, are you serious? This one's a joke."

"Do you know who that was?" Bailey asked Rachel. "That was Tommy Swift's mom."

"What did she say to you?" asked Savannah.

"She said she thought you should hurry up and pick a dress," Rachel said pointedly. "Come on. I don't want to be here all day."

Lucy settled on a sweet pink dress with slender straps and a flouncy hemline. Bailey and Savannah assured her it was "iconic." They'd both selected their dresses weeks ago. The Winters Dance, Bailey explained, was "like, basically bigger than prom."

The boys were still goofing around by the register, checking out cuff links and waiting for the last of them to get fitted.

What'd you get, Luce? Show us the dress. Did you enter the raffle? Come on. Admit it. The group agitated around Lucy as Rachel paid. She heard Bailey reprimanding them, telling them not to be so "hungry."

It was a funny bit of slang, Rachel thought.

Eventually Rachel herded the girls back out into the frigid grin of winter sunshine. Pale-blue bunting dangled plastic snowflakes at intervals down the street. Every store had a holiday wreath. The air smelled like woodsmoke.

She wondered idly how the Swifts would celebrate Christmas.

FOUR

We

Normally, school dances felt like parties thrown by the TSA. Normally we had to file past security stations posted at the entrance to the gym, emptying out every pocket and turning out our bags. Afterward we were barred from leaving except to use the bathroom—and even then we were likely to be aggressed by yet more chaperones who militantly made sure there was no more than one person in each stall. Dozens of teachers prowled the dance floor like bomb-sniffing dogs, scanning for even the faintest whiff of alcohol or twitch of pelvic thrusting.

But not that year. That year, the Winters Dance took on an almost medieval significance. Even though we were still slaughtering the competition statewide, the recent infiltration of the Market Catch website and the continued assaults on Coach Vernon's mailbox had transformed Woodward and its swimmers into a beleaguered minority. Ours was the besieged citadel, the mythical fortress; we recognized that the moat of deputy cars and the heavy delegation of security had been assembled to protect us from external attack.

We'd all come prepared, at least mentally, for a showdown. We'd heard rumors that the dance would be emptied by another fake bomb threat, or possibly a real one. We'd dreamed of what might happen if one of our enemies tried to disrupt the Balladeers' Auction. We'd heard that the Sharks were keeping baseball bats in their cars now—at least the ones who drove.

We were hailed as arriving heroes by the chaperones steaming breath into the cold, using glowsticks like air traffic control personnel to run us safely into the gym. Marauding packs of seniors sucked on vapes tucked behind their palms.

Most of the upperclassmen were at least a little drunk. So many people stashed alcohol in the locker room in the days before the Winters that fights broke out about space in the empty lockers.

We had to admit: Student Leadership had outdone themselves that year. String lights snaked up the walls to the scoreboards, and beachball-size plastic lanterns were rolling around, throbbing dully with color. Mrs. Steeler-Cox was planted next to the DJ stand almost as firmly as the bust of Coach Steeler next to her—now scrubbed of graffiti, crowned with a wreath of lights, and temporarily wheeled into the gymnasium to judge us for our dance moves. The Student Council Mafia was distributing glowstick necklaces and cheesy light-up bracelets, and we all agreed they were cringe. We took a bunch anyway and wore them ironically.

Lucy came late. From all over the gymnasium, we watched her shimmying off her coat next to the bleachers, smoothing her hair, tugging at her skirt. Her bare shoulders picked up the gloss of revolving lights and winked them back at us. The Sharks in tops and tails passed among us like dazzling members of an alien species, taller, handsomer, and more confident than the rest of us. We imagined the comforting astringent whiff of chlorine in their hair and clothing. We watched them touching and being touched.

There was Alec Nye in pale-blue sateen, hemmed close to the bleachers by adoring cheerleaders; Aiden Teller in vintage tails, surrounded by eddies of beautiful Echelon girls; Jeremiah Greene wearing double-breasted red plaid, tailed through the room by admiring freshmen.

We couldn't fucking believe it when JJ Hammill showed up with Kennedy Myers.

Kennedy fucking Myers.

First of all, she wasn't a student.

Second of all, no one ever showed up to the Winters with a date. It wasn't that kind of dance.

Third of all, Kennedy and Bailey were competitors on the pageant circuit and sworn mortal enemies for life. Their earliest tension dated back to a missing pair of ballet slippers and had escalated during the Miss Junior Indiana pageant when one of Bailey's pageant dresses was sullied with what appeared to be either dog or human feces just before the competition walk. It was an explosive controversy in eighth grade and had consumed us with horror for many weeks.

We saw Lucy pull Bailey to her and whisper something, her mouth briefly entangled in Bailey's hair. We'll never know what she said. But we knew somehow what it *meant. We felt it.*

An unthinkable suspicion ripened quickly into full-blown rumor: Bailey Lawrence was actually crying. Bailey Lawrence was crying at the Winters. We spotted Bailey fleeing into the locker room, her hand locked tight around Lucy's, with Savannah Savage and a small pack of friends trailing after her like fish surfing a wake. We could hardly believe it.

We held tight to our phones, as if we could squint through them for a glimpse of whatever might be happening in the bathroom. Some of us edged close to the girls' locker room door and debated finding an excuse to venture inside.

Instead we bridged the distance in our imaginations.

She doesn't look like she was crying, we pointed out when Bailey and her friends finally emerged from the locker room. *She doesn't even look upset.*

She looks . . .

Amazing.

Pissed off.

Over it.

Drunk.

We agreed that Bailey Lawrence was ten times hotter than Kennedy Myers, that JJ Hammill was an idiot, and that he and Bailey would be back together before Christmas.

~

There was no one on the dance floor when Lucy and Bailey stepped in front of the DJ stand, the lights briefly rotating colors through their hair. For a second, we saw angels haloed in blinding white; the next second, we saw demons silhouetted by a smoky red light.

On the dance floor, Bailey kicked off her heels and did a perfect pirouette in bare feet. She landed soundlessly on the beat of a new song, falling through the final repetition of a chorus we had tired of already. Mia Thompson was teasing Jeremiah Greene and Aiden Teller into attempting to twerk.

Suddenly JJ seized hold of Kennedy's hand. He trotted her to a spot on the dance floor directly next to Bailey and Lucy, even though there was a basketball court of unclaimed space.

We made jokes about end-times and hell freezing over. We felt a little drunk, even if most of us weren't drinking. We felt a little dizzy, a little sugar-high, a little delirious.

In all our accumulated years of school dances, we'd never seen JJ Hammill so much as nod his head to a beat.

Now he swept Kennedy into a dip and then twirled her. The incredible was happening. The impossible. The unheard of.

Something was changing, and it was *us*.

We poured onto the dance floor. We lost our shit. We discovered that we really *could* feel the beat, even those of us who obviously couldn't. We felt like we were part of a single throbbing heartbeat, a shuddering rhythm that soared up through the floor and trembled us all the way to the tips of our fingers.

The next song was our favorite. Until the song after that. That song was really our favorite, holy shit.

This is my song, we shouted at each other until we were hoarse from shouting how much we loved it and the lyrics, which we shouted even louder. *This is my shit.*

But no. No, no. Compared to the next song? Forget it.

The next song was our blood, our heartbeat, our whole life turned into a chorus and a bass line and a beat. It jacked all our nerve cells, exploded our hearts, burst us out of our bodies. It was a fist, and a fuck-you, thrown up at the walls, at the sky, at our parents, at our feelings. For almost forty-five minutes, we did transform. We *did* become something more beautiful. We became a single song, a single rhythm, nameless and wordless, without memory or fear.

We would be ourselves again as soon as we stopped dancing. The raffle was coming up, and we would all go back to our places, and then we would go home.

But for a little while, we belonged to the music, and the night belonged to us.

We saw Akash and Lucy dancing together. Lucy was laughing. Akash was skimming her waist with his hands as she twirled. Then they were standing close, and he had a hand in her hair.

We didn't see him try and kiss her.

FIVE

Rachel

Joaquin Turner, the swimmer from Jalliscoe who'd been questioned by Rockland County deputies after Nina Faraday disappeared, now lived in Ohio. According to his LinkedIn page, he was a middle school math teacher and curriculum expert.

After a bit of prodding, he agreed to speak to Rachel on the phone.

"We were just friends," he said almost immediately, as soon as the conversation turned to Nina. Even now, sixteen years later, he sounded exhausted by the topic. "We hung out a few times. That was it. Nina was off-limits."

It was just after nine o'clock on a Friday. Rachel was alone in the house; Lucy had packed off to the Winters Dance. Rachel could hear the clamor of Joaquin's kids in the background. "Off-limits how?" she asked. "Because of Tommy Swift?"

"Because of all of them." Joaquin sighed. "Look, I really didn't know Nina very well. After a few months, she told me that Steeler didn't want us talking anymore."

"Coach Steeler?" Rachel was startled. Immediately she felt uneasy. "How did Coach Steeler find out that you two were friends?"

"Oh, he knew everything about everybody. Nina told me Steeler was the reason Tommy dumped her in the first place. He thought she was a distraction. You've gotta understand, someone like Tommy was around Steeler more than his own parents. Nina too. She hung around practices, even tried to sneak onto the team bus to ride to meets sometimes. All those girls did."

"So what did Steeler think? That Nina was passing on trade secrets?"

"Don't know," Joaquin said. "That was the last I ever talked to her. After that, she ghosted."

The word "ghosted" touched off a shiver in Rachel's spine. She turned on a light, suddenly aware of the way that the house was accumulating shadows, pooling them in every corner.

"What was Nina like?" she asked. Reading about Nina Faraday in old Rockland and Willard County newspapers was like reading about two different people. In Rockland County, Nina was flunking biology, on medication for anxiety and depression, an attention-seeker, once suspended for having alcohol at a school event. In Willard County, she was a member of her church youth group, a talented cheerleader, and third-place winner of a state-sponsored writing competition.

"I don't know," Joaquin said. "She was just . . . normal. We liked the same kinds of movies. That's how we first started talking. I was between heats, and she complimented my Harry Potter T-shirt."

"Did Nina ever talk about other guys with you?" Rachel asked.

Joaquin chuckled. "She talked about plenty of guys. She knew all the team gossip. I remember she told me that one of Tommy's teammates got some girl pregnant, and Steeler paid for an abortion. That really bothered her. Nina was Catholic."

Rachel thought, fleetingly, of Coach Jack Vernon. He'd been Tommy's teammate—and one of Steeler's favorites. "What about boyfriends?" Rachel asked. "Did she ever talk about hooking up with anyone? Guys who she liked, or guys who liked her?"

"Not to me," Joaquin said. Rachel could hear the shrug in his voice. "To be honest, I kind of figured she was just using me to make Tommy jealous. The last time we hung out, she had a new bracelet. Like a tennis bracelet but with lots of little jewels in it. She said it was a present but wouldn't say from who. I figured Tommy gave it to her. That's why when she told me Steeler didn't want us talking anymore, it seemed more like an excuse."

"What about Nina's mom?" Rachel switched tactics. "Did Nina ever complain about her?"

"Oh, yeah. All the time. Nina's mom was intense. She hated Tommy Swift. Nina was always getting grounded for hanging out with him. Ms. Faraday went through Nina's phone to make sure they weren't talking. It drove Nina crazy. She told me she thought about running away sometimes."

A spark of energy lit up Rachel's chest. "She told you that?"

"I didn't take it seriously. Nina was too smart to do something that stupid. Besides, deep down, I think she knew her mom was right."

"What do you mean?" Rachel said. "Right about what?"

"Like I said." Joaquin sighed. "She hated Tommy Swift."

SIX

We

The five-minute break before the raffle was basically triage. We were gasping like drowned frogs, sweating like pigs, and our hair was unsalvageable. A lot of us were horrified to realize our deodorant was *not* working. There were meltdowns in the girls' locker room and a sudden frenzied bull market for gum, Altoids, and sweat-absorbent paper towels. We staggered back onto the dance floor like wounded soldiers—bruised, dazed, or fortified with alcohol, hoping for courage.

The raffle setup was cheesy, and we pretended to hate it like we pretended to hate the glowing bracelets slowly dulling on our wrists. Behind the table setup for the ticket draw, Mrs. Coates—who we were pretty sure had volunteered to man the locker room entrances just so she could go in whenever she needed to sneak a drink—kept nodding off in her chair.

Coach Radner and Judd French took turns announcing the Balladeers, reading off clues about each of the volunteering swimmers so we could guess who was next to the stage. The DJ fed us some *Jeopardy!* knockoff sound effects to build suspense, and then—bang!—one of the swimmers would burst into view from the locker room, arms up and grinning, and every time we fucking lost it, like each was a free cruise we'd picked from behind Door Number Three.

We were disappointed that Noah Landry wasn't among them. He was sitting alone on the risers, hunched over his phone, carving a protective wall with his posture. Well, not alone exactly; the Student Council Mafia had seized on him like pigeons on a breadcrumb.

Ryan Hawthorne drew Reese Steeler-Cox's name. We made jokes about how many tickets she must have purchased—*if* she and her mom hadn't devised some other way to rig the system. But Aiden Teller drew the name of a freshman named Maddie Lapinski who hadn't even been named one of the school's most desirable Minnows. She had blond hair so long it almost touched her waist and a pretty face that was the color of a fatal sunburn as she took the stage. We could swear she was even crying a little, like someone who'd just been given news of a lifesaving organ transplant.

@badprincess: Girl needs to breathe
@skyediva: Anyone know CPR??
@spinn_doctor: I do
@mememeup: no you don't

Jeremiah Greene drew Angie Peele's name—an enormously controversial pick since she was rumored to be hooking up with Ryan Hawthorne all fall. Then freshman Ethan Gregory drew Skyler Matthews's name, and we erupted. It felt like placing a team in the World Cup, watching her maneuver to the stage grinning like a maniac.

We suggested that the mods rename her handle to @cradlerobber, as a joke.

The raffle went on. Charlotte Anderson and Brianna Rourke, two of Reese's Student Council Mafia watchdogs, both got picked and joined Reese onstage in a bedlam of squealing. But Cole Hughes drew Shawna Locke's name, announcing it into the microphone with a slight cough, where it landed on the crowd like a hammer; Shawna Locke was a desperate hanger-on and a walking field of acne.

All in all, we were inclined to think the raffle was legit.

Then it was JJ Hammill's turn. "Give it up for JJ Hammill!" Coach Radner rolled JJ's name into a full sentence as the DJ cued JJ's entrance music, and a thudding bass line kicked out our eardrums.

We turned to the locker room doors expectantly.

Nothing.

The rhythmic thump of the music dulled into long seconds. We waited.

But the locker room door didn't open.

"Let's hear it for JJ!" Radner repeated, a little louder, which only made the microphone kick back a screech of reverb. Still, JJ didn't come. The applause petered off as we stood there in confusion.

Radner gestured for the DJ to cut off the music. For a brief, unnerving second, the room was silent.

"Hello? JJ?" Radner scanned the crowd as if JJ might be hiding among us. "Anyone know where JJ is? Anyone?"

We all turned instinctively to Noah. Only then did Noah look up and realize that we were all staring at him, waiting for his answer.

"No idea," he said.

Now Radner tipped the microphone away from his mouth a few inches. But it was still enough to land his voice at Noah's feet. "Well, can you try *finding* him?"

"Me?" Noah frowned. "Why me?"

"Unless you want to step in as a replacement," Radner said. "I'm sure the ladies wouldn't mind." He turned back to the crowd. "Would you, ladies?"

High-decibel enthusiasm kept Noah from responding for almost thirty seconds. "I don't dance," he said.

This was news to us.

Coach Radner was sweating under the lights. "Has anyone seen JJ?" he repeated.

Reese Steeler-Cox said loudly, "Has anyone seen *Bailey*?" That drew a laugh.

"Or Kennedy?" someone called out.

The word *threesome* surfed the crowd on a break of snickering. Someone shouted that the chaperones should check the parking lot. Mara Gaines, a senior on the cheerleading squad, announced that she'd seen lights in the construction trailer permanently moored between Aquatics and the rest of the athletics center. We saw a skirmish of discomfort work through the chaperones. Principal Hammill disappeared into the hall. Sofia Young, who had been sneaking to the parking lot to take swigs from a vodka bottle concealed behind the planters, announced that Kennedy had gone home with her parents. She'd left at the same time as Akash.

It was the first we'd heard that Akash had ditched out early.

@mememeup: does anyone know what happened?
@spinn_doctor: don't @ me.
@mememeup: we weren't
@bassicrhythm: wtf. His parents were supposed to be my ride ...
@pawsandclaws: did something happen, @goodnightsky? Details??

But Sofia didn't know, or was too drunk to remember.

Vice Principal Edwards stepped in to draw for JJ Hammill. When he announced Bailey Lawrence's name, we lost it. It was fate. It was toxic. It was true love. What were the odds?

"I guess Bailey owes me a dance," Edwards said, and we all laughed with him.

The locker room door burst open suddenly, and JJ slid out, arms open, giving off *I'm-sorry-to-be-so-awesome-you-had-to-wait-for-me* Coachella mainstage vibes.

Bailey materialized at the same time—from where, we couldn't say—and we fell aside in waves like she was Moses walking toward the Promised Land.

JJ bowed, and Bailey took his hand and did a spin that ended in mouth-to-mouth. Vice Principal Edwards leaped forward to separate them—a second and a half of gorgeous video that lived on for months as one of our favorite memes. Whatever he said had no prayer against the volume of the crowd.

There was no doubt about it: they were both nuts. Someday they'd probably kill each other. Their relationship was that psycho.

That's why it was fate.

And we had to admit, we were even a little jealous.

Doesn't everyone want to be loved like that?

Alec Nye was the last Balladeer to draw. By then the whole thing had the feel of anticlimax.

Then Alec Nye plucked a raffle ticket and read the winner into the microphone.

"Lucy Vale," he said and flipped the ticket around in his fingers to face the audience. And even though her name was way too small to see from even a few feet away, he stood there holding it up to the crowd—as if he knew somehow that proof would be important.

∼

Lucy didn't want to join Alec onstage.

"I didn't enter the raffle," she kept saying as a bunch of us were trying to steer her toward the stage. "Someone must have put my name in."

"Uh huh." Savannah Savage gave Lucy a nudge toward the stage. Even she didn't believe it. How could she? *Someone must have put my name in* was a punchline, a meme, like *asking for a friend*.

The Student Council had already whisked away the drawing table. Now we were all waiting for Lucy. Coach Radner took the microphone again and gestured for the raffle ticket Alec Nye was holding.

"Lucy Vale," he said, "come on up." A few people echoed him, shouting for Lucy.

"I didn't enter," Lucy said, raising her voice a little louder. The crowd opened up and then gobbled Lucy up, a physical pressure of bodies that kept her moving toward the stage. "Someone must have put my name in." Weirdly, the fact that she kept saying it seemed like proof it wasn't true—like someone loudly claiming an alibi for a murder that hadn't yet been discovered. Or the first person to sniff a fart and declare a culprit.

Lucy reached the stage just as the other Balladeers took to the dance floor with their dates. Briefly we saw her argue first with Alec Nye and then with Coach Radner, who made it clear with a hand gesture that the issue was below his pay grade. By then the DJ was softening the mood with the first chords of the night's final slow song. We saw Lucy shaking her head and Alec Nye's smile growing tighter and tighter, like it was stretched over a balloon.

At first we figured she was just embarrassed; she'd been claiming for weeks that she had no interest in Alec Nye. Or maybe she'd been hoping to dance with *another* swimmer—possibly Noah Landry. But the more Lucy argued, the more we wondered whether she really hadn't put her name in for the raffle. Maybe someone else *had* bought her a ticket.

Either way, she wasn't caving. Alec Nye's face was dark with anger as he followed her off the stage. Lucy tried to skirt the dance floor, hemming close to the bleachers where some of us were standing around, trying to make it look like we didn't care we had no one to dance with.

"Whoa, whoa, whoa. Not so fast." Nye caught up and stepped in front of Lucy. "You owe me a dance."

"I don't dance," Lucy said. She started to turn away again. This time when he caught her arm, he held it there.

"Come on, Lucy. Don't embarrass me." He was so much bigger than her, he had to bend over to get close. He looked like the wolf trying to convince Little Red Riding Hood to stay. "You're the one who put your name in the raffle."

"No, I didn't."

Alec Nye's smile looked sharp. "It's mandatory, Vale. No objections."

"I don't want to dance." She wrenched away from him.

It was maybe the first time in Alec Nye's life a girl had turned him down. Or maybe it wasn't. Maybe we just didn't hear about it. Maybe he wore them down. Maybe it was *mandatory*.

So this time when she turned again, Nye slid up behind her and put an arm around her chest so he could talk right into her ear. So she was pinned to his body. So that if we didn't know what he was saying—which we didn't until the following year—it would have looked like they were really close, like they knew each other, like this was normal. That *is* what it looked like.

Lucy said, "Let go of me."

Nye said, "Only if we can dance."

"Fine," Lucy said. "Fine."

"I mean it, Vale," Alec said. "I'm trusting you."

"I'll fucking dance with you," she said. "Just let me go."

He did. But he grabbed her hand immediately. "Come on," he said. "Relax. You might even enjoy yourself."

We couldn't tell what she was thinking while he led her toward the dance floor. She didn't look angry, or sad, or happy, or upset. She looked totally blank. Like the silhouette a painting leaves after it's been removed from a wall.

Nye went to pull her close.

And Lucy started doing the chicken dance.

She started *really* doing the chicken dance. She strutted and flapped. She knocked her knees together. She even squawked—right in his face.

For a second we were all too stunned to do anything but stare. Nye looked like he'd just gotten hit in the face with the back of a toilet seat. He looked *mortified*.

Lucy dropped her purse; it was interfering with the motion of her right wing. And she just kept on doing the chicken dance.

"Freak," Nye said finally. "You're a fucking *nutjob*."

She did look crazy, for sure. She looked totally, absolutely, gloriously out of her mind.

And we will always swear, to this day, that when Noah Landry came through the crowd toward her, he was moving inside a single beam of perfect white light, carving through the colors and the crowd and the laughter like someone surfing a perfect wave.

"Looks like you could use a wingman," he said. And Noah Landry—our Noah Landry, future Olympian, the boy who didn't dance, didn't break regimen, didn't even Balladeer for the charity raffle—put his hands on his hips, started strutting, and let out a single triumphant squawk.

It was legend. It was magic. It was a real-life happy ending. That's what we thought anyway.

Until almost exactly a year later when, sometime before midnight on New Year's Eve, in the Hawthornes' guest bedroom, something happened to Lucy Vale.

PART 6

ONE

We

Once Lucy Vale and Noah Landry officially started dating our sophomore year, they quickly became Woodward's it couple, even dethroning Bailey Lawrence and JJ Hammill. We didn't know how Bailey felt about being upstaged by her best friend, but no one could deny that Noah and Lucy were perfect. They were the kind of couple we saw in the rom-coms we denied watching and read about in YA books we pretended to find cheesy.

As southern Indiana slowly thawed from the clutch of winter, as the fields greened and the sun elasticized the daylight, our moods turned from rivalry to romance. The Sharks swept the state championships, drawing a record turnout of more than a thousand people. We'd all joined the flotilla of traffic traveling to the event in Morgan County with Shark decals plastered to our bumpers and school flags snapping from our trunks. So many people showed up that the crowd overflowed into the parking lot. Some of the late arrivals were stranded outside in the cold, trying to decrypt the action inside from the cadence of cheering and the muffled resonance of the loudspeakers announcing the results.

Noah Landry had beaten two of his own record-shattering times in the 50- and 100-meter freestyle events. But JJ Hammill, Alec Nye, Ryan Hawthorne, and even Aiden Teller were also at the tops of their games. Alec Nye accepted an offer to swim for North Carolina. Aiden Teller was heading to Michigan. It was the last time either boy would compete for the Sharks, and their swim caps were decorated with send-off messages written in Sharpie by girls more popular than we were.

They were gods in the water. We were vindicated, triumphant, and taking home the trophy for our third year in a row.

We said goodbye to the official swim season for another year.

We went out for new teams and swapped extracurriculars. Cicadas came up in heavy swells, burrowing up from the dirt like an upward-banking tide. They infested our trees, blurring the bark behind the motion of their bodies. We crunched over their discarded shells in the parking lot. Between classes, we made games of swinging at them with our book bags.

Spring was a season of sex and mating rituals.

Akash and Delancey McNamara started hooking up right before Easter. We were happy for him, even if we sensed that he had never quite gotten over Lucy Vale. It was almost compulsive how he kept track of Noah Landry and Lucy's relationship.

> **@kash_money:** did anyone hear that Noah and Lucy had a fight this weekend?

We hadn't.

> **@kash_money:** Does anyone think it's weird that Lucy goes to *all* of Noah's club team practices? It's like she doesn't even have a life anymore

We didn't think it was weird. We thought it was romantic.

> **@kash_money:** Rachel Vale ran into my mom at the post office today and they started talking about Lucy. I don't think Rachel likes Noah Landry

@gustagusta: why would she?

@gustagusta: Rachel Vale doesn't like the Sharks

It was a difficult truth to accept. But in the early spring, as the tension between Rachel Vale and the Steeler-Coxes exploded into open warfare, we were forced to come to the same conclusion: Rachel Vale had radical views about Coach Steeler, about the Faraday case, and about the swim team in general.

For that reason, when we heard people saying that Rachel Vale might be behind the troll account ANONYM1698—which for months had spammed the Sharks' social media accounts, the *County News* website, and the broader internet with conspiracy theories about steroid use and a culture of sexual violence—we assumed that the Steeler-Coxes were yet again to blame for the rumors. Rachel Vale had recently declared her intentions to protest the construction of a Jay Steeler Legacy Pavilion at the Aquatics Center, a controversy that besieged our parents and inboxes with all-caps emails and petitions to support one side or another.

But ultimately rumors were like every other virus: what made them deadly wasn't where they began but how contagious they were. The evidence that Rachel Vale and ANONYM1698 were the same person was circumstantial but convincing, at least among those inclined to distrust the Vales anyway. ANONYM1698 had first popped up online in July of the previous year—about a month before the Vales first moved to Granger. They didn't write like a normal online troll. Even more concerningly, they seemed to have a suspicious amount of inside information about the swim team, both past and present.

Only a journalist, the theory went, could write so dispassionately about hearsay, elegantly giving *rumor* the gloss of reported *fact*. Only a journalist could produce such detailed point-by-point references to accusations more than a decade old. Only a journalist could argue so persuasively that the system of booster funds, and the continued flow of big money tied to our high school swim team's ascendance, held

Administration hostage to their wins and incentivized the county to overlook their misdeeds.

Only a journalist—or someone waging a detailed and protracted campaign against our reputation, dedicated to spinning every story into damning proof and to displaying every failure in the most unflattering light.

Or both. The two possibilities weren't mutually exclusive.

It was always possible that Lucy Vale and her mother had taken the Faraday House with a hidden agenda and the intention to bring our swim team down.

Still, we championed Lucy Vale and Noah Landry's coupledom. We rooted for them.

To us, Rachel Vale's perceived disapproval of the Sharks made the Noah-and-Lucy endgame even more romantic. We loved a low-key Romeo and Juliet vibe.

We swooned over the way Noah decorated Lucy's locker on Valentine's Day. We made their Instagram posts our #relationshipgoals. We voted them onto junior homecoming court. We stood in a fan around them as they took to the floor after winning, shuffling awkwardly in circles under lights that glittered through their plastic crowns, and heckled them until they agreed to reprise the chicken dance.

We thought they would get married someday.

Somehow Noah Landry and Lucy Vale were not like other couples. For the most part, we tracked school romances by digital deduction. We knew whether Bailey Lawrence and JJ Hammill were on or off again by whether they were following each other on any given week. We could identify Savannah Savage's admirers by the accounts that left her heart-eyed and flame emojis. We knew who was hanging out and who was breaking up by the photos and videos they were tagged in. We were fluent in the Morse code of posted memes and chosen camera angles, hashtags and viral sound clips. We swiped and scrolled to a revolving picture of heartbreaks and hookups, feuds and friendships.

But Noah Landry and Lucy Vale's relationship was somehow obscure, even as they became the most watched couple at Woodward. They existed in their own space, in a dimension bounded entirely by his regimen and her devotion to him. They were the most private public couple we knew.

They were always together—in the SLD Tutoring Center between classes, in church on Sundays, in the lunch line. Lucy went to all of Noah's practices, doubling over her laptop in the bleachers while Noah swam endless laps, working milliseconds off his already deadly times. When we saw them in town or at the lake, they were always locked in private conversation or physically entwined, arms entangled, fingers interlaced, foreheads touching until they looked like a single being. When they showed up in JJ Hammill's or Bailey Lawrence's social media posts, they were always standing a little ways off from their friends, usually in the background. Touching. Always touching.

Noah walked Lucy to her classes. He walked her to the bus. Lucy stopped taking the bus. Noah Landry's parents began picking her up in the morning and dropping her home at night after Noah finished practice.

Every time we saw them together, they were holding hands. In the cafeteria, they sat practically on top of each other. We heard that when they were apart, even for half an hour, Noah Landry texted Lucy to check on her.

We didn't think it was weird.

We thought they were in love.

TWO

Rachel

Every Sunday, Noah brought Rachel flowers when he picked up Lucy for church. Rachel couldn't believe that her daughter was regularly attending services.

"What about becoming a Wiccan?" she teased. "I thought you said that organized religion was a tool to brainwash the masses."

Lucy looked a little embarrassed. "It's important to Noah," she said. It was a phrase that Rachel heard a lot that spring. *Mom, can you drive me to Wabash on Thursday for Noah's all-around? It's important to Noah. Mom, can I go to Noah's house for dinner after practice? It's practically the only time we'll have together this week. Please. It's important to Noah.* "Besides, I like the music."

"I just don't want you feeling like you have to become someone else," Rachel said, reaching out to ruffle her daughter's hair.

Lucy jerked away. "I'm not becoming someone else," she said. They were driving. She flipped down the passenger-side mirror to check her reflection. "I'm becoming someone better."

Rachel almost said, "According to who?" But she stopped herself. For the most part, Lucy seemed happy. Noah was nice to her, she said. Respectful. Not like her last "boyfriend," thank God. He'd tormented Lucy with those photos. He'd spread them around to his high school friends. Gossip had reached the middle school quickly. That's when Lucy's real torment began.

Noah Landry was different. Everyone liked him, according to Lucy—with the possible exception of Akash. Everyone knew him as a nice guy.

Still, Rachel worried. Noah had grown into Lucy's life fast and completely, in the way of young, early romances. His presence, his preferences, his swim schedule, his opinions seemed to invade their house, growing stalactite-like at the center of every conversation, every weekend plan, every thought for the future. Rachel found herself tracking Noah's schedule along with her daughter's, able to recite the dates and locations of his upcoming meets with the club team, aware of his swim times and the records he was trying to beat. She even knew what he ate, how many calories he needed to consume.

Lucy seemed to absorb Noah through a process of diffusion. Or maybe Noah had absorbed Lucy. And Rachel lay awake at night, fretting, trying to keep them distinct in her head.

And there were problems. Minor blowups. Nights when Lucy went to bed with her eyes puffy from crying because of something Noah had said, because he hadn't called after practice, or because he had called but sounded "weird." There was the time that Lucy came home fuming because she'd had her phone confiscated by Administration after texting in class.

"Why were you texting in class?" Rachel wanted to know.

"Noah had a question," she responded.

"Couldn't it wait?" she asked. "He knows you're not supposed to be on your phone in school."

"It was important," Lucy said. It was always important when Noah texted because Noah himself was important—not just to Lucy but to everyone at Woodward. *My boyfriend is basically our national hero,* Lucy told her mother once.

When Rachel asked her what that made Lucy, Lucy shrugged and said, *Lucky.*

Whenever Rachel worried that Noah and Lucy spent too much time together, she reminded herself that Lucy seemed healthy. Her grades hadn't slipped. Noah was a good student and cared about his schoolwork. (*He actually does his own homework,* Lucy had said, as if that were something to be especially proud of.)

The ground thawed early; it had been a mild winter with barely any snow. In early March, the Friskes had helped Rachel bag the fallen leaves and winter detritus from her two acres, carting away more than fifty bags to the dump. In the mornings after Lucy went off to school, Rachel wrote, made notes, made phone calls, and sent emails. In the afternoons, she gardened—yanking dandelions from between the paving stones, uprooting a sea of ferns that hemmed close to the front porch, clearing the rose beds and then reseeding.

It was a season of planting and sowing. Of ideas that barely sparked to life, then flowered into questions, hypotheses, leads to pursue. Slowly the veil of the new book fell over her, including ideas for the structure. She would write not about Nina first but about her mother. About the lawsuit and the claims she'd made about a cover-up. About her mysterious death. Then about Nina and Tommy Swift, about their volatile romance—the volumes of text messages, the obsession, the fiery arguments, the breakups. She'd begun to track down Nina's old friends—former cheerleaders, many of them still in town with young children of their own—and encountered the same haze of contradictions in their memories.

Yes, Tommy and Nina had broken up and gotten back together more times than they could count. Neither Coach Steeler nor Nina's mom wanted them to date.

True, Tommy Swift had a temper. But he would never have hurt Nina.

And Nina had changed in the weeks before her disappearance. That last time, it was Nina who'd ended things with Tommy. That last time, something was different. Something was truly broken. She was missing cheer practices. She withdrew. She seemed nervous about something.

Her grades slipped. Coach Steeler was worried. He was trying to help her. It was surprising perhaps that Coach Steeler had stepped in, given that he'd disapproved of Nina and Tommy's relationship. But it dovetailed with what Rachel knew about him: he was a man who liked to *fix*, to take control, to be at the center of things. Even now, several years after his death, Coach Steeler was, in a way, at the center of Rockland County life.

But not in her book. No, in her book Nina was the mystery at the center. Rachel would weave the narrative around the impenetrability of her final days, crystallize her through the stories people told about her. And slowly, through the fractal accumulation of viewpoints, of recollections and theories, she might assemble some splintered vision, some final insight, some truth.

And she would leave her own memories, her own experience, out of it. It didn't matter that she'd briefly encountered Nina in the dark all those years ago, watched her flying birdlike and barefoot across the lawn to greet Coach Steeler.

It didn't matter that Rachel had accepted a ride home from Jay Steeler that night, bored and flattered, heartsick over her ex-boyfriend. Young. Just barely twenty-two. Half-excited and half-sickened when the married father of two slid a rough hand up her bare legs and found her underwear with his fingers.

It was a brief affair. They'd met again only twice. Both times Rachel was nervous and drank too much at dinner. Both times they had sex in a motel room near I-69. Rachel could hear the 18-wheelers rattling the windows as Steeler grunted on top of her. She didn't come and didn't remember enjoying it. What she remembered was a desperate feeling of embarrassment, of having done something wrong, of having displeased him in some way.

She remembered calling his phone again and again on and off that winter, hoping to recapture some sense of power, some proof that he'd really meant it when he'd told her how beautiful she was.

She'd been stupid and naive without knowing it. She'd been desperate to be special.

But none of that belonged in the book. It would remain Rachel's secret—the small, tangled episode that had lived inside her for so long, it had grown roots and become its own source of strength.

All spring, Rachel knelt in the dirt, planted seeds, and sorted through the layers of the book taking shape in her head.

Lucy was rarely home. Too busy.

There was no rain at all.

THREE

We

Over the summer, we lost sight of Lucy and Noah a bit. We fractured into subsets and individual members. Loosed from Woodward's gravitational pull and the unifying force of shared homework assignments and social scandals, we drifted aimlessly through days of punishing heat.

Southern Indiana was suffering its worst drought in decades after a dry winter and a spring of puffed-up clouds and clear skies. Byron Lake was striped with brown as it gasped down to the sediment. The news tracked the Ohio River levels as they ebbed and denuded banks rifted into giant cakes of mud and then dust. The fields browned and crops withered. Our AC was always breaking, always dripping water down our windowsills, always on the fritz. Our parents yelled at us to turn off lights, to use a fan, to conserve the water when we were brushing our teeth.

Our only path to wholeness was through the internet, through our phone screens, through our fingers.

We used our phones practically naked in dark rooms, sweating next to the must of insufficient air circulated from our gasping fans. We constantly worried about what we were missing. We were sure that we were missing something vital—a boyfriend or girlfriend; a path and a purpose; the chance to be seen and to matter.

The girls on the server made a competition out of culling pictures of the Sharks with their shirts off. The boys claimed reverse sexism. The girls claimed retribution, payback for Luke Hawthorne's rumored Discord server, which none of us had actually been invited to join, where members ranked girls by hotness and exchanged their pictures.

It was news whenever we saw Lucy and Noah together—the town parade on the Fourth of July, for example, when Lucy and the Strut Girls shimmied on a float skinned with paper roses. They were just behind the open truck bed towing Noah Landry and the other star swimmers, sweating through their face paint next to a beaming Marnie Steeler, Jay Steeler's widow. Olivia Howard rang up Lucy Vale out at the PetSmart when she came in for cat food and reported Noah lingering several feet behind her, idly picking through the cat toys before settling on a squeaky mouse.

Mid-July, Akash reported that Lucy, Bailey, Savannah, and Mia were sunning in the backyard of the Faraday House. He snapped covert pictures of the four in their bikinis, barely visible behind the fan of green trees. The Vales were in trouble for their water usage that summer. An arc of sprinklers misted their lawn almost continuously. Riots of new roses climbed the trellises again, and the azaleas burst open blossoms the color of purpling wounds.

Akash told us that the Strut Girls had seen him and had hailed him over. They wanted to talk to him, he told us, about notes the Vales were receiving in their mailbox.

> **@ktcakes888:** what kind of notes?
> **@kash_money:** threats
> **@kash_money:** someone wants them to move
> **@lululemonaide:** move houses? Or move towns?
> **@kash_money:** towns, I guess. Lucy didn't really give me details
> **@lululemonaide:** ten bucks says the Steeler-Cox delegation

@lululemonaide: Mad because Rachel went public about naming the new pavilion after a known pervert
@nononycky: * alleged * pervert, please. Innocent until proven guilty lol
@badprincess: I bet it's Reese
@badprincess: salty because Lucy got Noah Landry
@meeksmaster: it could be anyone
@meeksmaster: I know like twelve people who think the Vales should have stayed up north
@badprincess: you know twelve people?

Conversation meandered, sputtered, and stalled over the summer. We lost track of time and each other. We lost service driving into the woods to find fishing holes, most of them down to puddles.

Peyton Neely lost her grandmother to a stroke. Sofia Young's father lost his job at the university after a student came forward with claims of sexual harassment.

We all lost our minds when Sofia Young took a break from Discord. Nick Topornycky lost his virginity.

Some of us grew beards. Evie Grant grew C cups. We were growing up, and growing apart, and getting our driver's licenses.

It was a summer of change. A summer of growth.

It was the summer we fought back and started a podcast.

FOUR

We

Shark Wars was a direct response to *Blood in the Water*, Apple's 1,241st most popular podcast, which by July had milked the Faraday mystery and rumors about our swim team across eight separate episodes with no signs of stopping.

We couldn't stand it.

Technically the podcast was Skyler Matthews's idea. For Skyler, the final straw came when the producers tracked down a previously unnamed witness who claimed to have heard an argument in the Faraday House the night Lydia died by suicide. A few hours before Lydia Faraday broke her neck on a belt, Housataunick native Jeffrey Hughes had been perched twenty feet in the air to repair the transformer on an electrical pole and became concerned by an escalating argument in the Faraday House. Sixteen years later, he was prepared to repeat the same impression he'd conveyed to the police that night: that there was trouble at 88 Lily Lane, that things were turning violent.

Of course, it was possible that Lydia Faraday had argued with someone before she decided to kill herself. But the fact that no one had ever admitted to being with her on the night of her death made the whole event suspicious and gave online conspiracy theorists plenty of juice to fuel their claims of a cover-up—or, at minimum, a sloppy and indifferent response from the sheriff's department.

There was, of course, another possibility: that Jeffrey Hughes himself was an agent of these same conspiracy theories, an anti-Shark agitator, and possibly a straight-up liar.

As soon as Skyler floated the idea for a podcast, we all volunteered to help.

We recruited members from the podcast and AV club and poached some of the best talent from the school's online newspaper, including junior Chloe Dawson, who'd done an infamous exposé on cafeteria beef expiration dates her sophomore year and was widely considered a rising star of the journalistic world, at least as far as lunch meat was concerned.

Allan Meeks recorded theme music, a deliberate rip-off of the ominous electronica that punctuated *Blood in the Water* with reverb. Scarlett Hughes designed the thumbnail graphics for the Spotify page. Alex Spinnaker offered Skyler and her guests use of his basement recording studio, which had gone unused since his father's alt-right political channel was suspended for violating YouTube's terms of service.

We began to dream that we would solve the mystery of Nina Faraday's disappearance once and for all. Forget Rachel Vale, a.k.a. R.C. Barnes. Rachel Vale was an outsider. An interloper. This was *our* mystery. It had belonged to us since we were old enough to lay a hand on the gates outside the Faraday House and whisper that old rhyme into the garden, like an incantation or a prayer.

Nina, Nina, where did you go? Lydia, Lydia, what do you know?

That summer we dreamed of our very own Netflix special.

We launched the first episode, a searing criticism of the major players in the online movement to get #justiceforNina, in August. Our first target was Ellen Faraday, supposedly Nina Faraday's long-lost aunt who'd recently started agitating for the reopening of Lydia Faraday's case. She'd launched a GoFundMe campaign to pay for ongoing legal fees related to the investigation. Skyler didn't turn up any hard proof that "Ellen Faraday" was a con artist, but she did point to a suspicious history of similar fundraising efforts tied to Ellen's cell phone number.

The episode was a hit, at least locally, and we all rode the wave of the new power it conferred. Suddenly there was a point to all our online sleuthing, our cyberwars and internet conspiracy theories. Suddenly we had an *outlet*. A channel.

A voice.

Our Discord swelled with new members, and our mods set up new channels for tips, snark, and crowdsourced character assassination. The mission was simple: to discredit everyone seeking to discredit us.

No target was too big or too small. Skyler Matthews assured us that in journalism, as in war, it was important to be fearless, thorough, patient—and exacting. We trolled the internet and tracked the worst offenders: super-Redditor bloodhounder22, who obsessively posted about the Faraday case on r/ColdCaseFiles and had even launched a spin-off Discord that Alex Spinnaker and Meeks infiltrated to observe; ANONYM1698, the online troll who badgered club team swimmers online and made insidious accusations about the Steelers and the long-time culture of the swim team; Linda Harpe, the fifty-year-old PTA hawk and secretary of the Rockland County School Board who had threatened to go to war with Woodward over their abuse of the booster fund system; even Maria Ramirez, the Jalliscoe graduate who, years ago, had accused swimmer Will King of drugging and assaulting her, then recanted her accusations when her own drug use came to light, and now was repeating claims that had been widely discredited ten years earlier; and, of course, the producers of *Blood in the Water* and their small cabal of brainwashed followers.

Following the trail of suspicion and accusation across Reddit, Discord, and even Facebook, we sloughed layers of rumor from the facts about Nina Faraday's final days in Granger and Lydia Faraday's subsequent campaign against the Sharks. The internet was divided cleanly into three camps: people who believed Tommy Swift had killed Nina, people who thought Nina's mother was to blame, and those who insisted that Nina Faraday had run off with a secret boyfriend who may or may not have killed her. Tommy Swift had the motive but no opportunity; Lydia Faraday had the opportunity but no apparent motive.

The only logical explanation, we agreed, was an unknown party. Likely a stranger. Possibly a covert boyfriend.

Definitely a psycho.

Not one of us.

Unwittingly we joined the legions of amateur detectives who'd determined to find #justiceforNina and became newly minted experts in the details of the case. On her last day at Woodward, Nina and Tommy reportedly had a blow-out fight in the cafeteria. Nina had accused Tommy of stalking her. Tommy had accused Nina of cheating on him. Afterward a tearful Nina had gone to her final class—a health elective taught by Coach Steeler—and been reprimanded for texting when she was supposed to be practicing CPR on a dummy. Police later determined that she had, in fact, been texting with her mother, a series of messages that later confirmed Lydia Faraday was pressuring her daughter to cut things off with Tommy completely and speak to Admin about his bizarre mood swings and possible use of steroids. A large and vocal corner of the internet held up this exchange as proof that Tommy was addicted to performance enhancers and desperate to prevent Nina from exposing him. An equally rowdy contingent argued that Lydia Faraday's texts were proof of an extremely, even narcissistically overprotective mother, possibly indications of a woman who would kill her daughter rather than lose her to a boy.

YouTube links about toxic boyfriends, and mothers, abounded. Alex Spinnaker became an overnight expert on psychopathy. Sofia Young returned to Discord and suggested that her father was a sociopath. We came to the sudden collective realization that our childhoods had been toxic, that our parents' questions were inappropriate intrusions on our God-given rights to privacy, that we were all victims just like Nina Faraday.

Unless, of course, Nina Faraday had run off with a boyfriend.

No one knew where Nina had been between final bell and the time Woody Topornycky saw her entering Aquatics just before 7:00 p.m. She'd skipped an after-school meeting of the Key Club and materialized briefly in the SLD Tutoring Center to ask a question about her chemistry homework. Her cell phone data later showed that she hadn't left campus until seven thirty, when she texted her mother that she was heading home and then, an hour later, sent her final cryptic message to her ex-boyfriend. By then Lydia Faraday had arrived home to find her daughter missing.

Tommy Swift, meanwhile, had been alibied by every member of the swim team and by Coach Steeler himself. After a grueling after-school practice, the club team swimmers had reunited with all the high school Sharks at Coach Steeler's house for a belated celebration of their championship season. Tommy Swift had opened the door to a pizza delivery guy with sixteen large pies and about an acre's worth of salad at exactly 7:16 p.m., and Nina Faraday's final text came in when Tommy was still planted in front of Steeler's seventy-two-inch flat-screen TV, enjoying a slideshow of swim team highlights. The party didn't end until close to 10:00 p.m., when Steeler shooed everyone home to get some sleep.

We dismissed the internet's fantastical theories about Tommy's "real" movements that night. But the rabbit hole of speculation brought us up against an unexpected problem: not everything that people were saying about the Sharks, and about Woodward, was off-the-wall lunatic.

In fact, some of it made an awful kind of sense.

The Sharks *were* gods at Woodward. The Steelers *did* have a lot of power in the Four Corners, including over the judicial system. Our swimmers *had* dodged a lot of trouble over the years. It *was* suspicious that Will King had illegal prescription drugs in his car, and it *was* believable that he'd actually dosed his date. Would she really have planted drugs and made up the assault story to punish him, all because she'd graduated from a high school with a long-standing rivalry with the Sharks?

But just because a story was simple—just because it was easy to believe—didn't mean it was true.

The truth was our swim team was under attack, and we were all Sharks in spirit. When there was blood in the water, we went for the kill.

FIVE

Rachel

The letters kept coming. Not with any rhythm or regularity, not with any pattern, but sporadically, even after Rachel installed a Nest security system and a series of not-so-subtle signs on the gates announcing that visitors were being filmed. At that point the letters, previously dropped off, began to arrive with postage stamps.

This made Rachel uneasy. Clearly they were being watched.

Nobody wants you here. You don't belong. Over time the messages grew lengthier and more unhinged. *You and your daughter just LOVE the attention, don't you? Isn't that why you chose to live in a house CONDEMNED BY EVIL? God have mercy on your sinning souls.* The day after Rachel attended a contentious town board meeting to discuss the dedication of the new Aquatics pavilion to Jay Steeler, she received a lengthy Bible verse: *There are six things that the Lord hates, seven that are an abomination to him: haughty eyes, a lying tongue, and hands that shed innocent blood, a heart that devises wicked plans, feet that make haste to run to evil, a false witness who breathes out lies, and one who sows discord among brothers.*

She thought back to the crowd that packed the small first-floor room at Town Hall. They were there to agitate for or against the new memorial pavilion. Was the culprit there? They must have been. It occurred to her that there might be more than one sender. She started imagining that people were looking at her strangely. That the woman who rang up her groceries gave her an odd smile. That Dale, their mail carrier, avoided meeting her eyes. That Mrs. Kowalski's curtains swished whenever Rachel drove by as if she was monitoring her movements from the window.

She took the letters to the police—not because she expected help or sympathy but because she had the sense that she would someday need the complaint on record. That it might prove important. Just in case. In case of *what*, she couldn't say. But she couldn't help thinking about the deluge of hate mail that Lydia Faraday had received even after her only child had gone missing—despicable letters accusing her of murder, of deliberately trying to implicate Tommy Swift, of a complex plot to exact revenge against Jay Steeler all because of a lingering obsession that dated back to high school. Some of the letters had been published online, leaked after Lydia's death by her family members. Rachel scoured them, looking for similarities. She couldn't help but wonder whether the same person—or people—had selected her as their new target sixteen years later.

The Rockland County Sheriff's Department was suffering from the aftershocks of several high-profile resignations the morning she drove to the small brick building next to the library. Two days earlier, Sheriff Cox had abruptly announced his departure. Several longtime officers quit in solidarity. The deputies who remained all had the mournful look of dogs abandoned too long in their crates.

In Cox's old office, Rachel found Rebecca Horne, previously an assistant district attorney in the county prosecutor's office and the first woman to hold the position, even provisionally, of Rockland County sheriff. Horne had a permanent squint and a monsoon of paper on her desk. She looked harassed and underslept, and she barely scanned over the stack of threatening letters that Rachel presented.

"I've gotta be honest," she said. "I'm not seeing the threats." She returned the letters to Rachel. "I wouldn't worry about it. Probably just someone who doesn't like you very much. You said your daughter is fifteen?"

"Sixteen," Rachel corrected. They had celebrated Lucy's birthday just the week before with dinner at the Round on the golf course. Rachel had been hoping for one night alone with her daughter. But Lucy insisted that Noah be invited, or Noah had insisted on it. Rachel couldn't tell.

"Maybe someone your daughter knows from school," Horne said. "Teenage beef. It happens."

That was Noah Landry's theory too. Rachel hadn't meant for him, or for Lucy, to learn about the letters. But a few days after the Fourth of July parade, a letter arrived addressed to Lucy. *When are you and your mother going to SIT DOWN?? Put lipstick on a pig and it still sleeps in shit. You should be ashamed of yourselves.* Lucy had confronted her mother, and Rachel had reluctantly told her about the other letters, dating all the way back to October. Just hours later, Lucy had a theory: it was Reese Steeler-Cox. According to Noah, Reese had been obsessed with him ever since they'd attended a church camp together. She was practically a stalker. That's why she hated Lucy so much, and why she'd tried to steer Lucy away from Noah.

It was in some ways a comforting theory. But Rachel didn't buy it.

"Teenagers don't write each other letters," Rachel pointed out to the sheriff. "They bully each other online."

Horne acknowledged that point with a tilt of the head. "You can fill out a report with the desk sergeant," she said. "That's about all we can do right now. We're stretched thin as it is." Then she added abruptly, "Did you know that Rockland County has one of the lowest rates of prosecution in the state?"

Rachel hadn't known that. But she wasn't surprised. No one knew exactly why Sheriff Cox and his dedicated lieutenant had vacated their positions so abruptly. But she'd heard whispers about an independent investigation by the state's attorney office and a long history of corruption. Cases seemed to flounder in Rockland County. People were arrested. People were released. Investigations dragged.

"Is it true you're thinking of reopening the investigation into Nina Faraday's disappearance?" Rachel hadn't meant to ask about the Faradays—not yet—but Horne had given her an opening.

"Who told you that?" Horne asked sharply.

Rachel shrugged. "It's just something I read online." The local theory about the shake-up was that the county was under pressure to do something about the Faraday case now that it was garnering statewide, even national, attention.

"The investigation was never closed," Horne said. Dimly Rachel was aware of the staccato radio static emanating from the main room. A sudden plaint of phones began to ring, one right after the other. Something was happening.

"What about Lydia Faraday's death?" Rachel asked. Horne's attention was drifting.

"I won't comment," Horne said impatiently.

"Even to a journalist?" Rachel said.

Horne registered no surprise; Rachel figured she'd heard all about the Vales by now. "*Especially* to a journalist."

Horne stood up, signifying the conversation was over. Rachel took her time, however, returning the notes to an envelope and the envelope to her bag, all while tracking the rising excitement from the officers on duty. She heard something about the drought and the Ohio River levels—lower, she'd read, than they'd been in decades. In certain places the river had curdled into a sludgy brown soup that smelled of wastewater and bacterial bloom. All summer the water had been relinquishing secrets, wheezing old trash onto its shores, coughing up submerged bikes and refrigerators.

She was just inching out of Horne's office when a deputy shoved past her, too impatient to wait until she was out of earshot.

"That was McKenzie from the French Island Marina," he said. "Someone found a body in the river."

SIX

We

The rumor that Nina Faraday's body had at last been found tore across social media for a few short days before the cops revealed the identity of the deceased: a fifty-five-year-old alcoholic from nearby Evanston who'd been reported missing by his family several years earlier after a Memorial Day barbecue. But by then, doubts had fomented across the far corners of the internet. Claims of another cover-up proliferated. In a misguided attempt to quell the rumors, freshmen swimmers Henry Rawlings and Jamie Greene infiltrated the memorial service and snapped pictures of the grieving family to prove they really existed.

We agreed afterward that Henry and Jamie were idiots but not that they should burn in hell like the internet was saying.

Meanwhile, we set out to verify another rumor that the sheriff's department was intending to reopen an investigation into Lydia Faraday's death by exhuming her remains.

But first we had to find where she was.

∽

The location of Lydia Faraday's grave was the subject of local debate. For months after her death, Lydia's headstone had been vandalized by outraged locals who blamed her for Coach Steeler's departure—her grave defaced with lewd graffiti, knocked down with heavy equipment, and at one point even stolen altogether. The county had briefly assigned a deputy to patrol the grounds at night to chase off anyone who came with spray paint and a vendetta.

But ultimately Lydia Faraday's grave was too expensive to maintain.

We knew that Lydia's body had been relocated from the cemetery behind St. Paul's Episcopal Church where some of the Faraday relatives were buried some short time after her burial; this formed the backbone of the many legends we'd heard as children about her wandering spirit.

Since then we'd heard lots of different stories about Lydia Faraday's final resting place. Some people said she'd been dumped in an unmarked grave behind the Granger Fire Department. Others said her ashes were tilled into the earth beneath the football field overlooking the Aquatics Center, as final torment. Some people said she'd been buried under the building itself and now wandered the chlorine-scented halls after dark, searching endlessly for Nina. We'd heard that her bones were sunk in Byron Lake, where skeletal hands would reach out and clutch you if you swam too far past the buoys, and that she'd been buried under a false name in Shady Glen Serenity Park, the county's largest cemetery.

This last story proved closest to the truth. Brent Manning had an inside source that summer: freshman Adelaide Burnes, infamous for being both chronically morbid and a D cup. Adelaide's family ran a massively successful funeral home that dominated an entire block in downtown East Granger and served more than 80 percent of the mortuary needs of the greater Four Corners area—at least according to their billboards.

The point was, when it came to dead bodies, we trusted Adelaide. The girl knew what she was talking about.

It was a sweltering July night when Brent Manning went to the cemetery to find Lydia Faraday's grave, to see whether there was proof of recent police activity. It was a crazy and pointless errand, but a bunch of us decided to join him when he floated the idea on Discord. We were itchy for something to do, somewhere to go, some excuse to get out of the house.

For days a thick haze had obscured our towns in a depressing pall of gray that refused to coalesce into badly needed rain. The pressure worked on our eardrums, squeezed our skulls, and lit flames beneath our skin. During the day, the temperature hovered in the nineties. Our towels mildewed in minutes. We drew our shades against the sun like vampires.

Plus, we needed more material for our podcast.

We asked Brent if he could score any beer.

He could.

Shady Glen Serenity Park covered more than thirty acres. It was intermittently lit and, as far as we knew, rarely patrolled. More importantly, the eastern entrance was a short half-mile walk from Valleyview Road, where Alex Spinnaker lived. His house served as a convenient cover and temporary base camp.

The rest of us followed the group's progress via thumbnail pictures and messages that came through Discord. Nate Stern had a new dirt bike and captured the trip through the woods—the rocky trail bucking the camera up and down, trees lurching into sudden view, thick clouds of gnats turned silvery by the touch of his headlights. Olivia Howard flooded our Discord server with inconsequential details and observations, such as several pictures of what she claimed might be the remnants of an occult ceremony but looked to us like someone's discarded chicken wings. Skyler Matthews recorded dramatic voice memos where she described the moon as "the color of old bone" and the gates of the cemetery as "looming forebodingly, like iron fingers pointing to a bad omen."

We were impressed and asked her what *forebodingly* meant.

We straddled realities as a group of us assembled at the eastern entrance of the cemetery, bridging the distance through photographs and video capture, comments and voice notes.

@mememeup: is @spinn_doctor wearing a moon suit? He looks like he's glowing

@gustagusta: wait, hang on guys aren't we missing @ktcakes888?

@ktcakes888: I'm literally standing behind you

@hannahbanana: wish I was there with you!! <3

@spinn_doctor: are we all here?

@highasakyle: where?

@spinn_doctor: by the east gate. Right across from the gun store

@highasakyle: I'm on my couch, bro

@badprincess: can someone ask @brentmann to change audio settings?

It was like that.

According to Adelaide, Lydia Faraday had not been buried under a fake name but simply under her initials. She'd pointed Brent to an area containing the cheapest plots in the cemetery, where stubby hills cracked with rows of slab headstones reared over County Road 11 and overlooked a dribble of fast-food chains and auto supply stores bleeding out from downtown East Granger.

Those of us who were there—Spinnaker, Meeks, Topornycky, Kaitlyn and Ethan Courtland, Olivia Howard, and a handful of others—followed Brent through the gates and up the hill under a suffocating silence, clutching beers that warmed almost as soon as they were open. The heat stuck to our skin like a plastic film that showed even through the videos we streamed back to the server.

The group split up on the hill, weaving among the headstones with camera flashlights burning like so many fireflies against the dark. It was Sofia Young who found the grave, halfway up the hill, set a bit apart from the other headstones. The whole server responded to her shout, which brought a tangle of messages to the general thread.

@badprincess: what was that? Did you guys hear that?
@brentmann: it's Sofia. She found something
@hannahbanana: hear what??
@badprincess: Wait, where are you?
@hannahbanana: I'm at home!!!
@badprincess: I'm talking to @brentmann
@spinn_doctor: I don't see you guys. Do you know how to do a duck call?
@highasakyle: did you find Lydia's grave??
@skyediva: ummmm … did anyone just hear that??? It sounded like a wolf??
@brentmann: I don't speak duck
@gustagusta: hello? @goodnightsky? Did you find Lydia's grave, or what?
@goodnightsky: It's not Lydia Faraday. It's some Vales
@hannahbanana: the Vales are there???
@goodnightsky: some of them are
@spinn_doctor: Bingo
@spinn_doctor: Jackpot
@highasakyle: which is it, Bingo or Jackpot?
@spinn_doctor: it's Lydia Faraday
@goodnightsky: where???
@spinn_doctor: right behind you
@spinn_doctor: turn around

Our group was gathering on the hill, flowing to where Sofia was shouting her discovery: half a dozen gravestones marked with Lucy's family name, indicating half a dozen of her buried relatives. A few graves down from Lucinda Vale Ellis, b. 1945, d. 2009, was a tombstone slightly apart from all the others, as if it had some contaminant associated with it. It was inscribed simply with the initials *LRF*.

We were stunned.

The coincidence, if it was a coincidence, was extraordinary. The Shady Glen cemetery was belted with swaths of untouched hillside and plenty of open land for burying whole generations of dead bodies. Yet somehow Lydia Faraday's body wound up spitting distance from a cluster of Vales.

Alex Spinnaker and Skyler Matthews took photographs of every headstone. There were six Vales in all, some dead half a century. We thrilled at each name, sensing in each another mystery, another online thread to unravel.

There was no sign of police activity at Lydia Faraday's grave. Not that we'd really expected any; in some ways, we'd instead been looking for reassurance, proof that Lydia Faraday was where she should be. But Evie Grant pointed everyone's attention to the bouquet of blue hydrangeas resting next to Lydia Faraday's headstone, visible in the photographs that Skyler had posted to our server.

@badprincess: what's up with the flowers??

At home we clutched our phones, refreshed our browsers, and maximized the grainy hydrangea image. They were bundled in what looked like newspaper, hardly wilted, and arranged with precision.

A gift for the ghost of Lydia Faraday.

@badprincess: helllooooo
@badprincess: Who brought the flowers for LRF?

Nobody knew. But for a second all of us unraveled a length of road in our imaginations, traveling down the slick of moon-skimmed streets to Lily Lane until we skidded to a halt at number 88—where, behind the iron gates, the Vales' garden erupted in color. Where newly painted trellises dripped with beaded roses and clutches of azaleas nodding off among their branches. Blue hydrangea bloomed like fat fists on great arms of green swaying faintly in the breeze, as if to the rhythm of secret music.

SEVEN

We

Lucy Vale refused an invitation to appear on our podcast, even though Skyler Matthews approached her directly. That summer Lucy took on shifts at the Granger Dairy Queen after senior Rory Adams got caught trying to manufacture CBD oil in the deep fryer. The Dairy Queen was always staffed with Echelon girls, possibly because it was a short walk from Byron Lake, where so many of the Sharks served as lifeguards. All summer long we gave our orders to an indifferent Savannah Savage, eagerly fed Bailey Lawrence our tips, and accepted coils of pillowy soft serve from Lucy Vale, thrilling when we grazed fingers over the counter.

According to Skyler, Lucy was trying to distance herself from the drama around the Faraday mystery. We were, in a word, unimpressed.

> **@stopandfriske:** if they wanted to stay out of it
> **@stopandfriske:** maybe they shouldn't have moved INTO it

To be fair, Lucy and her mom probably hadn't anticipated a groundswell of national attention around the case or veiled threats forked into their mailbox. They couldn't have known that an aggressive DA would shoehorn in a new sheriff to galvanize resources into the investigation of Nina's disappearance or reopen an inquiry into Lydia Faraday's death. On the other hand, we couldn't help but feel that the Vales were in large part responsible for all the ruckus. Before they'd arrived in Indiana, the Faraday House had been an old monument to mystery, a rotting relic that was firmly and visibly rooted in the past. By reinhabiting the house, they'd given new life to its stories.

Then there was the fact that Lucy *had* agreed to sit down with the producers of *Blood in the Water*—even after they'd dug up her lawn. Jackson Skye snipped that maybe if we asked her at shovelpoint in the middle of the night, Lucy would reconsider the offer. Either way, she'd had plenty to say about police incompetence and shoddy investigative procedure back in the fall. But now, when we needed her, she wanted to "let the sheriff's department do its job" and avoid "turning this whole thing into entertainment."

@badprincess: are you kidding??
@badprincess: she actually said that?

It was hypocrisy at best coming from the girl whose mom had parlayed an old tragedy into an actual Netflix deal, at least according to Wikipedia.

Besides, it was obviously too late. Hundreds of YouTube videos, scores of podcast episodes, and whole Reddit threads had already done the job.

Alex Spinnaker saw Lucy's refusal as typical of bleeding-heart liberals. We should have expected it from a family that drove a hybrid. No spine, no morals, and no loyalty.

That led to a skirmish about climate change and the government's response to COVID and a fretful and dissatisfied few hours of escalating tension on the server. In the end, we settled on one point of consensus: obviously we couldn't count on Lucy Vale to take our side.

Slowly, almost imperceptibly, our feelings about Lucy began to curdle, morphing into resentment and suspicion. It had been a year since the Vales had arrived in Indiana. One year since we'd first gone on a digital crawl for information about the new girl. And even though Lucy had become a fixture, an icon, a burning star in the universe of those we followed, liked, imitated, and talked about, in some ways her mystery had only deepened.

We returned again to the photographs captured at the Shady Glen cemetery and the names etched in stone above a row of sleeping bones. We found a decades-old memorial from the *Rockland County Register*, a newspaper that no longer existed, announcing the death of Lucinda Vale Ellis. According to the announcement, she was survived by her children and grandchildren, as well as two beloved nieces—one of them named Rachel. This should have satisfied us—Lucy had told Akash that she had family in the area and that her mother spent her teenage summers with a favorite aunt and cousin in Indiana—but we suspected a deeper significance to the Vales' connections to the neighboring county.

Our uneasiness deepened when Emma Howard reported seeing Lucy Vale and her mother eating lunch with the aging Mr. and Mrs. Swift at the Red Barn off State Road 16, a rambling nineteenth-century eatery in the nebulous stretch of unincorporated farmland between Clarion and Housataunick. First of all, nobody went to the Red Barn—at least no one who valued their arteries. Emma Howard had only popped in to wheedle a commitment to buy a half-page advertisement in the community theater's summer playbill from the owner.

She reminded us, not so subtly, that tickets went on sale in a week.

None of us were about to suffer through a two-hour musical devoted to *chess*, of all things. But we didn't tell her that. Instead we gently reoriented conversation to the Vales: What in the good name of Jay Steeler had they been doing breaking bread with Tommy Swift's parents? What could they have been talking about? What could they possibly have to say to one another?

@frenchkissesry: omg
@frenchkissesry: hold on hold on hold on

@frenchkissesry: I just thought of something
@badprincess: what?
@frenchkissesry: JUST HOLD ON

We held on. We were fretful and impatient. We developed heat rashes, and texts from our parents went unread. We didn't make our beds or load our dishwashers. In August we idled in the soporific heat and the dense pressure of rain that never fell.

Riley was back, this time with an old picture of Tommy, Nina, and Jack Vernon at a Halloween party, the one where Tommy had put his hands around Nina's throat. The picture had caused a litany of online static after Coach Vernon was appointed to the Granger Club Team. We didn't understand why Riley reposted it to the server until a second version appeared, this one maximized and cropped to zoom in on the background crowd.

@frenchkissesry: do you see it???

None of us were sure exactly what she meant. The resolution was terrible, a wash of distorted faces barely visible behind young Jack Vernon. But Riley was insistent.

@frenchkissesry: The girl in the red tank top
@frenchkissesry: with the black hair
@frenchkissesry: I think it's her
@frenchkissesry: I think it's Rachel Vale
@frenchkissesry: it looks exactly like her

Exactly may have been a stretch. Still, we all dutifully zoomed in and squinted until our eyeballs itched. We agreed it was very *possibly* Rachel Vale holding a SOLO cup that matched her tank top.

But we didn't understand what it meant.

Peyton Neely wondered whether Noah Landry knew that Lucy Vale had gotten friendly with the Swifts and what he would think about it. Akash replied that he must know; Noah Landry had Lucy Vale on a leash. In fact, he was surprised Noah hadn't been there, lurking under the table. He hardly let Lucy out of his sight. She wasn't even allowed to come over and play video games anymore.

We'd heard these complaints from Akash before and didn't think much of them or bother pointing out that Lucy might just have been using Noah as an excuse to avoid him. She'd moved beyond us. She'd ascended.

She'd kept her secrets for herself.

All afternoon we heard thunder. The sky was a low-belly gray, roiling with frustrated currents. Our dogs whined at the doors. Our air conditioners growled their exhaustion.

Still, the weather held.

PART 7

ONE

WE

We are not bad people.
 If anything is true, it's that we are not bad people. Most of us aren't at least. Most of the time.

We are positive of this. At least, we are reasonably certain. At least, we are reasonably certain most of the time.

We can prove it.

ONE

TWO

Rachel

In late September, Rachel had a startling realization: something was wrong with Lucy.

She was almost always in a bad mood. She complained that her antianxiety medication wasn't working. One night Rachel woke up to muffled sobs coming from the attic. The next she found wads of hair in Lucy's shower—clumps that looked as if they'd been removed by force.

It was Noah. She was sure it had to do with Noah. Lucy's frenzied texts, the whispered nighttime conversations. The way Lucy skulked off to school with barely a word and retreated to her room as soon as she came home.

For days Rachel felt as if she'd been jettisoned out of the nucleus of Lucy's life, landing back in a nightmare of confusion and helplessness. She skulked around the house like a foreign agent, looking for clues in Lucy's bedroom about what might have happened, scouring her daughter's Instagram account for indicators of trouble. She left two panicked messages with Lucy's old therapist. She considered driving to Noah's house to confront him about—what, exactly? She wasn't sure.

And then, abruptly, Lucy announced that she would need a ride to school that one day, and the day after that. Without a word or explanation, Noah stopped picking up Lucy before practice.

When Rachel asked whether something had happened, Lucy snapped at her.

"Noah's fine. We're fine. Things are just complicated." But Rachel took it as a positive sign when Lucy began to leak little complaints about her relationship, when she expressed irritation as opposed to simple despair. Noah was obsessed with body hair. He was even thinking of shaving his eyelashes. Who shaved their eyelashes? Or, Noah had terrible taste in music.

Then Sunday rolled around, and Lucy skipped church.

"What's the point?" she told Rachel, yawning. "I'm going to hell anyway."

"Is that what the pastor said?"

Lucy shrugged and looked away. After a pause she said, "Do you think I'm a bad person?"

Rachel's heart lurched. "Lucy, no. Of course not." She reached out and stroked her daughter's cheek. For once Lucy didn't pull away. "What gave you that idea?"

Lucy shrugged. She mashed the tines of her fork into her pancake. "When I came here, everyone thought I was so perfect. *Noah* thought I was perfect. He thought I was just as good as him."

"Noah is definitely not perfect," Rachel said.

Lucy sighed. "He kind of is, though. He's never done anything wrong. He's never even gotten a *tardy*. Ask anyone."

"Sounds pretty boring," Rachel said, earning her a wisp of a smile. "Besides, I don't believe it. Noah's only human. And humans make mistakes."

"Yeah." Lucy sighed. "But some of us make more mistakes than others." Lucy turned to the window, and for some reason Rachel found herself thinking of Jay Steeler and the way his hands looked touching her naked body. She remembered seeing the skin pouch around his wedding ring and feeling a vague sense of horror. Not because he was married—because he was old.

And yet she still met him again and then called his number over and over after he stopped returning her texts. Desperate to see him again. Desperate to know that it wasn't a *mistake*. She had even found his address months later and made the drive once all the way from Chicago just to sit paralyzed across the street from his house, debating whether or not to ring the doorbell and confront him.

And all these years later, she still remembered his cell phone number.

Rachel understood now that Noah and Lucy's brief and intense love was collapsing, that the center of their relationship had caved and they were now spiraling around an inevitable breakup. She ached for her daughter and at the same time felt unaccountably relieved. She couldn't say why. She'd never seen Noah mistreat Lucy. Still, she suspected that he picked at her, criticized her outfits, her friendship with Akash, the things she posted on social media. And there was something almost disconcerting about his talent and its effects on everyone around him. Even Noah's parents behaved as if he were a rare plant, an extraordinary natural phenomenon that needed constant placation. Dating him, Lucy had become simply Noah Landry's girlfriend, her identity reconfigured around its most "important" component.

She wondered if that's how it had been for Nina Faraday too—and whether she, like Lucy, had been so obviously lonely.

So she waited, she simply waited, for Lucy and Noah to fall apart. In the meantime, she traveled an imaginative line to the past, sifting through volumes of court records related to the Faradays. The county sheriff's department had applied for two separate search warrants for 88 Lily Lane. They'd searched Woody Topornycky's vehicle and his father's farm. They'd presented AT&T with a search warrant for information on Nina's missing phone. They'd briefly arrested two people, neither of whom Rachel had ever heard of: a local sex offender indicted on charges of statutory rape after lying to a high school field hockey player about his age and a poacher who was spotted with a shovel and a rifle in the state park the morning after Nina Faraday vanished, then bolted when a park employee tried to speak to him. At one point the police even petitioned to wiretap the phones of two known drug dealers, all because one of them was spotted on Lily Lane not long before Nina disappeared.

As she traveled through a tide of warrants, Rachel had the distinct sense of a police investigation curiously missing its center, concealing via a storm of activity the silent, obvious question within. It was as if the Rockland County Sheriff's Department had desperately stretched for something, anything, that would thread Nina's disappearance to a palatable storyline—a secret affiliation with dangerous criminals, a maniacal drifter, a stranger with a fetish and a fixation. It was a torrent of paper, a dizzying switchback of suspects and investigative maneuvers, exhausting to even read about. It wasn't true, she thought, that the sheriff's department hadn't tried to look for Nina. If anything, they had done too much—and possibly all the wrong things.

Most stories were so simple in the end. Plain, and sad, and simple.

Again and again she returned to what her agent had told her after eighth-grade Lucy had been persuaded by a high school sophomore to send nearly naked pictures.

It's always the same story with a few modern updates. It always comes down to a boy.

Rachel was sure, in her gut, that Nina's story began and ended with Tommy Swift.

The question was: How?

THREE

We

In October, Woodward announced a Casino Night fundraiser in honor of Mr. Cross, a beloved math teacher who'd been found dead over the summer with a needle in his arm.

We all pitched in to make Casino Night a success, temporarily making peace with the Student Council Mafia and the rest of the Student Leadership shills, and signed up for various committees. We designed graphics and drummed up new raffle items. Made cold calls to local businesses and wrangled donations of food, soda, and prizes.

Event attendance was open to Woodward students and their families. But our volunteers drew from all over. Big Lou, the cashier at the 7-Eleven off Route 12; Mrs. Harbor; and Hunchback Fred, who wasn't actually a hunchback but did have bad posture, suited up in formal wear to deal cards at the game tables. The new sheriff, Horne, with her hair slicked neatly into a bun, mixed drinks for half the night.

We dared each other to ask her about Lydia Faraday's case, whether she really thought Lydia might have been murdered.

The cafeteria was dazzlingly remade into a Vegas casino, glowing with green felt and sophomores in shimmering dresses who circulated with plastic martini glasses full of lukewarm pop. Poker tables dotted the hall, with crowds jostling to get into the games or heckle the players for bad bets. Mrs. Santiago's health classroom, STD poster and all, played host to several roulette wheels and even a craps table. The nurse's office across the hall, guarded strictly by both Vice Principal Edwards and Old McVeigh, was repurposed as a bar. Attendees who'd been properly ID'd and stamped at ticketing could find plastic tables draped with tablecloths, cluttered with donated Jim Beam, Gordon's gin, and Stoli vodka. We wasted a large portion of the night observing the entrance and trying fruitlessly to plot a way inside. Nick Topornycky and Will Friske, meanwhile, were being coy about whether or not they had beer in the car.

Most of the boys' swim team had rented tuxes from Angela's Formal in Housataunick, like they did for the Winters. It didn't matter that Angela's Formal hadn't been properly stocked this early in the season so that many of their jackets were too small, the cummerbunds held together with safety pins or abandoned altogether. We thought they looked amazing.

The girls wore sequins and high heels and showed off legs luminescent and pale from fall hibernation. They wore smoky eye shadow they'd applied in tandem, squinting over YouTube tutorials. Their hair was straight and a little frizzy and smelled of hair dryer static, and they were beautiful. The Strut Girls, including Lucy, dressed up like glamour girls from the 1920s. We side-eyed Lucy, checking her for evidence of embarrassment. A slick of whisper trailed behind her wherever she went. She kept her head high, a smile spackled to her face. We were impressed that she'd come.

It had been only two weeks since we'd all seen her photographs. The scandal had practically exploded county cell phone towers; for at least three days it had swallowed the whole school like a whale taking down a goldfish with hardly a burp. Lucy Vale, *perfect* Lucy Vale, had been keeping secrets from all of us. She'd been *lying* about what kind of girl she really was—or, at the very least, letting us believe something that wasn't true, which was almost the same thing.

We noticed she hemmed close to Bailey and that she and Noah were avoiding each other. We thumbed sly jokes about trouble in paradise and felt vaguely vindicated.

Apparently Lucy Vale was not so perfect after all.

The only bummer was the weather. The day before the event, the temperature plummeted, and a queasy mix of rain and sleet presaged the early arrival of winter. Frozen mud skid-marked across the hallway linoleum. The parking lot was sheeted with patchy ice.

This is important.

Because it is very, very possible that Lucy Vale only slipped.

∼

It was nine o'clock and we'd lost most of our money before we saw the SOS from Evie Grant on Discord.

There was something wrong with Sofia Young.

She was pounding on the door of the Aquatics Center, claiming she needed a swim.

She seemed confused. She kept claiming to be a dolphin.

Evie Grant was pretty sure she was on something.

@nononycky: no shit she's on something
@nononycky: what did she take?

Evie didn't know. But she needed help. Sofia Young needed water.

We absolutely could not breathe a word about this to Sofia Young's mom, or we were dead.

Nick Topornycky suggested we tell his uncle, Woody. He knew all about overdoses and how to reverse them. Evie Grant quickly nixed the idea. Woody was checking coats for new arrivals and was dressed in a suit jacket; for the night, he was as good as an Administrative appendage. We rushed instead to the refreshments table to get water and chips, which were being sold for an outrageous four dollars. We briefly complained about the price tag. Akash reminded us this was a fundraiser; Evie Grant told us to focus.

@ktcakes888: HELP
@ktcakes888: Mrs. Young just straight up asked me if I'd seen Sofia
@ktcakes888: what should I do?
@badprincess: what do you mean, what should you do?
@badprincess: MAKE SOME SHIT UP
@mememeup: #obviously

Evie reminded us that Sofia Young was our friend. She was our problem.

That was just part of our code.

We kept secrets. We kept quiet.

We lied, and we protected our own.

~

We hurried into the cold, slipping out from various exits to avoid suspicion and reconvening in the front courtyard. From there we navigated through the parking lot, clutching our phones for light and navigating slicks of unexpected ice. We found Evie Grant outside Aquatics, beneath the overhang of the construction scaffolding that had gone up over the summer, trying to wrangle Sofia Young away from the front doors.

"They're locked," Evie said when she saw us coming, as if that explained everything. She had Sofia by the waist, barely. Sofia squirmed and slurred that she needed to go swimming, she was too hot, she would die if she didn't get in the water.

Alex Spinnaker uncapped a bottle of water and slugged some of it at Sofia, barely grazing her face and mostly dousing Evie Grant.

"I'm trying to help," he said when we accused him of being a dick.

Sofia Young swiped for the water bottle, tipped some into her mouth, and then spit it out again in an arc.

"I'm a dolphin," she said. When she laughed, she nearly pitched off her feet. "No. No. I'm a *shark*."

We agreed: she was definitely on something.

We talked idly about finding her boyfriend, but nobody moved. Already we regretted leaving the cafeteria. It was deep dark where we stood, and the air was sharp with tiny points of sleet. Will Friske asked Sofia what she'd taken. That snuffed the laughter right out of her. She turned pouty.

"Ask Aiden," she said. We all looked at one another, bewildered. "Ask him about Mr. Cross. Aiden knows."

We felt something then, an unconscious shiver that ran back to Mr. Cross lying dead in a bathroom with a needle in his arm, and to Aiden Teller returning so quickly to the pool after injuring his shoulder in a fight.

Suddenly Sofia broke away from Evie Grant and started running. A few of us sprinted after her. Nate Stern caught up with her first, pinioning Sofia around the waist, spinning her back toward Aquatics.

A violent cataclysm seemed to shudder her whole body. Just as Evie Grant caught up, Sofia puked. She erupted. It was like something out of *The Exorcist*. Evie screamed as vomit patterned her face, her dress, her bare arms. We shouted, barely dodging the flow.

Evie started crying. Nate let Sofia go, pitching her toward the planters at the entrance to Aquatics. She fell to her knees, still retching. Everyone was talking. It was a mess. Olivia Howard and Hannah Smith left with a promise to find paper towels. Evie Grant wailed that she needed a new dress.

Peyton Neely hushed us sharply. She'd heard something.

Heard what? we wanted to know, and Peyton shushed us again.

"Voices," Peyton said. "Someone's coming."

Evie Grant was still crying softly. Kaitlyn Courtland was crouched next to Sofia Young at the planters, rubbing her back, murmuring indistinctly. The rest of us stood motionless, our fingers numbing against soda cans and bottles of water. The wind slid fingers down our necks. We imagined McVeigh prowling somewhere out of sight between the cars. Watching us. We scanned the parking lot for movement. Up on the hill, the darkness shuddered, rippled, and shook loose a pair of silhouettes.

"Do you think I'm stupid or something?"

Noah and Lucy. They were standing farther up the hill, a few hundred feet from where we were gathered, just outside the circle of light cast down from the overheads braced to the cafeteria.

"Answer me. Do you think I'm stupid?"

We heard the pitch of Lucy's voice in her response. But whatever she said was lost by the distance, muzzled by the fizz of indifferent rain.

Then Noah again, his voice edged with warning. "I know who you are, Lucy. I know everything about you. Don't forget."

We stood there helplessly, signaling to one another in the dark. Neither Lucy nor Noah looked in our direction. Even if they had, it wasn't clear that they would be able to see us where we were, lost in the folds of darkness that curved down the parking lot and puddled at the bottom of the hill.

From a distance we saw Lucy Vale step into the light, swiping her eyes with her arm. She wasn't wearing a jacket. Her voice canted suddenly down to us.

"You know what, Noah Landry? Everyone thinks you're so nice. But you're not. You're a fucking *asshole*."

She took one step. She took another.

"Don't you walk away from me," Noah said. He reached out. Grabbed her.

That's when it happened. Sofia's phone trumpeted a short blast of music from her bag, which she'd abandoned somewhere in the darkness.

Noah yanked.

Lucy slipped.

Or she slipped, and he pulled.

Later we could never tell the exact order of events. Everything happened too fast. Noah cursed. Lucy yelped. We were looking around for Sofia's bag, trying to silence the ringtone. By the time we looked up, Noah Landry was staring in our direction, and Lucy was on the ground.

"Hello?" he called out. "Is someone down there?"

After a long beat, Kaitlyn Courtland spoke up. "Sofia's puking. We think she took something."

Noah Landry said nothing. For a beat he stood there staring, maybe picking out our forms in the darkness.

"Lucy slipped," he said and bent down to help her to her feet. Then he put his arm around her, and she seemed to disappear into his jacket, engulfed inside his shadow. For a second something stirred again in our subconscious—a memory of something, an impression we couldn't name.

Yanked or slipped. A small difference but important. Critical even.

We were there. We'd seen it happen. But we didn't know for *sure*. The memory had already turned into a jigsaw of different pieces; we remembered it happening one way, then another. Noah had grabbed her, pulled her so hard she'd lost her balance. Lucy had lost her balance, and Noah had grabbed her, pulled her, trying to keep her on her feet.

Impossible to know. Lucy was changing—had changed—in our imaginations. Lucy was *slippery*.

Noah was probably just trying to help.

Sofia Young's phone began to ring again. Peyton finally located Sofia's bag, abandoned on the asphalt between two parked cars.

"It's my mom," Sofia said. She wasn't slurring anymore at least. "Don't answer it."

Up the hill, Noah was piloting Lucy back toward the cafeteria. She was moving carefully, limping with one hand on her lower back. We thought of calling out and asking whether she was okay.

Her voice thinned in the distance. We couldn't hear what she was saying, only Noah's response.

"Your funny bone's in your elbow, silly," Noah said. His voice sounded the way it usually did. Warm. Gentle. Sure. "That was your tailbone."

We were freezing. We felt suddenly anxious. We'd been gone for too long. Our parents would notice we were missing. Olivia and Hannah returned with rolls of paper towels for Evie Grant, pilfered from the auditorium bathroom, which had been mercifully unlocked.

"We saw Lucy and Noah in the parking lot," they announced. We said nothing.

Evie was still tearful. There was no way she could return with vomit all over her. It was all Sofia's fault for being such a fuckup.

We interceded before things could get ugly. We helped clean Evie and Sofia up. Sofia told us she was feeling much better. She hadn't taken much, she said. Just a few pills and some vodka.

We told her she would wind up like Mr. Cross if she wasn't careful. She didn't seem to remember that she'd mentioned him and implied that Aiden Teller knew something about the drugs and Mr. Cross's OD—just like the troll ANONYM1698 had been claiming online for months. And we didn't want to push it.

If Teller was wrapped up in something like that, we didn't want to know.

We scattered. Olivia and Hannah stayed with Sofia outside Aquatics, feeding her sips of ginger ale. We swore to fend off Ms. Young until Sofia was sober enough to return to the cafeteria. We promised to look around for Sofia's boyfriend. Evie Grant went to find her parents; she was done. By then most of us were tired. The night had soured. The cafeteria lights looked suddenly flimsy in the darkness, like a movie set, an illusion that would dissipate before morning.

It was close to midnight when we got a notification from Peyton Neely. A single message after hours of inactivity. By then most of us were sleeping. But a few of us saw our phones light up, casting a small neon window into the dark of our bedrooms.

@geminirising: hey. do you guys remember all those storm birds years ago?

We knew at once what she was talking about. Four years earlier, back-to-back tornadoes had driven the Ohio River over its banks. Floodwaters had sheeted the streets, spun away mailboxes, uprooted whole gardens. The same water had fingered through porous gaps in the drywall of Akash's old house and floated their living room furniture on four-foot eddies. As a result, Akash's parents had decided to relocate to Lawrence Place where it intersected with Lily Lane at the Faraday House.

But the Sandhus' old house was just one of the many casualties of that storm season. The winds had blown hundreds of nests from their branches. Dozens and dozens of infant birds, not yet grown enough to fly, had died inside a hundred-mile-an-hour centrifuge of debris, dirt, and loose trash. Some of the birds had tried to fly anyway; their wings were cleaved apart, stripped from the jointing of their spines, flayed in crazy directions.

In the morning, we'd found them. Dozens of them. Dark, all dark, with grit and storm sludge and blood. Who knew what color their feathers had been? All of them broken, their wings cracked in strange directions or almost entirely ripped away. They had lain with small, sorry faces turned into the pavement under a sweep of dirty feathers. They had almost looked as if they were covering their eyes. As if they had died mourning something they were too horrified or embarrassed to face.

@mememeup: yeah, i remember the birds
@mememeup: why?

We waited for an answer, but none came. We figured maybe Peyton had gone to sleep. We tried to sleep too, but our thoughts were full of agitation, the sweep of dark memories.

We hadn't thought about those birds in years. Not until Peyton Neely reminded us. Not until Lucy Vale, beautiful Lucy Vale—we agreed she was beautiful now—limped up the hill on Casino Night, pinioned beneath the dark wing of Noah's tuxedo jacket, her face invisible, turned into the shadow of his arm.

FOUR

Rachel

A few days before Thanksgiving, Rachel came home from the grocery store to find her daughter, face pulpy from crying, huddled on the couch among a scrum of wadded-up tissues. She was so alarmed, she nearly dropped the bag with the eggs.

"What is it?" she said. "What's wrong? What happened?"

Lucy blew her nose. It was like the toot of a mournful trumpet. "I broke up with Noah," she said. Her voice was thick with mucus.

"*You* did?" Rachel asked.

Lucy glared at her. "Yes, *I* did. Is that so fucking hard to believe?"

"*Lucy.*" Rachel deposited the bags on the coffee table and took a seat next to her daughter on the couch.

"Sorry," Lucy grumbled. She blew her nose again, extravagantly. "It was so sad. But I had to. He's been so weird ever since—"

She broke off abruptly. Her hands spasmed in her lap.

"Ever since what, sweetheart?" Rachel reached out to stroke Lucy's hair back from her forehead. Lucy's skin felt warm, clammy. She recalled then the time that Lucy had gotten strep throat and a fever that had briefly touched 105. Rachel had stayed up all night monitoring Lucy's fever and her agonized thrashing as she shivered under mounds of blankets in the June heat. Rachel remembered the smell of the bedroom—ripe, fruity, almost exotic, as if some strange fungal organism had taken over her daughter's body.

Lucy fidgeted. "He knows about what happened in Michigan," she said finally. "He saw the photos."

Instantly Rachel's blood pressure spiked. Her thoughts splintered into a whirl of alarms. "What? *How?*"

"I don't know. Someone found them."

"*Who* found them?" Rachel got up and began to pace. Or more like prowl. She was suddenly enraged. Lucy had been only thirteen when she'd sent those photos to the boy she believed cared about her, a seventeen-year-old junior she'd been talking with over Snapchat. Soon everyone in the high school had seen them, and Lucy, already struggling in middle school, was the subject of bathroom graffiti and physical assaults in the hall. People started spreading rumors: Lucy gave out hand jobs for twenty dollars; Lucy had lost her virginity to everyone on the basketball team. Rachel had fought to hold everyone who'd circulated the photographs accountable, and eventually two seniors, both over eighteen, were charged with trafficking child sex materials and forced to register as sex offenders. But it had taken close to a year, and by then Lucy was ninety pounds, wizened like an old lady and picking at her skin until it bled.

"I said I don't *know*." Lucy was close to tears again. "See? This is why I didn't want to tell you. I knew you'd freak out."

"Of course I'm freaking out." Rachel forced herself to sit down again. "When did this happen?"

"Forever ago," Lucy said. "Like in September. Before Casino Night even."

Now it made sense to Rachel—that time she'd found a clump of hair in the shower drain, those nights when she'd heard panicked whispering and muffled sobs from Lucy's room. She'd been dealing with the fallout of those photographs—again. Noah must have seen them. *Everyone* must have seen them.

She couldn't believe that Lucy hadn't told her. They'd sworn they would have no secrets.

"Casino Night," Rachel repeated. "When you and Noah had a big fight? When you came home in tears?"

Lucy looked away. She was silent for a bit. "It doesn't matter anymore," she said finally, almost ferociously. "So what? So now everyone knows what I am."

"Those photos," Rachel said, "are not who you are."

She reached out to place a hand on Lucy's knee.

Lucy squirmed away. "Just forget I said anything," she said. "Please."

Rachel shook her head. "If those photos are still out there, still circulating—"

Suddenly Lucy clapped both hands over her ears, squeezing as if she could cave in her head. "Mom, please. Please. I just broke up with my *boyfriend*." Her voice pitched to a desperate wail. "Noah's like the only person who ever even loved me."

"Noah's not the only person who ever loved you," Rachel said. She ached to put her arms around Lucy, to hold her like she would have when Lucy was a child awoken by a bad dream. To rock her until the billows of feeling rolled through, until the dream was fully dispelled. "I love you. Alan loves you. Your friends love you."

"You know what I mean," Lucy said.

They sat in quiet for a bit—Lucy still sniffling, shrunken into her oversize hoodie, turtle-like. The winter sun was dwindling on the floorboards even though it was barely four o'clock. The radiators hissed at the cold that blew through the gaps in the window frames.

"How did Noah take it?" Rachel asked once Lucy's breathing had settled. "Was he angry?"

Lucy's laugh was mangled. "Noah's never angry," she said bitterly. "Noah's just *disappointed*."

Rachel knew the type. Greg, her college boyfriend, had been like that: withdrawing into wounded silence when he felt Rachel had slighted him, punishing her with small cutting comments about her writing or her friends or her hairstyle. He had even used his warmth as a weapon, turning it on their friends and even on strangers so that Rachel could detect it landing on someone else.

"Do you think you'll stay friends?"

"I don't know. Maybe. I'm not sure that I want to," Lucy said. "I *love* Noah. But . . ."

"But what?" Rachel prompted.

"I don't think he's that nice to me," Lucy said.

Rachel felt a surge of love for Lucy that was almost overwhelming. There were so many ways to learn about parenting—so many books and websites and experts to consult. But no one could prepare you for the love, and how often it felt just like pain.

"I'm proud of you, sweetheart," she said. This time, Lucy let Rachel kiss her on the forehead.

Later, when Lucy went upstairs to nap, Rachel finished unloading the groceries. She felt unaccountably light, almost exuberant. Without realizing it, she'd been carrying around a weight about Noah and Lucy's relationship, about how it was reshaping Lucy's goals, attention, even her selection of a summer job. Lucy had initially pondered volunteer work, possibly for the Indiana chapter of Planned Parenthood. But working at the ice-cream store near Byron Lake had been convenient for seeing Noah—and Rachel sensed, although Lucy had never said so, that Noah and his family might be pro-life. Unconsciously she had feared that Lucy might continue to wrap her interests and schedule around Noah's, especially when it came time to apply to college. Lucy still hadn't totally found herself academically. On any given week, she might profess a thousand interests or none at all.

In some ways, Noah had been the ultimate distraction—a way of defining herself without actually finding herself.

But now it was over, and Lucy herself had made the choice. Rachel had little fear that she would change her mind. Lucy often hesitated, waffled, and even agonized before making a decision. But once she did, she stuck to it. She was a committer.

The thought flashed: Lucy wasn't like poor Nina Faraday. Lucy would never linger in a toxic relationship like the one Nina had with Tommy Swift.

Just as quickly, she chased the comparison away, ashamed by it. It was ridiculous to hold Lucy up to Nina and to judge Nina unfavorably for it. Whatever had happened to Nina Faraday, it was something that had happened *to her*. It wasn't Nina's fault or her responsibility. It wasn't the result of a character flaw—at least not *her* character flaw, like so many people in Rockland County had implied or assumed. Besides, she was troubled by the idea that Lucy and Nina had followed parallel paths, even briefly. This, too, was yet another source of worry that she had been trying to ignore for many months.

It was over now, Rachel told herself in a singsong. She would have to deal with the photographs, of course. Lucy might wish to forget the whole episode. But if someone at Woodward had distributed them, they would have to be identified and punished.

But not yet. First Rachel would make Lucy something yummy. Something she could eat in bed with a broken heart. Maybe mac and cheese—Rachel was getting pretty good—or an egg and cheese sandwich. Tomorrow they would again do a double Thanksgiving, first at Rachel's aunt and uncle's, then at the Sandhus'. But at least they wouldn't have to make a stop at the Landrys', where all the conversation, like the decor, was belabored with references to Noah's swim career.

She turned on the tap and began to fill a stockpot, encouraged by the cheerful drum of water against copper. She thought of her daughter lying upstairs, surrounded by a fleecy pile of tissues, probably torturing herself with old photos and social media posts. She thought of the slow and fitful way that broken hearts repaired, straightened out, and pointed you in new directions.

She thought they had much to be thankful for that year.

FIVE
We

To be clear, we don't know what happened at that party. Even at the time, we didn't know. How could we? We saw through the narrow windows of our perspectives, shaving the night into fragments.

And whatever happened or didn't happen to Lucy Vale happened behind a locked door, inside a room we couldn't access.

Rumors about a New Year's Eve party at Ryan Hawthorne's house seemed to materialize alongside our desire for one, like we'd all collectively given birth to the idea. Nate Stern heard that Mr. and Mrs. Hawthorne were going away for the weekend. Nick Topornycky heard something about a keg. Sofia Young heard that Ryan Hawthorne, who would be out of the pool for at least a month, had painkillers. Slowly the party grew in our awareness like a vein of mold, colonizing our attention until we were obsessed; we had to go.

It was the tail end of Christmas break. Indiana was locked in a cold front that sucked the air from our lungs and shocked the world into stillness. Our cars sputtered and wheezed in the mornings. Our eyeballs gummed to our lids. For days we'd been locked in our bedrooms, trapped in a prison of YouTube, TikTok, and porn.

We needed out.

Ryan Hawthorne lived in Green Gables Ridge, one of the fancy neighborhoods that backed up to the golf course, not far from the Steeler-Coxes and Alex Spinnaker. Driving up to the party, we half expected to be seized and interrogated. Most of us felt like interlopers in a different world.

But we convened without incident in packed cars with the heat blasting so hard it fried our eyeballs and the sting of cheap alcohol burning our throats. Cars backstopped the driveway and flowed all the way down the street. The lawn was rutted with tire marks. Every window scalded with light. We could hear the music reverberating in our lungs as soon as we climbed out of our cars.

Instantly we'd arrived.

The living room was hot, and eddying with classmates mysteriously transformed by the environment into strangers we didn't know and didn't know how to talk to. We shed our coats and scarves into a bedroom, into *the* bedroom where Lucy Vale would later go to sleep off her drunken night.

We didn't remember seeing Lucy arrive, only that we knew she was there, and drunk.

Very, very drunk.

For us it was like a scrim came down at that party, revealing Lucy's true self. Lucy was wearing heavy makeup and laughing too loudly. She kept asking around for cigarettes. It was as if she'd somehow collapsed into the rumors that had spread since we'd all seen her old photographs, as if Lucy Vale in real life had finally submitted to the Lucy Vale of our imaginations.

As if finally, at last, we *knew* her.

We felt vaguely sorry for her and slightly vindicated. Lucy Vale had been notched incrementally down the power chain, which meant, in some ways, the rest of us had climbed it.

A few of us saw Lucy Vale taking shots in the kitchen. Olivia Howard asked Bailey Lawrence if Lucy was okay when, a little while later, Lucy appeared to be nodding off on Bailey's shoulder. JJ Hammill came into the kitchen looking for an extra trash can in case Lucy needed to throw up. Akash saw JJ and Ryan helping Lucy into the first-floor bedroom, the one that served as a home office for Hawthorne's mom. The door stayed closed afterward. We remembered hearing that Lucy Vale had passed out.

We remembered that Holly Markeson, a senior, was puking in the downstairs bathroom and that the upstairs toilet was clogged. There was an empty pack of cigarettes puddled in a nest of soiled toilet paper and piss across the toilet seat. The boys were peeing outside behind a trim wall of boxwood near the patio.

We remembered Jeremiah Greene shouting that the music was too loud, that the cops would come if we weren't careful. The threat of cops was an undertow that kept pulling us into periodic panic. The cops were coming. Someone had called the cops. The cops would bust us for drinking. We had to run. No one could be outside. We had to get the beer off the patio. The neighbors had complained.

Rumors bloomed and dissipated. Still, more people arrived. At times we couldn't move. We were rat-packed between walls of people, clotting the stairs and the hallway, weaving in and out of the bedrooms. Breaking things. Stealing things. Getting tossed out and beaten up.

It was chaotic and liberating. We were there. We were part of it. We stood in line for the keg, submerged in a trash can full of ice on the back porch. We tried to get drunk, quickly. We needed to forget our discomfort. We needed to forget that we didn't quite belong.

None of us knew that Noah Landry had come. None of us remembered seeing him. All we knew was that the door to the first-floor bedroom stayed closed for hours after Lucy Vale had entered to sleep it off, and none of us could get our coats.

∼

Later Peyton Neely and Sofia Young saw Lucy Vale stumbling through the snow, flanked by some of the swimmers, who were practically carrying her toward a waiting car. What car, they couldn't say. But Akash was positive that Bailey Lawrence had told him that Lucy Vale was going home with Noah.

Of all of us, Akash was the most concerned about Lucy's drinking. Even though he and Lucy barely spoke anymore, he still couldn't quite shake her. He'd noticed she was missing at the party for a while. He'd heard, like the rest of us, that she was lying down in a bedroom.

Around eleven o'clock, he'd worked up the courage to ask Bailey whether Lucy needed a ride home. Bailey had told him that Lucy was fine, and Noah Landry had come to get her.

So Akash left to drive the Courtlands home and thought nothing more about it. What was he supposed to do?

If Lucy wanted to go home with her ex-boyfriend, she wanted to go home with her ex-boyfriend.

SIX

RACHEL

Later Rachel would obsessively replay the night in her mind, wondering where she had been, what she'd been doing when her daughter was staggering into a downstairs bedroom, leaning on her ex-boyfriend's best friend. Trusting him. What had Rachel been doing when Lucy woke up in flashes, in brief snapshots, to find Noah on top of her and his friends watching them from the corner, egging him on? Had she been brushing her teeth or on the phone with her cousin while Lucy was slipping in and out of consciousness?

Where was she at the exact moment that her daughter was being raped?

For some reason this felt important—critical even—in the brutal early days of the new year. If she could only think her way back to the precise moment when her daughter's life was slipping off its tracks, shoved in an entirely new direction, she might somehow avert it, might rivet Lucy back to herself as she puttered obliviously around the house, enjoying one of the few New Year's Eves she'd ever spent at home as a single woman. Rachel was sick afterward, remembering how much she'd enjoyed herself—how pleased she'd been, even, that Lucy had had plans with her friends.

A sleepover at Mia's house, Lucy had told her. Just the girls.

And Rachel had believed her.

Idiot.

She had suspected something was wrong, something was off, when Lucy had texted at eleven o'clock to say that she was going to bed as soon as she and her friends were done watching a movie. The message was full of typos; Rachel had asked point-blank whether she was drinking and then demanded that Lucy call.

Lucy wouldn't. But her subsequent texts seemed more lucid, and she'd promised to call as soon as the movie was over. Rachel suspected now that one of Lucy's friends had taken her phone, concerned that Lucy might tip off her mother about the party.

Lucy herself didn't remember; she didn't remember texting her mother at all. Whole portions of the night, she said, were missing as if they'd been removed with a gigantic ice-cream scoop. Instead she had only fragments. Feelings.

A sore throat, raw feeling, possibly from throwing up. Mysterious bruises on her arms and thighs.

Pain between her legs.

And Rachel had been—where? Surfing Netflix, trying to decide on a movie to watch. Texting with friends from graduate school. Spooning ice cream into the little glass cups she and Lucy had found at a yard sale over the summer and wondering why pharmacies had once doubled as soda shops, what the connection was. She had stayed up to watch the ball drop in Times Square, counting down with the crowd and blowing a kiss to the TV screen at midnight. *Goodbye and hello.*

She texted Lucy again. **Are you asleep?** And then: **Be honest. Have you been drinking?**

She checked the last message she'd sent to Bailey. **Can you please have Lucy call me?** No response. But she still wasn't too worried about it. Mia's parents weren't her favorite people—country-club types, disengaged—and she couldn't imagine that they would have stayed home to supervise the girls on New Year's Eve. But even if Lucy and her friends were drinking, Rachel had no reason to think they were in danger—not with the four of them together, not at a girls' sleepover.

So she turned off the lights. She treated herself to a face mask, a Korean clay treatment that Lucy had insisted they buy after hearing about it on TikTok. She thought she would read for a bit—one of her old colleagues from *VICE* had written a new book about the Murdaugh case—and she was just preparing to climb in bed when her phone lit up. She lurched for it, assuming it was her daughter at last.

She felt her first real pull of anxiety when she saw Noah Landry's number.

"Noah? Is everything okay?" Right away she could tell that Noah was in a car. She checked the time: 12:35 a.m. As far as she knew, Noah had a strict curfew. Something must have gone wrong.

"Um, I think so?" Noah's voice—so familiar, so casual—was instantly reassuring. "But, um, Lucy's pretty wasted . . ."

"Where is she? Where are you?"

"I have her in the car. I'm on my way to your house right now. I just thought you should know. She keeps saying she has to puke . . ."

"But where was she? Where's Bailey?"

Noah hesitated. "They're still at Ryan's house," Noah said finally.

It finally clicked. "What is it? Some kind of party?"

"I wasn't there," Noah said quickly, all but confirming it. "I only went because JJ called me about Lucy. He said she was passed out."

Now Rachel felt a spike of anger. So Lucy had simply lied to her from the beginning. Mentally she cycled through a list of appropriate punishments. She would take Lucy's phone. She would ground her for a month. "Well, just pull over if she has to puke. And Noah—please drive safely. The roads are icy."

"Yes, ma'am," Noah said. Rachel had never convinced Noah to call her anything else, even after months of seeing him almost as much as she did Lucy. She'd always felt that it was somehow retrogressive—gendered, of course, and so old-fashioned. The way he lilted the syllables brought to mind southern belles and statues of Confederate heroes. But right then she experienced a rush of real fondness for Noah, for his manners and his strict moral code. He was bringing Lucy back home, where she would sleep off whatever she'd consumed in her own bed, safe. She briefly wondered how Noah must be feeling, coming to Lucy's rescue so soon after she'd dumped him. She sympathized with him, felt sorry for him even.

He was a good guy. And Lucy . . .

Well. Lucy had her own issues to work out.

When Rachel saw headlights through the kitchen windows, she slipped on a ski jacket over her pajamas and shoved her bare feet into Lucy's UGGs. Outside the air razored through her lungs. The sky was clear, pristine with stars hanging like shards of ice against the black. She crunched down the driveway toward the garage, where Noah was just coaxing Lucy out of the back seat.

"Come on, Luce," he was saying. "Almost there."

"Did you talk to my mom?" Lucy's voice was still thick with alcohol. She could barely keep her head up. She didn't seem to register Rachel approaching. Her eyes slid from Rachel's, bounced over the house, rolled back toward the sky. She reeked of liquor, and something else; Rachel saw vomit on her sweatshirt, which engulfed her all the way to her bare thighs.

"I don't know what happened to her jacket," Noah said apologetically as Rachel took Lucy's arm and helped steer her back toward the house, half-relieved and half-furious. Lucy still had her bag at least, but she was wearing flip-flops. Underneath the sweatshirt, a ridiculously short skirt was twisted around backward. What the hell had she been thinking?

Noah helped Rachel maneuver Lucy up the stairs to the back door. Lucy stirred into sudden motion when he reached for the door handle, swatting away his hand.

"Go away," she slurred. "I don't need you."

Noah took a step back, looking wounded. Again Rachel felt sorry for him and furious with Lucy—the chunks of vomit tangled in her hair, the acerbic breath.

"I'm sorry, Noah," she said. "You should get home. It's late. Your parents will be worried."

Noah nodded. Still, he lingered, shoulders hunched to his ears, his hands shoved deep in his pockets. The porch light threw his shadow, huge, almost back to the garage. "Is she gonna be okay?" he asked uncertainly as Rachel wrestled with Lucy at the door, trying to get it open.

"She'll be fine," Rachel said.

Lucy dropped her head on Rachel's shoulder. She said, "Mom. Mom, I don't feel good."

Noah said, "I bet she won't remember anything, though." At the time Rachel didn't think much of it.

Then Noah turned and headed back to his car, which was still running, spitting exhaust into the cold. Rachel got Lucy to the kitchen and made her drink some water. She guided Lucy up the stairs and into her bedroom. Lucy belly flopped onto the mattress.

"I'm sorry, Mom," she said into the pillow. "I didn't mean to."

"We'll talk about it tomorrow," Rachel said. She sat Lucy up to get her out of the filthy sweatshirt. For a moment Lucy, now wearing only her bra, clung to her mother.

"I'm sorry," she repeated. Her skin felt cold and slick like something left out in a storm drain.

"Just go to sleep," Rachel said. She leaned Lucy back onto the pillows. Even after Lucy was asleep—or passed out—Rachel got a comb and spray bottle from the bathroom and tried to tease out some of the vomit in her hair. She couldn't sleep anyway.

She wondered what on earth had happened to Lucy's shirt.

SEVEN

WE

Sometime during the holiday break, in the brutal, icy headlock of midwinter, Lucy Vale and her mother went to the police to report that Lucy had been sexually assaulted at a swim team party on New Year's Eve.

Slowly the whispers curdled into terrible, poisonous accusations. Noah Landry had done things to Lucy Vale when she was passed out. JJ Hammill and Ryan Hawthorne had watched.

There was a video.

Lucy Vale was devastated.

Lucy Vale was lying.

Noah Landry was off the swim team. Noah Landry was going to jail.

Lucy Vale wanted revenge because Noah had dumped her in October.

Noah Landry wanted revenge because of the photos from Lucy's old school.

It took days for the rumors to compound with any certainty. For a while we lived with shudders of suspicion, hoping desperately that there had been some mistake—that Lucy Vale would come back to school, sheepish but smiling, ready to admit that she'd punked us. But after

Kyle Hannigan saw Sheriff Connelly and Lieutenant Steeler talking with Principal Hammill and Noah's parents outside Administration, we knew.

Something had broken. Something had gone terribly wrong.

A national cold front dropped temperatures to below zero. The wind was as sharp as a razor. The sun was almost macabre, grinning in a frigid sky. We felt as if we were sleepwalking through an alternate reality, as if the worst imaginings of the internet had come to life around us.

We couldn't bear to see what people were saying on the internet. We jumped whenever we got a new alert on Discord. All the news was bad—a darkening, a thickening of signs, all pointing to disaster.

> **@gustagusta:** the sheriff was at Noah Landry's house last night
> **@gustagusta:** My mom saw the car on her way back from the grocery store
> **@badprincess:** did you guys notice that the Strut Girls aren't following Lucy on TikTok anymore?
> **@meeksmaster:** the Sharks' Facebook page is a blood bath
> **@meeksmaster:** you should see some of these comments
> **@nononycky:** the Sharks have a Facebook page? lol
> **@meeksmaster:** it's not funny
> **@meeksmaster:** these people are unstable
> **@meeksmaster:** they should all be rounded up and shot
> **@hannahbanana:** this is like Jalliscoe's wet dream
> **@brentmann:** do we know for sure Lucy has no ties to Jalliscoe?
> **@badprincess:** you really think she's making everything up??
> **@brentmann:** that's what Bailey thinks. And Bailey's her best friend
> **@ktcakes888:** * was * her best friend
> **@spinn_doctor:** I told you that Lucy Vale wasn't as innocent as you guys thought
> **@nononycky:** you told us that the Vales were con artists from Canada

> **@spinn_doctor:** close enough

We didn't know what Lucy Vale was doing or thinking during that time. We didn't know whether or not she intended to come back to school. Nick Topornycky tried to wheedle information from Ceecee, Lieutenant Steeler's wife and our front office mole, and reported uncharacteristic pushback and a completely novel commitment to following Administrative protocol.

> **@nononycky:** she practically bit my head off
> **@gustagusta:** nah. that would have involved standing up

Akash reported movement in the Vales' house and lights burning in the windows. But other than that, the place might have been abandoned. There was no movement in or out. The Toyota hybrid and Lucy Vale's used Honda Civic remained immobile in the garage. Lucy Vale's bike stayed on the front porch. When it snowed, the front walk went uncleared. Although Akash did report seeing footprints around the house, as if someone had been circling late at night. The trash bins never even made it down the driveway on collection day.

We debated texting Lucy. But we couldn't. We all felt too awkward. By then we carried around the contaminant of guilt; from our server had seeped the old rumors about *Loosey Lucy*. Not a nice girl at all. Not trustworthy. A loose cannon. Prone to picking fights, starting shit, getting into trouble. Troubled.

Of course, we all felt at least partially responsible, although none of us said so, not out loud. Earlier that fall, as rumors about Lucy's connection to the Faraday case had continued to fester, breeding gaseous suspicion that soured our moods, we'd turned on Lucy Vale.

She had rejected us. She'd leveraged our friendships, our welcomes, to stratospheric heights of popularity. She'd humiliated Akash at the Winters Dance. She'd claimed for months that she had no interest in dating, and especially no interest in dating a swimmer. She'd pretended not to have entered the Balladeers' Auction, then brilliantly manipulated the draw to her benefit. She'd refused to contribute to our podcast.

Slowly our resentments had stirred into whispers, creeping insinuations about Lucy and her mom.

Our fixation with Lucy had taken a darker turn, turning petty and vindictive. We'd snarked about Lucy in private. We'd floated insinuations about her in text threads and DMs. Lucy Vale had still been a Strut Girl, immune from direct attack, protected by the buffering force of Bailey Lawrence's popularity. But within our Discord, we'd seethed. We were like a body suddenly inflamed with allergy; the Vales' presence was an irritant, a foreign object. Dangerous.

We'd criticized what Lucy wore to school. We'd trolled her performances with the dance team—Lucy nearly always fumbled her moves—and reported on every awkward hallway interaction between Lucy and Noah Landry. When we heard that the threatening letters had tailed Lucy back to school, found their way into her locker, we'd been unpitying. Instead we'd ridiculed her for complaining to Administration—a sign of weakness and, in our opinion, hypocrisy.

> **@highasakyle:** funny that Lucy's crying to admin now about bullying
> **@highasakyle:** she and her mom weren't so hype on making friends when they spent all summer protesting the Steeler pavilion
> **@spinn_doctor:** what do you expect from democrats?
> **@spinn_doctor:** they're always changing their position

Whereas over the summer we'd hunted for proof that would discredit our online attackers, now we tried to prove a connection between the Vales and the Faradays, tried to find evidence that the Vales might be profiting from the media around the case.

The more we leaned in to an ugly picture of the Vales and their intentions, the more Lucy's reputation was colored with stories about why she'd left her old school and muddied with rumors about her family's connection to the Swifts and the Faradays, the more Noah Landry sharpened in contrast into a figure of almost biblical perfection, we forgot our temporary misgivings about Casino Night, dismissed the memory of Noah's voice rapping out across the parking lot as he seized Lucy. The impression of Lucy, huddled pitifully at his feet, evaporated.

Only Akash still insisted that Noah Landry was, in fact, a fraud.

> **@kash_money:** he's a predator
> **@kash_money:** he only went out with Lucy because he made a bet with Nye just before the Winters
> **@kash_money:** it's all about the win with him
> **@geminirising:** who told you that? Lucy?
> **@kash_money:** Savannah Savage
> **@hannahbanana:** I still can't believe she follows you
> **@geminirising:** okay, but Savannah probably heard it from Lucy
> **@spinn_doctor:** say it with me, people
> **@spinn_doctor:** CHECK YOUR SOURCES
> **@spinn_doctor:** sounds like more #liesbyLucy
> **@brentmann:** what do you expect her to say? She just got dumped
> **@kash_money:** first of all, please don't ever use that hashtag again @spinn_doctor
> **@kash_money:** second of all, Noah didn't dump Lucy. She dumped him
> **@spinn_doctor:** see above re: #liesbyLucy
> **@kash_money:** what happened to #believeallwomen?
> **@spinn_doctor:** rationality?

We didn't want to side with Alex Spinnaker sheerly on principle, and definitely not in public. His hashtags were dumb. But we couldn't argue that he was right about Lucy.

Lucy Vale was not on our side.

But we couldn't imagine what had compelled Lucy Vale to go to the police. It felt to us like a dramatic miscalculation—an attempt to regain some degree of power over Noah Landry that had badly backfired. It was impossible to believe that Noah Landry, our Noah Landry, was responsible for hurting Lucy. The accusations were outlandish, almost cliché, direct parrots of the rumors our swimmers had been dodging ever since Nina Faraday had vanished. If something had happened to Lucy Vale on New Year's Eve, we felt sure it was a mistake. A misunderstanding.

After all, we were all there. We were all jostling around the beer pong setup in the basement, or refilling SOLO cups in the kitchen, or packing bowls and smoking cigarettes on the back porch.

If something had happened to Lucy Vale—something bad, something *wrong*—then surely, surely, we would have known. We would have felt it. We would have heard something. We would have seen a disruption at the party, a sudden thrust of people, a clamor to help out.

We were not bad people.

We would never, ever simply stand by if a girl were getting raped.

EIGHT

We

In the aftermath of Ryan Hawthorne's party, we suffocated. Every day was dulled by the dread of something terrible arriving. Information came in gasps. Whispers about the new sheriff covertly investigating. Rumors that Ryan Hawthorne had been placed on suicide watch. Reports that Noah Landry had been called to the sheriff's department twice.

Our parents spoke in whispers about the *poor boys' families*. The Landrys went to church. The Hawthornes hired a lawyer. JJ Hammill and Bailey Lawrence came to school holding hands.

Bailey Lawrence and Savannah Savage blocked all of Lucy Vale's socials.

For days the gates of 88 Lily Lane stayed closed. Again Akash reported seeing phantom footprints in the light dusting of snow outside the house and lights on in the upstairs windows. But no one answered when Mrs. Sandhu finally insisted on walking over to check on their neighbors. The second time she attempted, ever the gates were locked.

Someone had taken a marker to Lucy's mailbox. Mrs. Sandhu wasn't sure that the Vales had noticed; junk mail was overflowing in the snow. So she directed Akash to go out there with bleach and a toothbrush.

He almost lost a finger to frostbite, he told us, just trying to scrub off the first *whore*.

Lucy did, eventually, try and come back to school. That was in the early days of January, before the Investigative Committee announced its involvement—when the rumors about Lucy Vale's report were still nebulous and the details unclear.

Sofia Young was the first person to see her. Sofia was late to school that day, as she often was junior year. She'd started smoking weed behind the athletics complex before school with some of the senior stoners. Her new crowd.

We were surprised to see her back on Discord. She'd dropped off the server again right after Casino Night, soon after she first started hooking up with Harry Oakes, who sold pills to half the upperclassmen. But suddenly she was back, with no apology and no explanation for why she'd logged off. Nothing.

Still, we forgave her right away when she told us that she'd just run into Lucy Vale at her locker.

@goodnightsky: so awkward
@goodnightsky: what was I supposed to say?
@badprincess: oh my god. Did she try and TALK to you??
@goodnightsky: no tfg
@goodnightsky: she didn't even look at me
@lululemonaide: how does she look??
@goodnightsky: she cut her hair
@goodnightsky: other than that, normal
@ktcakes888: what is she thinking??
@gustagusta: you gotta give it to her
@gustagusta: she's got some balls
@badprincess: that's sexist
@gustagusta: save it for the Investigative Committee

All week Lucy Vale moved through the halls on a tailwind of whispers. The athletes fired verbal bullets at her through clenched teeth. *Whore. Liar.* It was as if the rumors calcified around her, took solid form, persuading us by her presence: Lucy Vale had accused Noah Landry, our star swimmer, one of the nicest guys in school, of doing terrible, unthinkable things. She'd made accusations against JJ Hammill, her best friend's boyfriend. She'd roped Ryan Hawthorne into it.

She was trying to get them in trouble. She was trying to get them expelled.

Lucy Vale had an agenda.

Day by day, graffiti thickened on her locker. We were too afraid to talk to her, to ask her what she was doing, to ask why, to beg her to tell us it had all been a mistake. Talking to Lucy Vale, acknowledging her in any way, was social suicide. The Strut Girls stared her down in the halls. At lunch they piled their belongings on the cafeteria chair that had once been hers, a clear signal that there was no space left at the table. We heard that Noah Landry had been warned to avoid her at all costs. We heard that he'd asked Coach Radner to bring his lunch down to Aquatics, where he and the other Sharks took refuge during their free periods. They needn't have bothered. We never saw Lucy between periods. We heard that she'd started hiding out in the nurse's office or the library to eat her lunch.

We couldn't have talked to Lucy even if we'd wanted to. But we didn't.

We'd welcomed her to Woodward. We'd nominated her to the homecoming court. We'd made her a Minnow, one of the most desirable girls at Woodward. We'd believed that Lucy Vale had deserved it all. We hadn't even been jealous when she'd started dating the most popular guy in school.

And all along, Lucy Vale was pretending to be something and someone she was not.

To us, that was the same as lying.

By then, we had agreed: we couldn't trust a word Lucy said.

NINE

RACHEL

Rachel had dreaded going to the police. Early on in her career, she'd covered a sexual abuse scandal at a tony private school in a small town, and she knew all too well the way these stories played out—the way that small systems under threat united in defense, the victim-shaming, the victim-blaming. Lucy had been drunk. At times she'd blacked out. Her memory of the evening was spotty. She'd been assaulted by an ex-boyfriend who subsequently drove her home, seemingly with Lucy's consent.

Even Lucy seemed confused, uncertain about what had happened. On the morning after the party, Rachel had watched the clock crawl past eleven o'clock and then past noon. Finally she'd taken pity on her daughter for what she'd assumed was a hangover. She'd mounted the stairs to the attic with orange juice and a Tylenol and found Lucy curled in the fetal position, staring at the wall, shivering despite the space heater.

"Lucy?" Rachel took a seat on her daughter's bed. "Lucy? Are you feeling okay?"

For a second Lucy just lay there, trembling as if her body were trying to physically shake loose her words. Finally she said in a voice that barely scraped above a whisper, "I think—I think something happened last night."

Instantly Rachel felt pricks in her spine like a touch of electricity. "What do you mean, something happened?"

"I mean with Noah." Lucy's voice was barely audible. Rachel had to lean closer just to hear her. "I think . . ."

"You think what? What happened with Noah?"

Lucy reluctantly turned to look at her. Her eyes brightened with tears. "I think . . . I think he raped me."

Raped. An unfathomable word, like a scalpel that cleaved the breath from Rachel's body.

Rachel knew the police would never believe Lucy's story. Even Lucy's *friends* didn't believe her story. In the days that followed the party, Rachel had taken Lucy's phone away as Lucy's notifications turned cruel, thickening like dark snow across her accounts. Bailey, Savannah, and Mia weren't speaking to her. One day, as if by silent agreement, they all unfollowed her at once.

Lucy seized hold of the idea that the police would hear her truth, that the police would make things right. That they *had* to. She was terrified that JJ Hammill had filmed the entire event, that this, too, would end up online, forever memorializing her horrific night. Lucy swore that JJ Hammill had been holding up a phone at one point, that she'd heard him tell Noah that he needed a better angle.

Rachel didn't know what to believe. If there was a video, at least it might corroborate Lucy's story. It might help them hold Noah Landry, the county's golden boy, to account.

But she doubted it. She doubted anyone would look in the first place.

Still, what could she do? How could she explain to her daughter, still sixteen and inflamed with ideals about right and wrong, that not all victims were victims in the same way? That people would say that Lucy had compromised her right to be taken seriously, first by drinking too much, by dressing the way she had, then by going into a closed bedroom with Ryan Hawthorne, and finally by accepting a ride home from Noah? She couldn't. Lucy, already paranoid, barely functional, had latched on to the idea that she would prove that she was telling the truth. That Noah might be punished and Lucy redeemed. Rachel didn't dare shatter that slender hope.

So she promised Lucy that they would hold all the boys responsible. Doubly so if they'd been the ones to circulate Lucy's old pictures.

But deep down, Rachel didn't actually believe it could happen.

Still, she took Lucy to the county sheriff's department to make her report. She hoped, at least, that they could speak to Sheriff Horne, still the only woman, other than a dispatcher, in the office. Instead they were directed to the sergeant who'd shoved past Rachel over the summer to announce that a body had been discovered along the river. Will Erickson was his name. In the intervening months, he seemed to have grown in both height and arrogance—but Rachel wondered whether this was simply a trick of perspective, the way he seemed to expand to fill the interview room while Lucy shrank further and further into her clothing.

Rachel sat beside her daughter, gripping her hands tightly in her lap, letting all the usual questions fall on her Lucy like blows from a fist.

How much did you have to drink that night?

Do you remember saying no to your boyfriend? Sorry, to your ex-boyfriend?

Were you already in the bed when Noah arrived?

Do you think maybe he might have had the wrong impression?

Was this your first time being sexually active with your boyfriend?

Sorry. Ex-boyfriend.

Rachel wanted to stop it somehow. She wanted to scream. But it was as if she were paralyzed, frozen inside that room with her daughter, watching every question chip away at some facet of her story, whittle it all down to nothing.

They would speak to Noah Landry and the other boys who'd been there, Sergeant Erickson told her. But it would likely come down to a classic case of he said, she said.

At least, Rachel thought, Erickson sounded apologetic.

After the interview, Rachel waited while Lucy lingered in the restroom, dousing her face and hands in ice-cold water—a calming trick her old therapist had encouraged for when Lucy was in danger of dissociating. The interview had ended with Lucy in tears, practically hysterical, demanding to know why the police were treating her as if *she'd* done something wrong.

He raped me, Lucy had choked out. *I don't care what he says. I don't care what you think. He raped me, and his friends stood there and watched.*

Coming out of the interview room, Rachel and Lucy had passed by a whiteboard hung with grainy photographs of Nina and Lydia Faraday. Rachel could hardly stand to look at them. For a second, she'd imagined Lucy's image hanging next to theirs—her daughter reduced to a handful of pixels, shrunk down forever inside the worst thing that had ever happened to her.

She'd imagined Lydia Faraday's voice like the whisper of paper in the wind.

I told you so.

For the first time since moving to Indiana, she dreaded going back to that house.

~

Rachel began to have dreams that she was hurting Noah Landry. In one she was elbow-deep in his entrails, which were made of metal ducts and insulation like the walls of a house. In another she was bludgeoning him with a shovel in the middle of a construction site she recognized, even in the dream, as lifted from photos of the first expansion of the Aquatics Center. She kept swinging and swinging, and Noah's head kept getting smaller, shrinking to the size of a fly until he was a fly and he buzzed off, and she turned to see an animal carcass baking in the sun.

She called Lucy's old therapist and left a message. Lucy started sleeping in Rachel's bed again. She began complaining about phantom symptoms—stomach aches, vision problems, numbness in her hands and feet. She begged to stay home from school.

Rachel didn't argue. She felt helpless, even ashamed. She was sure that this was somehow her fault. She hadn't protected Lucy in Michigan; now again, here in Indiana, she had failed to keep her safe. Once might be an accident. But twice was a pattern. Twice was negligence.

She was haunted anew by what her mother had told her after discovering Rachel was pregnant. *You can't take care of a child. You can barely take care of yourself.*

Maybe her mother had been right all along. Rachel was too selfish, too career-focused, and her life was too unstable. She'd never even been married.

She called Alan from the parking lot of the local Kroger, practically hyperventilating after spotting Noah Landry's mom in the produce aisle. Rachel had turned around and walked out—abandoning her cart already half-full of food she was hoping to tempt Lucy to eat—to keep from walking right up to the bitch and punching her.

Alan sounded worried. His girlfriend was in the car; Rachel heard her kids in the background. He pulled the phone from his ear to conference with her briefly. Then he was back, volunteering to come down to Indiana for a night or two.

"I just have to be back by Wednesday," he said. "Katie has knee surgery."

Katie. The way Alan said her name cracked Rachel's heart all over again. She imagined the girlfriend, whom she'd seen only once and from a distance, graciously giving Alan consent. Permitting him a short pit stop back in his old life, a quick tour of the damage he'd left behind. Lucy had once twirled her fingers in Alan's beard and called him Daddy

Al. Rachel had inched her fingers over his back, examining his moles one by one for signs of melanoma.

And now he could slide in and out of her life like a parenthetical remark. For the first time in a long while, Rachel realized she was about to lose it. Not just cry but lose it—scream, curse at him, drive her car into a lamppost, something.

"Don't worry about it," she heard herself say. "We're fine."

"Are you sure? I'd really like to see Lucy—"

"I said we're fine." Rachel was shouting without intending to. "Lucy doesn't want to see you. She hates you, remember?"

Immediately she regretted it. She couldn't breathe. She was sweating in her car while outside a winter darkness fell on the afternoon like judgment.

There was a long sluice of silence.

"Call me anytime, Rachel," Alan said. He sounded sad. She hung up.

Once upon a time, he'd called her Rach.

∼

She was afraid to leave Lucy alone for too long. Only when Lucy slept—at intermittent hours, usually during the day—did Rachel venture into the gasping cold with the sense she was breaking free of prison. Those January days seemed always blanketed by darkness. The weak winter sun barely touched the house before it was already wheeling away to the west. In the soupy, elastic weeks since Lucy had first made her report, Rachel found herself pulled again and again toward the same behaviors: driving to the sheriff's department in the four o'clock darkness, demanding answers that didn't come, actions that she knew on some level would never materialize.

Every time, she greeted the pictures of Nina and Lydia Faraday—still hanging on the bullpen whiteboard as if to advertise new commitment to the case—with gathering dread and even resentment. She remembered what she'd read about Lydia after her daughter's disappearance, how she'd made herself a nuisance on the one hand and turned reclusive on the other. How she'd been arrested for erratic driving. How she'd started drinking too much. Once she'd set up camp outside the sheriff's office, with a tent and everything, until she was booked on charges of public nuisance.

Rachel hated that she could understand, even a little, what Lydia must have been thinking. Sometimes in the middle of the night—sleepless, tormented by guilt and anger and a desperate desire to claw her way back to the night of the party, to undo it—she even imagined that somehow the Faraday House was responsible, was *complicit*. Maybe the curse was real. Maybe by returning there, she and Lucy had somehow become infected.

By now Rachel thought she detected the same pity—or was it contempt?—from a rotation of new recruits who blockaded the front desk, all of them with blandly generic names and interchangeable faces. There was a Smith. There was a White.

"Let me see if they're available." This time it was Smith who greeted her. She didn't wait for him to return with the news that Horne was out on patrol or Erickson was on a phone call. Instead she ducked around the desk and tailed him into the squad room.

Catching sight of her reflection in the big windows, she felt alarmed. Her hair was crazy, a mess of static beneath her beanie. She couldn't remember if she'd showered. All morning she had scoured social media, screenshotting comments about her daughter.

Rachel thought she might be losing her mind.

Erickson was at his desk. When he spotted Rachel, he stood and ducked into Sheriff Horne's office without saying a word. Seconds later, Sheriff Horne emerged.

"Ms. Vale." Sheriff Horne's tone was unreadable. "What can I do for you?"

"You can help my daughter," Rachel said. She was aware of the room's quiet, the muted whisper of papers turning at the few occupied desks, the shush of feet against the carpet. But there was no point in keeping her voice down. Everybody knew. She imagined everyone in the county knew by now. "You can tell me what you're doing about Noah Landry and his friends."

She thought she saw Sheriff Horne grimace. "Why don't you have a seat in my office?" Horne said, reaching out a hand as if to shepherd Rachel through the door.

Rachel pulled away. "I don't want to have a seat," she said. On some level she knew she was being childish. She understood that the sheriff's department could do little if the county prosecutor had decided there was no case. She knew all this. And yet she also knew that her daughter's world was upside down and she needed help righting it. "I want Noah arrested."

Sheriff Horne managed to draw Rachel into an adjoining office that seemingly doubled as overflow for old files and evidence boxes. She closed the door. Rachel felt a little like a child about to be cautioned by the principal.

"Noah claims that what happened that night was consensual," Sheriff Horne said in a low voice. "His friends are supporting his version of events."

"His friends watched him sexually assault my daughter," Rachel said. It was hot inside the police station. She had the oddest sense that she was in a theater, playing a role that had been scripted for her some time earlier. "They should be arrested too."

"I understand how you feel," she said, and Rachel almost said, *Do you?* "We've spoken to the Administration; everyone is taking these allegations seriously. But this is a process. Our investigation is ongoing."

"Ongoing," Rachel repeated. "Like your investigation into Nina Faraday's disappearance? That's been *ongoing* for seventeen years." She gestured to a box in the corner labeled **FARADAY**.

Sheriff Horne didn't like that. "I can't speak to what happened before my time," she said stiffly. "All I can do is try to move forward."

"But we're not moving forward, are we?" Rachel said. "Noah Landry won't be punished. He's too important to the swim team. Just like Tommy Swift."

Sheriff Horne looked at her sharply. "Tommy Swift was cleared as a suspect," was her only response. "There's no indication that he saw Nina again after fourth period when they shared a classroom. In fact, there's plenty of evidence that he *didn't*." Rachel thought back to the walks she'd taken with Tommy's mother and the time they'd sat in Tommy's living room looking at photographs from his childhood. Tommy would have done anything for Nina, she'd said. If she'd asked him, he would have stopped swimming. He would have gotten a job. They could have gotten married. It occurred to Rachel that it was a funny thing to say. Why, she wondered, would Nina have wanted Tommy to quit swimming?

Rachel stood up. She felt unsteady on her feet. It was too hot in the room; there must be some problem with the radiator.

"If you're not going to help us, or you can't, just say so," she said.

Sheriff Horne leaned back. She looked at Rachel as if she were a stubborn child, as if she were the one being unreasonable.

"Things happen at parties," she said. "Kids make bad decisions, especially when alcohol is involved."

There it was: not the truth exactly but the new story. The party line. Lucy had been drunk; Noah's friends had been drinking too. Something unfortunate happened. Mistakes had been made.

The best thing to do, the easiest thing, was to forget and move on.

A small tremor worked through Rachel's body. She wondered if Sheriff Horne could see it.

"I see." She was surprised to hear that her voice was steady, almost calm. Then she added, "I think your phone is ringing."

Horne stood up, obviously relieved for the excuse to leave the room. Rachel hung back for just a second, slowly shunting on her big winter coat—Alan's initially, discovered in a plastic bin only after she and Lucy made the move to Indiana.

Stories were powerful things. She had been telling stories all her life. Supposedly she had been reporting facts. But facts on their own had no value. Facts happened. But truth meant something. And in the end, it came down to whoever could tell the best—or the loudest—story.

Noah Landry had a story. But Rachel had one, too, and so did Lucy.

In the half second that she was alone, she reached into the box labeled with Nina Faraday's name, removed the evidence binder, and slipped it under her coat.

TEN

We

The weeks of the school's investigation into the party at Ryan Hawthorne's house was, we imagined, a little like living under occupied rule. Nebulously we understood that the Investigative Committee was related to the sheriff's ongoing investigation but independent. But to us the committee was everything—imbued with authority we didn't understand, empowered to interrogate, to interrupt, to demand evidence, to disrupt our class schedules. An external investigator was appointed by the school board, a man named Jerry Marbles who had once played quarterback for our football team. We sensed an Administrative gambit in the selection of a former football player; the football team had long been the neglected little cousin of the swim team and, back in the early 2000s, had even been forced to cede its mascot to Sean the Shark. The message was clear. Jerry Marbles would be neutral, a fair evaluator. He would have no special affinity for the swimmers.

Mrs. Steeler-Cox was the only woman appointed.

The Investigative Committee convened daily for two weeks in the media room just off the SLD Tutoring Center. Even when we saw no proof of their activity, we could feel their foreign influence. It was in the muted quiet of the halls between classes as we shuffled fearfully past one another under the watchful stares of the hallway monitors, whom we were sure had gone turncoat. It was in the uneasy sensation of being watched and the paranoia that made us spin around in empty hallways and clam up in crowded ones. It was in closed doors and open ones. It was in Principal Hammill's disapproving squint and the fact that Ceecee in the front office no longer had a candy bowl on her desk or smiled and called out when we passed by Administration.

It was in the seat, mounded with jackets and backpacks, that Lucy Vale had once occupied at the Strut Girls' lunch table. It was in the way the Strut Girls closed ranks, moving in a tight huddle, often gripping hands as if they were facing an invisible menace. It was in Lucy's locker, now defaced with graffiti.

Periodically, turning the corner to grab a soda from the cafeteria or a book from our locker, we were startled by a vision of a sheriff's deputy lingering outside the front office, or of Ryan Hawthorne somberly pulling on his winter jacket as if layering up for an outdoor funeral. We came to dread the announcements that spiked our days with adrenal shots of anxiety. *Savannah Savage, please report to the front office. Jeremiah Greene, please report to the vice principal. Nick Topornycky, please come to the front office after your next class.* The sound of the intercom cracking to life puddled our stomachs with dread. We grew to despise the sound of reverb.

Bailey Lawrence was called to give her account. Lucy was upset, she said, because some old photos of her had spread around the school. She and Noah had been fighting about it. It was one of the reasons they'd broken up. It was Lucy's idea to go to Ryan's party. Lucy was embarrassed and angry.

She wasn't going to just stay home and cry about it.

Savannah Savage reported that the morning after the party, Lucy Vale had seemed confused about what had happened the night before. Uncertain. She'd said she *thought* she and Noah had done things in front of Ryan Hawthorne and JJ Hammill. She *thought* that she'd been raped. Maybe.

Noah Landry said Lucy had called him three times in a row from the party. He was worried about how drunk she'd sounded. His friends had texted him to come get her.

Lucy Vale had wanted to get back together, he said. It was her idea to hook up that night. It was her idea to go all the way.

He denied that JJ Hammill or Ryan Hawthorne had been in the room.

Ryan Hawthorne and JJ Hammill denied that there was a video.

Still, they were all suspended from competition until further notice.

The news was as good as nuclear. It exploded our lives right before championship season. Our hopes of another state trophy vanished in a mushroom cloud of Administrative interference.

Right away we spoke of protests, of organizing a picket line, a sit-in, or possibly a hunger strike. We wondered if the Investigative Committee had violated any fundamental rights. We dangled the possibility of suing.

@stopandfriske: this is bullshit
@stopandfriske: what happened to innocent until proven guilty?
@spinn_doctor: the woke mob
@lululemonaide: do you have to make everything political?
@lululemonaide: this is about money
@lululemonaide: admin is just afraid of losing booster money
@spinn_doctor: you think money isn't political?

We tried to distract ourselves, but it was no use. During January, the gravitational pull of Lucy versus the swim team was so heavy, it warped every conversational thread, every piece of gossip, somehow back to the same place.

@stopandfriske: have you guys talked to Hannah Smith?
@badprincess: which Hannah Smith?

@stopandfriske: the one who got called into Committee this morning
@badprincess: that doesn't help
@hannahbanana: we both got called
@hannahbanana: we both showed up, anyway
@geminirising: what did they ask you??
@hannahbanana: they wanted to know about the pictures
@hannahbanana: they wanted to know where they came from
@badprincess: please tell me you lied
@stopandfriske: That's it?? They didn't ask about the party?
@hannahbanana: they did. They asked me if I knew that Lucy Vale was drinking
@badprincess: lol

Even time seemed to deform, pulling us backward into the past, into the slow horror of sheriff's deputies materializing in the Woodward hallways, squinting when we passed as if they suspected us of something. We lived in terror that the press would get wind of the story: another girl and her mother with another claim about the swim team.

Another championship season lost.

We all suffered. We felt our suffering keenly; we googled articles about collective trauma and confirmed that we all shared symptoms of PTSD. Administration was traumatizing us. Our parents' questions, their insensitivities, their insistence that we do our homework and stop obsessing over school gossip, was a form of gaslighting. We felt minimized and marginalized, both victims of and incidental to the drama. Evie Grant confessed that she'd doubled up on her antianxiety medication and was now running low. Allan Meeks kept having dreams that he'd been called to the SLD Tutoring Center to report to the Investigative Committee but couldn't find his way there. Will Friske started smoking weed daily before school just to get through the day. But the idea that he might encounter the sheriff on campus made him panicky, which meant he needed more weed and couldn't focus on any of his classes.

His parents were threatening him with therapy, or rehab.

Aubrey Barnes said she would pray for him at church. Friske told her to go to hell, then apologized. Evie Grant asked Will Friske if he could get her more antianxiety medication.

Our anger deepened, gathering force, buoyed by Noah's insistence that everything that happened at the party was Lucy's idea. Of course we couldn't know what had happened behind the locked door of that first-floor bedroom. And we believed in accountability. We were champions of transparency. We demanded it—from our brands, from our churches, from our teachers, about their politics and their grading system. We were feminists. Well, most of us were. Brent Mann was a sexist. Alex Spinnaker was a conspiracy theorist and a proud Libertarian.

But this was different. It was personal. It was about *us*. The swim team was ours. Noah Landry was ours. We knew him. We'd fished tadpoles with him from the murky shallows of Byron Lake in elementary school. We'd jostled next to him at the Fourth of July parade for a better view of the floats. We'd sung in youth choir with him, yawned next to him in church.

We'd known Lucy Vale for barely a year and a half.

And as it turned out, we hadn't known her at all.

Still, the summons kept coming. *Ethan Courtland. Alex Spinnaker. Evie Grant. Akash Sandhu.*

Please report to the front office.

Please report.

Report, report, report.

One by one, we waited to be called.

ELEVEN

We

We didn't know which of us was idiotic enough to mention our server to the Investigative Committee, only that soon afterward the Student Leadership Department began an email campaign about Discord's perverting effects on young minds.

When Mrs. Steeler-Cox's first letter to our parents was posted on the student portal, our stomachs curdled. We had the disconcerting sense of hovering above our laptop screens. It was like one of those dreams where we were naked at a pep rally, or like coming home to find one of our parents rooting in our drawers where we stashed weed and Adderall or kept condoms in the hopes that they might someday be necessary. We felt exposed. Violated. Helpless.

Right away we went on a hunt for the traitor.

@stopandfriske: who told Steeler-Cox about Discord??
@pawsandclaws: maybe she just knows about it from Reese?
@nononycky: afraid not.
@nononycky: the Investigative Committee asked me about our server
@nononycky: They warned me the sheriff's department might want access

@badprincess: TO OUR SERVER?????
@gustagusta: you're fucking joking
@meeksmaster: we've got 54 subs right now
@meeksmaster: can we be sure we don't have an administrative mole?
@badprincess: no way
@badprincess: @ktcakes888 is tracking usernames
@badprincess: right??? @ktcakes888
@ktcakes888: um, I think so
@badprincess: what do you mean, you think so??
@meeksmaster: do we know everyone on this server, or not?
@spinn_doctor: I told you we needed a double-verification system
@ktcakes888: I mean I'm pretty sure I know everyone
@meeksmaster: who is @flywheels12? Who is @lululemonaide?
@lululemonaide: um, hello? I've had this username since seventh grade
@spinn_doctor: but who are you??
@lululemonaide: Layla
@spinn_doctor: can you prove it??
@badprincess: this is stupid
@meeksmaster: seriously, who is @flywheels12?? They're lurking

We panicked. We sensed disaster—or, at minimum, a lifetime of detentions.

@spinn_doctor: we've got to delete
@ktcakes888: delete our server????
@badprincess: OVER MY DEAD BODY
@spinn_doctor: it will be, if admin gets access
@spinn_doctor: ** message deleted by user **
@nononycky: what?
@spinn_doctor: nothing
@nononycky: you just deleted a message

@spinn_doctor: what message?
@nononycky: the one you just deleted, you cockwipe
@spinn_doctor: I have no idea what you're talking about
@spinn_doctor: see how that works?

Later it turned out that our Discord was not, in fact, the impetus for the Student Leadership Department's sudden hysteria, which roiled our parents into long-winded and nonsensical speeches about group think, online predation, and the benefits of exercising outdoors. Apparently someone had alerted the Investigative Committee to a private server, the one putatively launched by Ryan Hawthorne's older stepbrother, the one where Woodward girls were ranked according to their hotness and willingness to give blow jobs.

But it didn't matter. The next few days saw an exodus of subs from our Discord. Coraline Winters had been one of the last to join; now she was one of the first to leave. We didn't fully blame her. Coraline had been selling forged permission slips, doctors' notes, and even midterm teachers' reports. After initially deleting almost her entire archive of exchanges, she sent a final cryptic message:

@winteriscoming: I was never here. And I'm not Coraline Winters.

Then she went dark.

The rest of us erased as much as we could. When deleting wasn't sufficient, we attempted revisionist history. Will Friske made a last-ditch attempt to redeem the validity of his cousin's landscaping business just in case our server fell into the hands of the cops or, God forbid, a DEA agent.

@stopandfriske: if anyone needs help this spring/summer
@stopandfriske: please consider Friske Landscaping
@stopandfriske: for edging, planting, clean-up, tree removal, etc.

@brentmann: how about WEEDing? Does your cousin do any WEEDing?
@stopandfriske: not sure what you mean
@stopandfriske: it's a super legitimate business
@stopandfriske: five stars on Yelp

We sifted through avalanches of conversation and gutted whole threads. Thousands of messages selling homework. Hundreds of messages about being stoned. Pleas for Nick Topornycky's older brother to get us more Adderall.

Obsessive threads about Lucy Vale, dating from before she'd even moved to Indiana. Speculation about Lucy and her mother. About Lucy and Noah Landry. Blurry photos of the two of them together.

@kash_money: does anyone think it's weird that Noah texts Lucy like every five seconds?
@stopandfriske: did you guys see the video of Landry talking about the dress code?

Delete.

Sideways snapshots of Lucy Vale chewing on a pen cap in homeroom. Points awarded for intel about the new girl.

@mememeup: ten points for an Instagram photo older than six months
@nononycky: twenty for a secret Instagram account. Hers is sus

Delete.

Spinnaker was adamant. Everything about Lucy had to go. Otherwise we would be accused of fixation. Harassment. We might even get roped into an investigation about the threats Lucy and her mom had been receiving for months.

We would lose our chances of going to college. Worse, we might lose our driver's licenses.

@pawsandclaws: Lucy said that Alec Nye rigged the raffle at the Winters
@pawsandclaws: she says the whole team knew about it, even Landry

Delete.
We knew nothing. We'd seen nothing. We'd tell nothing.
Otherwise we were fucked.
After all, we were the ones who'd found Lucy Vale's old photos and leaked them to the swim team.

TWELVE

Rachel

*A*t first everyone agreed that Nina Faraday was a good girl. Later they began to have doubts.
It's possible that Nina Faraday was cheating on her boyfriend. She may have used drugs. Or not. Memories are fickle, colored by the interpretations we assign them in any given present. And points of view are just that: points. Individual components of a puzzle that mistake themselves too often for the whole.

From the beginning, the investigation into Nina Faraday's disappearance centered on a single question: What kind of girl was she really? Was she the kind who was likely to run away, to get in trouble, to pull off a stunt for attention?

Was she the kind of girl worth worrying about?

See, we often assume that the crime makes the victim. But causality is slippery, and often it's the other way around. A good victim makes for a good crime, or at least an obvious one. But a bad victim, an unsympathetic victim, a victim who isn't credible?

Well, with the wrong kind of victim, it's hard to know whether a crime was committed at all.

So for now let's forget about issues of identity. For now let's stick to the facts.

For now let's go back to that March morning eighteen years ago, in the southwest corner of Indiana where a seventeen-year-old Nina Faraday is running late for school. It's a Tuesday, only a few weeks before spring break. Woodward High School is in the middle of a $20 million renovation to the pool facilities, all thanks to one of the most generous booster funds in the state. Club team swimmer Tommy Swift has recently broken his third national record.

Possibly he has just broken Nina Faraday's heart for the last time.

Just before 8:00 a.m., Nina receives a text from her best friend, Shannah Groves. She wants to know why Nina hasn't made it to homeroom. Nina responds that she accidentally slept in. She hasn't been feeling well. But she assures Shannah that she's on her way and hasn't forgotten that they have a math test first period. Shannah thinks little of it. Nina does indeed make it in time for their test. Later Shannah will insist that Nina seemed "normal."

But Nina was anything but normal that morning. We can imagine that she might well have been nauseated. We can imagine that she might have been struggling with exhaustion, with new weight gain, with a body that felt suddenly foreign.

You see, the night before her disappearance, Nina made two calls to a hotline for pregnant teenagers—information that has been sitting with the Rockland County Sheriff's Department since her phone records were subpoenaed six months after Nina vanished.

But perhaps it's understandable that this information was never revealed. Because Nina didn't only call the hotline the night before her disappearance. She also made four phone calls to a local number—the same number she dialed only an hour before she was last sighted at the high school the following day.

Likely the number she was calling was a disposable cell phone, commonly known as a burner. I came to that conclusion many years ago—around the same time as Nina's disappearance actually, when the number I'd been calling for months was abruptly disabled.

As a journalist, I'm supposed to disappear behind the facts, to leave myself out of the story. But I can't. Not this one.

You see, I know who that number belonged to.

I wonder. Is it possible that the police did too?

PART 8
We

ONE

Lucy dropped out of school right around the time the Investigative Committee concluded that the school had no further role in what happened at Ryan Hawthorne's party. There was no official confirmation that she had, in fact, withdrawn. But that's what everyone was saying. Her absences hung closer and closer together, until they beaded into a week, and then two. The surface of her locker was bleached clean until only the barest trace of graffiti remained.

The Investigative Committee, and all proof of its activity, evaporated. The loudspeakers patched into silence again, except for morning announcements and the occasional reminder to stay clear of the active construction site on the north side of Aquatics. The SLD Tutoring Center reopened its media room for student use. Slowly we saw it repopulated by the LARP crowd, acting out their fantasy worlds in relative privacy between periods.

The paranoia that had roiled us since February broke suddenly into relief, followed quickly by exhaustion.

@badprincess: after *all* that drama, nothing??
@badprincess: no explanation, no apology, we just act like nothing ever happened?
@spinn_doctor: because nothing DID happen
@ktcakes888: we don't know that for sure
@spinn_doctor: ??

@spinn_doctor: that's what the Investigative Committee decided
@badprincess: oh, so NOW you trust admin??
@spinn_doctor: so now you trust Lucy Vale?
@badprincess: I just think it's weird that the committee is just DONE
@highasakyle: I gotta be honest
@highasakyle: I'm pretty done too

Ostensibly the investigation was now entirely in the hands of the county sheriff's department. But as weeks passed with no news and no updates—as Noah Landry began making headlines again, this time for simultaneous early admission offers from Berkeley and UNC; as Lucy Vale dematerialized, withdrawn into the Faraday House like something submerged in water—so, too, did the lingering threat of charges. We understood that the investigation of Ryan Hawthorne's party had dissipated along with Lucy Vale's material presence.

Instead we heard new rumors—that Administration was quietly planning the next phase of their war on Discord; that the cops were looking into whether there were, in fact, pictures of underage girls circulating on a private server associated with our school and possibly our swim team; that Sheriff Horne was focused on bringing a conclusive end to Nina Faraday's cold case and, for the first time in eighteen years, calling up old and new witnesses, interviewing Nina's teachers, reaching out for tips, and trying definitively to establish where Nina had been before and after Woody Topornycky saw her entering Aquatics by a side door.

In the raw early months of spring, after Lucy simply slipped away from Woodward like something lapsed in our memory, the sheriff's department's dual investigations became confused. Muddled. Past and present became curiously indistinguishable, like the reflection of sky thrown up by a palm of water.

@bassicrhythm: hey @nononycky

@bassicrhythm: did Woody tell you why he got called in to talk to the sheriff?

@nononycky: because the cops are finally doing their job

@nononycky: they're taking him seriously for once

@safireswiftly: why are they talking to Woody about Ryan Hawthorne's party?

@safireswiftly: was he there??

@lululemonaide: I hear they talked to Coach Radner too

@nononycky: not about the party

@nononycky: about Nina Faraday

@nononycky: they think he was the last person to see her before she "vanished"

@safireswiftly: and they think Coach Radner knows something??

@lululemonaide: no, no

@lululemonaide: I thought we were talking about Lucy

@bassicrhythm: my cousin says they're reviewing all her old phone records, too

@safireswiftly: Lucy's, or Nina's??

@badprincess: probably both?

@bassicrhythm: Lydia Faraday's, sorry.

@badprincess: this is so confusing

Rumors sifted to us, one after the other, until all the rumors were just stories and all the stories were just comments turned over on our server, through our fingers, into tidbits of data to digest and regurgitate and recycle and forget.

We moved on. As a raw spring wind began to scrub the green from the ground, we felt the fierce grip of the events on our subconscious begin to loosen. With it, almost imperceptibly at first, came the slow unraveling of our obsession with the swim team. The state championships had come and gone. We'd felt nothing but relief when they were over; none of us had bothered to attend the meet. Without some of our best swimmers, Woodward placed third behind Willow Park and Nyack, giving our enemies something to crow about on TikTok.

We pitied our rivals for their obsessive preoccupation with a single competition. We had other things to worry about: college, and whether we would get in or could afford to go; the looming threat of the SATs, which suddenly edged into every conversation with our parents and every lecture from our teachers; whether or not we would be able to see Taylor Swift in concert. We'd grown up and gained new perspectives. It was as if the swimmers and their wins had slipped down the length of a telescope, grown increasingly distant from us.

Toward Noah Landry, our feelings turned fickle. Fitful. With no punishment on the horizon, we were stirred by currents of unease. His social media, we felt, was insensitive. His headphones were outdated. His easy smile, suspicious. We detected no signs of shame, no crippling grief, no self-flagellation or regret. Spinnaker pointed out that Noah's behavior was evidence of a clear conscience. Evie Grant floated the word *sociopath*.

Noah just kept swimming on the club team, and left all the bad feelings for us to work through.

We studied for our PSATs. We were buried under an avalanche of homework. We started having dreams about college where college was a maze and we couldn't ever find the dining hall. We put our phones on "Do Not Disturb" for hours at a time. We hunted for new Discord servers dedicated to our favorite gamers, our favorite channels, our favorite books. We were hopeful, for once, about our basketball team. We heard that freshman Theo Davis had sunk thirty points in one game. We followed him on TikTok.

In March we heard that Administration had been tipped off about a cheating ring that fed homework to the athletes for cash. Alex Spinnaker warned us not to say anything. He threatened to infiltrate our hard drives and leak our personal data if we even thought of confessing.

@spinn_doctor: no body, no crime
@spinn_doctor: remember that
@nononycky: whoever killed Nina Faraday did
@mememeup: that's not funny, man
@lululemonaide: wait—do we really think Nina Faraday is dead???
@nononycky: no, we think she went on a 17-year-long vacation

We relaxed our imaginative hold on Lucy. We let her slip away, lost inside the Faraday House, drowned somewhere out of sight. The longer she stayed away from school, the less clear our memories of her were. When we tried to get our imaginations around her, it was like plunging our hands into a stream to catch something we saw streak beneath the surface—a fish, a frog, a newt stirring in the mud. Our fingers went quickly numb. Something vital slipped through the dark places in our memories.

Even Akash stopped reporting on the lights burning in the house or the twitch of a hand at the window, cinching the curtains shut. He logged on only intermittently, usually with a question for Spinnaker and Meeks about a video game that had stymied him or an expletive about homework. He spent most of his time with his new sort-of girlfriend. He'd even moved lunch tables to sit with her.

And then, one day, without a word or a goodbye, his username disappeared.

Without Akash, our server began to fray.

Then Kaitlyn Courtland rocked us when she announced she was giving up the moderator role. We weren't convinced by her excuse either. According to Kaitlyn, her parents wanted her to spend more time on her homework. This was equivalent to announcing that Kaitlyn Courtland *had* parents. It was our parents' most common refrain, the rhythmic undercurrent that powered a whole generation of internet use. We were always supposed to be doing our homework, or our chores, or getting outside, or making real friends. True, Mrs. Steeler-Cox's aggressive marketing campaign about the poisonous effects of Discord on young minds and moral development made things trickier. Still, we wouldn't have pegged Kaitlyn for a quitter.

Ethan Courtland had an alternate explanation for his cousin's abdication of her responsibilities.

> **@mememeup:** She feels bad about Lucy Vale
> **@badprincess:** what do you mean? Bad how?
> **@mememeup:** she just feels bad about what we did to her
> **@spinn_doctor:** are you crazy?
> **@spinn_doctor:** am I crazy?
> **@spinn_doctor:** does anyone listen to me?
> **@spinn_doctor:** do I exist?
> **@nononycky:** unfortunately
> **@spinn_doctor:** we did absolutely nothing to Lucy Vale
> **@spinn_doctor:** we are innocent bystanders
> **@spinn_doctor:** to a tragic devolution of power dynamics that have absolutely nothing to do with us
> **@mememeup:** right, exactly
> **@spinn_doctor:** thank you
> **@mememeup:** no, I mean, this is exactly why @ktcakes888 is taking a step back

Discord was different once Alex Spinnaker took on the sole moderator role. At least, it was quiet of conversation, more of a monologue. Spinnaker went on frequent long-winded rants, changed themes and channels with obsessive frequency, and often cluttered the open channel with coding tips none of us could use. A paranoid tone prevailed. Conversation bubbled up and fizzled out as if depressed by the heavy atmosphere. We frequently woke to ominous warnings about everything from an institutional shortage of Dr. Pepper to the imminent collapse of civilization. We silenced notifications to avoid spam: links to articles about Russian trolls, government cover-ups, and bacterial outbreaks in national salad bars. Every time we signed on, we had to dodge a litter of Spinnaker crazy. In the end, it was easier to disengage.

Week by week, we shed subscribers.

We lost Skyler Matthews only a few days after Alex Spinnaker became moderator. Skyler's podcast had been on hiatus since January, when the news of Lucy Vale's allegations had paralyzed us. It hadn't helped that, shortly before then, a cabal of Jalliscoe haters had tracked down Skyler's YouTube channel and started flagging her en masse for violating YouTube's terms of service under the pretense that she'd been distributing fake news.

Skyler originally railed against the bullying, refusing to be cowed. She wrote impassioned Tumblr posts about the dangers confronting United States journalists and celebrating the value of free speech.

But that was before Ryan Hawthorne's New Year's Eve party and its fallout swallowed our lives. After, Skyler's attitude was fitful. Uncertain. We perceived flickers of doubt. It was as if all the time she'd spent researching our most insistent critics had turned her slowly in their direction, confusing her, leaving her mired in doubt. She was distrustful of the Investigative Committee's bias. She was the one who'd pointed out that Mrs. Steeler-Cox was its only woman and that several other appointees had signed on to support the new Jay Steeler Legacy Pavilion, helping push the project past the town board, in opposition to Rachel Vale and a small community of dissenters.

Skyler had doubts, she told us, that Lucy Vale had gotten a fair trial. We pointed out that Lucy Vale hadn't been on trial at all.

Then Skyler said we were either dumb or in denial. It was harsh and unexpected criticism, especially from Skyler, to whose podcasting efforts we'd been critical. Meeks suggested that Skyler was PMSing. Skyler called Meeks the "walking embodiment of toxic masculinity." Meeks replied that comments like that were the reason so many people hated feminists.

Skyler said that our server had gone to hell and she was out.

Our numbers continued to dwindle. We dropped to thirty. Then twenty. Then twelve.

We sensed the end of an era.

In a way, it was a blessing when Lucy returned to torch our mascot a few weeks later.

TWO

It was late March when the alarm pierced our third-period classrooms, pitched lower and more urgent to signify the lockdown. The sound crawled up our spinal cords and touched off immediate thoughts of death. The automated message that spat through the loudspeakers instructed us to observe lockdown procedures and report to safe zones immediately.

We'd practiced lockdowns before—but never like this, never without warning, never with our teachers ghostlike and shaking as they locked the doors, drew the blinds, and shunted us away from the windows. We suffocated with fear. We imagined blood-slicked hallways, a vengeful classmate prowling the halls with his dad's AK-47.

We assumed it was a gun.

We assumed it was a him.

None of us were thinking of Lucy Vale. We listened for gunshots and startled at the report of distant locks clicking into place. We heard the panicked drumbeat of sneakers in the hallway as other students rushed for safety from the cafeteria and the SLD Tutoring Center. We touched our crosses and confessed our sins. We gripped hands and phones.

We were herded into closets, huddled like cattle for the slaughter, breathing the must of stale breath. We sent texts to our parents. We cursed the spotty service in our various hiding places—the art closet, the boiler room.

We really had to pee.

Minutes eked by. The hum of our nerves began to idle with boredom.

For the first time in weeks, our Discord server began sparking with conversation. *Does anyone know anything? Can anyone hear anything? So typical of admin to go silent during a lockdown. Cowards.*

Our hearts leapt when we saw @ktcakes888, @skyediva, and @kash_money asking for permission to rejoin the server. The alert electrified us into sudden herd activity, like the touch of a cattle prod. We crouched over our phones in locked classrooms. We ignored the imminence of death. We stood strong in the face of a nameless terror who might be prowling the grounds with an AK-47, looking to take revenge for some nameless infraction or indifference.

We fired off messages to Spinnaker. *Akash wants in. Let Akash into the server.*

As usual Spinnaker was truculent, even during lockdown.

> **@spinn_doctor:** Akash has to be verified, just like everybody else
> **@mememeup:** screw your security, Spinnaker. This server is dying
> **@badprincess:** we're dying
> **@badprincess:** we literally could be shot any second
> **@nononycky:** heyyyy @badprincess is back
> **@badprincess:** I never left
> **@badprincess:** just haven't been on
> **@mememeup:** LET AKASH IN THE SERVER
> **@spinn_doctor:** I'm not just going to roll out the red carpet now that he's decided to grace us with his presence
> **@mememeup:** good thing all you have to do is click admit

Spinnaker caved. We welcomed Akash with a confetti of emojis.

> **@nononycky:** welcome to the lockdown party

@kash_money: are you guys okay? Do you know what's going on?
@mememeup: I don't hear any shooting
@badprincess: me neither
@lululemonaide: I wish they'd tell us what's happening ...
@goodnightsky: did you guys miss me?
@goodnightsky: is everyone alive?
@mememeup: unfortunately
@mememeup: this closet is rank

We were miserable and elated. It was horrible and historic.

It was, we found out, a fire in the recycling bin and death to our beloved mascot. An abomination, but a relief nonetheless.

Once Administration released us from our classrooms and an encirclement of police cars and fire trucks logjammed our parking lot, we milled around while sheriff's deputies cleared the buildings and members of the fire department clustered around the evidence: a blackened, still-smoking ruin, which we joked should be buried with a proper funeral for Sean the Shark. We were electric with excitement, disaster narrowly averted.

We thought of Jalliscoe. Of podcasters. Of vengeful online agents persuaded by reports that the Sharks' star swimmers had been doping for years.

Over the next two days, our Discord swelled again to forty-seven members. Spinnaker was forced by a vote of the returning majority to yield sole power as mod. Kaitlyn Courtland came back, reconfigured the server, and restored sanity to the threads.

Once again we were alive, powerful, and tethered to our phones, where the world was compressed to a typeface, flowing steadily to us through a stream of message alerts.

We had theories. We had arguments. Scarlett Hughes had pink eye, which she was convinced she'd picked up from the gym's moldering equipment room, her refuge during the lockdown.

We quickly zeroed in on the idea that the fire had been an act of protest against the construction of the new Jay Steeler Legacy Pavilion. We'd heard that the recycling bin had been removed from the construction site before it was taken to Administration—to us a clear signal of meaningful intent. The mascot, which had been adopted by the school during Coach Steeler's reign, was an obvious and pointed target.

Then there was the timing, only days after *Blood in the Water* had dropped its last episode of season 2. For the season finale, the hosts had interviewed Daniel Frisker, who'd actually swum with Tommy Swift under Coach Steeler for a few years. According to Daniel Frisker, competitive high school swimming was rife with various forms of doping, at least at its most elite levels. Tommy Swift, Daniel claimed, was on a regimen of illegal supplements that he thought would improve his swim times. Coach Steeler encouraged it. He had total control of all his star swimmers' lives, Daniel said. What they ate, where they went, and who they went out with. The boys got used to asking Coach Steeler's permission before making any decisions of their own.

Daniel Frisker was sure Coach Steeler would have lost his shit if he'd found out Nina and Tommy were still talking.

True, the night Nina vanished Tommy was with the team at Coach Steeler's house having pizza. True, Tommy hadn't left the house until after nine o'clock, by which point Nina had already sent her last text: Don't look for me.

No, Tommy hadn't mentioned receiving a text from Nina. And so far as Daniel knew, he'd never tried calling her cell phone, even after he'd heard from her concerned mother that Nina wasn't at home. Tommy later claimed it was because he'd found out that Nina was sleeping with somebody else.

But at the time, Daniel had thought it odd.

Daniel Frisker hadn't come forward sooner, he claimed, for the same reason Nina Faraday's friends had walked back their statements: Nina was afraid of Tommy's temper and worried about the supplements Coach Steeler was encouraging his star swimmers to take. The reason?

There was no point. The Steelers had too much power, too much pull with the police.

Besides, for years Daniel had suffered from a kind of Stockholm syndrome, a bond of shared trauma that yoked him to the pact he'd made with the rest of the team. They'd agreed to alibi each other—and had sworn to never mention that Coach Steeler was late to his own party, that he was missing for about an hour and a half on the evening Nina Faraday was last seen alive.

THREE

We felt it fitting that Akash, who had reported the first sighting of Lucy Vale, brought us our last solid news about her. It was a Saturday, a few days after the fire, and we were all bleeding time away on Discord. That's how the weekends felt spring of our junior year. On Saturdays we congealed inside our boredom, coagulating on our beds and sofas and laptops. On Sundays we were gutted, spilling unchecked toward the school week. Our parents were newly suspicious. They scented trouble in every text alert. They hovered around us constantly, like a foul smell.

We were dissatisfied and disconcerted. That morning we'd been batting around theories about Reese Steeler-Cox's latest TikTok video, an unexpected tirade about the swim team and the special privileges they enjoyed from Administration. We were baffled. We were nonplussed. We were jealous that she'd gotten so much organic engagement.

Reese Steeler-Cox was one of the most dedicated swim team shills. She was a Student Council princess. A student hallway monitor. Practically an Administrative appendage.

She was in love with Noah Landry, for Christ's sake. That's why she'd defended Lucy Vale to the Investigative Committee back in January—to get back at Noah Landry for picking a different girl.

It was known. It was the only thing that made sense.

Like the fact that you couldn't trust a girl from Jalliscoe.

Like the fact that Lydia Faraday was a nutjob.

Like the fact that she'd been found hanging in the apple tree.

These were the stories we'd grown up with, and the stories that had grown us.

We didn't need proof. Some things, we just knew.

April had the raw, wild smell of manure and new things growing out of sight.

Akash logged on.

@kash_money: Has anyone heard from Lucy?

It took all of us a second to get over the shock of seeing Lucy's name. We seesawed momentarily over a bad feeling, like we'd been tipped down into a pit.

@memememeup: ?
@badprincess: what do you mean?
@lululemonaide: why would we have heard from Lucy?
@spinn_doctor: does anyone still talk to her?
@kash_money: that's what I'm asking. Has anyone talked to her?
@nononycky: the answer is no. no, we have not talked to Lucy.
@memememeup: the question is why are you asking?
@kash_money: the sheriff is looking for her
@memememeup: ummm . . . try the Faraday House?
@meeksmaster: why? What's she done now?
@kash_money: she's not home. Her mom hasn't seen her. The car is missing
@kash_money: she set fire to our mascot, for one
@meeksmaster: the Toyota?
@geminirising: wait WHAT
@geminirising: that was LUCY VALE???
@kash_money: no, the civic. The one her mom bought her when Lucy passed her test.
@geminirising: can we STICK TO ONE CONVERSATION AT A TIME

@kash_money: The cops think Lucy was the one who set our mascot on fire
@kash_money: I guess the school had security tapes
@kash_money: They came looking for her last night
@kash_money: But she wasn't home
@kash_money: Her mom doesn't know where she is
@kash_money: She filed a missing person's report last night

In the silence, we saw new alerts: @sunshineandhugs, @blackrainbows, and @swifty99 were asking to join the server. Soon requests from unknown usernames thickened in the waiting room.

It was only a matter of time before Spinnaker had a meltdown.

@spinn_doctor: who are all these people? Where are these requests coming from?
@highasakyle: look, we can't trust anyone named @sunshineandhugs
@highasakyle: that's a fact
@kash_money: I told everyone to meet here.
@spinn_doctor: confirm we have verification procedures in place @ktcakes888
@kash_money: we have to find her
@spinn_doctor: this server has protocols
@mememeup: FUCK YOU, SPINNAKER
@mememeup: LET THEM IN
@mememeup: LET'S FIND LUCY VALE

We scrambled to keep track of the inundation of new subscribers. A rapid volley of new requests quickly exposed problems in our infrastructure, namely that Spinnaker was a control freak. He proposed a system of verification questions that would ensure the new subscribers at least attended Woodward. We scrummed first over the system's viability, then over what the questions should be. Akash accused us of wasting valuable time. Evie Grant reminded us sanctimoniously that the first seventy-two hours after someone's disappearance were the most important. We told her we'd all seen old episodes of *Law & Order*. Allan Meeks expressed doubt that Lucy Vale was missing at all. He suggested she might simply be seeking attention once again, trying to leverage our sympathies. Spinnaker said we should locate her just so she could be properly booked and charged with destroying our swim team mascot. Hannah Smith lamented that we had so little compassion for mental illness. Spinnaker called her a gullible simp. Meeks told her to go pop some Zoloft and cry about it. Kaitlyn Courtland blocked him from commenting and threatened to boot him from the server until he apologized and, preferably, sought help. Nick Topornycky recommended he try Zoloft.

Meanwhile, a backlog of new users were idling, waiting for our permission to join.

> **@nononycky:** who is @reesespieces1698?
> **@sunshineandhugs:** that's Reese.
> **@badprincess:** um, I'm sorry? Reese . . . ?
> **@sunshineandhugs:** Reese Steeler-Cox.
> **@spinn_doctor:** very funny
> **@badprincess:** RSC wants to join OUR server??
> **@spinn_doctor:** and who are you @sunshineandhugs? Who let you in here?
> **@sunshineandhugs:** it's Charlotte.
> **@sunshineandhugs:** Charlotte Anderson.
> **@sunshineandhugs:** we heard Akash set up a Discord server to help find Lucy Vale

Even Spinnaker didn't dare correct her. It was an extraordinary turn of events, completely unprecedented. We were, of course, suspicious. All of us knew that Charlotte Anderson and Reese Steeler-Cox had once catfished Harper Rowe in seventh grade, permanently icing her out of the

Echelon. We couldn't believe that a single member of the Student Council Mafia would deign to grace our server with her presence, much less two of them. On the other hand, only someone like Charlotte Anderson—a Hello Kitty fanatic and Pinterest apologist—would choose a handle as flagrantly banal as @sunshineandhugs.

We rounded on Akash. We weren't sure whether to count it as a coup or a betrayal. First Savannah Savage, Bailey Lawrence, and the other Strut Girls started following his socials. Now, suddenly, he was friendly with the Student Council Mafia.

@highasakyle: dude, since when do you know Reese Steeler-Cox, @kash_money?
@kash_money: since I found out who was putting threats in Lucy's locker
@badprincess: it was RSC?? I KNEW IT
@sunshineandhugs: it wasn't Reese!! She would never
@kash_money: no, Ceecee
@badprincess: ??
@nononycky: our Ceecee?
@nononycky: from the front office?
@kash_money: she's not *our* Ceecee
@kash_money: she's married to a Steeler
@sunshineandhugs: can we please admit Reese?
@sunshineandhugs: she's texting me
@badprincess: this is so chaotic
@brentmann: I thought Reese hated Lucy
@sunshineandhugs: Reese doesn't hate anyone
@sunshineandhugs: she's worried about Lucy
@sunshineandhugs: she tried to warn her to stay away from Noah Landry
@sunshineandhugs: she was afraid something like this would happen

For a moment we were all ricocheted back to January and the blow of cold air in our chests. Charlotte Anderson wasn't done.

@sunshineandhugs: the Vales should never have come back here
@badprincess: what do you mean, back here?
@sunshineandhugs: you didn't know?
@sunshineandhugs: Lucy's mom used to spend summers down here
@sunshineandhugs: she knew Coach Steeler
@sunshineandhugs: I mean she *knew* him, knew him
@sunshineandhugs: she published on substack about it
@badprincess: link please

Charlotte sent us the link.

That was it. That was the moment. In a split second, the foundation of our entire lives—our image of the swim team, of the legendary Coach Steeler, of Woodward, of the whole county—caved. It came crashing down on the Sharks and the club team, on Noah Landry and his wins, on Alec Nye drawing Lucy's name at the Winters Dance because he'd made a bet that he could get with her first, on Noah Landry cutting in because he wanted to win. It collapsed in an upward plume of all the rumors we'd been trying to discount and ignore.

Woodward swimmers can get away with anything.
They never get in trouble.
They make the county too much money.
They could literally get away with murder.
They already have.

@badprincess: HANG ON HANG ON HANG ON
@safireswiftly: are you saying Coach Steeler slept with Lucy's mom??
@sunshineandhugs: I'm not saying it. Lucy's mom is saying it
@sunshineandhugs: she's saying he slept with Nina Faraday, too

@badprincess: I might actually puke
@sunshineandhugs: can you please let Reese in now?
@sunshineandhugs: we're literally wasting minutes

We were too shaken to respond. Even Spinnaker went silent.

Then Nick Topornycky pointed out that Reese's handle, @reesespieces1698, looked familiar. Why, he asked Charlotte Anderson—or at least the user claiming to be her—had Reese chosen those specific digits for her username?

@sunshineandhugs: bc they're the last four of her cell phone number
@sunshineandhugs: easy to remember

We knew then what he was angling at. Nick's question had touched off a series of associations that hopscotched us through the archives of the internet and landed us back in time, before the Vales had even arrived in Indiana—back to when an unknown user, ANONYM1698, first blinked into existence and slowly began to spread the gospel of the swim team's dirty secrets.

We'd been looking for a mole, someone with insider access to the team and the Administration.

We wondered now, though, if all along we'd been looking in the wrong direction.

By almost unanimous vote, we welcomed Reese Steeler-Cox onto our server and vowed to track down Lucy Vale.

FOUR

In a way, the days after Lucy Vale went missing were our Discord's finest. We soon counted more than two hundred subscribers. Our server swelled to include members from every grade and social group, and even a handful of recent graduates.

We gave up on trying to verify identities, but we all agreed on one thing: no swimmers allowed.

Spinnaker, of course, was apoplectic. But the impact of his rants was attenuated by the sheer volume of conversation, which overwhelmed our phones, inundated us with new alerts, overflowed into our dreams and dinner conversations. We were consumed, obsessed.

We were convinced we would find Lucy Vale.

On Reese Steeler-Cox's recommendation, Kaitlyn Courtland rearranged the server and its threads to make tracking tips and sightings easier. We pinned the sheriff's official APB, which included a description of Lucy's outfit and aggregated photos from her social media. We reached out to the Strut Girls. On a singularly memorable day, all three of them—Bailey, Savannah, and Mia—logged on.

Even in real life, we felt unusual solidarity, as if Lucy's disappearance were a tidal pressure that gathered all of us on the same beach. We hadn't felt such unity or purpose since Aiden Teller has been surprised by Jalliscoe Wolverines outside the Lucky Strike.

But this time—for the first time—the swim team was excluded.

We frantically swapped theories. We speculated that Lucy may have heard that the sheriff suspected her as the arsonist and fled town rather than face up to what she'd done. We wondered if Rachel Vale was only feigning ignorance about her daughter's whereabouts. We hypothesized that Lucy had dipped off to Mexico and would soon reunite with her mother on the white sand beach of some tiny Central American town.

But one look at Rachel Vale—who wandered the Four Corners like a loosed spirit, distributing flyers, hunting for leads—put that theory to bed. It was obvious that Rachel had no idea where Lucy Vale was.

Unfortunately neither did we.

We combed through Lucy Vale's social media for clues. By that time, she hadn't posted since December. Still, we scoured for evidence. Items in the background of photos that might indicate where she'd gone, trinkets from her room. A Grand Canyon postcard visible on a cluttered corkboard that briefly inspired us to look in Arizona. A copy of Jack Kerouac's *On the Road*, around which Olivia Howard claimed to see a dark aura that proved Lucy had planted it the previous August, a clue about her future intentions and unannounced road trip. We clutched at straws. Someone had seen a van on Three Hills Road, only a quarter mile from Lily Lane, the same afternoon that Lucy Vale had vanished. For a few hours we went wild with the idea that a kidnapper was on the loose—until Richie Dale confirmed that his neighbors were reshingling their house and the man who'd been skulking around the yard was only there to give an estimate.

As our server grew, blowing together hundreds of different perspectives and voices like so many errant leaves, we began to assemble a fuller picture of what Lucy's life had been over the past few months. Since she'd walked into the sheriff's department with her mother and reported rape.

Maria Gomez, a sophomore who worked part-time at the CVS in North Granger, reported that Lucy had come in several times just before closing. Each time she'd spent nearly an hour wandering the bright fluorescence of the deserted aisles, sniffing shampoos and body lotions, spinning the revolving display case full of sunglasses and trying on different pairs, reading the greeting cards in the stationery aisle. Maria's impression was that Lucy was bored and simply looking for an escape. As far as she could recall, Lucy never purchased anything but Advil and ChapStick.

Senior Ally Mack had been seated behind Lucy Vale and her mother at the Waffle House late on a Thursday when the restaurant was half-empty. Rachel, she'd noticed, was doing most of the talking. Lucy's waffles remained largely untouched. Ally had noticed and wondered whether Lucy was becoming anorexic.

Freshman Julia McGraw had intersected with Lucy and her mom in the waiting room of Bright Smiles Dentistry, the one in Camden Shopping Center. Rachel Vale had been inquiring about getting her daughter Invisalign. Something about that almost gutted us. The idea of Lucy and her mother discussing orthodontic options—the idea of Rachel Vale worrying about her daughter's teeth—was so basic, so inconsequential, so indisputably true. It scared us to imagine that Lucy Vale's life had been playing out even when we weren't there to look at it. We were seized by sudden fits of dread. We were gripped out of nowhere with the impression that we had forgotten to do something—turn off our car engines, turn off the stove, lock our doors, do our homework.

We had to remind ourselves that no one knew the truth about what had really happened to Lucy Vale that night in January. Even the sheriff's department hadn't come to a conclusion. The case had simply unraveled, frayed, loosened into accusations and counteraccusations, story after story after story.

We sickened when we saw Noah Landry posting about his swim times, or his regimen, or his six thousand calories a day. We thought it was inappropriate, even disturbed.

We insisted on hanging Lucy's missing person poster directly outside Administration and all over Aquatics. We discussed protesting the Jay Steeler Legacy Pavilion. We insisted we had to stop it.

We persuaded Skyler Matthews to release a final podcast episode, this time about Lucy's disappearance. It dropped like a stone down the empty cavern of the internet the same week Rachel Vale went public with her story about how she met Jay Steeler, the fabled former Olympian, at a party. She was just twenty-two years old.

We told ourselves that whatever had happened to Lucy Vale, it wasn't our fault. We had done nothing wrong.

We were not bad people.

In April we stayed up late and found each other online at strange hours.

In April we had trouble sleeping.

FIVE

Rachel Vale held a press conference. She appeared on CNN. We watched the clip on YouTube. The chyron identified her as *journalist and true crime author R.C. Barnes*. We felt stupid, like the last people to have gotten a joke.

On-screen Rachel Vale looked like a different person. Composed. Almost clinical. She was wearing a suit jacket with her hair slicked back in a bun. She spoke in the voice of a reporter, leaning heavily into her words for emphasis.

She begged us all to remember her daughter, Lucy. She talked about Lucy's smile and her devotion to her cat, Maybe. About the sticky notes she left for her mother all over the house with smiley faces and inside jokes written on them. She showed pictures—of Lucy at Halloween, vamping as Marie Antoinette; of Lucy cuddling with Maybe on the sofa.

She talked about Lucy's problems in Michigan. How she'd started acting out. How they'd hoped to find a new start in Indiana. How excited Lucy was to be making friends, to be finding her place, to have a boyfriend everyone admired. A boyfriend who said he loved her.

But nowadays, she'd said, *bullies aren't bound by geographical constraint. They find you online. They found Lucy online.*

She teared up, speaking about topless photos of thirteen-year-old Lucy that had circulated back in Michigan and then again at her new school. She mentioned nightmares Lucy had been having shortly before her disappearance. That Lucy was convinced her life was over. That she was convinced she would never escape those photographs or the mistakes she'd been trying to outgrow.

We were leaden, paralyzed with terror. Discord was silent. There was nothing to say.

It had occurred to us too late: we were not the heroes of this story.

SIX

Everyone we knew, and hundreds we didn't, turned out for the search party in Rockland County State Park. We navigated a thicket of local and state reporters angling for a view with their cameras, all of them trained on the crowd like lidless eyes.

We reported on the reporters' reporting and captured videos of ourselves being filmed.

Bailey Lawrence, Savannah Savage, and Mia Thompson clutched hands in the parking lot, faces shadowed by matching dance team hats. They stood with heads bowed like mourners while we received instructions from orange-clad volunteers. Akash came with both of his parents and even his older sister who was home on college break. He stayed apart from us, fists balled in his jacket, his eyes raw with grief.

It was possibly the first time we understood: he really had loved Lucy Vale.

Coach Radner and Coach Vernon were there, wearing matching blue-and-red windbreakers. The Steeler-Coxes were noticeably absent. According to Reese, the Steeler-Cox delegation was considering legal action against Rachel Vale for her claims about Jay Steeler. Rachel Vale wasn't the first person to accuse Jay Steeler of being a predator, but her report was the first to explode in the news cycle. Since then, Reese told us, all of the Steelers had been receiving death threats online. Mrs. Steeler-Cox's beloved Facebook page, where she rigorously hyped the perfect family image, had gone mysteriously dark. Reese Steeler-Cox, meanwhile, made furtive TikToks from her bathroom and sent sporadic messages to the server that carried the slightly hysterical tone of someone trapped in a bunker at the end of the world.

That day was no exception.

@reesespieces1698: who's there?
@reesespieces1698: tell me everything
@reesespieces1698: I only have a few minutes
@reesespieces1698: it's like a war room downstairs
@highasakyle: think Coachella
@highasakyle: but depressing
@pawsandclaws: Coachella *is* depressing
@reesespieces1698: is Noah Landry there for his photo opp?
@mememeup: haven't seen him
@reesespieces1698: just look for the biggest camera
@reesespieces1698: and the tallest liar
@lululemonaide: where is this coming from?
@reesespieces1698: experience
@reesespieces1698: I tried to warn Lucy away from Noah Landry
@reesespieces1698: I told her to stay away
@nononycky: you stuffed her sweatshirt down a toilet bowl
@reesespieces1698: We were making a point.
@spinn_doctor: Landry was cleared.
@mememeup: True. Due process by a jury of school board shills

Reese Steeler-Cox was right about Noah. Minutes later, Alyssa Hobbes spotted him being interviewed by the crew from *Spotlight Indiana*. Noah kept his hat ducked low over his eyes and his shoulders hunched forward, as if he had a stomachache. His parents and Coach Vernon ringed him on either side; Alyssa snuck a picture, and we all had the impression of someone pinned into place.

@badprincess: wow. it's like . . . now he suddenly gives a shit about Lucy?
@bassicrhythm: Hammill and Hawthorne are here too
@badprincess: that's convenient
@colonelmustard: I think it's nice that the swim team showed up
@colonelmustard: you know, considering
@badprincess: please. all of them showed up for the publicity
@badprincess: meanwhile, they didn't care at all when they were trashing Lucy's reputation
@highasakyle: sure
@highasakyle: but you could say the same about us
@pawsandclaws: maybe they're here because they feel guilty
@nononycky: what do you mean?
@pawsandclaws: why did Lucy burn our mascot?
@warcraftlordandlegend: idk. Because she's deranged?
@hannahbanana: I thought we agreed that Lucy Vale has serious problems
@hannahbanana: right? Didn't we all agree on that?
@hannahbanana: hello?

No one answered. We didn't know what to say.

It seemed like Lucy Vale had problems, for sure. But standing there in the thin spring sunlight, hemmed in by the crowd that had come to search for her, we realized: we really had no clue where Lucy Vale might have gone.

In the end, we really didn't know much about her.

∼

We fanned out through the woods, staying arm's lengths from our neighbors. "No point in getting a second person lost in these trees," Deputy Stern joked. We didn't laugh.

The sky was the chafed color of old denim. The woods were full of desperate daffodils, pushing valiantly through a scrum of rotting leaves. The trees were eking out their first green onto water-parched branches. The ground covering was so dry, it cracked beneath our footsteps like the report of a gun. The late winter snows had done little to resolve Indiana's drought. When we gathered at the lip of Fallow's Creek, we found it gone. The water was down to its last filthy dribbles, leaving a hollowed-out rut of sludge and fallen branches that whipped out of sight.

Four separate volunteer groups searched the state park, an unruly twelve-thousand-acre swath of woods and campgrounds, fishing ponds and bird sanctuaries. Other volunteers gathered at a constellation of trailheads that bracketed the densest part of the forest, cordoning off a three-square-mile portion of the park where a hiker had reported seeing a girl who matched Lucy's description, apparently headed north through the woods. We learned later that more than eight hundred people convened over three days to search for Lucy.

We tried not to think about the Lucy we might find. We steered clear of the cadaver dogs straining at their leashes. We snuck messages to one another, trying to lighten the mood.

@mememeup: did anyone bring snacks?
@mememeup: I'm already hungry
@badprincess: I can't believe Mrs. Devane brought her kids
@badprincess: this isn't, like, a field trip??
@warcraftlordandlegend: depends on what we find

The woods rebounded Lucy's name as we called out to her. We slogged through the dry rot of winters past, pushing through tangles of witch hazel and chokeberry bushes that clutched our jeans as we navigated the slopes parallel to the exposed creek bed. Volunteers in lurid orange looked like flames along the trails. The trees thinned the sunlight into pinwheel shafts that barely warmed us. A sharp wind rose, carrying the smell of ice. Minutes cycled by, marking the repetition of our calls. *Lucy. Lucy Vale. Lucy.*

We lost track of time. Lucy's name began to sound foreign, losing its tether to the girl, to the point. In the echoing shouts of distant search teams, we imagined a conversation. A call and response that held the mystery.

Lucy. Lucy Vale.

Where are you?

Suddenly there was a scream, a sharp wail—from our left, from our right, from behind us.

We broke rank. We shook loose from our assigned positions, forgetting what we had been instructed, and followed the thread of sound.

It was Olivia Howard, gasping, standing with both hands over her mouth.

"Look. Look at what they've done to her," she was saying as we approached, crowding past the volunteers trying to herd us back in line, saying, *It's okay, it's nothing, it's just a deer.*

Actually it was a fawn. A carcass. Long limbs, eyes open, blackened with swarming insects. Its stomach was missing, gutted by sharp teeth. Probably coyotes. Maybe a bobcat.

We were annoyed at Olivia, and told her so. Why had she screamed like that?

It was a deer, for Christ's sake. Had she ever seen roadkill before? Hadn't she been to Alex Spinnaker's house and seen the deer hooves used to mount a rifle? It was one thing to be a Wiccan and a vegan. It was another to make her problems everyone else's.

We thought she'd actually found something. When we heard the scream, we thought for a single electric second that she'd found Lucy Vale.

"Of course I didn't find Lucy Vale," Olivia fired back. She seemed annoyed. "You really think we're going to find Lucy? You think she just—what?—wandered off? For no reason?"

Maybe. Maybe not. The state park was vast. The trails were poorly kept and wandered off like lapsed sentences into the obscuring underbrush. As the afternoon wore on, we began to understand why Deputy Stern had counseled us to always stay in our places, to keep one another in sight, to move slowly in a single line, like a human tide. The pine trees thickened. Great-bellied clouds cast a pall over the sun. We lost our sense of direction. If it wasn't for the hollow of the creek bed, gouging an enormous rut between the trees, we might have been circling.

We paused every so often to sip from water bottles, even though we weren't thirsty. Our fingers numbed from cold. We could barely thumb messages to each other.

@**badprincess:** anything over by you guys?
@**bassicrhythm:** just more trees
@**lululemonaide:** I'm freezing
@**lululemonaide:** how long do we have to stay out here?
@**mememeup:** shit
@**mememeup:** shit
@**badprincess:** ??
@**mememeup:** give me a minute
@**mememeup:** I'm pretty sure they found something . . .
@**badprincess:** oh my god
@**hannahbanana:** please tell me it's not Lucy

In the distance, we heard the sharp rap of a dog barking. The sound was quickly silenced. The command to hold where we were shuddered down the line. We idled in groups, checking our phones, anxious about service, which for many of us had winnowed down to a single bar.

@**badprincess:** what's happening??
@**skyediva:** ugh my battery is low. Any news??
@**mememeup:** idk
@**mememeup:** There are deputies heading down to the creek

@mememeup: They're looking at something
@ktcakes888: something?? Or someone??
@mememeup: something
@nononycky: maybe it's another deer
@pawsandclaws: not funny @nononycky
@mememeup: It looks like a backpack or something
@badprincess: ugh @bassicrhythm can you ask your cousin??
@mememeup: wait no
@mememeup: not a backpack
@mememeup: a duffel bag
@mememeup: yellow and black
@badprincess: like a Woodward duffel bag????
@hannahbanana: did Lucy even have a Woodward duffel bag?
@mememeup: not sure
@mememeup: but Nina Faraday did

SEVEN

The discovery of Nina Faraday's dance team bag during a search party organized for Lucy Vale almost broke the internet. It was so extraordinary, so unprecedented, that rumors immediately began circulating that the entire search effort had been orchestrated by an anonymous tipper who knew where Nina's bag had been dumped. We even wondered if Lucy Vale was said tipper. We thought she might have reported that a girl who matched her description was walking north along the creek—not because we had any hard evidence but because it fit with the picture of Lucy we were reassembling.

Even then, after everything that had happened, Lucy Vale was still malleable—more so now that she was gone, occupying a blank space we could populate with our imaginations.

Maybe, we thought, Lucy Vale had planned the whole thing. Maybe even with Rachel Vale's help.

> **@gustagusta:** it's brilliant. Think about it.
> **@gustagusta:** burn the mascot and get the police looking for you
> **@gustagusta:** then disappear
> **@gustagusta:** then point the cops to Nina Faraday's duffel bag instead
> **@pawsandclaws:** if the Vales knew where Nina's stuff was dumped, why wouldn't they just say so?
> **@gustagusta:** maybe they didn't think the cops would listen

@bassicrhythm: that seems highly unlikely
@gustagusta: really? Does it?
@safireswiftly: idk. I mean, is Lucy really THAT devious?
@safireswiftly: she couldn't even keep up with the dance choreography
@safireswiftly: even when it was just twerking
@spinn_doctor: Lucy's just a patsy
@spinn_doctor: my money's on the mom

Within days, national media channels had picked up the story. News vans from all over logjammed traffic in downtown Granger and circled outside the high school for interviewees like prowling scavengers. We saw our school fractalized across dozens of news stories and then thousands of subsequent video commentaries. TikTok was virulent. Nina Faraday's name began to trend. Lucy Vale's too. *Blood in the Water* rocketed to number forty-five on the Apple Podcast charts.

The Sharks' Facebook page was apparently inundated with so much hate speech that Administration disabled comments and then removed it altogether. Alex Spinnaker reported a near constant flow of traffic in and out of Green Gables Ridge, the gated community where both the Steeler-Coxes and Ryan Hawthorne lived. Reese's messages were erratic in those days, her TikToks almost unwatchable. We felt sorry for her. We sent her heart emojis.

So much had changed since January.

In early May, as the search for Lucy Vale stuttered, petering into sporadic and largely worthless online tips, we peeled away from Rachel Vale's grief, from her continued agitation to get answers, explanations, some closure that we knew would never come. Ominous graffiti appeared on the side of the Aquatics Center: **WHERE ARE THE GIRLS?** Days later, the message had spread like some kind of fast-growing mold to colonize downtown buildings and even the Byron Park gazebo. **WHERE ARE THE GIRLS?**

We weren't even sure whether to blame the graffiti on outsiders. As news about Coach Steeler's relationship with Rachel Vale and possibly Nina Faraday exploded across the internet, our attitudes toward the swim team cracked, exposing a rot of hidden resentment. We sent pictures of our windshields, denuded of their Sharks decals after hours of work. We soaped and scrubbed our bumpers to clean them of their Sharks stickers, leaving a film of shredded plastic behind as evidence. It wasn't unusual in those days to see garbage cans full of Sharks merchandise dragged out to the curb for pickup. It even became a trend to demonstrate support for the Vales and the other women who seeped forward to report creepy interactions with Coach Steeler—at Woodward High School and later at the University of Arizona, where he'd taken a position after Nina's disappearance.

Of course, many people shifted the opposite direction, shaking out Sharks banners, staking team colors in their yards—even displaying posters of Coach Steeler in their windows to gaze benevolently down on us like some long-dead cult leader. We rifted across generational lines. The athletes banded together and largely threw in with the Sharks. Riley French attempted to strike some middle ground by suggesting that Coach Steeler's questionable behavior over the years had been the product of his environment and the backward morals of the world twenty years earlier. She was roundly ridiculed on the general thread for being an apologist. Charlotte Anderson reportedly had a screaming fight with her grandfather, who referred to both Nina Faraday and Rachel Vale as home-wreckers. She didn't see how she could bring herself to cash his graduation check.

We told her to go ahead and spend his money.

We shuddered and lurched toward the end of the school year. We reported to school bleary-eyed, paranoid, shell-shocked, like soldiers to another day at the front.

We eked through our homework. We drove with our windows down. We scraped bird shit off our windshields.

A slow seep of rumor darkened around Noah Landry and the reason for his record times. *Noah Landry uses steroids. All the club swimmers cheat. Coach Vernon knows.* Swimmers marauded through the halls looking ferocious and beleaguered like starved pack animals. We heard that the Aquatics booster fund was in danger of drying up; if the money vanished, so would our swim program.

Skyler Matthews dyed her hair.

Sofia Young came to school drunk and puked in third-period English.

Charlotte Anderson began picking out her eyebrows.

Reese dropped the Steeler from her last name, insisting that we call her Reese Cox.

Even Spinnaker began distancing himself from the swimmers after years of clamoring for their approval like some deranged lapdog. He wouldn't go so far as to say that he believed all the stories about Coach Steeler. He reminded us that Rachel Vale had been twenty-two years old and an adult when she claimed he'd pressured her to have sex. He pointed out that being a dirtbag and a cheater weren't the same as being a predator.

@badprincess: what about Nina Faraday?
@badprincess: she was seventeen
@spinn_doctor: we don't know that he ever touched Nina Faraday
@spinn_doctor: all we have is Rachel Vale's word for it
@swifty99: Nina was definitely pregnant
@bassicrhythm: there was a used pregnancy test in her duffel bag. She had it wrapped up in plastic
@badprincess: a used pregnancy test, gym shoes, and an SAT test prep book ☹
@swifty99: ew
@swifty99: why
@badprincess: I guess she was studying for the SATs?
@swifty99: no I mean why the pregnancy test?

@skyediva: maybe proof? Or she didn't want to throw it out at home
@spinn_doctor: just because Nina was pregnant doesn't mean Steeler's the one who knocked her up
@lululemonaide: Rachel Vale is a well-respected journalist
@lululemonaide: I doubt she'd lie
@spinn_doctor: jfc
@spinn_doctor: you people really never learn, do you?
@spinn_doctor: have I taught you NOTHING?

Still, as finals approached, Alex Spinnaker wound down the homework ring. For years we'd pushed assignments to the athletes in exchange for spending money and the occasional smile or acknowledgment in the hall. Unsurprisingly Spinnaker blamed liberal culture for souring the atmosphere and making it too dangerous to conduct successful business.

@spinn_doctor: admin is going to come down hard
@spinn_doctor: just wait for it
@lululemonaide: so it's official? Administration knows?
@highasakyle: that the swimmers don't do their own homework??
@highasakyle: of course they know
@highasakyle: when's the last time you've actually seen Hammill in class?
@spinn_doctor: fair. But now they actually have to do something about it
@kash_money: better than admitting that our best swimmers are hopped up on human growth hormones and veterinary medicine
@spinn_doctor: everyone uses performance enhancers nowadays
@spinn_doctor: it's the only way to stay competitive
@kash_money: "and the sun never sets on the empire..."

We tried to keep up with the outpouring of new information, a cataclysmic volume of new headlines, TikTok videos, hashtags, and podcast episodes. Our server was a deluge of informational threads—about supposed sightings of Lucy Vale, about advances in the Faraday case, about the penis now defacing the statue of Coach Steeler in Byron Park, about the growing clamor to have the statue removed. Nate Stern told us the cops were still combing the state park with cadaver dogs. We didn't know which girl they were looking for anymore.

Woody Topornycky—town drunk, petty criminal, UFO enthusiast, and occasional drug dealer—was suddenly a local superstar. Nick told us that his uncle had spent an hour walking the sheriff around the Woodward parking lot, detailing the spot where he'd last seen Nina Faraday. He was, according to Nick, the key to the entire investigation.

@nononycky: he's our most important witness

@bassicrhythm: no offense, but he was tripping balls that day

@nononycky: doesn't matter. He knows what he saw

@safireswiftly: right. An alien landing craft

@nononycky: He saw lights. Machinery. Activity on the construction site

@nononycky: and a man taking Nina's car

@brentmann: I thought the cops cleared all the construction workers

@brentmann: they were off-site by 5 pm

@nononycky: exactly. So why did Coach Steeler tell the swimmers that he was delayed because of construction issues?

@badprincess: is that what he said?

@nononycky: according to Daniel Frisker.

@stopandfriske: do we trust Daniel Frisker?

@nononycky: do we trust Coach Steeler?

@lululemonaide: what about the texts that Nina sent after she left campus?

@bassicrhythm: the cops aren't sure she sent them at all

@bassicrhythm: could've been someone else, using her phone
@lululemonaide: omg. So something happened to Nina ON CAMPUS?
@pawsandclaws: I knew it
@pawsandclaws: swear to goddess, the aura in Aquatics is so dark

Rumors thickened, tightening around our necks, keeping us in a choke hold, bound to each other and our phones. We heard that the IHSAA had questioned Coach Vernon about rumors that his club swimmers were using performance enhancers to improve their times. We heard that the sheriff's department was hunting down the Sharks who'd been at Coach Steeler's house the day Nina Faraday vanished and reinterviewing them one by one. We heard that work on the Jay Steeler Legacy Pavilion might at last be suspended. But day by day, construction continued, sending up a fine silt of red dust that coated the parking lot and clotted our lungs, made breathing difficult. Mornings smelled like machine oil. Our heads ached with the sound of jackhammers. We'd all but given up on sleeping.

We began to wonder if maybe our parents were right about Discord. Maybe we did spend too much of our time online.

We got our yearbooks. In one of the full-page photos, Lucy Vale was practicing with the dance team. We spent hours staring at that picture, as if we could draw out of the pixelation some clue about Lucy Vale's final act and what she'd been thinking.

In the picture she has one hand on her hip, the other thrown into the air, fist clenched, as if in triumph.

In the picture her head is tilted back, her eyes narrow, barely glancing at the camera. Her hair is loose. She's laughing.

EIGHT

The police did eventually locate Lucy's car, a used Honda Civic that Rachel Vale had bought her right around the time Lucy and Noah broke up. It was in an impound lot in Warren County, Ohio, two hundred miles from Granger. It had been abandoned in a nature preserve parking lot not far from the Jeremiah Morrow Bridge, which carried I-71 high above the Little Miami River gorge, one of the Ohio River's tributaries.

The news came from Evie Grant, who'd found out about it on TikTok even before we'd tracked down the official sheriff's bulletin.

According to Evie, Jeremiah Morrow Bridge was one of Ohio's most popular suicide spots.

> **@ktcakes888:** you think she jumped??
> **@badprincess:** I'm just telling you what I read online
> **@lululemonaide:** was there a note in her car or anything?
> **@geminirising:** what about her wallet? Rachel Vale says she left home with her wallet
> **@pawsandclaws:** why would you bring your wallet to commit suicide?
> **@nononycky:** tolls? Snacks?
> **@pawsandclaws:** this isn't funny
> **@badprincess:** why would you leave your cell phone behind to run away?

@geminirising: maybe she just wanted to . . . disappear for a while

@lululemonaide: if she'd decided to kill herself, she would have left a note

@lululemonaide: she would have told somebody

@lululemonaide: right?

We didn't know. It was possible that Lucy had ditched her car and jumped. But she'd emptied her checking account at an ATM in Cincinnati the day before her car was abandoned. And a long-haul trucker had reported seeing a girl who matched Lucy's description at a rest stop outside Columbus two days later.

We held on to hope that Lucy Vale would soon be found, would soon return, would soon show up online, make contact, make things right again. We prayed that the story wasn't over.

But after that, the leads dried up.

The rain came at last just before Memorial Day. Indiana sucked it up in sheets and spit back violent explosions of green. For days heavy winds took down the missing posters that Rachel Vale had distributed patiently over weeks, covering miles of open farmland with a shock of red flyers. Heavy rain bled most of them into a pulp.

Over the long weekend, Mr. Mole, the adoptive cat who lived in the Student Leadership Department Tutoring Center, died. Reese Cox told us her mother had discovered him stiff-legged and staring blankly outside the computer center where the Investigative Committee had convened earlier in the semester. He was at least eighteen years old; still, we batted around theories of foul play. It was a sign of the times that our minds went immediately to poison.

@sunshineandhugs: Reese thinks Mr. Mole was poisoned

@sunshineandhugs: it's gotta be retaliation

@mememeup: why? What did he do?

@sunshineandhugs: not retaliation against *Mr. Mole*

@sunshineandhugs: it was a message to Reese's mom
@sunshineandhugs: because she refuses to back down about this dumb Steeler Pavilion
@gustagusta: "where Sharks are born, and girls go missing"
@sunshineandhugs: she loved that fucking cat
@highasakyle: really?
@highasakyle: huh
@highasakyle: is that a thing?

As it turned out, it was.

Mr. Mole's death sent the whole school into a brief and inexplicable period of mourning. Grieving Student Council members tied black ribbons to their ponytails and painted whiskers on their cheeks. The school chapter of PETA agitated about what Administration had done with the body; there was some rumor that he'd simply been tossed out in one of the dumpsters. Another rumor suggested that Old McVeigh had buried Mr. Mole down by the construction pit, not far from where he'd first been discovered wandering the drainage pipes shortly before Nina Faraday disappeared.

Jackson Skye reminded us of the rumor that we'd heard growing up that Lydia Faraday's body had been buried beneath Aquatics—a final torment for her troubled soul and punishment for the claims she'd made about Tommy Swift. Punishment because Lydia Faraday had tried to hold the swim team accountable.

For the first time, we wondered whether there was some truth to the story after all.

Maybe, we thought, we simply had the wrong Faraday.

NINE

We rushed into the summer gaspingly with an enormous sense of relief. We fragmented back into individual lives, into babysitting gigs and jobs scooping ice cream at the Byron Park concession stand, into video games and gamer communities, into fandoms and new Discord servers.

We saw each other infrequently and mostly by accident. There was the Fourth of July parade, missing its usual Shark floats, grim and securitized, ringed by so many sheriff's deputies that it felt like the opening salvo of a world war. There were afternoons at Byron Lake and swimmers who worked as lifeguards scowling at us from their chairs, shrilling every infraction with the blast of a whistle, as if in retaliation. There was talk of parties that never materialized, the suggestion that we should all visit Lucy's mom, welling up and dispersing again like bubbles in a stream.

Slowly Lucy Vale became less and less real to us. It seemed impossible to imagine that she'd once sat next to us in biology, one leg folded underneath her other, doodling on the sole of her sneaker. The more internet famous she became—the more her picture, and Nina's, were circulated by strangers—the less she seemed to belong to us. We bled her slowly out of our system via transference that instead enshrined her story forever online.

It was late July before the sheriff's department got permission to dig for Nina Faraday's body under the Aquatics Center, where she was last seen alive. Sofia Young, who'd been forced into summer school after flunking two classes, brought us the news of police activity on campus.

> **@goodnightsky:** um, does anyone know why there's a militia outside of Aquatics?
> **@goodnightsky:** it's crazy—the whole building is roped off
> **@goodnightsky:** and like twenty state troopers on the construction site
> **@goodnightsky:** hello?
> **@goodnightsky:** ??
> **@goodnightsky:** is anyone alive??
> **@goodnightsky:** jfc

It took us hours to see the messages. By then our server was a carcass, gutted of all but a handful of active members, bled of its purpose and our pleasure in it. Every so often a comment or meme sparked a few fitful minutes of chatter. But for the most part our Discord was dark, the conversation intermittent at most. Threads that had amassed thousands of comments grew listless, dark for days at a time. The swell of new subscribers logged on less and less, placing an agonizing pressure on the rest of us to keep the server going.

But what was our Discord with no news of Lucy Vale and no real hope of bringing her back? Every thread raveled us back in time to the edge of the Jeremiah Morrow Bridge and a free fall into darkness. We prayed for more news of Lucy—another sighting, a potential breakthrough, something to prove definitively that she had not left the world in a swan dive.

We powered on for Lucy and for our Discord server. We did it so that we would have something to talk about. Something to discuss. More threads to follow. More mystery to unravel.

We were not bad people.

Still. We were only kids.

We didn't know how to let go of our stories when the truth was merely sad.

~

Almost exactly two years since we'd first heard that a new girl was moving to town, two dozen of us gathered in the football bleachers to watch Nina Faraday's body exhumed from the ground. It was a hot day and muggy with flies. A bald sun scoured the parking lot, making distant mirages of the asphalt. Some of us came with flasks of alcohol siphoned off from our parents; some of us came with sandwiches and snacks. Olivia Howard showed up with flowers. It felt like that kind of occasion.

We couldn't see much of the activity from our vantage point, just a cordon of police cars and deputies milling around the entrance to Aquatics, trying to shoo away the arriving press. The construction site, where work on the Jay Steeler Legacy Pavilion had been stalled by growing national outrage, was invisible from where we were sitting. Instead we had a sweeping view of the parking lot and traffic slowing to a long-tail crawl at the school entrance as word of the operation spread through the afternoon. We saw Old McVeigh prowling like a caged animal between the press vans. Skyler Matthews pointed out Principal Hammill and Coach Radner, hemmed behind a bright rope of police tape, angling for a view. In the far distance, drifts of green massed among the hills marked the easternmost portion of the state park. From campus it was at least an hour to the spot where Nina's duffel bag had been discovered. Still, it would have been easy enough to stash her stuff in an empty locker, then get rid of it in the days after her disappearance—maybe during a long hike or even a fishing trip.

An hour seeped by, then two. The sun heated the metal bleachers to an agony. We ran through all our snacks. We grew bored and impatient.

"How do they know where to dig?" Evie Grant wanted to know. The Aquatics Center was a thirty-thousand-foot complex, and nearly half of it had been under construction the night Nina Faraday went missing.

No one knew the answer. Nate Stern suggested that the sheriff was working with old blueprints. Will Friske suggested that they might have been tipped off like they had been to the duffel bag's location. We wondered what Coach Steeler's swimmers had known, or at least suspected. It was no wonder, we said, that Tommy Swift had gone off the rails.

We got sunburned. We grew bored, impatient for something to happen. Nick Topornycky tried to sneak into Aquatics for a closer look but got busted by Nate Stern's cousin, who threatened to write him a ticket—for what, we didn't know. Nick Topornycky and Nate Stern got into a fight about who was the bigger asshole, Nick or Nate's cousin.

We scratched our mosquito bites until they bled.

One by one, we lost interest and drifted home, back to our air conditioning. Olivia abandoned her bouquet of flowers to brown on the top row of bleachers. We agreed that it had been a gigantic waste of an afternoon.

We doubted the cops would find shit, no matter how long they kept digging.

But we were wrong.

Two days later, Reese Cox wrote us with the news: Ceecee was blackout drunk, and her mom was crying into a kitchen towel.

That morning, the sheriff's department had found bones.

More than eighteen years after she had vanished, Nina Faraday had come home at last.

TEN

We'd long graduated high school by the time Rachel Vale released her book about the Faraday murders and her relationship to Jay Steeler as a young woman. This time she published under her own name.

The book's release drew some of us back to Discord for the first time in years. Senior year we'd disintegrated, as so many things had—our booster funds, our swim team program, the Steelers' reputation. Our final year at Woodward felt grim and embattled as an interminable series of investigations swallowed Administration, froze our athletics funds, and blackened our reputation with endless bad press. Mrs. Steeler-Cox abruptly resigned. Principal Hammill retired early. Our only decent math teacher was fired in the cheating scandal that engulfed the athletics department.

Still, the club team swimmers kept competing. Noah Landry kept winning. Some people are like that. Untouchable.

At least for a time.

It was weird being back on Discord, like walking through an abandoned graveyard overrun with dead threads and years-old comments.

@stopandfriske: whoa. This is trippy
@courtlandia: it's like a time machine in here
@stopandfriske: who are you?

@courtlandia: oh, sorry. It's Ethan Courtland. I got rid of my old handle

@ktcakes888: who posted all these links about Noah Landry qualifying for the Olympics last year?

@courtlandia: someone named @ninjaterrier, apparently

@nononycky: who's @ninjaterrier?

@ktcakes888: a Noah Landry fanboy, obviously

@nononycky: Welp, that narrows it down

@nononycky: to half the country

@spinn_doctor: you're still a mod, aren't you @ktcakes888?

@spinn_doctor: you should know your own subs

@ktcakes888: um, I have a life

@ktcakes888: besides, last I checked, you're still a mod too

@spinn_doctor: and I have two other ACTIVE servers

@nononycky: so that's where all the far-right fringe theories are these days . . .

@spinn_doctor: sure. since the far-left bought out mainstream media . . .

@lululemonaide: what did you guys think of Rachel Vale's book?

@lululemonaide: did anyone else read it?

@courtlandia: did you?

@lululemonaide: it's on my dresser

@lululemonaide: but this semester has been crazy

@moonovermatter: I hear she got pictures from the Swifts

@ktcakes888: maybe we should all read it together

@lululemonaide: ohhh. Like a book club??

We agreed that yeah, sure. We could read it together, like a book club. But after finals wrapped up. After we finished our crit lit essays, our biology labs, our coding assignment. Maybe over the holidays, or after the holidays, which were always nutty.

We skirted uneasily around the subject that had made our server, broken it, and then brought us together again after all that time, verbally sidestepping the topic of Lucy until the omission itself became a kind of presence. Finally Evie Grant spoke up.

@badprincess: did you guys see that post from Lucy Vale?

Just like that, the tension collapsed.

@lululemonaide: um YES
@lululemonaide: I almost died
@lululemonaide: she tagged Noah Landry !!
@courtlandia: WHICH post?
@courtlandia: I've seen like 20 accounts claiming to be her
@ktcakes888: only 20?

We'd noticed the accounts popping up soon after Rachel Vale's book hit the bestseller list. *I am Lucy Vale*, read the bios. All of them featured the same profile picture: a graphic of a single flame burning against a dark background. *I am Lucy Vale.* One account posted a picture of the Las Vegas strip. Another, a mountain overlook. A third, the Chicago River. Faster and faster they thickened online as more and more people changed their profile pictures to match, changed their bios to read, *I am Lucy Vale.*

We didn't know whether Lucy Vale was really behind it or whether her story had simply fractured, germinating new voices, new stories, new victims who were now coming forward under her name, new survivors. Either way it felt like a gathering storm, like a pressure massing from all corners of the internet, like Lucy Vale's story was about to explode from a thousand different directions.

@spinn_doctor: It's not her
@spinn_doctor: someone's trolling us
@courtlandia: I'd say more than one someone
@courtlandia: #IamLucyVale was a trending hashtag last week

@lululemonaide: I don't think it's about us
@lululemonaide: not everything is about us
@nononycky: speak for yourself
@lululemonaide: I'm serious
@lululemonaide: people just identify with Lucy
@stopandfriske: I think she started it
@stopandfriske: she's out there somewhere, living her best life
@stopandfriske: laughing at us
@badprincess: GOOD
@badprincess: I hope she is
@lululemonaide: me too
@courtlandia: co-sign on that

We dawdled awkwardly around the server for a few days. We sent pictures of our dorm rooms or our employee badges. We made plans to hang out over break that we knew would never materialize. We joked about a party at the Faraday House—empty again after a fast rotation of tenants had cycled through after Rachel Vale moved away.

We asked whether anyone had listened to Skyler's new podcast. Whether it was true that Reese Cox was no longer speaking to her parents and had gone goth, or whether she was just playing for her TikTok followers. We wanted to know whether Sofia Young was out of rehab yet or whether anybody had seen Charlotte Anderson's baby. We asked about Akash and how he was enjoying the University of Michigan. We missed Akash. We hadn't talked to him in years.

@spinn_doctor: the Kash machine? He's killing it
@spinn_doctor: his girlfriend's premed, and a smokeshow
@courtlandia: tell him I said hey
@courtlandia: and that I still need some lumber. it's an inside joke
@spinn_doctor: wow, you still play Catan?
@courtlandia: just tell him

@lululemonaide: do you think that Akash might want to join our book club?
@spinn_doctor: doubt it
@spinn_doctor: he's moved on.
@ktcakes888: Lucky him.

As far as we know, it was the last message sent on the server.

ELEVEN

If we imagine Lucy Vale now, we like to picture her in motion. Sitting on a train, her reflection slurring with the landscape outside her window. Or riding in the back of a Greyhound, headphones in, hoodie up, smiling to herself.

Sometimes, though, she falls unexpectedly through our dreams. Down and down, smaller and smaller, like a star drowning in our imaginations, like a star reflected in the eye of a fish. Down and down, smaller and smaller, until she disappears into a river's worth of silence; she is absorbed, at last, into the dark crush of our stories.

If you're out there, Lucy Vale, we want you to know that we forgive you for burning our mascot. We're sorry about the photos. We're sorry for whatever happened to you.

We're sorry you never got to tell your side of the story.

We want you to know that it's safe now. It's safe to come forward. It's safe to come back.

And if we ever see you—at a gas station, on a wind-whipped corner in Chicago, or standing at the river with sunlight at your back—we want you to know you don't have to be afraid.

We promise we won't say a word to you.

We promise to let you go.

ACKNOWLEDGMENTS

This book was such a challenge to write, for reasons I both understand and don't. At many points, I became so discouraged I was persuaded that I no longer knew *how* to write and almost gave up on my career entirely.

I want to first thank Stephen Barbara, my faithful agent, who stood by me through some of the stormiest, most fitful, and most frightened days of my writing life. A big thank-you, too, to Sidney Boker for her thoughtful reads and careful notes.

I am deeply grateful for my mom, to whom this book is dedicated, who took care of me through both a divorce and breast cancer, happening simultaneously, even as I was trying to finish a draft. She proofread pages multiple times and encouraged me to believe that I could finish the book and that it was worth completing. Thank you also to my father, who read several versions as it came together and whose work ethic has always served as an inspiration.

I'm deeply grateful to Carmen Johnson, who gave me the final and radical editorial push I needed to transform the manuscript into a satisfying book and provided that magical balance of guidance and freedom that all authors crave. Thank you for believing in *What Happened to Lucy Vale* and helping me get it over the finish line.

To Lyndsey Blessing at Inkwell Management and Howie Sanders, plus my team at Anonymous Content: thank you for your endless support and your impressive dealmaking skills!

Lastly I want to thank my various fans and readers, whose behavior online is as different from that depicted in the book as can be imagined. I can't tell you all how much your support has meant and continues to mean, even as I am only intermittently online, or struggling with writer's block, or trying out new kinds of writing. You are the loveliest and most loving people, and I am grateful to each and every one of you.

Keep a look out for *New York Times* bestselling author Lauren Oliver's newest mystery thriller . . .

THE GIRL IN THE LAKE

Coming autumn 2026